The item should be returned or renewed by the last date stamped below.

Dylid dychwelyd neu adnewyddu'r eitem erbyn y dyddiad olaf sydd wedi'i stampio isod.

To renew visit / Adnewyddwch ar
www.newport.gov.uk/libraries

ALSO AVAILABLE FROM GARRY DISHER AND VIPER

Bitter Wash Road
Peace

CONSOLATION

GARRY DISHER

VIPER

First published in Great Britain in 2021 by
VIPER, part of Serpent's Tail,
an imprint of Profile Books Ltd
29 Cloth Fair
London
EC1A 7JQ
www.serpentstail.com

First published in Australia in 2020 by
The Text Publishing Company

1 3 5 7 9 10 8 6 4 2

Typeset in Freight Text by MacGuru Ltd
Printed and bound in Great Britain by
CPI Group (UK) Ltd, Croydon, CR0 4YY

The moral right of the author has been asserted.

A CIP catalogue record for this book is available from the British Library.

ISBN 978 1 78816 817 5
eISBN 978 1 78283 858 6

for Juliane Römhild

1

Did Hirsch own the town?

At times he felt he did—was making it his, at least, as he prowled the streets at dawn. When he'd begun doing this eighteen months ago, he was mapping the place. Fixing the police station in relation to the little school on the Barrier Highway, the general store, the side-street lucerne seed business, the tennis courts, the painted silos at the defunct railway station—and the houses, mostly built of the stone found hereabouts. Wheat and wool country, halfway between Adelaide and the Flinders Ranges.

That achieved—context established—the cop in him began to emerge. Protector and enforcer. He watched over the teen siblings who cared for their manic-depressive mother, the old woman whose husband wandered off if her back was turned, the Indigenous kid who'd come halfway to thinking Hirsch wasn't the bashing kind. And he watched for stupidity, cunning and plain malice. Recasting old crimes and cockeyed fate until a veranda post here and a driveway there were imprinted with blood, regret and if-only—so that next time he might anticipate it. The glint of craziness in a man who was, at first glance, a solid citizen. Or where on First Street he'd be able to head off an escape attempt. Or how, on Canowie Place, he'd eventually nab the snowdropper. Every place was porous. Badness—goodness—seeped through and linked them all.

The snowdropper. Hirsch turned off Mawson Street and headed down Canowie Place, this frosty Wednesday morning in late August, frost dusting the grass, blades of ice reaching down from dripping garden taps, frost and ice splitting into prisms and diamonds as the sun struck. A bright, still, freezing day ahead. Snow reported on the Razorback yesterday, and Hirsch was prepared to believe it, his eyes watering right now, his cheeks and toes frozen.

Strange to think that 2019 had started with bushfires all over the country. Nothing could top that. He hunched his shoulders, stamped his feet, pulled his head in, a swaddled figure under an Icelandic beanie, rolling down Canowie. Past the Uniting Church, now home to a retired geologist, past a transportable kit home, smoke rising straight up from the chimney, past more stone houses, their roofs made of faded red or green corrugated iron, their shrubs and Holland blinds keeping the world at bay. Like any country town: a mishmash of the old, the new, the restored and the forsaken, and he could feel the chill in each of their bones.

He paused at Mrs Lidstrom's, 9 Canowie, giving himself a sightline along her side wall to a quadrant of backyard clothesline. A tea towel and a pair of the navy polyester pants she liked to wear. They'll be ice-stiff in this air, he though. He imagined flicking them with a fingernail: the little snap, like cardboard.

He lifted his gaze to the eaves. After the snowdropper had struck numerous times in the district—here in Tiverton, down in Penhale, over in Spalding—targeting some victims more than once, the district police budget had covered the installation of a discreet CCTV camera at one house in each town. No incidents reported in Redruth, leading Hirsch and his boss, Sergeant Brandl, to theorise that the guy lived there. That was ten weeks ago. Since then, grainy video footage had been obtained from Mrs Lidstrom's camera and the one in Penhale. A male figure in motorcycle leathers and a helmet. 'Come to think of it,' neighbours had said, 'I did hear a bike last night.' No face, only an impression of a stocky build—stocky in leathers, anyway.

Hirsch's electrician friend, Bob Muir, had installed the cameras at each location. Mrs Lidstrom, standing with Hirsch in the side yard, watching Bob up a ladder, had used a word Hirsch had only ever seen in print.

'Who would want to steal my old lady's bloomers?'

'It's your cutting-edge taste, Betty,' said Bob, looking down from the ladder, a pair of brass screws bobbing between his lips.

She snorted. She was round, comfortable and white-haired; sharp and mostly amused by the world. 'Not to mention my bathers and best bra.'

'Bathers?' said Hirsch.

A little twist of annoyance: keep up, Paul. 'Water aerobics. Redruth pool.'

As she'd once said to Hirsch, she wasn't one to let the grass grow under her feet. Probus Club lectures, walking holidays in New Zealand, volunteering, fitness. 'Right,' he said.

'Keeps me young. Not that young, though. I repeat, who'd want to steal an old lady's underwear?'

'It's called snowdropping,' Hirsch said.

Betty Lidstrom looked at him. He saw the snap and crackle of her mind. 'A fetish?' she said. 'Psycho-sexual?'

Hirsch raised his eyebrows at her. She punched his upper arm lightly—don't go making assumptions about old women—and he smiled and nodded. 'Probably.'

They both stood there, and Bob Muir in his overalls stood there on his ladder, the three of them thinking their way into the head of a man who stole underwear from backyard clotheslines. Why he did it. What he did with his trove of old lady's bloomers. And whether he was building up to something else.

He'd be hard to catch. And if he was caught, he could talk his way out of it, say he'd bought the underwear in an op shop. Embarrassing, but not theft. Then something about the authorities having no business in the bedrooms of the nation, et cetera. So each victim had been supplied with marked underwear: a hole punched in the top left corner of the waistband label in case he did it again.

Just then a light went on in Mrs Lidstrom's rear side window: kitchen. Hirsch walked on, securing the town, burning away his overnight aches and stiffness, feeling good to be alive despite the cold, the tedium. He'd probably spend the morning witnessing a stat dec or two; writing up last weekend's pub brawl between windfarm workers; chipping away at the clods of mud inside the wheel arches of his SA Police 4WD—the nasty, clogging, adhering red-soil mud of the mid-north plains.

Up the side path of a little brick-veneer house on the highway. A habitual good-luck knuckle-rap on the windscreen as he edged past his old Nissan. In through the back door. Then, showered, second breakfast inside him, he opened the connecting door and stepped from his suite of three cramped rooms into the room facing the highway.

This was the police station. A ceiling fan for summer, a useless bar heater for winter. Community notices on the walls, an out-of-date calendar of spring wildflowers east of the town, a counter separating his desk, computer, swivel chair and filing cabinet from the waiting room. People rarely waited. Crimes occurred now and then, perpetrators were about, but mostly a local or a stranger could be sure of immediate service—if Hirsch was there, at any rate; if he wasn't out on patrol or answering a call. A sleepy country town. Mostly.

Seated at his desk, scorched-dust odours rising from the bar heater, his shins barely warm, he tackled his in-tray, read emails and checked the Tiverton WTF Facebook page. The snowdropping was an ongoing What the Fuck item, the commentary sometimes amusing, sometimes faintly off-colour; occasionally nasty. Hirsch supposed Betty Lidstrom knew about it. He couldn't protect her from it. Police everywhere were fighting losing battles with social media.

Three items of interest this morning: photos of the Razorback with its spine of snow; reports of a pair of Irish roof repairers floating around the district—*A con?*—and an anonymous query regarding Quinlan Stock and Station, a Redruth agency that specialised in the buying and selling of land, livestock, wool, agri chemicals and equipment: *Anyone find this mob to be slow payers?*

The desk phone rang. 'Paul?'

Hirsch didn't recognise the voice. 'Speaking.'

'It's Clara.'

Hirsch assumed he should recognise the name and voice; knew it wasn't his strong suit. Not a good look in a country policeman: the job description included friend and counsellor, as well as law enforcer, to everyone. The name Clara was a wisp of smoke in his mind, sent up by something remote in time and place.

'Hi.'

She read him. 'Clara Ogilvie.'

Nothing. 'How are you?' he asked, concentrating madly.

'Caledonian Dreaming?'

Ah. A loose group of fiddlers, guitarists, pipers, tin-whistlers and singers—border ballads, edgy folk, Appalachian mountain music, anything vaguely Celtic. Once a month in an upstairs room of the Woolpack, in Redruth, half an hour down the highway. Hirsch had gone twice, dragged along by Wendy Street and her daughter. His second time there, back in June, he'd closed his eyes against every penetrating eye in the room and given a short, deeply self-conscious vocal performance of 'Dirty Old Town', from an old Pogues LP his parents had owned when he was a kid. He had the words in his head; what he didn't have was a rasp in his voice from whisky and cigarettes.

And suddenly he was able to place Clara Ogilvie. Mid-forties, slender, vivid, the kind with a permanent current buzzing inside her. She'd touched his forearm afterwards—Wendy looking on with a sleepy half-smile—and told him he had a lovely tenor voice. In a small community that was code for passably pleasant.

'Clara, right. What can I do for you?'

'I'm ringing because...' She trailed away. 'Have you got a minute?'

'I have.'

'It's not one of your patrol days?'

Hirsch would have been on the road by 7.30 a.m. if it was.

'You're good,' he said, and a corner of his soul tensed. She wanted him to sing again, maybe in the concert mooted for the Redruth Show in September.

'I'm calling because...Look, it's complicated.'

'Take your time.'

'I'm concerned for someone's welfare.'

The last time Hirsch made a welfare check, he'd stumbled on a mother and son shot dead in a home invasion. The blood, the bodies: instantly there in his head again. 'Uh-huh. Who?'

'Background,' Clara Ogilvie said. 'I teach English at Redruth High—that's how I know Wendy. She said I should talk to you rather than bring in Child Protection just yet.'

A kid in her class? Didn't schools have welfare officers?

This was becoming a round-the-block-and-up-over-the-hill kind of conversation. 'Someone you teach? You think it's a police matter?'

'I hope not, but I am worried.'

A child sexually abused, he thought. Coming to school with bruises. Acting out. Neglected. On drugs. Dealing drugs...

And why call him? The Redruth police station was two minutes from the high school, Hirsch thirty minutes. 'Perhaps ask Sergeant Brandl to look into it.'

'You're closer.'

'How about you tell me the circumstances.'

A pause, as if he'd been short with her. Then a sense of a deep breath taken. 'In addition to teaching at the high school I do a bit of online work with home-schooled primary age kids, monitoring their progress.'

'Okay.'

'For the Education Department.'

'Okay.'

'It's a requirement.'

'Mm.'

'This week I've been online with a girl in her final year of primary school. Lydia Jarmyn, eleven years old, home-schooled by her mother, Grace.'

'Okay.'

'Well, I touch base with these home-school kids a few times a year, monitor their progress in various different subjects, curriculum check, and all week Lydia's been distracted. Yawning a lot. Zones out all the time.'

'We're talking about Skype? Zoom? You can see her?'

'She looks thin and pale. Drifts off, gives a little shake as if she's trying to wake herself up, then just drifts off again.'

'Have you spoken to the mother? Maybe she spends all night on the computer. TikTok, whatever it is now.'

'There's something else going on, I think. I asked her if anything was wrong and she said she's hungry all the time. Said she's only allowed a small bowl of rice a day. And she can't get warm.'

Hirsch ran through the likely scenarios if he called Child Protection: thirtieth caller in line, or someone promises to get back to him but doesn't, or it's allocated a case number for attention next month, or they need more evidence, or they promise to act and don't...And the child dies.

Or we're looking at a kid having a whinge.

'Do you know where the Jarmyns live?'

He heard paper rustling and then Clara Ogilvie recited an address: Hawker Road. Hirsch pictured it: a gravel track up in the Tiverton Hills. 'Any reason why she's being home-schooled?'

As against Tiverton Primary School, across the road from his police station.

'If the parents can satisfy certain requirements, they're allowed to home-school their children.'

Which was an answer, but not to the question he'd asked.

'Okay, thank you, I'll check it out.' He paused. 'You did the right thing.'

Diplomacy: it was half his job.

Ogilvie's voice changed: light and chatty. She was looking

forward to the Caledonian Dreaming get-together on Sunday afternoon; she named a couple of songs she thought would suit his voice. Hirsch swallowed. From their titles alone they were epic ballads of feuds, raiding parties and supernatural come-uppance. He dodged and weaved and got off the line without committing.

Hirsch pinned his mobile number to the front door and backed the police 4WD onto the highway. Cars were streaming into the side-street entrance to the school, and he wondered again why Lydia Jarmyn was being educated at home. He waited for the Broken Hill bus to trundle through, then trailed it north through farmland.

Wheat, oats and barley shoots in thick, vividly green rectangles on either side of the road and reaching in broad brushstrokes up the hill slopes, stopping where the soil gave way to stone reefs. Distant rooftops on these hillsides: farmhouses and implement sheds. He thought about the march of the seasons. He'd not much noticed it when he lived in Adelaide. The weather was hot, cold or in-between, that's all. He didn't register plants and birdsong, pollen and blossom, life and death. Only what to wear, did he need a jacket and was it hot enough to swim. But up here, three hours from the city, and quite high above sea level, there were two extremes: cold green winter and droughty summer.

A speck in the sky resolved itself: a crop-duster, short, stubby, the cabin a prominent bubble above the wings, side-slipping and straightening for a run across a wheat crop. Hirsch slowed, signalled, pulled onto the verge, and watched it drop, leapfrog the powerline, drop again and howl from fence line to fence line, releasing a thick stripe of chemical spray, climbing before it ploughed into the hill, tilting onto one wing and coming around again. Drop, hedge-hop, spray-bomb, climb, turn.

Timing it so he wouldn't get a lungful of chemicals or a roof-rack full of landing gear, Hirsch pulled the police HiLux back onto the highway. Fifteen minutes later he turned left, a gravel road taking him up and then across the flank of a hill. Finally a driveway, sealed by twin galvanised iron gates padlocked together.

He parked and got out; stared balefully at the lock. The driveway wound between silvery gum trees to a 1970s tan brick house set among pine trees. Tremendous view, he thought, turning around to confirm it, seeing the world through the eyes of anyone who lived here, high above the valley.

Should he, or shouldn't he? Between first and second thoughts Hirsch was climbing the fence and trudging up to the house. The wind was fierce. It reached deeply into his bones and the eucalypts bent to it, moving above his head in a ceaseless rushing sound. A shut-up look about the house, curtains drawn on every window. No vehicles that he could see. He knocked: no answer. He didn't like this. He didn't want to do this.

Not a place abandoned, though. The veranda was clean, pot plants healthy, garden beds weeded, window glass spotless. No mould on the downpipes. And a sheepdog in a kennel watched him, unconcerned. Chooks pecked and scratched in the backyard. A little pink tricycle stood neatly in the carport. The householders are out, Hirsch thought. They'll need to come back and feed the dog.

Leave a note? And then, alerted by a hint of a whisper of a sound or a movement, Hirsch took a second look at a caravan parked inside an open implement shed at the far end of the farmyard.

He crossed the yard. It was an older style of caravan on rotting tyres. Subject to the weather blowing in, because here at last was the grime and mould. A slip bolt had been mounted on the door, wire grilles over each window. As nice a prison as you could hope for.

Hirsch knocked and said hello and didn't wait but slid open the bolt, opened the door and stepped inside.

2

And jerked back reflexively. He turned, took a bite of the chilly fresh air blowing in from the wider world, stepped down to hook the door flush against the metal flank and tried boarding the caravan again, swimming against a rank tide—piss and shit odours drilling into his sinuses.

Shallow-breathing, he slid open a couple of windows for the cross breeze and took stock. Down at the bottom end was a mattress and a tangle of blankets. Closer to, on a grubby fold-out table between bench seats, was an atlas, a dictionary, foolscap booklets and pens and a wooden ruler in a glass jar. On a nearby sink, a plastic bowl ready to be washed, one pale maggot of cooked rice glued to the rim.

Hirsch scanned the rest of the interior. The walls—a thin metal skin that would be no defence against mid-winter temperatures—were finger-marked and mostly bare apart from a scrawled-upon whiteboard mounted between over-head cabinets halfway down the room. He saw that it was a list of rules in black and red, the words butting furiously against each other:

Bad behaviour is not rewarded in this family
Remember who is boss (hint: its not you)
You fit in with us, we do not fit in with you
You break it you fix it
Learn to take no for an answer
It might surprise you to know your not the centre of the universe
You get respect when you earn respect

Hirsch moved on and stood looking down at the bedding. A thin foam mattress, stinkingly yellow, askew on the bedframe. Two threadbare grey blankets with blue piping bundled at the foot of the mattress, stained and worn through here and there; probably poor comfort in the night.

A faint shift in the equilibrium of the caravan. As if it lived.

Hirsch went at once to a floor-to-ceiling wardrobe and opened it and the stink rolled out at him and, shrinking into the floor, was a girl, caging her head in her hands and forearms. Matted brown hair, a grimy woollen pullover and oversized explorer socks for warmth. But her legs were bare, and a disposable nappy was straining to protect her midsection.

Hirsch reached out a hand to her shoulder and rested it there. She jerked violently and ground herself deeper into the floor. He couldn't see her face.

'My name is Paul. I'm a policeman. You're safe now. Is your name Lydia?'

A stillness came over her. Not acquiescence: a willingness to listen? Give him the benefit of the doubt? He stroked her forearm and relayed some low, soft, calming nonsense for a couple of minutes: Isn't it a cold day! Want to go somewhere warm? You must be feeling a bit uncomfortable there. Ms Ogilvie's worried about you. Shall we find you some warm clothes?

It didn't work. At each statement she flinched, curling herself more tightly into a ball.

Hirsch realised how tiny she was, skin and bone. Eleven? She looked about six or seven.

'Now I'm just going to make you more snug and comfortable,' he said, lifting her out in one motion. She stiffened but didn't struggle. He spread one blanket over the stained mattress, sat her on it, wrapped the other around her shoulders.

She no longer hid her face in her arms but looked at the floor rather than meet his gaze. A smudged jawline, sharp cheekbones, mouth ajar. She sniffed wetly. A rattly cough. She's not well, Hirsch thought.

She dragged a forefinger across her nostrils. It glistened, a new mucous trace upon old, and a ring glinted, fake ruby, fake silver, and that made Hirsch sadder than ever.

'Is anyone home, Lydia?'

Nothing.

'I knocked at the house but there was no answer.'

This time she shrugged.

'Have they gone to the shops?'

She seemed to consider the question and whispered, 'In Clare.'

'Okay. For shopping?'

A pause and a shrug.

'Would you like to go over to the house and have a nice warm bath and change your clothes?'

She shrank against the enormity of that. 'Stay here,' she said.

'Is this your bedroom?'

She was very still; then a tiny nod.

'Shall we see if we can find you a change of clothes?'

Nothing.

'I could warm up some water so you can wash and change in here. I'll wait outside.'

She hunched herself, wanting to disappear again.

'Perhaps it would be best if I phoned your mum. Do you know her mobile number?'

It was as if she hadn't heard him. Then her hand shot to her scalp and her fingernails dug in. Nits? She coughed, and it left her weak.

Hirsch said, 'I don't think you're very well. Let's get you to Doctor Pillai in Redruth. Do you know her? She's nice.'

Lydia Jarmyn shook her head. 'Stay here.'

'I'll leave a note at the house to explain.'

'Stay here,' she croaked, and coughed again, sad and feeble and helpless against it. Worn out, she fell against Hirsch.

He wrapped her deep within his arms and the grimy blanket and carried her out into the air and some kind of future. Her struggles were those of an old dog insisting she be allowed to walk. The air was a rejuvenating force around them, with only a faint underlay of the child's wastes. Then just as Hirsch passed from the shed gloom to the wintry sun a pinprick of red caught his eye. A CCTV camera was trained on the caravan.

Oh well, he thought. I'm the cops, so you can fuck off. And he hoped that if there was film of him snatching Lydia, there was also film of those who'd harmed her.

Note to self: obtain CCTV footage.

He belted Lydia Jarmyn into the passenger seat, cracked open the window a couple of centimetres and rolled down the hill and out onto the highway. The sky was vast above the shallow valley and an eagle hung there and sunlight glinted on a distant windscreen. The world was washed clean.

He glanced often at the child as he made his calls, steering with one hand. Dr Pillai, at the Redruth Medical Centre, suggested he take the girl to the town's little hospital. 'Text me as soon as you arrive.'

'Will do.'

Then his boss at Redruth, Hilary Brandl, who wanted a lot more detail.

With a glance at Lydia, Hirsch said, 'In due course, sergeant.'

A pause. 'She's there? She's listening?'

'That's correct.'

Another pause. 'I'd like to check the place with my own eyes before I get Child Protection or CIB involved.'

'Understood.'

'Jarmyn, Hawker Road?'

'Yes.'

Hirsch heard the clack of a keyboard. 'Checking now…No callouts to that address. No outstanding warrants, no traffic offences…Nothing.'

'We should see what the neighbours have to say.'

'Yes, Constable Hirschhausen.'

Uh-oh. Telling her how to do her job. But she'd said it warmly. They'd grown to trust each other. There were those in the force who didn't trust Hirsch.

'What's your gut feeling?' she said. 'Neglect, or something worse?'

She meant sexual abuse, slavery…'I don't know, sergeant,' Hirsch said. With a glance at Lydia he said, 'I think there could be at least one other child living there.'

'Also in the caravan?'

'Not that I could tell. I don't know about inside the house.'

'You knocked? Peered through windows?'

'Nobody home. They've gone to Clare, apparently.'

'Be nice if we could be there when they get back.'

'Except we don't know when that will be,' Hirsch said.

'Mmm. Perhaps one of the neighbours has a mobile number for them. Otherwise we leave a note telling them to call the station.'

'Sergeant.'

'Text me as soon as you get to the hospital.'

Redruth, spread over seven small hills, was thirty minutes south of Tiverton. A pretty town, pastoral these days but settled in the late 1840s by Cornish miners, who'd built cottage rows as a reminder of home. The copper mine was now a bottomless, deep-blue pit of water surrounded by stone chimney stacks, powder magazines and engine houses on the hillslopes. Lydia Jarmyn was asleep, or Hirsch might have told her some of this as he rolled through the outskirts.

Down into the town square, an irregular patch of lawn around a red and yellow rotunda and out along the Adelaide road to the hospital, a small, understaffed place more aged-care centre than anything else, and reliant on doctors from the town's only medical clinic to take up the slack.

Hirsch parked, texted his arrival to Doctor Pillai and Sergeant Brandl, walked around to the passenger door and reached in. Lydia stirred, her eyes fluttered, then she fought him feebly as he lifted her out. She was rigid in his arms, panicked to be carried across a strange car park, past strange cars to a strange building. Fight or flight, and somehow that rendered her feather-light.

But when they stepped into the foyer and crossed to the reception desk she was overwhelmed and glued herself against him, a dead weight now. The receptionist, a scowling woman with short grey hair, watched him as if nothing in her experience or the rule book allowed for a policeman to advance across the foyer and stand before her with a grubby child in his arms. A smelly, grubby child. She sniffed and looked away and said, disobligingly, 'Help you?'

'I'm meeting Doctor Pillai.'

The woman looked across at the waiting room as if Hirsch might soil it, then down along the main corridor. 'She's busy.'

'She's already here?' Hirsch said.

'What does it concern, if I may ask?'

Take a wild guess, Hirsch thought, and was saved from more time-wasting when a voice called, 'Paul.'

He turned. Doctor Pillai, her black ponytail swinging, scarlet-rimmed glasses flashing, was slipping one arm and then the other into a white surgeon's coat as she emerged from the corridor. White runners on her feet—how would that go down with the receptionist?—black trousers and a navy top. Gold here and there: earlobes, wrists and fingers.

Her eyes met his for the duration of the hello but now she was standing close, peering at Lydia Jarmyn, touching a hand to her forehead. 'How old did you say?'

'Eleven, apparently.'

'Huh.'

'Exactly.'

'Let me take her from you,' Pillai said, reaching with both hands, but the child squirmed, dug her head in under Hirsch's chin and burrowed against him.

'Okay, she's latched onto you,' Pillai said. 'Come with me.'

To a room along the corridor, where Pillai and a nurse named Ella poked, prodded, peered, stood Lydia on scales, took a blood sample. The little girl whimpered; Hirsch felt useless.

Then Pillai said, 'We need to bathe her now.'

The implication was: to see what might lie under the grime. 'I'll be out in the waiting room,' Hirsch said.

But a minute later Pillai was back. 'Sorry, Paul, I think she'd be calmer if you were with her.'

She led him to a spacious tiled shower room with a hoist and pulley arrangement for non-ambulant patients. He stood in a gap in the curtain and smiled at Lydia as Ella and another nurse stripped off the nappy, socks and jumper, Doctor Pillai watching. The stench rose and Ella said, 'Oh, you poor little thing,' and Hirsch didn't look but he could visualise: caked wastes, sores.

'That nappy's been there for a while,' Pillai said, confirming the image.

A showerhead on a chrome flexi hose in one hand, a washcloth in the other, Ella began to dab at the bony limbs and torso, Lydia succumbing but her eyes fixed hard on Hirsch. He tried a smile or two; her expression didn't alter. She was trusting him, and he didn't know if he could live up to that. The suds turned brown; pink skin emerged.

Then a shampoo and rinse, three times, Ella finally saying, 'Clean now, but she's got headlice.'

Pillai nodded. 'Treat that later. Right now I want to finish examining her, then get her into some warm clothes and something to eat. You hungry, sweetheart?'

Lydia, lost in a giant towel, shrank away.

The hospital boasted a small comfort room: a sofa and armchairs, TV set, a poster of kittens on one pastel wall. Magazines on a coffee table, children's books, and a box of plastic tip trucks, soft toys and Lego. Hirsch and Pillai stood behind the sofa watching Lydia, in roomy blue pyjamas and a pink dressing gown, building a Lego tower. Her eyes flicked ceaselessly from the next Lego brick to Hirsch's face. Now and then she'd reach out to a plate of crustless sandwiches, nibble, and return the sandwich until next time, as if luxuriating in the meal, making it last.

A knock, and Hilary Brandl entered. Hirsch's sergeant was slender and wiry, an early-morning-jogger type, with short, fuss-free hair. Her gaze fixed on the child and Hirsch saw her mind working: was this a Child Protection case? Would Port Pirie CIB take over? What charges might the parents face?

She shook hands with Pillai, then Hirsch. 'Sorry I'm late. First impressions, Sandy?'

'Severely malnourished,' Sandali Pillai said. 'She only weighs twenty-one kilos, which is about fourteen under the average for her age.'

A murmur now: 'Any signs of sexual interference?'

'No immediate signs.'

'Cuts, bruises, old breaks, restraint marks?'

'No.'

'Anything else?'

'We've tried to talk to her, but she's frightened and wary. Unwilling to say what's going on.'

Brandl looked at Hirsch. He could feel the full force of her concentration. 'She's been home-schooled, so presumably she's not intellectually challenged?'

'Not according to the online tutor whose been monitoring her.' Looking to Pillai for confirmation, Hirsch added: 'But if she's been kept in isolation her social skills probably haven't developed.'

The doctor nodded. 'If she continues to be underfed and

kept isolated and in filthy conditions, she's not going to develop properly—physically, mentally or emotionally.'

Sergeant Brandl swung her lean face back to the child. 'I hate this kind of thing. Okay, constable, work to do.'

It was cruel to leave the child. She wailed and was help-less on the floor when Hirsch crouched to say goodbye and stood to go. In the end, Doctor Pillai called for Ella, the nurse who'd bathed her, Hirsch's closest substitute.

3

Late morning now. Rendezvousing on Hawker Road, they divided the task: Hirsch to call in at the properties uphill of the Jarmyn house, Sergeant Brandl to take the ones between the house and the highway. 'But first,' she said, climbing over the gate, 'I need to check the caravan for myself—no offence.'

'Sarge,' Hirsch said. Start at the top and work down, he decided.

At the top was a maintenance depot for the windfarm turbines that marched like mounted sentries along the valley in both directions. A high razor-wire fence surrounded equipment sheds, empty drums, muddy white LandCruisers and a semi-trailer loaded with a turbine blade. He drove in. The place seemed deserted.

Then Graham Fuller emerged from one of the sheds, amiably quizzical, wiping his hands on a rag. A solid man in his forties, who'd retrained as a wind-turbine mechanic when his little farm no longer supported him.

'Howdy,' Hirsch said.

Fuller nodded, stuck out his hand and then thought better of it. Examined the offending limb front and back. 'Wouldn't want to get those soft indoor fingers of yours all dirty.'

'No offence taken.'

Fuller grinned. 'You here about the graffiti?'

Spray-painted slogans and dripping skulls on the white towers, up and down the district: *eyesore*; *silence is golden*; *bird killer*. 'Sorry, no,' Hirsch said.

'Do for you?'

Hirsch asked about the Jarmyn property—who lived there, unusual activity, rumours, phone numbers—as Graham shook his head.

'I'll ask the boys at knock-off, but all I can tell you is, the gate's usually shut, and I've never seen anyone coming or going.' He paused. 'I did hear the husband works up at Roxby, that's about the extent of it.'

Roxby Downs. Five hundred kilometres north of Adelaide, near the opal mining town of Andamooka and the old Woomera rocket range. A modern town built in the 1980s to service the copper and uranium mine at Olympic Dam. Local men had found work there; Fuller himself had been offered a driving job but turned it down, telling Hirsch that fly-in fly-out wasn't for him; he'd rather go home to his wife and a home-cooked dinner at the end of the day.

Hirsch thanked him and retraced his route, calling at the first property downhill from the maintenance yard. A small stone bungalow sitting in a permanent pine tree shadow, mould on exposed surfaces, pine needles clogging the gutters. A black Valiant in the carport, more rust than duco, and a frenzied kelpie wanting a piece of him, throttled by a collar and chain at each lunge.

'Come behind, you bloody red whore.'

Hirsch heard something like that every week: *Sit!* and *Come behind, you mongrel* and *Down, you useless bloody cur*. He traced the voice to an elderly man emerging from the deeper shadows of a woodshed, an axe in one hand. An army greatcoat over knee-patched baggy pants held up by braces. A face like a scrotum with sparse thickets of whiskers here and there on his cheeks and neck, smudged glasses, ancient rubber boots. Hirsch visualised the fate of the yellow-taloned toes if the axe should slip.

'Jonas.'

'Chief superintendent.'

Jonas Heneker was the sole carer of his wife, who was sweetly demented and mostly bedridden. Hirsch checked in on him once or twice a month. They shook hands, and Heneker said, 'To what do I owe the honour? Not your usual day, is it? Admittedly, my mind is going.'

He continued to shake, his grip strong, prolonged, as if hanging on for dear life. A bloke with few visitors, fewer distractions, Hirsch thought, waiting it out.

Finally he was released and asked about the Jarmyns.

'Keep to themselves,' Heneker said. He patted his pockets, pulled out tobacco, papers and a match, settling in for a chinwag.

'Who lives there, exactly?'

'Husband, but he's away half the time, works up at Roxby Downs, then there's the wife—Grace—and a toddler.'

'Just the three?'

Heneker gazed down the years, his tongue busy with a tobacco fleck. 'I did hear they took in the husband's kid a while back.'

'From a previous marriage?'

Heneker shrugged. 'Heard she shot through on him when the kid was a baby. Years go by and she gets hit by a bus and he gets lumbered with the kid.'

Hirsch felt a first flicker of understanding. A loathed ex-wife and a child who reminds him of her. Take it out on the child.

'Do you ever see them to talk to?'

'Not me. I wave if I pass them in the car, but you see them stiffen up like I've got shit on my shoes.' He paused. 'Which I usually have.'

Hirsch grinned. He guessed Heneker waved to the Jarmyns for the sheer pleasure of discomfiting them. 'You're pretty well informed.'

'Stand still long enough,' Heneker said, 'everything comes around again and you hear everything there is to know.' He cocked his head; twinkled. 'How's that gorgeous sort of yours? Get her car fixed?'

Early in the week, on her way to work at Redruth High School, Wendy Street had lost power in her new second-hand Golf. Told Hirsch afterwards that she hadn't been able to go faster than thirty k's. 'There's even a name for it: I was in limp-home mode, the garage man said.'

'I hear rats got into the engine,' Jonas said. 'Chewed hoses? Some kind of vacuum leak?'

'Remarkably well informed,' Hirsch said, shaking the old man's hand goodbye.

He called at three more properties, then found Sergeant Brandl waiting for him outside the Jarmyns' locked gate. 'Developments,' she said, her breath white in the chilly air, ears and nose tip red. 'Doctor Pillai called me. Lydia started disclosing, so they decided to get a social worker involved, and the social worker notified Child Protection.' She shrugged. 'The guidelines are clear. I would have done the same thing myself. The state the poor kid was in, the state of that caravan.'

'What did Lydia say?'

Brandl blew on her fingers. 'Could be worse. No hitting or sexual abuse, but she was never fed properly, too cold in winter and too hot in summer, never allowed out to play, made to wear a nappy all the time.'

'That means CIB are taking over?'

'Yes. We're to wait here for them—or for the Jarmyns, whoever arrives first.'

Could be hours, thought Hirsch. 'Learn anything from the neighbours?'

The sergeant glanced down along the road. 'Woefully uninformed. Except one person said the girl was a niece and another said she was retarded.'

'She's not retarded,' Hirsch said.

'And a third person said, quote, "The husband's under the thumb."'

Hirsch stared out at the folds of hillsides lit green by the wintry sun, working that fact—if it was a fact—into his theory of the dynamics in the Jarmyn household. Then the sergeant's phone buzzed, and he watched incuriously as she muttered, 'Why's Brian texting me?' and poked at the screen. He grew interested when her face stiffened, whitened: distress writ large. 'Sergeant?'

She swallowed, wouldn't look at him; diminished in some way. 'I have to go.'

'Is everything okay?'

'I have to take some personal time. A couple of days.'

'Anything I can do to help?'

She was edging away. 'You're in charge. Keep me in the loop.'

'If you like I can call in tonight and—'

'I won't be at home or at the station. I'm going to Adelaide.'

Her tone said: *No more questions.*

'Sergeant.'

Hirsch watched her shoot off. Racing to deal with something momentous. Something private.

He climbed into the Toyota and waited. Hoped and prayed that CIB would arrive first, with a social worker. Who knew what might happen if the Jarmyns arrived first? His orders were clear, arrest and caution, but what if they got aggressive? Ran for it? Dissolved into hysteria? He was only one man.

The whole area of child protection was murky. To report suspected instances of child endangerment was a clear and mandatory obligation, but often the nature of the endangerment wasn't so clear. Careless neglect, intentional neglect, abuse, sexual abuse, enslavement? Should it be a police matter or a social work matter? Or both? What precise charges should be laid? It seemed obvious to Hirsch that police attention was necessary here—the imprisonment, for a start—but had the Jarmyns' intention been criminal in nature or were they merely poor or under-educated or with addiction or mental health issues, and deserving of support and counselling, not trial or imprisonment.

He was musing on these and other matters, occasionally running the engine for warmth, when a bulky white 1980s wagon, a Falcon, nosed fearfully at the locked gates. Two heads on board: the driver had a little girl asleep in a booster seat behind her. Hirsch got out; the driver got out. She wore ankle boots, jeans and a sleeveless puffa jacket over a dark blue skivvy. Glancing at him with a doleful lack of curiosity, she unlocked the gates, swung them open, got behind the wheel again and drove in.

Right.

Hirsch trailed the Falcon up the driveway, slowed as it coasted into the carport, and parked hard behind it. By now the woman was bending into the back seat, fussing with straps, backing out with a wispy blonde toddler all in pink: boots, tights, corduroy dress, jacket and hair ribbon. The child blinked at Hirsch and at the world as she woke up.

'Mrs Jarmyn? Grace?'

The woman ignored him, moving mechanically, just a mother returning from another shopping trip in the car.

'Are you Mrs Jarmyn?'

She was without affect, gaunt with disappointments and privations. She looked to be in her forties but was probably younger. Painfully thin. Slender, shapely hands, he noticed, when she set her daughter down—and, as if they were her only vanity, she'd had the nails done: silvery blue, with a speckled pattern.

Hirsch stepped right up to her and said, 'Mrs Jarmyn, please.'

She glanced past his ear at the caravan in the shed, turned her back on him and took her daughter by the hand to a side door leading into the house. Gave the child a little push, watched for a moment, then returned to the car and hauled open the tailgate.

Uh-huh, thought Hirsch, watching her reach in and emerge with an apple carton containing carrots, potatoes and pumpkin. She'd been to a roadside stall?

Then, backing away from the car, she jerked her head at the rest of her shopping: a Mitre 10 bag, a Coles bag and a Target flatpack.

Okay. He gathered it all and followed her into the kitchen, a tidy space, clean but tired looking. A scorch mark beside the gas burners, wooden tabletop faintly engraved, as if from years of heavy-handed crosswords, a shuddery round-shouldered fridge: everything brightened by a sprig of eucalyptus leaves in a white vase. Hirsch placed the shopping bags on the table and the flatpack against a chair leg and all the while was trying to work her out. She knows why I'm here and she's playing dumb; or she hasn't the capacity for curiosity or speculation; or she's straight out beaten down by life.

Then she spoke. 'Cup of tea?' A soft, melodious voice.

'Thank you,' Hirsch said, 'but first I need to confirm that you are Grace Jarmyn?'

'I am.'

Hating the whole procedure, Hirsch placed her under arrest and advised her of her rights. 'Other police will be here shortly,' he told her. 'Formal charges may be laid.'

She was filling an electric jug with water. 'Okay,' she said.

Not confident that she'd taken any of it in, he repeated what he'd said. 'I need to hear you say that you understand, Mrs Jarmyn.'

'I understand.'

She placed the jug on its base, flicked a switch. The jug gave a little jolt of surprise; slowly began to boil. She fetched down mugs from an overhead cupboard and teabags from a drawer beside the dishwasher. Meanwhile, glimpsed through an archway to the sitting room, the child was crouched over a colouring book on a coffee table. Everything was seriously weird.

'Sit please Mrs Jarmyn, while the kettle boils.'

She glanced uneasily around the kitchen as if vital house-work tasks awaited, then at her daughter, and finally eased into the chair opposite him. Shifted the shopping bags to the far end, wet the tip of a forefinger and rubbed at a spot on the table.

'You're entitled to legal representation at any time, Mrs Jarmyn, and I don't intend to question you, but it would help matters to know where Mr Jarmyn is at this time. Is he at work up north?'

Grace Jarmyn gave Hirsch her full attention, her face mobile at last. Stripped of its bony flatness, her manner was wry. 'For all I know, he's in Outer Woop Woop.'

'He's not working at—'

'I haven't seen my husband for at least a year. He could still be working up at Roxby; he could be in Outer Woop Woop.'

So much for Hawker Road intel, thought Hirsch.

She cocked her head. 'He left me lumbered with his daughter. That's why you're here, isn't it?'

'Mrs Jarmyn, you really should—'

'He said he couldn't cope; it was too much for him. Alex is a very weak man,' Grace Jarmyn said, getting to her feet as the jug switched off. Another glance at her daughter, then she busied herself making the tea.

'Mrs Jarmyn, if you intend or wish to make admissions, I should record them.'

She said, over her shoulder, 'I have nothing to hide or to fear.'

An air of unreality attended as Hirsch placed his phone on the table and recorded time, date, location, persons present, the circumstances that had led to the involvement of South Australia police. Arse covering.

Meanwhile Grace Jarmyn was setting mugs of tea, a small milk jug and a sugar bowl on the table. Then she fetched biscuits. With another glance through to the sitting room, she sat again, saying, 'I've been feeding, clothing and home-schooling Lydia for a year and a half now. I assume you've taken her away somewhere?'

'Mrs Jarmyn, you do realise that when I found her, she was—'

'Hmm, yes. Do you know what state she was in when we got her? Skin and bone. Her mother was an addict. Lex's first wife.'

Was that going to be part of her defence? 'Even so, to keep a child locked in a caravan...'

'For her own good. She kept running away.'

Hence the CCTV. 'A bowl of rice a day isn't very nourishing.'

'Lex left me with debts. I've been doing everything myself, no help from anyone. I have no family and his is useless. Centrelink is a complete nightmare. I go without some-times, just so my daughter, *and his*, are fed and clothed.'

So, a bit skewed in her thinking. Hirsch watched as she examined her fresh new nails. Hands out, stiff-fingered, an assessing frown creasing her brow. Nonplussed, he turned to glance at the child with her colouring book, and Jarmyn caught it. 'You're not taking Naomi away from me.'

Hirsch was expressionless. He wouldn't, but Child Protection might.

He was saved by the sounds of vehicles arriving, doors slamming. He left the house through the carport and found a Port Pirie CIB detective named Comyn standing with two women: a colleague and a social worker. Comyn, a squat plug of a man mostly gristle and sneers, said, 'Just come from Redruth. Saw the before and after photos and spoke to the kid. Now we need to see this so-called prison.'

He always addressed Hirsch as if he believed anything Hirsch did or said was suspect. 'This way,' Hirsch said.

Asking his colleagues to go indoors, Comyn followed Hirsch to the caravan. Walked around it, examining the barred windows and the door with its external lock, then climbed aboard. 'Pongs.'

Hirsch said nothing. He waited outside, gazing at the wintry yard and the cars with their skirts of grime, feeling the coldness of the afternoon creeping into his bones.

Presently Comyn reappeared. 'See what you mean.'

Hirsch jerked his head. 'Mrs Jarmyn started making admissions.'

Comyn flared up. 'What the fuck? Did you—'

'It's all on tape, including the required preamble. I'll email you the file.'

Comyn stalked across the yard, muttering, 'Spare me from small-town uniforms.'

As Hirsch trailed behind, his phone buzzed. He glanced at the screen—*Tiverton Primary School*—and accepted the call. A tense voice in his ear: 'I need you to get here straight away. A parent's going mental.'

4

Hirsch tore away, taking the slippery road at speed, the HiLux fishtailing. Relieved to reach bitumen at last, one eye on the sky for kamikaze crop-dusters, he ran the name Leon Ayliffe through his mind. A farmer; lived with his eighteen-year-old son—Jake? No, Josh—on a wheat and wool property south of the town. Two dealings: last summer, when Ayliffe had barred entry to an RSPCA inspector acting on a tip-off, and at the end of autumn, when Ayliffe had rammed his wife's car. Diana Ayliffe had been in the process of leaving him, her Mazda crammed with boxes, eleven-year-old daughter, Chloe, in the passenger seat. Mother and daughter now lived in a rental house on First Street. Hirsch saw them walking to and from the school sometimes.

Leon was a drinker, Diana said. A brooder. Hard one moment, sentimental the next.

If there was an issue at school, why had the estranged husband turned up and not Mrs Ayliffe?

The school supported two teachers and a part-time

admin clerk. The principal, Julian Roskam, taught the upper primary grades, Vikki Bastian taught preps and juniors; it was the admin clerk, Glenys Fife, who'd called Hirsch. He'd heard shouting in the background: '*Coward...Mongrel...Piss weak the lotta ya.*'

Ten minutes later he was parking the Toyota next to a muddy silver Holden ute angled crookedly over two of the school's visitor-parking slots, 'Ayliffe Pastoral' scrolled on each door. The numberplate read OZ4US: great, thought Hirsch. As he crossed the yard, he could see into one of the classrooms. It looked crammed; Vikki Bastian, standing at a whiteboard, gave him a rueful smile and wave. They'd placed all the children in one room while the drama played out, he realised.

He entered the foyer, Glenys watching him tensely from the reception desk. She pointed along a corridor and said nothing—not that Hirsch needed directions: just follow the voices.

Drawings and class photos pinned to the corridor walls— and a poster for the inaugural Clonmel Run music festival next week. From Friday evening until Sunday afternoon, and Hirsch would be on duty for a part of that time. Kids smuggling in booze and drugs. Kids overdosing. Pissing down with rain, probably. Awful music.

Reaching the principal's office, he switched his phone to silent, knocked, walked in. Two men stood there: Julian Roskam between his desk and the back wall, Leon Ayliffe squaring up as if to hurdle at him. Roskam, mid-fifties, was plump, balding, anachronistic in a straining grey cardigan over a white shirt and a strangling blue tie. He looked frightened, but with a tinge of hauteur, as if outraged at what he was being subjected to. He shook his head at Hirsch. 'Finally.'

Hirsch gave a curt nod. He concentrated on Ayliffe. A slight man, tightly wound, hands clenched, wisps of grey in his demoralised bushman's beard. A man for whom nothing was ever quite right—the temperature of his tea, the state of the roads, government policies. And right now Hirsch had come to his attention. He swung around, disgusted: 'Fucking outstanding. The cops are here.' Turning back to Roskam, he snarled, 'You piece of piss.'

'Why don't we all sit down,' Hirsch said, 'and sort this out.'

Ayliffe took a step towards him, puffed up at this fresh outrage. 'Sit? That's all any of you pricks do is sit. How about some fucking action instead?'

Hirsch recoiled. The man had been drinking. 'Mr Ayliffe, the kids can probably hear you. It'll be upsetting for them. Think of Chloe.'

Ayliffe swelled again. 'Chloe's why I'm here!'

The principal shook his head. 'Au contraire, Mr Ayliffe, you're here because—'

Hirsch marched up to the desk, stuck out his hand, and Roskam, astounded, shook with him. Then Hirsch turned to Ayliffe, hand still extended. 'Mr Ayliffe?'

Ayliffe, equally astounded, also shook, nudged by some trace of propriety. But it defused him. And Roskam looked defused too.

'Let's sit,' Hirsch said, reaching into a gap between filing cabinets and fishing out two metal folding chairs. With a flick he had them facing Roskam's desk. He sat, gestured at the other chair, and Ayliffe sat. Roskam settled, like a blimp coming down, behind his desk.

'Okay. Let's start at the beginning.'

Roskam, safe now, leaned over a pristine blotter bordered by green leather. 'He came barging in and—'

Hirsch cut him off. 'Perhaps if we start a little earlier than that? Mr Ayliffe? May I ask why you came to the school today?'

Ayliffe gathered his thoughts. Seated, he was less menacing. In profile he had a starved look, as if anger depleted him of flesh, leaving only bones and sinews. 'Well, it started with...No, I tell a lie, it started with that deadshit Quinlan.'

Hirsch was lost. The stock and station agent?

'Adrian Quinlan? How's he involved?'

Ayliffe looked uncomfortable now, as if beginning to regret the past thirty minutes. 'Ask around. The prick owes money right, left and centre.'

'He owes you money?'

'That's what I've been saying. I've used him for years, selling sheep, buying rams, sourcing hay, et cetera, et cetera. Never a problem. But the last cheque bounced: three thousand. Bastard won't return my calls.'

There was a link to be made between Quinlan, the bounced cheque and the school...

Hirsch made a leap: 'You owe school fees?'

Ayliffe was exasperated. 'That's what I've been saying. The wife—Di—calls me half in tears, half pissed off. She's upset because this prick'—he indicated Roskam—'made Chloe stand out the front of the whole school, and pissed off because I was supposed to pay the fee at the beginning of term. It's a *voluntary* fee.'

Throwing a challenge at Roskam, who sat, elbows on desk, fingers tented, and said, 'This school, like most public schools, is not in a position to cover a pupil's book, stationery, sport or excursion costs. We expect parents to contribute. Take that trip to Broken Hill early in the year: bus travel, accommodation...' He did something he shouldn't have done. He shrugged. 'It's the convention.'

Ayliffe was quivering. 'It's the *convention* to punish kids if a parent overlooks something, is it?' He looked at Hirsch, spitting chips. 'At morning assembly on Monday, Chloe and another kid were bailed up and made to stand out the front because the fee hadn't been paid. What a cunt act, humiliating a kid like that.'

Hirsch thought he had a point. 'Mr Roskam?'

The principal rolled his shoulders, faintly uncomfortable. 'We can't carry the cost. Some things need to be nipped in the bud.'

'I'll nip you in the—'

'Mr Ayliffe,' cautioned Hirsch.

Encouraged, Roskam said, 'I should point out that the school council is on board one hundred per cent with my taking steps to rein in the budget.'

'You pompous fucking arsehole,' Ayliffe said.

And a few other choice terms Hirsch could think of. He glanced at Ayliffe. Already smarting because his wife and daughter have left him, down three thousand dollars in income—sporadic income, since he's a farmer—the man suffers a last straw, the public humiliation of his daughter.

'Perhaps we can work out a payment plan?'

Hirsch the mediator. He seemed to spend most of his time as father confessor, therapist, social worker, fixer and go-between. What he'd give for a plain old criminal and a plain old vanilla arrest.

Three-thirty now. As he stepped outside, kids were pouring onto the grounds, shrugging into parkas, backpacks bouncing, many of the boys in short pants, oblivious to the cold. He thought about Roskam as he got into the Toyota and drove back to the police station. Roskam had replaced the previous principal at the beginning of the school year. He'd joined the tennis and football clubs, arranged an art fair, promised a bigger and better end-of-year school concert. Nothing to explain why he'd humiliate a couple of kids whose parents hadn't paid—or been able to pay—a two-hundred-dollar levy for equipment and excursions. Maybe it was to do with where he'd taught previously. A tough inner-city school? Maybe some cashed-up private joint. Where would you be more likely to punish kids for something their parents had neglected to do?

Then he thought about Adrian Quinlan. If there was a big shot in this corner of the mid-north, it was Quinlan. Sixties, portly, flushed in the face. Liked to dress up as a pastoralist—moleskin pants, R. M. Williams boots, tweed jacket, Akubra hat—the works. Donated to the hospital and to local schools and sporting clubs; drove a Range Rover Evoque; lived in a lovely 1920s homestead on a hillslope overlooking Redruth; and ran a small fleet of cars, utes and trucks marked *Quinlan Stock and Station Services* from a depot near the stockyards on the northern edge of Redruth. A big, warm, back-slapping, hand-pumping, grinning man, exactly the kind of guy to make Hirsch's soul retreat. Although, being Hirsch, he assumed the inadequacy was with him, not the backslappers.

Two references in one day to financial irregularity on Quinlan's part. Was the district full of pissed-off citizens?

He parked in the police station driveway, got out, looked glumly at the mud coating the Toyota's tyres, undercarriage and side panels—just his luck if the area commander dropped in unannounced. Then it began to spit with rain: a bloke couldn't be expected to work outside when it was raining. Rather than wash his official police vehicle he went through to his kitchen, switched on the jug, made a cup of tea and took it to his office. Remembered his mobile. Two missed calls and a text from Sergeant Brandl: *Call me asap*.

She answered, sounding jittery. 'Just checking in. Did CIB turn up? The Jarmyns?'

'Mrs Jarmyn arrived first,' Hirsch said. 'The husband's out of the picture apparently. Then CIB arrived.'

'Okay, okay,' she said, already losing interest. 'Look,' she added, her jitteriness increasing, 'I need to go.' A grudging pause. 'I'll try to be back by the weekend.'

'Hope everything's okay, sarge,' Hirsch said, but she'd already cut the connection.

He shrugged, made a start on letters and emails, and had barely begun when someone knocked on the front door. Usually people let themselves in. He yelled, 'It's open.'

Vikki Bastian stood there as if reluctant to enter. Early twenties, wearing a charcoal woollen dress, black tights, smoky blue pullover, hair dotted with rain. She darted a worried smile at Hirsch, another over her shoulder at the school across the highway, and finally strode in, pulling off leather gloves, creating a little disturbance: public notices— most of them out of date—rustled in her wake.

Stopping at the counter, she gazed around Hirsch's office. She didn't look inspired, and Hirsch couldn't blame her. 'Cold in here,' she said.

'I'm waiting for someone to break the law,' Hirsch said, 'so I can get warmed up running them in.'

'Ha ha. No central heating?'

'Bar radiator the size of a tissue box.'

She gnawed her bottom lip briefly. 'About earlier. Mr Ayliffe...'

Hirsch stood. 'Come around here. It's marginally warmer.'

Settled into a chair that faced his desk, she said, 'Marginally being the operative term. And if someone comes in and sees me sitting here?'

'I've been gossiped about since I arrived,' Hirsch said. 'I like to keep the locals on their toes.' He cocked his head at her, genially expectant.

'Several things,' Bastian said briskly. 'First, Leon Ayliffe was totally out of line. He was scary, I thought he was going to hit someone. Before he barged in, he was roaming around outside for half an hour, swearing, kicking rubbish bins. Then when Julian went out to see what the matter was, he started bumping chests. It would've been comical if it wasn't so serious. The kids were frightened.'

What's she saying? thought Hirsch. That I should have arrested him? 'I had to make a judgment call,' he said. 'I didn't want things to escalate.'

'No, no, you did the right thing, the payment plan,' Bastian said. 'Good solution in the circumstances.'

'Mr Roskam told you?'

'Leon did, actually. Came up to me and apologised.' She paused. 'And it's not as if Julian didn't have some warning. Leon's been phoning and emailing the school since Monday.'

Some warning. How often did coppers hear those words...

She went on. 'It's a good school. Too small to be a bad one. But you do learn to spot the problem parents. You know, overprotective, always hovering, always on the phone about the smallest thing impacting on their little darlings. Or their little darling is the centre of the universe and deserves your undivided attention. Or you have parents who're on some kind of power trip—I'm an easy target because I'm young and I'm new. And you have disengaged parents: it's *your* job to provide discipline, guidance and care. And then you have fathers—mothers too, actually—like Leon Ayliffe, cranky and aggressive. If you punish their kid, you're punishing *them*.' She shrugged. 'You do hear things that explain it sometimes. A messy divorce, mental health issues, drugs...'

Hirsch saw her pause, narrow her gaze, wondering if she'd

said too much and he'd start demanding names. He waved her misgivings away. 'How can I help?'

'It's more in the way of *me* helping *you*,' she said, giving him a look.

'Okay...'

But she didn't get to the point immediately. 'About the services fee. If you want to be a stickler about it, it *is* voluntary, but everyone pays it—except two families this time around. Hard times, you know? It happens. But Julian didn't handle it very well.' She hunched a little, as if a shot had been fired at her. 'I feel bad, saying that. I do have to work with him.'

'Is he somehow—'

'No, no. Just poor judgment.' Vikki was busy with the hem of her dress, the lie of the fabric along her thighs.

'So, tell me what's on your mind. I'll be discreet.'

She said in a rush, 'It's what Leon said about Adrian Quinlan.'

Quinlan reference the third. 'Okay.'

'Leon shouldn't have behaved like he did, clearly he's got anger management issues, but the thing is it's probably true he's owed money by Mr Quinlan.' She paused. 'So is my father, and I bet others are, too.'

Wondering where she was going with this, Hirsch said, 'Your father sells sheep through the agency? Wool?'

Vikki Bastian gave him a confused look. 'I'm talking about the music festival,' she said. 'Clonmel Run?'

Hirsch connected: Hedley Bastian was the grazier who'd made his property available for the festival. He made another connection: the main sponsor was Quinlan Stock and Station Services.

He thought about joking that he'd be on duty, patrolling with sniffer dog and machine gun, but there was something faintly humourless about the daughter. 'Your father hasn't been paid for leasing his place to the festival? Perhaps he gets paid when it's over.'

'He hasn't even been paid the deposit. He's spent thousands getting the paddock ready, slashing the grass, clearing stones, fixing the fences. Liaising with suppliers, marquee people, caterers...A few people have been paid some money, but not enough to cover up-front costs, and meanwhile Quinlan keeps fobbing everyone off.'

Hirsch said carefully, 'It's not a police matter at this stage. Perhaps if your father and the others got legal advice? A civil suit?'

A flurry of nods. 'I've already told him that, but he says Mr Quinlan's a mate, they've always had fair dealings. I hate to see Dad worried. And what happens if no one's paid, or the festival doesn't go ahead?'

Hirsch shrugged a little. There really wasn't anything he could do.

But Vikki Bastian wasn't finished; she tilted her nose a little. 'I just thought I should tell you in case someone does something that makes it a police matter.'

5

Thursday, patrol day.

Hirsch walked around the town, pinned his number to the main door and was on the road by 7.30. He made two long-range patrols each week, east of Tiverton on Mondays, west on Thursdays—crime waves or other factors permitting. Mostly he called in on the lonely and the vulnerable—a widow and her Down Syndrome daughter, an elderly couple stubbornly running sheep on marginal land, a sharefarmer with a wheelchair-bound wife.

Today he'd barely started when he remembered the Jarmyns' dog. He called Comyn, who said, 'This'd better be good.'

'I was after an update on the Jarmyns.'

Comyn was clipped. 'The caravan kid's in hospital, the little one's with Child Protection, the mother's having a psych eval.'

'Will she be allowed back home?'

'Not for me to say. Anything else?'

'Did the CCTV show anything?'

'Grace Jarmyn coming and going with food. Couple of times with a laptop.'

For the sessions with Clara, thought Hirsch. 'Have you heard from the husband?'

Irritable, Comyn said, 'You talked to her. She tell you he walked out on them a year ago?'

That would be a no, Hirsch thought. 'What about the dog?'

'What dog?'

'There was a dog in the kennel.'

'Mate,' Comyn said, 'call the RSPCA or check on it yourself.'

So Hirsch checked on it himself, parking at the Jarmyns' gate, climbing over, walking a zigzag route around driveway mud and potholes, until he reached the house. The kennel was empty, the lead lying in the damp grass. He had to presume Grace had taken care of it. But to be on the safe side, he tramped around the property. It was about ten hectares in size. No crops, no animals, only grass, old sheds, the house and its well-tended garden beds. The sheds were mostly empty: hessian sacks, a dented five-litre fuel can, a cobwebby aluminium ladder, a couple of bald, perishing tyres.

Beyond the sheds, two grassy paddocks rose in a gentle upslope on the flank of one of the Tiverton Hills. Hirsch set out for the far corner, where a windmill—rusty, vanes missing, unmoving despite the wind—leaned exhaustedly as if yearning for the embrace of the grass. A holed and rusty galvanised iron tank. A rusty trough. He peered in: scummy water, blooming with algae. He turned, scanned the stretches of grass, all spirit draining suddenly out of him.

When had he realised he was looking not for a dog but a dead husband? Where would you begin to find a body here anyway, in the country of the unseen and the unheard? Country he barely felt tethered to, sometimes. And why was he thinking the husband was dead and buried? Because his ABC of policing said: assume nothing, believe nothing, challenge everything. Trouble was, you were perpetually pushing against a headwind when you did that.

Bank records, he thought. Phone records.

He resumed his patrol. It was rain-shadow country out east, and he was struck by how rapidly the district's new winter-green tones fell off the further he ventured. Significantly drier within just a few kilometres. Stragglier.

He made his home visits, turning on the dashcam at each location, just in case; stopped for a while to watch three eagles floating speculatively. Two hundred and ninety kilometres and half a day later, one hour short of getting home, his mobile rang.

A male voice, young, peeved. 'There was a note on the door of the police station.'

'I'll be back by four,' Hirsch said. 'But if it's something I can deal with by phone...?'

The caller was named Andrew Eyre, he was the district council's environment protection officer and he needed Hirsch to attend while he investigated a possibly illegal land-clearing issue. Still peevish, he added, 'I called at Redruth first. They told me Sergeant Brandl's taking some personal time and I should call you.'

'Okay. Can you give me the address and some details?'

Leon Ayliffe, a property near Penhale.

Well, that made Hirsch's day. 'He's felling trees illegally?'

'That's just it. I can't be sure. Someone reported him so I went there yesterday morning and was denied access. Couldn't get past his front door. Told to turn around and not come back. He was very aggro. They both were.'

'Both?'

'Father and son.'

'Aggro in what way?'

'The father shoved me. Shouted. Swore. The son went back in the house and came out with a shotgun. Said he was off to shoot rabbits—and he did go off, but the meaning was clear.'

Hirsch arranged to meet Eyre at the entrance to the Ayliffe farm. 'Park out on the road. Don't try to go in. I should be there by four.'

Hirsch accelerated, wondering what an environment protection officer did all day in an area like this, long since cleared and settled by grain and wool farmers. Approved or disapproved applications for windfarm turbines, roads or dams? Or were they planning issues? Approved or disapproved large-scale weed-clearing programs? Culling—foxes, rabbits, kangaroos? Or were they health and safety issues? Progress implied dispossession, though, so forms of protection were needed. Too late for the Ngadjuri people. Too late for the trees indigenous to the area—and therefore too late for the creatures that lived in them. Hirsch glanced right and left as he drove: hillslopes and paddocks, denuded of trees. Some years the topsoil blew away in summer and washed away in winter.

He left the land of the back roads and emerged onto the Barrier Highway north of Tiverton. Drove right through the town, sixty k's, accelerating to a hundred once he was past the grain silos. Five minutes later he had the Razorback on his left. Snow? No. Yes—a smear of white lingered along the stony spine.

Twelve minutes later he was in Penhale, a town midway between Tiverton and Redruth and one of the smallest settlements in his patrol area. Turning left, he took Nautilus Road into undulating farmland, a mix of new green wheat shoots, fallow ground and occasional homesteads set back from the road. Taking more notice as Ayliffe's driveway appeared, he realised that what appeared as a khaki patch on a distant hillslope behind the house was a stand of gum trees several hectares in size.

One of the white Ford twin-cabs favoured by the district council was parked outside the dispirited stock ramp that marked the entrance to the Ayliffe property. The driver got out as Hirsch pulled up. Andrew Eyre was in his late twenties. Faintly hipster-bushwalker in appearance: jeans, top-of-the-range hiking boots, Gore-Tex jacket and designer eyewear. The farmers around here would take one look and think *greenie*.

They shook hands. Hirsch asked for the backstory.

Eyre pointed to the smudge of trees that Hirsch had identified as the likely source of trouble. 'I think those are the trees in question,' he said, wisps of condensation curling from his mouth. 'On the other side is a house in a little gully and the woman living there rang us last week to say men with chainsaws and bulldozers had started clearing.'

Hirsch took notes. The wind cut through him and his fingers were going numb. He wanted essential information as quickly as he could get it. 'Her name?'

'Amy Groote.'

Hirsch asked for the spelling and wrote it down. The Penhale snowdropping victim was Maggie Groote. Family connection?

'The trees are protected?'

'Put it this way,' Eyre said. 'You'd need council permission for large-scale clearing.'

'So you don't know if Mr Ayliffe has cut down one tree or a dozen?'

'Given his reaction yesterday morning,' Eyre said, 'I'd hardly say he'd stopped at one. He didn't want me investigating.' He paused. 'Look, I don't intend to make a song and dance about the aggro behaviour, I just want to do my job. I want to inspect, write up a report, and issue notices or fines if required. Without getting shot.'

Humour? Hirsch peered at him. No.

He turned away, stared out across the damp paddocks, seeing, in his mind's eye, the aggrieved glint in Leon Ayliffe. Imagining the son, a younger feral-bushman version of his father?

'Did Mr Ayliffe confirm or deny that he was chopping down trees?'

'All he said was, "This is my land and I'll bloody well do what I like with it."'

Heard throughout rural Australia. Urban Australia, too. 'Okay, let's see what happens. You follow me.'

Eyre, glancing at the service pistol on Hirsch's belt, returned to his car. Hirsch climbed into the police HiLux, called in his location and bumped over the ramp and up the driveway. Drooping wire fence, potholes filled with water, then an ugly low-slung brick house. Diana Ayliffe had left her husband three months ago, and now the place looked sad and hopeless. Untamed lawns, misshapen shrubs, drifts of leaves on the veranda. Dismal tea towels and a lonely sock on the clothesline.

He got out, waited for Eyre to join him on the weedy gravel. 'Hear that?'

Eyre nodded. Distant chainsawing. The rumble of a heavy vehicle. Bulldozer?

Hirsch knocked anyway. No answer. He checked the car shed. No vehicle, but serious equipment: power and hand tools, ladders, ropes, winches and cables, tarpaulins, a tent and poles, car batteries hooked to a charger, fuel and water cans. Ready for the apocalypse?

They left the Ford and took Hirsch's 4WD through a back gate and along a vehicle track that wound among stone reefs concealed in wet grass. 'Lovely old trees,' Hirsch remarked, as they drew nearer. He felt a twinge of protectiveness.

No sign yet of men or vehicles so he drove along one

flank, the ground sloping down now to a fence and a little house in a hollow. He pointed. 'Is that where Amy Groote lives, the woman who reported it?'

'I guess so,' Eyre said.

Hirsch kept going, swinging into the space separating the trees from the fence, and here was activity at last. Eight raw stumps, a truck, the Holden ute Hirsch had seen at the primary school, a dirt bike, a tractor fitted with a blade. Leon Ayliffe was leaning over a felled tree trunk, chips flying as he trimmed it. The son was prowling in the tractor, nudging offcuts into a growing mountain of twigs, branches and leafy canopy.

Ready for the match, Hirsch thought. 'Stay here,' he warned, turning on the dashcam and getting out.

He waded through the grass and stood where Leon Ayliffe was bound to see him. Ayliffe froze mid-cut, then nodded, finished sawing and shut off the motor, straightening his back, stretching it. 'Oof,' he said, grimacing in pain, whipping off his earmuffs and goggles and setting the chainsaw on the ground. Beard, nose and home-knitted pullover were flecked with pale moist sawdust. 'What can I do you for?'

'I think you know, Mr Ayliffe.'

Ayliffe glanced past Hirsch at Eyre in the passenger seat of the HiLux. 'Like I told your pal, this is my place and I'll clear it if I need to. Plant it with wheat, run sheep on it, whatever I like.'

'It may be that you'll be allowed to do that in the long term. Meanwhile there's the matter of bylaws and permits and rights and obligations. Paperwork.'

'Rights? Like I said, I've got the right to farm my own land. Just as my daughter has a right to a free education.'

The tractor was idling nearby. Hirsch turned, made a slicing gesture, but Josh Ayliffe, seeing Andrew Eyre get out of the Toyota and aim a camera at the felled trees, opened up the throttle and made a slow feint. Eyre scrambled back into the Toyota. Leon Ayliffe laughed; Hirsch wanted to, then regretted it. These guys could be dangerous.

Josh switched off and climbed down from the cabin. Taller than his father, wiry build, hair in a ponytail, Indiana Jones hat. Grinning at the Toyota.

His father called, 'That's enough now, Josh.'

The kid kept striding across the grass, stabbing his finger at Hirsch. 'You leave my dad alone.'

'Rules and regulations, Josh,' Hirsch said tensely.

'You're all the same.'

Tears in his eyes, Hirsch realised. Another dimension opened. He blames his mother for leaving? She'd asked him to go with her? He wanted the old family unit back again? Meanwhile he was living with his father in that atmosphere you got sometimes in these situations. Toxic masculinity.

Hirsch held up his hand, addressing both men. 'Mr Eyre has a job to do. Let him do it and we'll be out of your hair in a jiffy.'

As if he'd heard Hirsch, Eyre emerged from the Toyota again and aimed his camera. Leon Ayliffe shouted, 'I give you permission to do that?'

'Formality,' Eyre shouted in return. 'I'll be opening a file.'

Poor choice of words, thought Hirsch, as Leon bristled.

'This is my land. Mine. I can chop down trees if I want to.'

Eyre lowered the camera, came a little closer. 'It's not just your land though, Mr Ayliffe. It's everybody's, isn't it? People driving by, visitors, neighbours, even those who never pass by this way. You live in a community. A neighbourhood. In a sense, you—'

'I'll fucking give you sense,' Leon said, sprinting across the grass.

Hirsch chased after him, grabbed an arm, swung him around and blocked his access to Eyre, who had backed up and fallen on his backside. 'Cool it, Leon, okay? I don't want to arrest you, but I will if you continue to make threats, or harm Mr Eyre—or myself—in any way.'

There was a red-mist wildness in Ayliffe. Hirsch almost touched the butt of his pistol for reassurance but feared it might set Ayliffe or his son off again. The wind was cold and moaning through the treetops and up over the hillslopes.

'Dad!' Josh Ayliffe said.

The father blinked. He backed away. He poked a forefinger at Eyre, who was examining the wet seat of his pants. 'Stay away from me and my son. Don't come here again. You want to communicate with me, do it by post.'

Hirsch drove Eyre back to the Ford. 'They'll keep chopping down their damn trees,' Eyre said, frustrated, as he got out.

'Maybe not,' Hirsch said. The air behind them was silent. 'I suggest you make a hundred per cent sure what the legalities are, and then send them whatever forms are required to stop them or keep their actions within the law, but do it quickly. And if you need to serve paperwork on them, don't come out here by yourself. Contact us, but I warn you we can't always be available for your protection. If you need to monitor their activities, maybe do it from Amy Groote's side of the fence.'

'Speaking of which, I think we should go and see her,' Eyre said. 'She's had her own hassles with those idiots, apparently.'

And why didn't you tell me that earlier, thought Hirsch. 'Such as?'

'Phone calls late at night. A shotgun shell in her letterbox.'

6

To reach the little house below the Ayliffes' gum trees they followed each other back down to the highway and up Hubert Wilkins Road, on the southern edge of Penhale. Hirsch parked beside Eyre's Ford and got out. He could hear motors, but not the chainsaw. Shading his eyes, he peered uphill. The tractor was trundling out of sight, trailed by the ute.

The house was old, careworn fibro-cement, a fringe of rust on the roofing iron and rust holes in the gutters. But cared for otherwise, with severely pruned and skeletal orchard trees on one side, herb and vegetable beds on the other. A pile of newly delivered loam; freshly pulled weeds accumulating in a wheelbarrow. The sound of tines on soil.

They found Amy Groote in the backyard, an area crammed with beds marked *beans*, *carrots*, *radish* and *silver beet*. She was a thickset woman in overalls and rubber boots, trying to dig out a patch of bamboo. A round, flushed face and an expression of lofty calmness as she worked. When she saw them her hand went to her billowy chest. 'You startled me,' she said, not looking startled at all.

They explained who they were, the reason for their visit, and she offered tea and scones. 'Baked this morning.'

Up concrete steps to the back door, where she said, 'Please remove your shoes.'

An entryway led to a laundry on one side, a time-warp kitchen on the other. Baking odours lingered; tidy old appliances and furniture; tea cosies and doilies. And it was freezing: Hirsch kept clenching his toes as he sat with Eyre and watched Amy Groote make the tea. Eyre was also cold, hunched deep into his coat. Groote seemed oblivious.

Words poured out of her as she fussed. When her husband had run out on her last year, leaving her with nothing, she'd been taken in by Aunt Maggie. Maggie Groote, did Hirsch know her? Unfortunately she and Maggie didn't really get along, and Maggie was finding the property hard to manage anyway, the garden in particular, so in March it was decided she'd move down to the town to live.

Amy stopped to turn and look at Hirsch. 'Of course you know her. That trouble she had.'

Underwear nicked from the clothesline. 'Yes.'

'You had that camera put in.'

'Yes.'

'I'm not sure I quite like that whole idea,' Amy Groote said. 'Big Brother and all that.'

Anyway, she continued, she and her aunt got on better *not* living together. 'I'm into a self-sustaining lifestyle, and there she was with all her packaged supermarket stuff. I grow and make everything I need. Anything left goes into compost or I drive it down to Adelaide to feed the homeless.'

Hirsch took in more of the kitchen as she talked. An anti-windfarm flyer under a fridge magnet; a herb calendar on one wall; bay leaves and garlic hanging from twine at the entrance to the pantry. Eyre wasn't part of the conversation. He sat opposite Hirsch, poking at his phone.

'Naturally this isn't my house, though. It's Maggie's. I feel like a custodian, really.'

Enough of a custodian to object when the Ayliffes started clearing a stand of trees on her boundary fence, Hirsch thought. He wondered if she expected to inherit. Had she and Maggie always been close? 'Ms Groote—'

'Call me Amy.'

Hirsch wished Eyre would put down his phone. 'Amy, about the tree lopping. Did you talk to Mr Ayliffe first, or go straight to the council?'

Groote plonked a bowl of scones and three chipped mugs of milky tea on the table. 'I don't back down from things. I talked to Leon and Josh first up and they told me in no uncertain terms where to go. To hell with that: I kept on at them, the next day, and the next.'

'And?'

'I started to get anonymous phone calls late at night. A shotgun cartridge was left in my letterbox. My bike tyres were slashed. That's when I informed the council.' Groote glanced at Eyre. 'I'm not usually keen on involving official-dom, but I'm just one woman, living on her own, and the Ayliffes are in the wrong.'

Hirsch had once found a 9mm cartridge in his letterbox. The creepy feeling it gave him. A permanent sense of cross-hairs trained on his back.

Eyre spoke at last. 'We'll take it from here, Amy.'

'Ms Groote,' she corrected. She clearly didn't think Eyre was up to taking on anything.

'How about Maggie?' Hirsch said. 'Was she involved in any way? Did she ever have dealings with the Ayliffes?'

Amy Groote shook her head. 'Not them.' The eyes in her plain round face were burning bright now. 'Her dealings with the other neighbours is a whole other story.'

'The other neighbours?'

Amy Groote gestured north and east at the world beyond the kitchen. 'Not the ones in town, the ones out here, up the top of the hill there. The Fearns. They ignore her for years, and now suddenly it's like they're her new best friends. Dropping in on her all the time, bringing her stuff, taking her to doctor's appointments. Makes me sick.'

Hirsch saw Amy Groote in all of her vulnerability. 'Are we talking undue influence?'

Amy Groote examined the garden dirt under her finger-nails. 'Some might call it that.'

The day had got away from Hirsch. He left Eyre quizzing Amy Groote on dates and times and drove down to Penhale, the light leaking from the sky, the setting sun a weak, red-yellow streak along the tops of the Tiverton Hills as he parked behind Maggie Groote's Nissan Micra in the drive-way of her house on the northern edge of the little town.

61

'Just saying hello,' he said, when she opened her door.

A thin, stooped woman with fine, sparse white hair. Slippers on swollen feet, a heavyweight blue cardigan over a grey woollen dress. About eighty. She blinked at Hirsch, for the briefest moment unsure of how he fitted into her life.

'Oh, Paul.' She looked past him at the gathering darkness. 'You're letting the cold in.'

She took him to the sitting room, an overheated, overstuffed den: two electric radiators, fat armchairs, thick carpet, creepy-looking dolls perched on the mantelpiece, and a sideboard so dark and massive it swallowed light. A little table set with a meals-on-wheels dinner was parked beside an armchair that faced a flickering game show on a boxy old TV.

She seemed surprised to see the meal, the TV. 'I'll just...' she said vaguely, then recovered herself sufficiently to mute the sound.

Had she really wanted to move away from her home on the hill below the Ayliffes? Had the niece driven her out? 'Finish your dinner, Maggie,' Hirsch said. 'Sorry to bother you.'

She eased stiffly into her chair. 'Sit a moment.'

He positioned a stiff-backed chair to face her. And suddenly she was ten years younger, spry and canny as she looked at him. 'Caught that blessed fellow yet?'

'Not yet,' Hirsch admitted.

'I don't want a scrap of it back.'

Two bras, tights, several pairs of underpants. 'I don't blame you,' Hirsch said.

Then her mind drifted again, her eyes growing vague. She seemed surprised to see the plate of food there.

'Eat up before it gets cold,' Hirsch said, rising to his feet.

Relieved, she said, 'Thank you, I will.'

'Anything I can do for you before I go?'

'Is it Friday? Sylvia Fearn comes to see me on Fridays.'

'It's Thursday,' Hirsch said. He smiled. 'I'll check in again soon. I can let myself out.'

'Give the door a good slam,' Maggie Groote said. 'If you don't, the latch doesn't catch properly.'

'Will do.'

Hirsch tested the door on his way out: she was right. Making a note to come back soon with some tools, he took the highway north. Headlights in the queer half-darkness, a set behind, another ahead. Then the oncoming car was past him, the one behind turned onto a side road, and he was alone in the world, only his puny lights probing.

He reached the sparse streetlights of Tiverton and a minute later was parking in the police station driveway. Switched off, locked, and walked to the front door to remove the card pinned there, advising callers of his mobile number, just as his phone rang.

Andrew Eyre, advising Hirsch that he intended to lay some paperwork on the Ayliffes the next day and could South Australia Police arrange a detail to accompany him. A *detail*? thought Hirsch. You'll be lucky to get *me*. 'Can't you just post it?'

Eyre gave an empty laugh. 'We all know how that scenario

plays out. They deny getting it, I post it again, so on and so forth, and weeks go by.'

Hirsch muttered an okay and then, gloomily contemplating the contents of his freezer, he was interrupted by another call. Clara Ogilvie, hoping he'd forgive her, but she was wondering if there'd been any follow-up to her notification that Lydia Jarmyn was possibly being mistreated in some way. Polite, but a reproving thread of icy precision and strained patience in her voice, and Hirsch screwed up his face, a soundless groan: Christ, I should have rung her.

He recovered and said, 'I'm glad you called. We all owe you a big thank-you. She was clearly endangered and has been removed from the home situation.'

It was the right thing to say. When Ogilvie said, 'She did look in a bad way to me,' he sensed a relaxation in her, an acknowledgment that he'd repaid his debt.

'She was,' he agreed. 'I can't go into the details, but she'd clearly been neglected, over quite a long period.'

'But she's safe now?'

'Yes.'

'Was she sexually abused?'

Should he divulge anything at all? 'I'm afraid it's out of my hands now, Clara,' Hirsch said. He paused; he should give her something back. 'But not that I was aware of.'

'Beaten?'

'Not that I'm aware of.'

Other questions came flying at Hirsch, as if he was her pupil and falling short with his answers.

'The parents? They've been charged?'

'Sorry, Clara, it's out of my hands now. I expect there will be formal charges, though. I did mean to call you earlier with an update but as you can imagine, it's been pretty full on.'

Her voice turned sunny. 'See you in the pub on Sunday. Might we hear your voice again?'

Hirsch winced. He mouthed the words: not if I can help it.

7

First thing Friday morning, Sergeant Brandl called him.

'I'll meet you at the Ayliffes'.'

Phone tucked under his ear in the backyard, scraping yesterday's mud from his shoes, Hirsch said, 'I was just about to leave. But I thought you were going to be—'

'I got back last night,' the sergeant said. Terse, telling him not to pursue it.

'Okay.'

'I found a message telling me what Mr Eyre has in mind. I don't want you there by yourself if Leon Ayliffe goes off half-cocked.'

Hirsch was relieved. 'I'm meeting Eyre at the front gate, eight-thirty.'

'See you there.'

That was the plan. It failed to account for sheer bloody-mindedness.

Hirsch headed south along the shallow valley, the green hillslopes on either side darkened by misty rain, then on to Nautilus Road, passing the same sodden paddocks, the Toyota's wipers on an intermittent setting, smearing the windscreen. Johnny Cash singing 'Hurt' on the Old Farts CD that Wendy's daughter Katie had made for him. Played, replayed, and Hirsch decided to dub it the best song ever. At least for this month.

He came to a small rise, tyres churning the muddy crown of the road, and braked in a careful panic on the slippery surface. No sign of Eyre or his Ford, but Sergeant Brandl had parked the Redruth patrol car on the grassy verge and was standing in the broad middle of the road, her back to Hirsch, gesturing *stop/slow down* at Josh Ayliffe, whose gleeful elbow was hooked out of the open side window of his father's Holden ute, his other hand deftly steering it into burnouts, spraying mud over the sergeant, over her car, the grass.

The kid stopped when he spotted Hirsch; grinned, the ute idling side-on in the middle of the road. Turning on the dashcam, Hirsch pulled over, switched off, got out. Calling, 'Sarge!' he walked along the road to join her. She didn't turn, simply raised a hand to indicate that she'd heard him.

Hirsch's advance seemed to flick a switch in Josh Ayliffe. He planted his foot and powered the ute in a giddy circle again, bellowing, '*Yee hah,*' the idiot. Hirsch made his own *slow down* gestures, and, just as he reached Sergeant Brandl's elbow, saw Ayliffe switch manoeuvres, throwing the ute into a figure-of-eight. The tyres gripped poorly; the mud was slick. The ute began to slide, a movement that looked slow, almost inevitable, but must have been fast as a whip snap, the motor screaming, the side panel looming, oil leaks stinking on the redlining motor. Hirsch made a grab at Sergeant Brandl's rain-dampened nylon sleeve, found no purchase, and felt himself backpedalling, toppling, one muddy hand breaking his fall while the sergeant froze. He didn't say any of this to the major incident officers later, his language was bland, but, in his dreams, he couldn't stop the ute's slide, he couldn't stop hearing the meaty thump.

Sergeant Brandl was on her back. The ute twitched, righted itself, stalled. The kid got out. Hirsch got up. He looked at his hand, wiped it on his trousers. Looked at his shoes. For a moment, he wasn't sure what to do first. Then he was sure, and knelt beside the sergeant.

She was unblinkingly still, and Hirsch thought she was dead. But the sky, indifferent, continued to drizzle and presently she did blink, shedding rain from her lashes.

Relieved, Hirsch said, 'Where did he hit you?'

She blinked again. 'Left leg.'

'Can you get up?'

She tried, fell back. 'Unless I'm mistaken, it's broken.'

Josh Ayliffe was standing there, abjectly working his mouth. 'It was an accident. You saw. I didn't mean it.'

Hirsch said, 'Don't go away,' fished in his pocket for his phone and called 000. Advised not to move the sergeant, he hunted in his mind for a way to shelter her from the rain. There was a tarp in the Toyota. Park both vehicles beside her, spread the tap over the gap.

'Can I go home now? It was an accident, right? You saw.'

'No, you can't go home now. You just knocked over a

police officer in the execution of her duties, for Christ sake. I saw her trying to stop you, Josh. So, no, you can't go home.'

The kid teared up. 'I didn't mean it. It was an accident.'

'Help me cover her.'

But Josh Ayliffe had turned his attention to a vehicle coming over the rise and said venomously, 'We told him not to come.'

Hirsch turned: Andrew Eyre's Ford twin-cab. It was hugging the centre of the road as if to avoid the worst of the mud and stickiness, and, for a moment, seemed about to plough over them all. Then Eyre, hanging on for dear life, turned the wheel and chugged to a halt a metre away from Hirsch and the sergeant. He looked shocked, his eyes switching from Hirsch to Josh Ayliffe to the sergeant on her back in the mud. He switched off, got out and, ignoring the others, said, 'Joshua, is your father here?'

The kid backed away, kept backing away as Eyre advanced uselessly, a manila envelope in one hand. 'Joshua, answer me,' Eyre said. He turned to Hirsch. 'Will someone tell me what's going on?'

'The sergeant's been hurt,' Hirsch said. 'Help me put a tarp over her.'

A tiny knot between Eyre's eyebrows, as if he felt put out. 'Let me hand over the paperwork and I'll be right with you.'

Josh Ayliffe went rigid. Shouting, 'You can just fuck off,' he retreated for the ute.

'Leave it, Andrew,' Hirsch said, but it was as if Eyre hadn't heard him.

'Joshua,' Eyre persisted. 'Is your father home?'

'Up yours,' the kid said, yanking at the door, slipping behind the wheel, gunning the motor. Another spray of mud and he was through the gateway, headed for his house.

Eyre turned to Hirsch. 'Coming?'

'Mr Eyre, my sergeant's been badly injured. You can help me by—'

'I'm no good at first aid.'

'I don't need you to be. Just help me put a tarp over her until the ambulance gets here. You park on one side of her, I'll park on the other.'

Hirsch could see Eyre thinking it through. A plan that would tie up his vehicle for God knew how long.

'I'll be quick, okay?'

'Mr Eyre—'

He was ignored. Eyre returned to his Ford and, with a gentle flip of mud, pulled away and swung through the gateway.

Murmuring, 'Fuckwit,' Hirsch positioned his police Toyota beside Sergeant Brandl, rummaged for and unfolded the tarp and trapped one corner in the driver's door, the other in the door to the rear compartment. His sodden spine was the final prop, the tarp flowing down his back to the ground as he crouched beside Brandl. The rain, tapping and pattering, was the only sound in the world.

Until the gunshot.

Hirsch glanced towards the gateway uneasily but stayed put. Sergeant Brandl was cold to the touch. Shock, hypothermia, what did he know? His immediate duty was to her, so he put in an urgent call for backup and then fetched the space

70

blanket, tucked it around her. He heard a vehicle. He figured it for the Redruth ambulance but then realised it wouldn't arrive for at least another twenty minutes. He tensed in his wet shelter as the Ayliffes' Holden ute appeared, fishtailing towards the road. It slewed through the gate, no intention of stopping, Leon Ayliffe not bothering to look at Hirsch, his son beside him, holding a rifle barrel-up, both men wearing camouflage jackets. The tray was heaped with drums, crates, boxes, ropes, cables.

On the run. In for the long haul, guessed Hirsch.

8

Hirsch radioed again, this time giving the Ayliffes' registration number and descriptions and warning that they could mean harm to Adrian Quinlan, Diana Ayliffe and Julian Roskam. To make doubly sure, he made personal calls to all three.

Quinlan was at an auction in Brinkworth. 'Stay there till you hear from me,' Hirsch said.

'I don't understand. Leon intends me harm?'

Play it that way, thought Hirsch.

Then he called Diana Ayliffe, who said, her voice rising: 'He what? And Josh is with him?'

'Yes. I suggest you collect Chloe from school and take her somewhere safe, somewhere they won't think to look for you.'

'Chloe's home with me today. I'm thinking of enrolling her in a different school.'

Hirsch didn't care about that. He cared that mother and daughter should go somewhere safe. He repeated his advice.

Cooler now, she said, 'I can handle Leon.'

That sounded like famous last words. 'Just keep an eye open,' Hirsch said. 'I'll drop by very soon.'

Then, still watched dully by Sergeant Brandl, he called Glenys Fife at the school. 'Mr Roskam, please.'

'Julian's teaching at the moment. Can I take a message?'

Hirsch decided that she had to know. 'It's urgent, Glen. Leon Ayliffe's flipped out and he and his son could come to the school.'

She didn't reply but he heard her footsteps and traced them to a classroom. She'll monitor the kids while Roskam takes the call, Hirsch thought. He waited. He realised he was holding the sergeant's hand, and then he heard a heavier tread and Roskam's voice was in his ear. 'What's this about Leon Ayliffe?'

Hirsch explained, and Roskam, a man who'd had a lifetime of dealing with pests, said curtly, 'Well, there's been no sign of them, and why would they bother with me anyway?'

Hirsch could think of one good reason. 'Mr Roskam, if they do come to the school, and decide to teach you a lesson, others could be hurt. The children. I'm advising you to close for the day. Send the kids home.'

'That could take hours!'

Hirsch doubted it, but could see that logistically it would be a nightmare. Parents who worked all day. Parents who couldn't be contacted. He put grit into his voice, got a grudging acquiescence and now he slumped, his energy draining into the mud.

A pressure in his hand: Sergeant Brandl squeezing. Having

gained his attention she said, her voice scratchy, 'I'll be out of action for a while.'

'Probably just a bruise, sergeant.'

'Don't make me laugh. I want you in charge. And be nice to the children.'

The sergeant's 'children' were the Redruth constables, Jean Landy and Tim Medlin: barely two years' experience between them. 'Of course,' Hirsch said.

Just then, as they waited in the dismal shelter, the rain stopped, the clouds parted, and sunlight poured in. Hilary Brandl, pale with pain, gave Hirsch a crooked grin. 'A stairway to heaven?'

Hirsch swallowed. 'A joke, boss? In your condition?'

The clouds merged and they were wrapped in grey light again. 'Good, not my time after all,' Brandl said. She paused. 'I heard that shot. Our environment protection guy?'

Hirsch said, 'I'll check on him as soon as the ambulance gets here.'

'Go now. I'll be okay.'

Hirsch shook his head. 'The ambulance won't be long.' And he hated to think what he'd find.

Sergeant Brandl gave him an anguished look. 'Sorry I've been in such a shit mood the past couple of days.'

'That's okay.'

'Not okay. Or rather, I had a good reason but shouldn't have taken it out on everyone. My boyfriend, for want of a better word, sent me a text to say—'

She was interrupted by the yip-yip of a siren as the Redruth police SUV came over the rise, Jean Landy at the wheel, Tim Medlin in the passenger seat, an ambulance hard behind. The world was full of noise now, and all Hirsch had registered were the words 'boyfriend'—he'd thought Sergeant Brandl was married?—and 'text'. He crawled out from beneath the tarp, pointed the SUV into the Ayliffes' driveway, gestured for Jean to wind down her window and said, 'There could be a gunshot victim up at the house. Let me know immediately, before the ambulance drives away.'

'Sarge. I mean, Paul,' she said, flustered. 'Is it safe?'

'I think so. The shooters drove off—but keep an eye open.'

He watched them go, then guided the reversing ambulance and helped lift the sergeant onto a stretcher and slide her in.

'I need you to wait a minute,' he told the paramedics, explaining why.

'No problem,' the driver said. 'She's not in immediate danger.'

'Immediate pain,' the sergeant said, from inside the ambulance, and Hirsch liked that. He liked quippery.

Then his phone buzzed. Tim Medlin, saying: 'Gunshot victim, still alive.'

'One more customer,' Hirsch said.

He followed the ambulance along the track, seeing it twitch and right itself in the mud. He parked beside the Redruth SUV and crossed the yard to where Landy and Medlin were crouched beside a sodden, motionless scrap on the ground.

Then his view was blocked briefly by the ambulance, and Eyre was being loaded by the time he reached the others.

'How bad?'

'Shoulder's all busted. Unconscious,' Jean Landy said.

She'd been a paramedic before applying to join the police. 'I figured it would be safer,' she once told Hirsch, 'than dealing with ice addicts every night.' Hirsch thought it probably was, on the whole, especially in a backwater town—until someone went rogue with a firearm.

There'd be a manhunt now. A father and son declared armed and dangerous, not to be approached. Not killers—not yet. But don't push them too hard, in other words. Apply reason. Then apply force.

The ambulance left. Hirsch told Landy and Medlin to remain at the house—'This is a crime scene, so no one in or out, and keep your eyes peeled in case they come back'—and raced down Nautilus Road to the highway. Then north to Tiverton, knowing he'd arrive before any backup could get there and feeling ill prepared for a shootout.

He'd struck it before, the fallout when a man fucks up but feels his wife or girlfriend—or boss or workmates or the system—have let him down. A man like that might wipe out his family, boss or workmates, then turn the gun on himself. Or some, like Leon Ayliffe, might simply turn one or more of the children against their mother—spread the toxicity around that way.

Soon the Tiverton silos were on the horizon: the towers of a fortified city on a misty plain. Then he was past them, unchallenged. Passing the general store and the police station and turning right onto First Street. No Holden ute outside Diana Ayliffe's rented house.

He parked, ran to her door, knocked, feeling eyes on his back. The sensation was powerful, and he turned to scan the street, but it was just a quiet side road in a forgotten town. Dripping slightly but otherwise lifeless. A key turned in a deadlock, the door opened and Diana Ayliffe said, 'Paul.'

'Any sign of Leon?'

He eyed her closely, trusting in his ability to sense if she was being coerced—to sense if her husband was standing behind her, the tip of his rifle against her backbone. 'No,' she said, sounding vaguely fed up. 'But he called. Didn't say anything about Josh, just said he'd done a stupid thing, but that I shouldn't believe everything I hear about him.' She stood back. 'Come in.'

The hub of the house was the kitchen, a room refurbished half-heartedly a couple of decades ago. 'Tea? Coffee?'

Hirsch shook his head. 'I still have to check the school. What else did Leon say?'

'Nothing. The line just went dead.'

'He hasn't driven past?'

'No,' she said, stiff with tension now. She'd cropped her hair since the last time he'd seen her. An old tracksuit hung loosely from her torso and waist so that you wouldn't know the shape of her. An attractive face if you took a second or a third look, but it wasn't immediately apparent. Toned down in some way. Pale, anxious, not wanting attention.

'I need to ascertain that Chloe's here and that she's okay,' Hirsch said. 'You understand.'

A brief flicker of annoyance, but then she tipped back her head and called, 'Chloe? You're wanted.'

A voice shouted from the end of the main passageway, 'I haven't finished packing.'

Grumpy-sounding, put-upon. Not frightened. 'It's okay, I believe you,' Hirsch said. 'I need to check the school now, if I could just have details of where you'll be staying…?'

She scribbled on a notepad with the letterhead *Tiverton Primary School*. A slender hand, noticed Hirsch, with a simple, pretty ring. He'd been told by an old girlfriend that he was a 'hand man'.

'A cousin in Adelaide,' Diana Ayliffe said, tearing off the top page.

Hirsch folded it into his pocket. 'Won't Leon think to look for you there eventually?'

'I doubt it. Distant cousin. We connected on Facebook a few months ago and got close. It was her told me I should leave him.'

Hirsch nodded. 'Keep your phone charged and turned on. Police officers more senior than me will want to ask you questions.'

She'd been blank but now looked surprised. 'What about?'

'Who Leon's friends are. Who Leon might have a grudge against. Where he likes to hunt. Was he violent to you. That kind of thing.'

It was all getting too much for Diana Ayliffe. 'He never hit me, but he was pretty controlling—what I thought and what I did and who I saw and what I spent.'

An old story. 'The ute was piled with what looked like survival gear,' Hirsch said. 'Ropes, tents, jerrycans of water, tinned food. And Josh was holding a rifle.'

'Probably not the only gun they've got with them. You need to be careful. They're both good hunters—kangaroo and wild goats, mainly. They can live off the land. They know where to hide, all that.'

'Good to know,' Hirsch said.

He turned to go, and she grabbed his arm so hard that he stumbled. 'I need to tell you something.'

Hirsch glanced at his watch, feeling jittery. 'Be quick.'

'I had this fling, if you could call it that, with Julian Roskam.'

A few things fell into place. 'And when you broke it off,' Hirsch said heavily, 'he took it out on Chloe.'

She looked irked, as if her secret hadn't been a secret after all. Recovering, she said, 'Not a very nice man, all things considered.' She paused. 'Something a bit off about him.'

Hirsch returned to the highway. Vehicles and people were massing at the school, so he pulled into the police station and walked across, still antsy as he scanned the streets, houses, trees, vehicles. Only the school thrummed: the rest was benign, hunched against the gentle, dreary rain.

A car swept out of the school car park with gleeful, confused kids and a scowling mother on board. A car entered, couldn't park anywhere, headed for the oval, where the tyres of other cars had already scored the soft turf. People were milling around the main building, Vikki Bastian and Glenys Fife crossing off names, trying to answer questions. No sign of Roskam.

'He went home,' Glenys said sourly.

It was an old-style primary school with a home for the head teacher behind a hedge in one corner of the grounds. Hirsch skirted around the huddle of classrooms, a water tank and a shelter shed, through a squeaky gate and pounded on Roskam's front door.

No answer. The house sat in sulky dampness, curtains drawn, paint flecking from rotted window frames, bricks fretting and gutters drooping. He walked around to the rear, tried the back door, tried to peer inside the locked garage, gave up and returned to watch the tail end of the evacuation.

His phone rang: Jean Landy. Thinking, Christ, the Ayliffes have come back, he accepted the call. 'You okay?'

'We're fine. But the place is crawling with ninjas and we find ourselves surplus to requirements.'

CIB from Clare and Port Pirie, she said, plus a STAR Group team from Adelaide. 'And the guy in charge wants to know why, quote unquote, you pissed off from a crime scene.'

'Yeah, yeah. Tell him I'll be there soon. You two can head back to Redruth and rescue kittens from trees.'

'While you single-handedly bring down a couple of maddened gunmen.'

'It could happen.'

Half an hour later, Hirsch was knocking on the door of a major-incident caravan on a vacant lot just outside Penhale.

'Yeah?' A senior constable, all in black, wearing a nametag: *J. Beulah*. Mid-twenties, bullet-shaped head; bright, endlessly assured dark eyes that flirted with a smirk.

'I'm here to see Inspector Merlino,' Hirsch said.

Beulah stood aside. 'Better come in then.'

Wall monitors, laptops, comms, desks, chairs and a couple of other STAR Group ninjas who ignored Hirsch. The inspector stood, beckoned. Tall, lean, short-haired, unimpressed, a man with the loose-limbed restlessness of an athlete.

Showed Hirsch to a chair and began to grill him. Why hadn't he made the wife and the daughter, not to mention the teacher, available for interview? They'd each have to be located now, and time was of the essence. Why hadn't he accompanied Mr Eyre to the house? Why hadn't he and Sergeant Brandl taken additional officers along with them? Who did the Ayliffes hang out with? Where would Hirsch go, if he were them?

'I'm fairly new to the area,' Hirsch said.

'Fairly new? You've been here a year and a half.'

So, he knows my story, Hirsch thought. 'They were well provisioned when they left. I'm told they have bush survival skills. They like to hunt.'

Beulah, standing behind Merlino, said, 'Like to hunt,' as if the Ayliffes' proclivities were all down to Hirsch.

'Where?' barked Merlino.

'Out east. Where out east I don't know.'

The inspector glanced eastwards, as if he could visualise slogging through mud and rain out there, in the emptiness. He said tersely, 'A doorknock of the neighbours might turn something up. I've put you with a Port Pirie suit, name of Comyn.'

Oh joy, thought Hirsch.

9

'You drive, hotshot,' Comyn said.

Hirsch preferred Comyn when he was perfunctory and bloodless. Today the detective was edgy, as if rattled by the slick, complacent martiality of Merlino's ninja squad. Still capable of taking a bite out of me though, Hirsch thought.

They checked the farms along Nautilus Road first, Hirsch engaging four-wheel drive on the steep section beyond the Ayliffe farm. As the road curved, he looked down: glimpses of distant, blue-suited figures removing computers and files from the house and searching the outbuildings. Maybe some scrap of paper, some email or reference on a 4chan board, would indicate where father and son were headed.

Four kilometres to the first house, where they found a note on the front door. The occupants were not sticking around with a madman on the loose, and here was a contact number.

'Christ, already? Word gets around quickly,' Comyn said, his expression marinated in disdain. He was wearing a suit under an overcoat and had realised too late that he wasn't in suit-and-overcoat conditions. Distaste twisted his features as he viewed the soles of his shoes. 'You know these people. Call them.'

Hirsch didn't know them but called anyway. A reluctant voice said, 'We're staying with relatives until Leon and Josh are caught.'

And no, they didn't know where the Ayliffes might go or who might give them assistance. A similar story at the second and third farms. Notes pinned to the door, reticence or lack of knowledge. It seemed no one had a beef with the Ayliffes, but Leon had turned weird a while back and gone all doomsday prepper. Now his son was wrapped up in the conspiracy nonsense as well.

The fourth house was a mouldy weatherboard within a square of pine trees that blotted most of the sunlight. The garden was overgrown; the grimy windows looked in on bare floorboards. No vehicles, no tracks: clearly abandoned. Comyn flipped a page of his notebook, and said, 'Okay, now we check properties on Hubert Wilkins Road.'

Hirsch held up a finger. 'One suggestion. The Ayliffes will know about this place. It should be checked once or twice a day, just in case.'

'You think?' said Comyn. But he made a note.

Driving up the little gully to where Amy Groote lived, Hirsch said, 'The place is owned by Maggie Groote, who lives in town now. Amy's her niece.'

'And that's crucial how?'

Hirsch counted to ten. 'Maggie might know more than Amy, who only moved in a few months ago. And you heard about our snowdropper? Maggie's one of his victims.'

Comyn said nothing. Hirsch parked and they found Amy gardening again, turning soil with a fork. 'I did hear the shot yesterday. Didn't think anything of it, those two are always shooting at something.' She kept working, the tines stabbing close to Comyn's shoes as she talked.

'Watch what you're doing.'

'Sorry.'

'So you heard a shot. Did you see anything?'

She stopped, leaned on the fork. 'Perhaps it's escaped your notice, but there's no clear view of their house from here.'

'How about in recent days or weeks,' Comyn said. 'Things out of the ordinary. Visitors, that kind of thing.'

'Like I said—'

'How about rumours,' Comyn said.

'I mind my own business,' Amy Groote said. She pointed to a house on the distant upslope on the other side of the gully and added waspishly, 'Try the Fearns. They seem to know everyone and everything.'

Hirsch drove a short distance to a board marked *S & J Fearn* bolted to a milk churn letterbox, then up a steep, freshly gravelled driveway that wound between stony outcrops to a sprawling farmhouse. Green corrugated iron roof and deep verandas, the front and side yards neat, orderly, with closely cropped couch lawns and pruned rosebushes. A LandCruiser and a Renault SUV in the carport, and a car Hirsch recognised in the driveway: Maggie Groote's Nissan Micra.

Comyn was bitching, this was a waste of time, they could be out searching, so Hirsch was able to tune him out as he parked, stood on the turning circle and looked across the gully to the Ayliffe property, then down at Amy Groote's house. Much of the Fearns' land was steep and stony, at least from this aspect, only good for grazing sheep. Maggie Groote's property, on the other side of the road, was gently undulating and unmarked by anything but lush grass, a creek and a dam.

Desirable.

'Daydream if you like,' Comyn said, 'but I've got work to do.'

Hirsch followed him onto the veranda, watched him knock, wipe his shoes on the mat with the energy of an angry man; knock again.

'Yes?'

Sylvia Fearn was stocky, late forties. Dressed with surprising formality in a dark blue woollen skirt and a pearl-grey twinset, her straight, blonde hair pinned back from each temple. She seemed to be composed of two women, one youthful, the other dully middle-aged. She recognised Hirsch from the tennis club and gaped in alarm to see him in uniform. A hand reached tensely for her throat. 'Is it about Leon Ayliffe? Has he come back?'

'May we come in, Mrs Fearn?'

'My manners. Of course.'

Separate flower patterns clashed in the sitting room: the carpet, the sofa and armchairs—even an orchid in a weak pool of sunlight from a skylight. A coffee table set with a teapot and flower-pattern cups and saucers, milk jug and sugar bowl. Oatmeal biscuits on a plate.

But mostly Hirsch was interested in John Fearn and Maggie Groote. Fearn was wearing a tie, no less, and balancing a plate on his knee, Maggie perched at the edge of the sofa, upright, sipping tea. She, like the Fearns, had dressed for the occasion, whatever it was. Someone's birthday?

Hirsch made the introductions and let Comyn take over. Refusing tea and biscuits, the detective said, 'We're gathering intelligence on Mr Ayliffe and his son. Anything at all that might help us find them.'

'They'll head for New South Wales, would be my guess,' John Fearn said.

'And why is that?'

'Leon has family over there somewhere, I believe.'

Fearn was eyeing the biscuits now; a man in tight clothes, his stomach and thighs stretching the fabric. His face was forgettable, a blur of clean, pink flesh. Hirsch watched the flicker of thoughts and feelings as he reached a decision, then a slow eruption as he struggled forward, reached out, grabbed and subsided.

Making a bad job of hiding his irritation, Comyn said, 'Know anything more about the relatives? Hunting friends? Fishing shack? Holiday house?'

'Wouldn't have a clue. We didn't really mix. Maggie might know. Her property joins theirs—on the other side.' He raised his voice, spoke slowly: 'Maggie, can you fill these gentlemen in? They want to know about Leon Ayliffe.'

Maggie smiled vaguely at Hirsch. 'There have always been Ayliffes in the district.'

Hirsch said, 'What about brothers or sisters or cousins who don't live locally?'

'That I wouldn't know, dear. Leon was an only son, I know that much.'

Comyn said tersely, 'If any of you know anything at all, please let us know. Friends, family, places they liked to visit. Anything at all.'

Sylvia said, 'They liked to go out east and shoot kangaroos and wild goats.'

That was the sum of anyone's knowledge and Comyn left with curt thank-you nods. Out on the front step, he said, 'Greetings from 1955, eh? All dressed up for afternoon tea.'

Hirsch nodded. None of his business. 'Where now?'

'Hold your horses,' Comyn said. Putting up a don't-interrupt finger, he checked with the incident caravan. Completed the call and smiled at Hirsch. 'We can knock off. The Ayliffes have been spotted in Broken Hill.'

The rain eased and the light was fading as Hirsch headed north to Tiverton. He pulled into the police station, called Redruth and learned that Sergeant Brandl had been taken to hospital in Clare, Andrew Eyre medivacced to Adelaide. Still seated in the Toyota, he turned on the radio. The Ayliffe incident was a breathless news item and he wondered who'd call him first: his parents? Wendy and Katie? Town friends, like the Muirs?

He got out, locked the Toyota, opened the main police

station door and instantly the landline rang. Wendy or his parents, they'd call his mobile. Curious about the timing, he lifted the handset. Clara Ogilvie, in a burst of words, said, 'Thank goodness you weren't hurt.'

10

Clare hospital, Saturday afternoon, Hirsch walking along a broad corridor in search of Sergeant Brandl. He found her in a private room, propped up against pillows and reaching awkwardly for headphones in the bedside cabinet. The room's prevailing colours were pastelly whites, pinks and greys, which offset the more garish primary colours of well-wishers' flowers, cards and heart-shaped helium balloons.

'Thank God. Let's hope you're more interesting than Brahms' Fifth Racket.'

'Can I sign your cast?'

'No, you can't sign my cast. I expected grapes, by the way, and you bring roses.'

'Slightly shopsoiled.'

Seeing him compare his Woolworths roses with the other bouquets, she said, 'I do have friends, you know. Family.'

'Where are they, then?'

'Ha, ha. I think there's another vase in that cupboard.'

Hirsch found it, filled it, spent a moment fluffing the

roses into order and placed it on a tiny shelf under the TV—
mounted at neck-strain height to keep the hospital's physios
in business.

Then he dragged a chair across and said, 'I quite like being
in charge. Don't hurry back.'

'Rack and ruin, is what I heard.'

'So, how are you feeling? How bad is it?'

A grimace on her thin face. 'They reckon the towbar or
the rear bumper got me.'

Which would make the break below the knee, but it
seemed to Hirsch that most of Hilary Brandl's leg was in
plaster. 'Just as well it wasn't your knee or your hip.'

'Just as well I didn't get shot.'

'I've always liked that about you, your sunny disposition.'

'Okay, hotshot, tell me what's been going on.'

Hirsch outlined his actions, concerns and theories and
the sergeant listened as if itching to get out and fight crime
again. At the end of his account she said, 'You'll need more to
convince me, or CIB, that Mrs Jarmyn buried her husband in
the backyard. But contact Roxby Downs and see if he's still
working there, and, if not, when and how he left, and did
he leave a forwarding address. The usual. As for our undies-
snatcher, maybe he's lying low because he saw himself on
Facebook. Nothing we can do but wait. And follow up on
the music festival. The daughter of one of the doctors here
sings in a band that's supposed to be playing on the Sunday
morning. She's been hearing rumours it won't go ahead.
Take one of the children with you and speak to Quinlan. He's
the main sponsor.' She paused. 'Any news of the Ayliffes?'

'Spotted in Broken Hill.'

A voice said, 'Hills, sweetheart! Are you okay?'

Hirsch saw the sergeant's face go flat. He glanced around; recognised the face in the doorway from a photograph on her desk at work. He'd always assumed 'husband', but apparently his status was 'boyfriend'. And last Wednesday he'd sent her a text that had her tearing off to Adelaide in distress.

'Brian, what are you doing here?'

A man who ignored inconvenient questions. Advancing across the room as if parting the waves, he said, 'You sure took some tracking down.' Stopped to shove a hand at Hirsch: 'Brian Cottrell. Can you give us a minute, er...?'

Hirsch found himself shaking a slim, bony hand and offering his name. Cottrell was probably an athlete, like the boss. Tall and fit, an impression of energy suppressed. Wearing a scarf, a leather jacket, tan boots and new jeans. The scarf was unnecessary in the cloying warmth, but it set off the engaging planes of the self-aware face.

'I'll be, umm...' Hirsch said, feeling inadequate.

'Hilary and I go way back, and I couldn't believe it when I heard. She's a special person. It kills me to think how it could have turned out.'

One of those men, thought Hirsch. Fluent in admiring and sympathetic phrases with no content at all. The emotional intelligence of a house brick. Glancing at the sergeant as he left, Hirsch read desolation and emptiness on her face.

He wandered in search of the cafeteria, bought tea and

a chocolate muffin, and claimed an abandoned copy of the *Advertiser*. Visitors and hospital staff wandered in and out but only one other person was seated there, and she looked awkward: both uneasy and far too glossy for the room. He sipped, chewed and had a go at the cryptic crossword.

The solution to the other puzzle—the woman—came when Brian Cottrell charged in and gathered her up. 'Sorry, babe.'

Seeing Hirsch, he saluted, said, 'Nice to meet you, Pete. Got to rush, we're making a winery weekend of it. Places to go, reds to taste...'

The woman simpered. Hope you both get heartburn, Hirsch thought. Hope the local plods pull you over.

The sergeant was bleak and raw when he returned to her room. 'Sorry about that,' she said.

'Sorry it happened to you,' Hirsch said, for want of something more profound. He'd grown halfway fond of Brandl over the past year, but they were not close. Friendly, joshing; mutual regard. But she was his boss.

'You deserve an explanation.'

'None of my business, sarge.'

But Hilary Brandl wouldn't be stopped. 'I was at high school with Brian, known him forever. We went out for a while but lost touch, the usual, and then ran into each other at a forensics conference—he works for a lab, he's not police. Long story short, we started going out again.'

She looked closely at Hirsch. 'I don't know about you and Wendy, but relationships develop a rhythm, right? A pattern.

One of our things was texting every day, especially with me working in Redruth and not seeing him all week.'

She shook her head. Blinked wet eyes. Hirsch said, 'It's okay, you don't have to tell me.'

She said, with heat, 'Jesus, Paul. Who else can I tell?'

Hirsch told himself to shut up. He smiled and squeezed her forearm.

'Two years go by. Then a couple of weeks ago I noticed his texts had become more...offhand? Perfunctory? I asked was there anything wrong'—she barked out a laugh—'by text, of course, and he texted back saying he'd been sleeping with someone else for a while and felt there was a real chance of a relationship with her.'

Hirsch didn't say it: As if what *you* were in wasn't a relationship.

She swallowed, a little choked. 'He was actually surprised that I'd twigged—he thought his texts were the same as usual.' She shook her head. 'I think it's because he can't read subtleties. He can't read people very well. He relies on them to tell him what they're thinking and feeling, and when they do, he's able to understand what they're saying but he doesn't *get* it. Not emotionally. He's a facts and figures man.'

'Sorry, sarge.'

'He mightn't be able to recognise anyone else's pain, but boy can he recognise his own. Now that I think about it, he was always going on about people letting him down...' She paused. 'Sorry.'

'A rant might do you good.'

'Not for general consumption,' she said, a touch of steel

in her tone. Then: 'Sorry. I do trust you. And sorry for saying "sorry" all the time.'

He squeezed again and she welcomed it. 'Brian's bright,' she said. 'I'd always admired his quickness. But as you can imagine, I've been doing some thinking since Wednesday. Underneath it he's very single-minded. Ruthless, really. Intense about winning, about being right. Always aware of the odds and the risks and the advantages. Zero humility, of course.'

Hirsch had met men and women like that. They ignored irrelevancies and tended to get what they wanted. But surely they missed out, too, if they never stopped to smell the roses? Did Brian Cottrell know that about himself?

He grew aware that the sergeant was looking at him. 'Sounds like you're well rid of him, boss.'

Hilary Brandl shook her head. 'I made a fool of myself last week, leaving you guys in the lurch, but I had to see him and talk about it.'

'No problem,' Hirsch said.

The sergeant shrank in the bed. 'I said to him, let's at least be friends, we've known each other forever, and he had to stop and think about it. Actually rubbed his jaw and said it could be possible, he did have a class of friends he saw every six or eight weeks.' She laughed. 'That says something about him, right? Then he said that, either way, he'd be sure to chat if he should ever happen to run into me. So much for knowing each other for twenty-five years. Made me feel really stupid as well as sad to think that for him there was nothing there.'

'His inadequacy boss, not yours.'

She patted the back of his hand. 'Thank you. And thank you for listening.'

They sat there and let the bad feeling drain away and then an orderly came in with afternoon tea and everyone rattled off a bit of nonsense and life went on. But in the quietness that followed, Hirsch saw that Hilary Brandl would go on gnawing at what had happened to her. Who could blame her, really?

'I wonder now if he didn't want people to know he was involved with me? I was never introduced to any of his friends; almost never saw him with his family.'

'When you're in the middle of something it's hard to see what's wrong,' Hirsch said.

'Tell me about it. I realise now he wasn't all that interested in getting to know me.'

'Perhaps he doesn't know how to go about it.'

She shook her head and was silent for a while. 'He's good looking, right?'

'Not my type, sarge.'

'...good looking and clever, and people probably told him that from an early age. And the result is a self-congratulatory monster.'

'I'd say you're well rid of him.'

She sighed. 'Maybe you're right. But some habits are hard to break.'

Hirsch thought about some of his own experiences. He'd remained friends with most of his ex-girlfriends. Not the sociopaths and axe-murderers, of course, but most of the others. 'A combination to avoid, boss. Self-absorbed; can't read people; doesn't know how to empathise. Someone like that will always roll right over you.'

Hilary Brandl gave him a flicker of a wounded look. 'Mister Experience.'

Hirsch smiled sadly and they were silent, looking back along their messy histories.

11

'I observed a certain urgency to the sexual activity, constable,' Wendy Street said, on Sunday morning, propped on an elbow, slowly trailing her fingertips up and down Hirsch's chest. 'Not that I'm complaining.'

The shared, unspoken thought, last night and again this morning: thank God he'd survived to have sex with the woman he loved and wasn't in some hospital or on a slab at the morgue.

Katie was at a friend's, so they took their time. Afterwards, showered, dressed, freshly combed, Wendy said, 'Will we be hearing your pleasant tenor voice this afternoon?'

Hirsch, giving himself a final check in her wardrobe mirror, said, 'Not funny.'

'The pipes, the pipes are calling...'

'Seriously, not funny.'

'From glen to glen...'

'I mean it. Shut the fuck up. I hate that fucking song.'

She wrapped her arms around him from behind and rested

her cheek between his shoulder blades. He succumbed, feeling the emotion flow through him. Tilted back his head, rubbed his skull against hers. The air, faintly stirred, was fragrant: shampoo, scented soap.

'She'll be expecting you to sing, of course.'

'Who will?'

Wendy retreated a fraction and kneed the back of his thigh. 'Don't play dumb.'

'Okay, okay,' Hirsch said.

By now he knew what made Wendy tick. This wasn't a touch of jealous heat; she had something to say about Clara Ogilvie and was building up to it. He waited there, Wendy's slight form warming his back.

Presently she said, 'A heads-up. I got talking to her after school on Friday and got the distinct impression she's disappointed you didn't tell her more about that girl you found in the caravan.'

Hirsch pictured the Redruth High School staffroom, everyone milling around, shoving weekend marking into backpacks and briefcases. He pictured Clara Ogilvie, feeling—frustrated? Entitled?

'I did tell her some of it. I'm not obliged to tell her everything,' he said, turning around in Wendy's arms.

She tilted her head back, looked up at him. 'I realise that.' She bumped her forehead gently against his chest, looked up again. 'I like Clara, but she can be...intense.'

'Don't get on her bad side, in other words.'

Wendy gave it some thought. 'Can't say I've ever seen a bad side. But she does get this little frown.'

He'd seen the frown. 'To be avoided.'

They ate soup and bread at the table in the sunroom at the side of Wendy's house, wintry light coming in at a shallow angle over Bitter Wash Road. And suddenly Hirsch felt the emptiness of the house. Being able to spend time with Wendy, especially a few hours at a stretch, was rare, and they'd populated it pretty well last night and this morning, but now he registered the absence of Wendy's daughter. A sleepover, in Redruth, with a schoolfriend. The house was hollow without Katie's clopping footsteps, music leaking from earphones, jokes and sunny insults. Wendy felt it, too. She looked subdued, almost as if she didn't know what to do with herself. He reached across and took her fingers.

She smiled and the mood vanished. She drained her tea and said, 'Let's get this show on the road.'

Hirsch stood when she did. 'Is your car working?'

'Good as new.'

'Are we collecting Katie on the way?'

A wry twist to Wendy's mouth. 'My darling daughter's final words to me yesterday were, quote unquote, a sleepover's a sleepover, Mum.'

Hirsch grinned. He'd attended two of the Celtic music afternoons and each time Katie had been...not stony-faced, exactly, but you could see her mind working darkly, suffering beside him, her snaky humour wanting an outlet. He reckoned that if he encouraged her, and she encouraged him, they could construct a pretty funny and not very nice riff on the Caledonian Dreaming crowd. Out of Wendy's earshot, of course—although even Wendy wasn't averse to an occasional dig. The old bagpiper with his Empire Line pants. And why was it necessary for all male fiddlers to grow a bushman beard?

By 2.00 p.m. they were heading south on the Barrier Highway. Through Penhale—the incident caravan gone now—and finally to Redruth and a parking slot in front of the Woolpack, an 1870s pub with deep verandas, a farmhouse-green roof and dun-toned walls, each stone delineated with thin black pinstripes. Up a massive wooden staircase to a well-used function room—club meetings, wedding receptions, Christmas work lunches and Probus lectures. Hirsch felt himself tighten. Wendy, reading it in him as they entered, tucked her hand in his elbow and snuggled against him. 'Be strong, be good.'

'Not sure I can do both,' Hirsch said.

'And thank you for coming with me. It means a lot.'

They were the stragglers. Men and women had gathered in front of a raised platform at one end of the room, tuning fiddles, setting up microphones and a drumkit, arranging a semicircle of stiff chairs for the musicians. Assorted friends, kids and loved ones lounged in club chairs or leaned their elbows on small tables, waiting. They all went quiet, watchful, when they saw Hirsch, knowing he'd been present when Andrew Eyre was shot.

He gave the crowd a general nod, said, 'Break a leg,' to Wendy, and did what he always did at public gatherings, made for the back wall. He cast back over his shoulder as he crossed the room, feeling her eyes pull him, reading the look: *Thank you. And—I don't need to check on a grown man...but keep the hiding and scowling to a minimum, okay?* He stopped, smiled, gave her a thumbs-up.

Hirsch was lost to dreams when the music began. It wound through him, taking him over—even the dreary nasal stuff. He liked to identify patterns, he liked to anticipate the direction a line of notes might take. At the afternoon tea interval he came out of his fugue and paced along the perimeter walls, browsing the photographs: stud rams, a stretch of wire fence hung with wedge-tail eagles, Ulooloo and Cappeedee station homesteads, Aboriginal stockmen, and one titled *Gin scrubbing shirts, Bundaleer Outstation.*

A man came in on his blind side. 'Pete Burroughs. We met last time.'

A young farmer with heavy glasses and the regulation Ned Kelly beard. Played guitar. 'Sure, Pete, how's it going?'

'Better than the Ayliffes, that's for sure.'

A tone, an attitude. Hirsch tried to read the man. Burroughs watched him with a hint of challenge.

'Do you know them?'

Burroughs felt he'd delivered part of a message. As he turned to go, he delivered the rest: 'I don't approve of what they did, but I approve of taking a stand.'

And he was gone. A stand against what, exactly? Greenies? District council environment protection officers? Governments? The police?

'There you are.'

Hirsch jumped as Clara Ogilvie came in on his blind side, carrying a lap dulcimer under one arm. 'Clara.'

She grasped his wrist. 'Are you sure you're all right?'

She was pretty in a pale, fine-boned way, and buzzing with the social, emotional and intellectual energy he remembered. Her fingers on his wrist felt charged. Not desire, exactly. And not neediness. Some other internal heat.

'Safe and sound,' Hirsch said heartily.

Too heartily. She registered the tension in him. Released him and stepped away. 'That's good.' Hunting around for a subject, she added: 'Anything new on Lydia Jarmyn?' Her gaze drilled him; she still felt entitled to know everything.

'I'm afraid not, Clara, sorry.'

She pursed her mouth and looked away, nodding her disappointment. 'Let's just hope the authorities know what they're doing.'

'Yes.'

'Child Protection have been known to drop the ball occasionally.'

'Yes, they have.'

She rested her hand on his arm again. 'You'll keep me informed?'

'Yes.'

'Good,' she said, removing her fingers. Hirsch glanced past her desperately; everyone was milling around a table, guzzling sandwiches and cakes. Wendy was chatting with a tin-whistler.

'Sit with me,' Clara said, touching his arm again. 'May I get you something to eat or drink?'

'I'm fine, thanks,' Hirsch said, joining her at one of the little tables, knowing he was in for the long haul. She had colour in her cheeks. Occasions like these exhilarate her, he thought. Drama lurks in every corner of her life.

She placed the dulcimer out of harm's way. 'Are we going to hear that fine voice of yours today?'

Hirsch shifted in his chair. 'I haven't actually...'

She set a tote bag on her lap. It was marked Clonmel Run Music Festival. He wondered where she'd bought it, but before he could ask, she'd fished out a songbook. 'I thought I'd sing this Emmylou Harris song, if you're up for a duet?'

Hirsch peered: 'Little Bird'. He coughed, said: 'Sorry, the old voice is a bit rusty today.'

There was that little frown. Thinking that he should give her something, mend this bridge, he said, 'I love the song, though. I used to have the CD.'

'*Stumble into Grace*. What happened to it?'

He leaned forwards. 'Have you ever noticed how books and CDs can sit on the fault lines of failed relationships?'

Hirsch knew he was taking a chance. According to Wendy, Clara was single. She'd been married, though, and surely had a history beyond the marriage?

It worked. She beamed in recognition. 'God, yes! With me it's books. Favourite books. Too many of them, frankly. You can't really ask for them back, that's the trouble.'

'For me it was *Stumble into Grace*. Except there was no grace—or stumbling, really. She skipped out without a backward look.'

Another little frown, but one of confusion. Not everyone got it when he joked, he knew. Not everyone got jokes full stop. For some people the world was a completely literal place. 'Before that, it was Dire Straits. Before that it was...'

Now she laughed. He liked the sound of it.

Into the pause that followed, she said, 'You and Wendy seem to hit it off quite well.'

Hirsch grew wary. 'Yes.'

'It can't be easy, her job. Being a mother. *Your* job.'

'We manage.'

'The hours you work.'

'True.' To change the subject, Hirsch indicated the tote bag. 'You going to the festival?'

'I'd like to think I am. There are rumours it won't be going ahead.'

A voice called, 'Ladies and gents, take your places. Clara? She here?'

'Love you and leave you,' Clara Ogilvie said, slipping gracefully from the chair, uplifted and blushing faintly. Like a guileless girl in love.

12

On Monday morning Hirsch checked for Ayliffe updates—the car they'd stolen in Broken Hill had been found burnt out in Mildura; no further reports—then he advised everyone on his Monday and Thursday patrol routes why he wouldn't be dropping by for a couple of weeks, and finally pinned his mobile number and a note to the front door: *Temporarily based at the Redruth police station.*

Reversing onto the highway, waiting for a bus marked *Wilpena Pound Tours* to pass, he glanced across at the school. Permission had been given to reopen; parents were dropping kids off.

He headed south through misty rain. At Redruth he skirted the town square, turned left into a side street a short distance out along the Adelaide road and parked behind the police station, a dreary, utilitarian brick place with aluminium window frames. He entered, said hello to the auxiliary support officer—a retired shearer named Pickett—and stepped through an inner door to the main part of the station. Sergeant Brandl's 'children' had the briefing room ready: pastries and freshly brewed coffee freshening the bland interior, blessedly warmer than the Tiverton police station or the great outdoors. Hirsch took the end chair, flanked by the others, and said, 'Dearly beloved...'

They grinned, perky, laptops and notebooks ready, not sure what to make of him in this role, not sure what he'd be like as a boss. He grinned back and said, 'Might as well follow the same procedure as our esteemed sergeant. Tim?'

Medlin outlined the week's reported crimes, accidents and incidents in a stumbling voice. Then, more confident, he tapped laptop keys and said, 'This video clip came in over the weekend.'

They eyed the wall monitor. Images flickered. Hirsch peered, trying to decipher murky black and washed-out grey patches in the foreground, backlit by a faint glow in the top left corner. A distant streetlight, he guessed, its illumination barely reaching a rickety back fence, which itself cast a dense shadow over a little metal shed, a wheelbarrow, a bulky figure reaching both hands to a pair of knickers on a rotary clothesline. One hand to remove the peg, the other to claim the prize. The process was repeated: a bra this time.

'Anne Pierce's house in Spalding?'

Medlin nodded.

'Tell me both items had the marked labels?'

'Yep.'

They all felt it, a kind of controlled elation. Hirsch frowned: 'But that looks like it's taken from inside the house?'

Medlin nodded again. 'Rats chewed the CCTV cable. Apparently Mr Pierce doesn't sleep well. He heard a motorbike outside, immediately twigged and went to the kitchen with his mobile phone.'

'Knew what to expect,' mused Hirsch. 'What time?'

'About two in the morning.'

Hirsch wondered aloud about work. Maybe their man had no daytime job—people knew that kind of thing in a rural community. Or maybe he'd begun to perform badly at his daytime job because he was out all night?

Jean Landy was taking notes, her fingers flying on the keyboard. She paused. 'We still have to tie someone to any or all of the marked underwear. And the question remains: how does he find his victims? You don't just drive down a street and look at a house and think: an elderly woman lives there.'

They'd all had a laugh about it, back in May—police and victims alike—but now a sense of unease had crept in. There lived among them a man who fetishised the underwear of elderly women. And according to Hirsch's research, the guy probably masturbated over the knickers and bras, finding it arousing to own and touch them, maybe to wear them.

He said, 'If we had more victims, we might find a link between them. In your spare time—I realise you won't have much until Sergeant Brandl is back on deck—could you both go over the incident reports of the past six months? Thefts, trespassing, anything that might in fact have been an actual or failed snowdropping incident but not reported as such. And keep your ears open for gossip, incidents that were never reported because the victim was forgetful or only targeted once.'

'Sarge,' Medlin said. Then, embarrassed: 'Paul. Constable Hirschhausen.'

Hirsch said, 'Just ordinary, everyday arselicking is appropriate. Anything else?'

'One last thing.' Medlin sent a photograph to the wall monitor. A nondescript brick building with a flat roof, a wooden door with *Quinlan Stock and Station* in gold lettering on the glass inset, and a shattered window. Another photo replaced it: an interior shot, a red house brick on a grey industrial carpet.

'Me and Jean were wondering if this is Troy Padfield up to his old tricks.'

Dumped by his girlfriend back in March, Troy Padfield had gone on a rampage: tossed a brick through her bedroom window, slashed her new boyfriend's car tyres and spray-painted *a slut works here* on the footpath outside Redruth Hair and Beauty. Hirsch barely knew the kid but had seen him a handful of times since. He always looked deeply ashamed.

'Does Troy have a history with Quinlan?'

They both shrugged.

'I'm wondering if something else is going on,' Hirsch said. 'There are rumours that Quinlan's business is in strife. A bounced cheque is one reason Leon Ayliffe kicked off. A question mark over the music festival. References on Facebook. Was there a note with the brick?'

'No note.'

'Either of you heard any rumours?'

Medlin shook his head. Landy said, 'I was in the newsagent's and someone came in wanting to buy a festival ticket and Mr McLean said, "You might want to hold off on that for a while."'

Hirsch rubbed at his forehead. Perhaps it was better to be a humble constable. Perhaps he wouldn't sit the sergeants' exam just yet. 'The festival's on Friday. It'd be good to know if it is in fact going ahead.' He took a breath, decision made. 'Jean, you come with me. Tim, you see what Padfield has to say for himself. Padfield or any other disaffected youth in the area.'

He smiled bleakly. Kids didn't stick around. They headed for Adelaide and jobs, a TAFE course, a night life.

Hirsch and Landy emerged into drumming rain. It cowed every leaf, bounced off tiles and corrugated iron, cars, bitumen, scurrying umbrellas and his uniform cap. It stripped the world of specificity. They ran to the Redruth patrol car, Hirsch into the passenger seat, Landy behind the wheel. Heater at full blast, they splashed out of the station carpark and through the town in a fug of clammy flesh, wet fabric, hot, demisting air.

'I just need to make a couple of calls.'

'Go your hardest,' Landy said.

He checked his notebook for the Roxby Downs number, got through, asked for HR. Stated his query and visualised an office at a mine site in the far north of the state. Was it raining there, or was it semi-desert, huge bites taken out of dusty soil by massive yellow machines?

'Jarmyn?' said a voice in his ear. 'First name?'

Hirsch didn't think there'd be that many people named Jarmyn working there. 'Alexander. Maybe Alex.' He paused. 'Or Lex.'

Silence on the line. Jean Landy steered expertly through the dripping air, listening with interest.

Then: 'We don't have anyone of that name working here.'

'How about last year? The year before?'

'I have to go into a different system...'

The woman's voice trailed away. Hirsch didn't know if going into a different system meant moving to a different room or building, or simply to a different window on her computer—but he did know that she wanted him to go away. He put some edge in his voice. 'This is a police investigation.'

Landy beside him grinned. The voice on the phone sighed, at the polite edge of irritation, and Hirsch heard the clack of keys. 'Alexander Jarmyn. Worked here for four years. Gave notice in September last year.'

'Any reason given?'

'No. He simply handed in his notice.'

'In person? In writing?'

'He simply handed in his notice.'

'Is there someone listed there as a manager, a supervisor, I could talk to?'

'The mine,' said the woman, 'is in full operation today. I can't just pull someone out to take a phone call. If you give me your number, I'll have someone ring you.'

Hirsch complied and the phone went dead. Jean Landy said, her voice light, 'That sounded like a fulfilling experience.'

'Welcome to the world of policing.'

They reached the stockyards on the northern outskirts and Jean slowed, steering into the carpark alongside Quinlan Stock and Station. Two men in overalls stood under the eaves looking phlegmatic and eyeing the rain as it beat against a windowpane clamped to a frame in the tray of a small truck marked Tuohy Glass. They grinned crookedly at Hirsch and Landy as if to say that life was one big joke.

'Wet enough?' one said.

Jean said brightly, 'Keeps the bad guys indoors.'

'Yeah.' The older glazier jerked his head at the building behind him. 'But that's where some of them do their best work.'

Interesting. Hirsch said mildly, 'Catch you later,' and followed Jean inside.

The brick had been removed; the grey carpet bore the stripes of fresh vacuuming. The receptionist was expecting them. Messy ponytail bouncing, she was fielding a phone call, clacking through files in the top drawer of a cabinet and pointing with her chin towards the corridor beyond her desk. Hirsch saw Quinlan standing at the end, waiting. Busy man.

'Sorry to hear about Sergeant Brandl,' he said, in a voice pitched to reach the corners of a vast arena.

They reached him, shook hello. He was about sixty and

solid, with bone-crunching hands, but his capacious size and voice were belied by a pale, small-featured, egg-domed head. He took them into a room stuffed with leather and chrome furniture and framed by wall-mounted pennants, sashes and photographs: Quinlan with politicians, footballers and golfers. Quinlan with Prince Charles. Seeing Hirsch lift his eyebrows, he said, 'I was fortunate to be invited to a garden party at the palace.'

Hirsch said nothing. In his view, the royal family was fucking ridiculous, but try telling the Australian public that.

'Sit, sit. Tea? Coffee?'

'We're fine, thank you. We won't take up too much of your time.'

Quinlan steepled his fingers on the other side of his desk and swivelled slightly, taking in his visitors. 'I'm flattered, but I don't know that a broken window is such a big deal that it needs half our police force,' he said, twinkling. 'A police incident number for my insurance claim and we can all get on with more important things.' He paused, shrugged. 'Kids, I assume. Maybe have a word with young Master Padfield?'

'Actually, Mr Quinlan,' Landy said, with certitude, 'we're here about certain rumours that have come to our attention.'

Quinlan pursed his bloodless lips. A deflector, Hirsch thought. Whenever a conversation strays anywhere difficult, he'll blandly redirect it. 'Rumours?'

'I understand that things are tight in the rural economy. We've had a few years of drought, nasty bushfires, unfavourable trade agreements, markets drying up...' She stopped and she waited. Hirsch, happy to let her take charge, waited with her, curious about Quinlan.

'I don't follow.'

'Liquidity problems,' Jean said. 'We hear it all the time. But when there's a flow-on effect...'

'Flow on?'

'When people get angry or agitated. They're relying on a cheque in the mail and it doesn't come. Or it bounces. Could that be a factor in your damaged window, Mr Quinlan? Just a thought.'

Quinlan tried for befuddlement, an open look, uncoloured by panic. Did it badly. Because we're the police? Hirsch wondered.

'Forgive me—what are you implying?'

Jean held up a hand. 'I'm not implying anything, merely asking: is it possible a creditor took matters into his own hands?'

Eyes moist with disbelief, Quinlan said, 'Creditor? Yes, I have creditors. But this is a business. We work on a sixty-day cycle, I've always worked like that. People are patient, they know me, they know they'll get paid. If someone asks me to sell a stud ram on a Tuesday and wants his money on a Wednesday, well, he'll have to be patient, it doesn't work like that.' He swelled a little. 'The business has been here in this town for decades. Decades. It'll still be here when I'm dead and gone, I should imagine.'

'Thank you. That's encouraging to hear. So, the music festival is definitely going ahead?'

Astonishment. 'Why on earth wouldn't it?'

'No reason, Mr Quinlan. Not that I'm aware of. Except if suppliers haven't been paid and no one turns up.'

Quinlan said stiffly, 'Everyone will be paid in full before the opening day.'

'But if it doesn't go ahead, and people don't hear about it in time, my colleagues and I could face some unpleasant surprises.'

'I have also hired private security, don't forget.'

'That's for sure? They've been paid an advance fee?'

'Absolutely.'

'And the kids who've bought tickets. Is there a refund policy?'

'Look,' Quinlan said, as if she was starting to grate on him. 'Everything's a go. And the kids will get their money's worth. Top-notch bands all weekend.'

'Good to hear.'

Hirsch said, 'There have been mutterings, Mr Quinlan. For example, Leon Ayliffe said a cheque you paid him bounced.'

'You're surely not blaming his...his whatever you call it, on me? I'd be very grateful if you could just give me a reference number for the insurance company. I've got a lot on.'

Jean Landy said roguishly, 'Didn't toss a brick through your own window, I hope, Mr Quinlan? For the insurance?'

Quinlan gave a desperate hurt chuckle and said, 'If the business *was* going down the tubes, I'd try something on a grander scale.'

'I'll pretend I didn't hear that,' Jean said, dropping the roguishness, and they left Quinlan and his sportscoat and moleskins in a puddle of doubt.

Back in the patrol car Hirsch said, 'I think you got him rattled, Constable Landy. Great job.'

'You know what that prick did a few weeks ago? Actually asked me to waive his daughter's speeding fine.'

'You told him where to go?'

'Very politely.'

Hirsch fished for his phone. He'd felt it vibrate during the interview. While Jean turned the ignition key and got the heater going, he checked the screen: a missed call and a follow-up text. Sophie Flynn, a teller at the Mid-North Community Bank, had been given his number by Maggie Groote. Maggie was in a state, asking for him.

13

Landy dropped him back at the police station, where he retrieved his Toyota and drove to the town square. The bank, sandwiched between the supermarket and Redruth Olde Wares, always seemed faintly desperate to Hirsch, its windows papered with offers and bold percentage and dollar signs that failed to excite greed in him, or even thrift.

He switched off, got out. The rain had eased but the runoff frothed along the gutters, paper cups eddying, plastic scraps massing. He stepped over the mess and entered the bank. A long, narrow room, with a couple of plain chairs and a wall-mounted counter on the left, two teller windows on the right. A closed door at the far end: wood and frosted glass, *Manager* in gold.

A man in overalls and a young woman with a baby strapped to her chest were waiting at the second teller window, but they, and the teller, were alive only to the drama playing out on one of the customer chairs. Maggie sat there sobbing in distress with Sophie Flynn crouched before her, holding her hands.

Hirsch joined them, crouching also, his damp knees brushing Sophie's. She flashed him a troubled smile, a young woman out of her depth. He smiled to reassure her. 'Thanks for calling me.'

'That's all right.' She touched his sleeve. 'I heard what happened on Friday. Are you okay?'

He smiled. 'I'm fine. How can I help you?'

'Maggie's in a spot of bother, aren't you, Maggie,' the young teller said, with the bright, innocent voice of a student nurse.

'Sorry to hear that, Maggie,' said Hirsch. He turned to Sophie, murmuring, 'Is Mr Cater in?'

'He had an appointment.'

Hirsch nodded, unsurprised. The manager struck him as a man who always had appointments. 'What seems to be the problem?'

Just then another customer entered the bank. Sophie, a kid from the district in her first job, looked up, torn between her duties. 'You go,' Hirsch said.

'I'll be right back,' she promised.

Hirsch creaked upright and sat beside Maggie Groote, who blew her nose and said, 'I feel like such a fool.'

'I feel like that every day,' Hirsch said, trying a smile on her.

She gave him a look: You're young and healthy; I'm not. Don't make light of it.

He tried for a little more warmth in his smile. 'Something happened?'

'I did something stupid.'

She looked at him as if he might allow her to have been stupid. He said, 'Was it something to do with money?'

'Yes.'

They'd hardly call him in if she'd overdrawn her account. 'Were you cheated, Mrs Groote?'

'Yes!'

'Okay. What happened?'

'That heavy rain last week...' She stopped.

'Go on.'

'There was a knock on the door and two men were standing there in those yellow coats and plastic helmet things...'

Hi-vis jackets and hardhats, Hirsh thought. And he knew where this was going. 'Were they Irish?'

'Yes! How did you know? Lovely accents, and so friendly. They said they'd been sent to fix my roof. They had a ladder against the side wall and everything.'

The cuffs of her blouse were grimy. She'd painted rouge on her cheeks, and she smelt stale. Her hand trembled. He clasped it briefly. 'Did they say what the fault was?'

'Water was pouring over the side of the gutter. I could see it. They said it had been happening for some years, probably, and would have rotted the timbers underneath. They said the ceiling could fall in on me.'

They blocked the gutter, then knocked on her door, Hirsch thought. 'Have you ever seen any signs of dampness inside the house? Walls or ceiling?'

'No, but they came in with their ladder and one of them poked his head through the manhole in the hallway and the other one had this gauge thing to measure the moisture in the air. They both said it was at a dangerous level and I could be breathing in spores and the ceiling could collapse at any minute.'

'Maggie, did it strike you as odd that they just showed up?'

She looked lost; shook her head. 'I thought the council might have sent them.'

'Then what happened? They offered to fix it?'

'They said they had special equipment in their depot that would blow hot air into the ceiling cavity and dry everything out.'

Hirsch said patiently, 'They wanted a deposit? Up-front payment?'

Maggie was weeping again now. There was movement in the bank; both tellers were temporarily free. Sophie came through to rejoin them, crouching beside Maggie's knees again.

Hirsch said, 'How much did they want?'

Maggie sank into herself. 'Seven and a half thousand.'

'Oh, Maggie,' Hirsch said. 'This was last week?'

Sophie looked up at him. 'It was me who served her. Then when she came in this morning and wanted another five thousand, I thought I should say something.' She patted Maggie. 'You looked a bit...self-conscious, Maggie, like you wanted me to step in.'

Perceptive, thought Hirsch. 'The same men? Did they say why they wanted another five thousand?'

Maggie shifted uncomfortably. 'Different men. The men last week they said they'd send in a special crew.'

'Okay.'

'They knocked on my door just after breakfast and were going to start work when they realised it was worse than they thought, and they'd have to get a more powerful blower.' She paused. 'I feel such a fool.'

It must work for them, Hirsch thought, taking a second bite from elderly people like Maggie Groote. 'Were they also Irish?'

'Yes.'

'Can you describe them for me?'

All four had been in their thirties, if she was any judge. Ordinary looking. Goggles and hi-vis; hardhats or beanies.

Harder to ID them, Hirsch thought. 'Did you see what they were driving?'

She hadn't thought to look. 'Sorry I can't be more help. But they had a long ladder.'

Sophie patted the old woman again. 'Could have happened to anyone, Maggie.' She turned to Hirsch. 'Two lump-sum withdrawals inside a week, and she said both times she needed it for personal reasons.'

'They told me to say that, in case I was queried.'

Sophie patted her. 'Anyway, I thought I should grill you a bit, Maggie, sorry about that.'

'Just as well you did, dear.'

'I'm afraid your seven and a half thousand is gone, but it could have been twelve and a half.'

'I know. I'm so relieved.'

'The thing is, there wouldn't have been enough in your account to cover the five thousand,' Sophie said gently.

The old woman went very still. She didn't look so vague

now. 'That's impossible. That's my special account, for large bills and holidays and car repairs.'

Sophie patted her forearm. 'Anyone can forget to keep an eye on their account. I do it all the time.'

Maggie sharpened. 'But I never use that account.' A long pause. 'Come to think of it, I haven't received a statement for some time.'

Bank business. Hirsch waited for it to play out, and asked, 'Maggie, are they still waiting inside your house, by any chance?'

She shrank. 'They had to get everything ready. Their ladders and drop cloths and toolboxes and that.' She shook her head and wept; an old woman tossed aside.

Hirsch stood. 'I'll go over there right now, Mrs Groote. Perhaps Sophie can make you a cup of tea? Or can we call Amy to come here?'

Maggie Groote looked up. 'Actually, Paul,' she gave him an awkward smile, 'I'd really rather not involve my niece, if you don't mind.'

Hirsch drove north through cheerless rain. At Penhale he turned into Maggie Groote's street and halted, peering through the smeared glass. There were no vehicles parked outside her house or in her driveway. He inched forward, parked, sprinted to the shelter of her veranda, and saw that her door was ajar. He knuckled it, stepped into the hallway. The manhole cover was open. No equipment, only a broad wet patch on the carpet. They simply poured a bucket of water over it, he thought. Ceiling and walls were bone dry.

Why did they leave, though? Because she was taking too long to return? They'd followed her and seen me enter the bank? He left the house, looked along the side wall at the CCTV camera under the eaves: the line had been cut.

A voice spoke from under a drumming umbrella at the front gate. 'I sent them packing.'

A large middle-aged woman in tracksuit pants, moon boots and a Crows football jumper; corkscrew hair gone crazy in the damp air. Hirsch joined her on the footpath. 'They didn't seem right to you?'

'The Irish accents, mate. Charm the birds out of the trees, but I didn't come down in the last shower. Plus, I read about it on Facebook.' She looked past his shoulder. 'That door sticks. You need to give it a good slam.'

Over a cup of tea next door he obtained no useful details. Just a couple of blokes, looked like tradies. A white van, she thought; she didn't get the plate number.

And then she pointed a chipped fingernail at him. 'But I wouldn't put it past the niece, you know.'

'She's working with a team of Irish conmen?'

'I wouldn't put it past her.'

Hirsch headed north again, through farmland to Tiverton, and into the police station driveway. A small paper bag leaned against the door, the top taped down, a black Texta smiley face below the fold.

He tore it open. A CD. Emmylou Harris, *Stumble into Grace*.

Well, it hadn't been left there by whatsername who'd skipped out on him.

14

Tuesday, 6.00 a.m., Hirsch walking the town. No rain but the sky was not hung with stars, meaning cloudy greyness later on. His way was lit by streetlights set far apart and a torch from the two-dollar shop in Redruth. He was the only fool abroad at this hour—but he was a creature of habit. If he didn't walk every morning, mischance and chaos would reign.

Back in his paltry kitchen at the rear of the police station he fixed breakfast #3: juice and muesli. Breakfast was a cup of tea when he first awoke, second breakfast coffee and toast an hour later. Mischance and chaos.

A short patrol today, but first some paperwork. Emails, envelopes. The registration was due on his Nissan. Rosie DeLisle, his only friend at HQ, had sent him a plain white card with *Horrendously uninspired all-purpose greeting card* printed on the front. On the inside, scrawled in blue biro: 'He never rings, he never writes...xxx'. He grinned, then felt chastened. Thought, not for the first time, about friendship.

Was he just shit at it? Did he know what it was? It required work he wasn't currently putting in, he knew that much.

Finally he checked the Tiverton Facebook page. A selfie of Gemma Pitcher, who worked at the general store, standing in a voluminous pink puffa jacket beside a strip of snow on the Razorback. No snow there today, he thought, after all the rain. Several delighted posts on the greening of the farmland and tracts of mallee scrub that had been burnt out last summer: game new shoots in the blackened soil and whiskery sprouts on tree trunks. It did Hirsch good, people seeing goodness around them. He considered himself an optimistic man, but he saw the opposite too often.

Irishmen. He flexed his fingers, ready to type up a warning post on the Facebook page, wondering how to express it. Irish roof-repair scammers were a thing—like Albanian ATM scammers. They flew into Australia, fleeced the locals of several hundred thousand dollars, flew out again. But the Irish roof guys were new to the mid-north. A team of at least four: two to make first contact, two to come along later as the repair team and ask for more money. Maybe a couple more men—or women—he couldn't be sure. They'd saturate an area, then move on. With any luck, they were still somewhere around.

He curled his frozen toes, blew on his fingers and began to type. Beware of men with Irish accents and charming manners who knock on the door and offer to carry out roof and other repairs, and please check regularly on elderly acquaintances, who are especially vulnerable to approaches from these men. They may look and sound official—hi-vis jackets and so on—but ask to see ID and ask for a written quote.

If you are approached, do not pay a deposit, do not hand them your account details, do not leave them alone in your home. If you are warned that a ceiling or wall is in danger of collapsing, get a second opinion.

Challenge these men if necessary, but do not antagonise them. Descriptions, photographs and plate numbers would assist the police, but, again, don't do anything to alert or antagonise. Finally, these men might be living out of a mobile home or staying temporarily in a motel, hotel or Airbnb. Please advise your nearest police station if you suspect you've spotted them anywhere in the mid-north.

He was about to switch off when the computer pinged for a new email. The South Australia Police Service was offering a range of short courses that would help him flex his leadership style and consequently develop pathways to success. A three-day workshop, or one evening a week for six weeks, run by accredited style coaches using conceptually supported and evidence-driven analysis that would enable Hirsch to understand the colour aura of the various management styles available for every workplace contingency.

Hirsch's aura was dark grey when he pinned his number to the door and headed out, and it turned black when his phone pinged and he saw the caller's name. He pulled over, checked as usual for kamikaze crop-dusters and said, 'Clara. I was just going to call you.'

Her voice was tight. 'You got the CD all right?'

'I did, thank you, it was very thoughtful of you.'

Should he have said that? Would it encourage her? Should he nip this in the bud right now?

'I was beginning to think,' she said, 'that someone must have pinched it off your doorstep.' Then, with a tighter voice, a strangled laugh: 'Or that you disapproved.'

Fuck, yeah, I disapprove. 'No, no, very thoughtful. It's just that with one thing and another—I'm temporarily in charge of Redruth *and* Tiverton right now—I've been snowed under.'

'All those terrorist invasions and bomb scares,' she said with a tinkling laugh threaded with something he couldn't place but didn't like.

'Exactly.'

'Well, better not keep you.'

'Thanks again, Clara,' Hirsch said, in his flattest voice.

Twenty minutes later he was asking Jonas Heneker about when he'd last seen Alex Jarmyn.

Bristles advanced, retreated, parried as the whiskery old mouth cogitated. 'You know, it could easily have been a year ago, now you mention it. Why, you think he's dead? In the wind?'

'Did you speak to him that time?'

'He'd barely give me the time of day, let alone talk. Not long after they moved in—what, three or four year ago?—he was at his front gate, putting up a mailbox. I stop and tell him, mate, no deliveries out here, you need to rent a slot down at the shop. Same with newspapers. That was about the sum total of my contact with the bloke.'

Hirsch made a note: check the Jarmyns' Australia Post box at the general store. Get a warrant and check the box. Or suggest it to Comyn and be ignored.

He allowed himself a stale Anzac biscuit and milky tea in the old man's kitchen and drove down to the highway. Through Tiverton to Penhale, where he turned into Maggie Groote's street. He didn't go in: the Fearns' Renault was parked outside her house.

Back onto the highway and out along Nautilus Road. He slowed as he passed the Ayliffes' driveway entrance: no fresh tracks in or out and the crime-scene tape was intact. He drove on, engaging four-wheel drive, until he reached the empty house that he'd doorknocked with Comyn on Friday. Nothing had been disturbed; no new tracks.

Finally he drove down to Redruth, where he spent most of the day writing reports, fielding calls and checking on Ayliffe updates. They were believed to have stolen a Pajero in Mildura, and New South Wales police were keeping watch over a house owned by an Ayliffe second cousin in Dubbo.

Then at 3.00 p.m. Hirsch was called to look at a padlock on a gate.

Rolf Voumard was worn down by the sun and thankless labour. Gaunt as a dustbowl survivor, he was about fifty and taciturn, clothed in threadbare but spotless work clothes under a bushman's oilcloth coat. His boots, planted in the muddy road outside the gate, had probably been polished that morning.

'I'm the caretaker,' he told Hirsch.

'Okay.'

They were halfway up a hillslope on the opposite side of the shallow valley from the Ayliffe property. Hirsch peered across; couldn't pick it out.

'Gardening,' Voumard said, 'mowing, getting in firewood at the start of winter, kind of thing. Check the power hasn't gone off. Check for break-ins. Feed the alpacas. I come by once a week at this time of the year.'

'Okay.'

The entryway was a broad, shiny cyclone gate between massive fieldstone gateposts. A short distance away, glimpsed through casuarinas and banksias, was a Cape Cod-style kit home. A weekender, a hobby farm, belonging to a North Adelaide dentist.

'So when I heard the news on Friday I came straight here. Nothing had been disturbed, and the police must've checked the place because I found a card stuck in the front door.' He paused. 'They must've climbed over the gate.'

'Probably,' Hirsch said, hunching his shoulders and stamping his feet. The hillslope was funnelling a nasty wind and the caretaker was slow getting to the point.

'But just now when I checked, I couldn't get in.'

Hirsch was slow to process that. Seeing his confusion, Voumard pointed at the chain and padlock. 'That's not mine—I mean, Mr Woollcott's. I didn't put it there.'

'Someone changed it since Friday?'

'Yes.'

'You're sure?' asked Hirsch, knowing it was a stupid question.

'See for yourself,' Voumard said, fishing a bunch of keys from a deep coat pocket. He counted them off for Hirsch: 'My house, my shed, Mr Woollcott's house, Mr Woollcott's shed, gate padlock.'

Hirsch tried the padlock key. It didn't fit, and a powerful sense spread through him of a shrewd mind at work.

The Ayliffes were back in the mid-north. How many other places like this existed? Ignored, overlooked, uninhabited, innocent-looking places where Leon Ayliffe had fitted his own lock and chain and could come and go as he liked?

'Would Leon Ayliffe or his son know about this place?'

'They sold Mr Woollcott some hay last year. For the alpacas.'

Hirsch glance up at the house uneasily. The Ayliffes were hardly likely to lock themselves in. 'Have you checked?'

Voumard nodded. 'Everything's okay, except someone's taken half a drum of diesel.'

For the stolen Pajero? 'You're sure,' Hirsch said, another stupid question.

'The pump's still in the drum. I never do that; I always take it out and put the cap back on.'

Hirsch thanked the caretaker and made some phone calls.

15

Neither the STAR Group inspector nor Comyn was overwhelmed by Hirsch's lock-and-chain theory. Perhaps the dentist was trying to tell his caretaker something? Like, your services are no longer required? And how old was the guy, anyway? Could he have lost his key or forgotten he'd replaced the lock and chain? As for the diesel...How old, again?

Anyway—duly noted, let us know if you see or hear anything.

In Sergeant Brandl's office first thing Wednesday morning, Hirsch called the dental surgery: Woollcott was at a conference in Singapore.

Hirsch fired off an email, then spent the next few hours attending to calls, reports and follow-ups. He was half-expecting the penny to drop at police HQ—that Constable Paul Hirschhausen had been placed in charge of a busy police station.

His mobile pinged. A text from a mobile number he didn't recognise. A question mark, nothing else.

He was pretty sure he'd made enemies over the years, and he was convinced that he managed to bewilder someone nearly every day of his life. But his only thought now was: Clara Ogilvie.

He called the number: a recorded message said, 'The number you are calling is not available.' Had she switched off as soon as she'd sent the text?

He blocked it.

Then he unblocked it, thinking: evidence.

Lunch was butter chicken from the Caltex out near the hospital. Butter chicken, tikka masala, rogan josh, chicken korma, saffron rice and naan bread steaming in a bain marie wedged between a stand of Goodyear tyres and a shelf of brake fluid and anti-freeze. Cooked by Harshida, the daughter of the Sikh owner; served by Darvesh, the son, and a demonstration, to Hirsch, of the world's resistance to classification.

After lunch he walked the streets of Redruth to stave off sleepiness and reassure the locals that the police were ever-vigilant. On the return leg he received a call from the Roxby Downs HR department.

'Alexander Jarmyn resigned by letter. Barely readable. It's in his file.'

Be interesting to examine the handwriting. 'Could you scan and email it to me, please?'

A pause. 'I am not comfortable doing that. I would need to seek permission. Mr Jarmyn has a right to confidentiality, as does the company.'

Hirsch counted to ten. 'All right. May I ask what the letter says? Paraphrase.'

Another pause. 'It says simply that he has found other employment and apologises for the short notice.'

'Did he have a locker?'

The pause seemed to ask: why can't life be simple? A stern cough, then: 'He did, but there is no record that he left any belongings behind when he finished here.'

'Did Mr Jarmyn empty it? A friend or family? The company? Any way of finding out?'

A chill came from Hirsch's phone. 'I have neither the means nor the time to find that out. But I remind you that we are a big and busy concern. Staff lockers are always in demand.'

Late afternoon—lamb korma for dinner in a bag in the passenger-side footwell—Hirsch called in at Maggie Groote's house on his way home.

She seemed vague in the stifling heat of her sitting room, focusing only when he asked about her depleted bank account.

'There should have been over two hundred and fifty thousand dollars in that account,' she said. Gesturing at the walls around her she said, 'I bought this house two years ago, with a view to living in it when the farm got too much for me.' A crooked grin. 'Of course, I hadn't counted on moving in quite so soon.'

Hirsch understood. She hadn't counted on Amy needing a place to stay, or that they wouldn't get along. 'The two hundred and fifty thousand was money left over?'

'It was. I sold BHP and Cochlear shares.'

'It wasn't your daily account?'

She shook her head. 'I set it up for special occasions but so far I haven't touched it. Promise. I'm not making it up.'

'I believe you,' Hirsch said. 'But if that's the case, you probably didn't check the balance very often.'

She seemed to fold in on herself. 'Probably. I'm a silly old woman.'

'Not silly,' Hirsch said. 'You didn't use the account, so you didn't realise you weren't being sent statements.'

Maggie was staring with a little frown at the mantelpiece. 'Sophie's looking into it for me.'

Struck by a new intensity in her, Hirsch followed her gaze. She was staring fixedly at photographs, her doll collection, or a glazed pot. 'Something wrong?'

'Could you straighten the pot for me, dear? The blessed woman who cleans for me uses a feather duster as if she's smiting her enemies.'

Smiting her enemies, thought Hirsch with a grin. He stood, crossed the room, turned the pot, and saw the name *Rory* on a tiny glazed shield. He faced it outwards. 'Your husband?'

'Passed away fourteen years ago, bless his soul.'

As soon as Hirsch was back in his chair, she patted his knee. 'Want to hear a story?'

'Always,' said Hirsch, thinking of his lamb curry, thinking of his empty rooms, thinking of his role in the community. But where was the person named Paul Hirschhausen in all of that?

'It was quite a big funeral, Rory was well liked, and when

it was all over it was the quiet time, you know? Just me. A few days later, I get a call from Driscoll's.' She peered at Hirsch. 'The funeral director? In Clare?'

Hirsch nodded.

'Apparently Rory's ashes were ready, I could pick them up whenever I liked. So I drive over there and pick them up and strap him into the passenger seat and spend a few hours out and about in the car. Chores. This, that and the other. Some of the spots we liked to go, the miners' dugouts along Redruth Creek, the Razorback, a picnic spot out east. And all the while I'm chatting away to him, there in the passenger seat. Talking and laughing—and crying, half the time.

'So I get home, put him on the mantelpiece—not in that jar, he was still in a plastic bag in a cardboard box at that stage—and still I'm talking and laughing and crying.'

She paused, humour and tears on her face. 'Bonding with ashes in a cardboard box. Then the next morning I get another call from Driscoll's. They've given me the wrong ashes.'

She looked at Hirsch. 'You're allowed to laugh.'

Hirsch was almost at Tiverton, 'Ode to Billie Joe' on his Old Farts CD, when Monica Fuller called. Graham hadn't come home.

135

16

The clouds had bunched into massive cotton balls during the day, letting in the sharp light of winter, and now, with the sun a low smear on the horizon, the turbines were blazing white along the tops of the Tiverton Hills. Hirsch flipped down the visor and slipped on his sunglasses as he climbed Hawker Road to the windfarm depot.

The gate was ajar. The workers' cars were gone. A white Nissan Pajero with Victorian plates stood, doors open, at an untidy angle outside the main workshop.

Hirsch radioed his location then, low in the driver's seat, he made a circuit of the place. Nothing disturbed the lengthening shadows on the sloping ground. Seeking cover, he parked in a muddle of fuel drums, pallets, small sheds and a van on blocks and got out, unholstering his pistol.

A fast, bent-over run took him to the rear wall of the workshop. He tested the back door: locked. Still keeping low, his heart hammering, he edged around to the side wall, darted a look and dashed for the front. Another quick look around the corner and he was crouched at the main entrance, watching, assessing.

Stillness inside. Dimness. Only a neon tube buzzing, and the odours of oil, petrol and greasy cold metal tools, axles and angle iron in his nostrils.

Then: 'You took your bloody time.'

Hirsch felt the tension ebb away. 'Well, I've got a lot on my plate.'

'It'll be *you* on a plate if you don't set me free.'

'Patience my friend,' Hirsch said, crouching to pick at the duct tape binding Fuller's wrists together. Another strip bound him to the upright of a work bench.

'Monica called you?'

'Yes.' Hirsch's fingers were blunt and useless.

'I could hear the phones going off. For Christ's sake, use a knife. There's a boxcutter on the bench.'

Hirsch found it in a tray of duct tape, tyre pressure gauges and cotter pins. 'It was the Ayliffes?'

'Yep.'

Crouching, slicing through the tape, Hirsch said, 'When?'

Fuller climbed stiffly to his feet. Swaying a little, he clutched the edge of the bench. 'About an hour ago. The other blokes had all gone home.' He paused. 'Like they were watching the place.'

'Both Ayliffes?'

'Yes. Look, I need to tell Monica I'm okay.'

Hirsch walked outside to give him privacy and called the STAR Group inspector, then Comyn, and waited in the chilly wind. Presently, hearing Fuller say goodbye to his wife, he went back in. Fuller stood with his back to Hirsch, both hands on the bench, head bowed, as if praying. Getting his strength back, thought Hirsch.

He crossed the grubby cold concrete floor and put an arm around the man's solid bulk. 'You okay?'

Fuller shook him off, embarrassed. 'Fine.' He straightened. 'I know you need to ask questions, but can I go home? Monica's in a bit of a state.'

And so are you, Hirsch thought. Console each other. 'Just a couple of quick ones. Other police will have more, but fuck it, they can call you at home.'

Fuller was resigned. 'Fire away.'

'Did they stay long?'

'Long enough to tie me up and steal one of the LandCruisers.'

'They say anything?'

'Apologetic, that's all. They had no beef with me, they just needed a replacement vehicle.' Fuller nodded towards the door. 'The one they arrived in was using oil and there was a knock in the motor. Thrashed it, probably.'

'Armed?'

'Pointed a damn sawn-off shotgun at me.'

'Did they give any indication where they were going next?'

'Not as such. I said, give yourselves up before someone gets hurt and Leon taps his nose like he's Agent 007 on a secret bloody mission and says, "Unfinished business." Whatever that means.'

Hirsch thought he knew. As soon as Fuller had gone, he called in the details of the stolen LandCruiser, then phoned

Quinlan and Roskam. Quinlan was in Adelaide. Roskam didn't answer.

Hirsch looped crime-scene tape across the entry to the workshop, and again at the front gate on his way out, and sped down Hawker Road to the highway. Almost 6.00 p.m., his headlights melding with the twilight that folded in across the road and the floor of the valley. Reaching the highway, he turned right and within minutes could see the faint glow of the town ahead. He glanced at the police station as he turned right into the little street beside the school. A grey Fiesta idling next to his driveway seemed to sense him and accelerated away.

He forgot about it and parked next to the admin block of the school. It looked shut down. He got out, ran once around and between the buildings and then through the hedge to Roskam's house.

It was also in darkness, a deeper darkness owing to the hedge, garden trees and its distance from the streetlights. Hirsch made a swift circuit of the house, checking a garden shed and a lean-to stacked with firewood. The garage door was up this time. Parked there, with workbenches, shelves, ladders and a saw table closing in on it, was a small white Kia sedan.

Hirsch drew his pistol and crossed the front of the house to the main door. Locked; no reaction when he knocked. Around to the back door: alarmed to find it open. He slipped inside, finding himself in an old-style sunroom and enough light to assess the dark spaces between a bamboo and glass coffee table and bamboo chairs with brightly coloured cushions. A faded Turkish rug on the floor.

He lingered a while, reading his senses for evidence of blood spilt, someone dying, the aftermath of violence. The house smelt faintly of toast—Roskam's after-school snack?—and the evening moaned around its old frames. Nothing else. He checked the corner of his mind that sometimes registered the uncanny and felt nothing there either.

So he swept through the house, room to room, checking under beds, in wardrobes, behind curtains and dressers. Empty.

He returned to the garage, switched on the overhead light and peered into the Kia. Also empty. Under the benches, into the corners. The head-high shelves were stacked with large document cartons marked *Tents*, *Sleeping bags*, *Colouring books* and *Upper primary stationery*. Snug-fitting lids, except for a gap where one corner had lifted. Hirsch wondered why you'd store a bra with sleeping bags.

A shadow fell over him and a voice called, 'Hello? Paul?'

Glenys Fife stood in the doorway. Hirsch said, 'Talk about giving your courageous local copper the fright of his life.'

'Sorry.' Her hand was at her throat, bunching the fabric of her shirt. 'Have they gone?'

Leon and Josh Ayliffe had made her sit on the floor of her office, she said, then taped her to a leg of her desk and disappeared.

'I was just about to lock up. Look at the state of my arms.' She rested them, palms up, on Roskam's kitchen table.

Then rotated them, palms down, palms up again. The skin was chafed, with pinpricks of blood. 'I rubbed up and down until the tape broke.'

Hirsch reached across and squeezed her forearms. 'Did they say anything?'

'Not a word, except to tell me to sit on the floor. But they looked apologetic, if that helps.'

Hirsch made a gesture. 'Mr Roskam's not here. Did you hear anything to suggest they took him?'

'I don't think they did. He must've heard them—I heard him drive away.'

'Are you sure? His car's here.'

'He was on his motorbike.'

Hirsch sat, and he thought. He said, 'Back in a tick,' and returned to the garage. Switched on the light, reached up and tugged on the bra strap. He felt resistance and then it jerked and slid free of the carton with a waft of laundry detergent. A hole punched in the bottom of the 'B' in Berlei. The bra had, until recently, been in the possession of Anne Pierce in Spalding.

He tucked the bra into one of his pockets and returned to the kitchen. Glenys was jiggling one leg and looked ready to snap. 'Paul, if you don't mind, I'd like to go home. Or maybe to the pub.'

Hirsch nodded. 'Someone will take your statement later.'

'Here?'

'That won't be necessary.' Hirsch smiled. 'Thanks for your help, Glen. I'd have found you eventually—I needed to check on Mr Roskam first.'

'Yeah,' Glenys Fife examined her wrists gloomily. 'I guess so.'

When she was gone, Hirsch called Betty Lidstrom. 'Just out of interest, have you had anything to do with Julian Roskam?'

He could visualise her sitting there, thinking. 'Just out of interest, my eye,' she said.

'Humour me.'

'Just out of interest, he gave a series of talks on Jane Austen for our Probus group in Redruth.'

Should he ask her to name her classmates, or should he call each of the snowdropping victims? She got there ahead of him. 'Just out of interest, apart from me there was Maggie Groote, Anne Pierce, Rose Wurfel, Leonore Drew and Alice Snell.' She paused. 'I should have seen it.'

She'd named four of the victims. 'Please, Betty, keep it to yourself for now.'

'My lips are sealed.'

Hirsch sat for a while then, the cold seeping into his bones. He texted Roskam to say it was safe to return, made tea from the man's tin of English Breakfast, and settled in to wait. His phone pinged and he stiffened: not Roskam but a smiley face, and when he called the number, he heard the same recorded message: unavailable, please try again.

He removed the bra from his pocket and draped it over the back of a chair. It would be the first thing Roskam saw when—if—he returned.

17

Inspector Merlino arrived first, with a reduced team.

'We've got a kid in a suicide vest waving a machete around in Enfield,' he said sourly. In his view, the Ayliffes posed a greater threat; he wanted a full-size team.

They sat in Roskam's kitchen nursing sweet black tea, hunched in their coats, a bar heater at their feet. It gave out less heat than the one in Hirsch's office, if that were possible. Merlino's ninjas had it worse: as a first line of defence in case the Ayliffes returned, two were patrolling the school grounds on foot and Beulah was watching from the back seat of one of the black SUVs.

Merlino said, 'I phoned your mate, Fuller. Didn't have much to tell me.'

'You won't get much from Mrs Fyfe either,' Hirsch said, 'and I think Roskam cleared out at the first whiff of trouble. The Ayliffes could be chasing him, but he's on a motorbike, so I don't like their chances.'

'But he's coming back?'

'According to the text he sent me,' Hirsch said. Behind him the old refrigerator shuddered and switched off. The air and the silence were frosty.

'Tell me about him.'

Hirsch complied. Merlino said, 'Is this an upstanding citizen we're talking about? Given the flick by Mrs Ayliffe so he takes it out on the daughter, which pushes Leon Ayliffe's button?'

'I think Leon was going to pop anyway,' Hirsch said.

'Uh-huh. And meanwhile there's something about Roskam you're not telling me.'

Hirsch hunched miserably against the cold. Had an education department anywhere ever heated a classroom or a teacher's dwelling? And Roskam was a poor housekeeper. A tap dripped; the tabletop had been swiped with a greasy sponge; sticky floor; crumbs around the toaster.

A buzz and Hirsch's phone vibrated, on its back beside his elbow. He glanced at the screen: a sad-face emoji.

'Constable Hirschhausen, I'm talking to you.'

'Sorry, sir, could you repeat the question?'

'Roskam. Married?'

'No, sir.'

'And no longer involved with Mrs Ayliffe.'

'Correct.'

'Then whose bra is this?' Merlino asked, reaching across, flicking a pale pink cup.

'I aim to ask him that, sir.'

'He's your snowdropper,' said Merlino.

Hirsch looked at him.

'Don't look surprised, constable. You think I go into a town without doing my homework? Was it in plain view?'

'Kind of, sir.'

Hirsch explained: the visible strap, hinting at a stash; the hole in the label.

'Clever. Your idea?'

'Yes, sir.'

'So you can get him on theft. But there's a pathology there, right? A rap over the knuckles isn't going to fix that. Get the court to order a psych eval.'

'I aim to, sir.'

Merlino leaned forward, his lean dark face boring into Hirsch. More animated now, he said, 'And it might pay to check where and when he's lived and worked in the past ten or twenty years and collate that against granny-related incidents.'

Hirsch had been intending to do some digging. 'Good idea, sir.'

Merlino leaned back and cocked his head. 'You've already thought of it.'

Hirsch's phone pinged again, and Merlino said, 'Will you for fuck's sake deal with whoever's calling, or switch the damn thing off? I can see from here it's not important. Girl-friend sending you smiley faces?'

Hirsch switched off and pocketed his phone. The wind moaned around the blighted house but not so determinedly that it drowned out the sound of a motorbike.

Hirsch didn't know it until later but Roskam's hoard numbered 823 pairs of knickers, 488 bras, a threadbare garter belt and a handful of camisoles. For the moment, though, one tired bra was enough.

The primary school head walked in, saw it draped over the back of one of his kitchen chairs, went white and swallowed convulsively, like a fish landed in the bottom of a dinghy.

'Hello, there, Julian,' Hirsch said.

'What...I mean...what...'

Hirsch picked the bra off the chair and waved it. 'Tip of the iceberg, right? Quite a hoard you've gathered over the years.'

The teacher shot a look towards his garage. 'I'm so ashamed. Please don't tell anyone. I'll quit my position and move away, I promise.'

'Hey, hey, hey,' said Merlino warmly, surprising Hirsch. 'Enough of that talk.'

He stood, placed an arm around Roskam's shoulders and settled him in the fourth kitchen chair.

'Mr Roskam, is it? My name is Inspector Merlino and I'm in charge of the Ayliffe manhunt—which I'm hoping you can help us with, okay? But first I'm going to make us all a cup of tea—how do you like it?—and Constable Hirschhausen is going to explain what happens next.'

Hirsch outlined the charges—theft and trespass—and told Roskam he'd be summonsed to appear in court at a later date. The horror grew on Roskam's face. '*Theft*? Trespass? Never. No, that's not me.' He squirmed in his chair. 'All right, yes, I collect, er, certain items—*purchase* them here and there, but I don't steal. I mean, why would I if I can buy them?'

146

Standing at the kitchen bench behind him, Merlino said, 'We can sort all that out later, Mr Roskam.'

He returned to the table with the tea and Roskam gave him a grateful smile. Merlino was friend, Hirsch was foe.

The three men sat for a while, their mugs steaming in the frigid air. Merlino said mildly, 'The main reason we're here is to catch Mr Ayliffe and his son. If that relates to you in any way, Mr Roskam, we'd be keen to hear it. Timing's critical, you understand.'

Roskam swallowed. He was greasy with perspiration, a whiff of putrescence in the dreary room. 'I want to help.'

'Constable Hirschhausen will record everything we say, for our mutual protection.'

'I understand. But I want to say...you understand...I'm not a bad person. I've got a quirk that perhaps most people won't quite understand.'

'A quirk,' mused Merlino.

'A kink.' Roskam squirmed in his chair. 'A fetish. Everyone's got one. I bet you have one.'

Hirsch was amused. He watched the STAR Group inspector, expecting an explosion, but Merlino seemed to concede the point. 'The privacy of your own home and all that.'

'Exactly. It doesn't make me dangerous or anything. I'm not a risk to anyone. It's not as if I'm a rapist.'

'Anyone can see that,' Merlino said. Then he turned cold and hard. 'But you are a thief. You did trespass on private property. You did cause a measure of alarm or distress.'

Hurt, betrayed by his pal, Roskam turned to Hirsch. 'Paul. You know me. I would never—'

Hirsch tossed him the bra. 'Check the label. See the hole in the letter "B"?'

Roskam recoiled. He didn't want to touch.

'You stole that from Anne Pierce a few days ago. Been a busy boy, Julian.'

Roskam began to rock. His voice choked. 'It's only underwear.'

'It's theft and it's trespass,' Merlino said. 'How did you choose your victims?'

Roskam looked hunted. 'Probus.' He gave a little clearing cough, said, 'Probus,' with greater definition. 'They attended a series of lectures I gave earlier in the year.'

Hirsch saw that he was hanging onto this scrap of prestige for dear life. 'You used their enrolment forms?'

A whispered, 'Yes.'

'Why some women and not others?'

Roskam gave a wondering look. 'Don't really know.'

'Why the motorbike and not your car?'

Roskam blushed. He found a smear on the table; rubbed at it. 'Quicker. Easier.'

'Why,' said Hirsch, 'women from this demographic?'

'What my young colleague means,' said Merlino, 'is why have you got a thing for old ladies?'

That was the turning point. Roskam shut down. As for the Ayliffes, all he could say was that he saw them arrive when he was wheeling his bin out and didn't waste any time, just got on the bike and sped off. Didn't engage. Had no knowledge of the Ayliffes' friends, family or favourite haunts.

As if he were the sane one in the equation he added, 'The father's a maniac. Son too, probably.'

'Just so that everything's formal and on the up and up,' Merlino said, 'we require you to show us your hoard of stolen underwear.'

'But I thought you—'

'Then I'll be out of your hair.'

'I'll show *Paul*,' Roskam said loftily, 'not you.'

'Suit yourself,' said Merlino expansively. He stood, said, 'Good work, constable. Keep your nose clean, Julian,' and left.

In the garage at the side of the house, Roskam said, 'Does the school council need to know?'

'It will come out, Julian.'

Roskam folded in on himself. 'This will kill my parents...'

'You never know, they might be very supportive.'

'Ha! Dad's ninety-five, Mum's ninety-three.'

Hirsch thought about that. Roskam was about fifty. 'I need you to come over to the station now to complete the questioning.'

'Then what?'

'You'll get notice of a court date in due course.'

Roskam shivered. 'I can't stay here.'

'That's up to you.'

'I'm too jittery to drive anywhere.'

'Can someone collect you? A friend?'

Roskam thought about it. 'My sister. She lives alone. I can stay with her.'

He wanted Hirsch to call. Avril Roskam, who lived near

Gawler, said tersely, 'It's going to take me ages to get there.'

'Come to the police station,' Hirsch told her.

The hours passed. After sharing his lamb korma with Roskam, Hirsch continued the formal interview. Then, leaving Roskam to watch TV, he hunched over the radiator in his office and pretended to do police work.

A knock on the door. Roskam's sister, a larger version of her brother, entered and occupied the place.

'I'm Avril. Where is he?'

Hirsch indicated the door that separated the office from his three miserable rooms. 'Through there.'

'God almighty, didn't you watch him?' she said, barging through.

But it seemed that Roskam hadn't hung himself from the light fitting. Hirsch heard murmurs; he prepared to wait. There was another knock and Clara Ogilvie was there on the front step of the police station, a bottle of red wine in one hand.

'I thought I'd drop round, see if you need a bit of unwinding,' she said with a light touch that didn't fool Hirsch. 'Your, umm, friend arrived just as I was parking the car. Anyway, we can easily split the bottle three ways.'

18

'Clara, you live down in Redruth. You're not just dropping around.'

Playfully reproachful, she explained that she did have a legitimate reason for being in Tiverton. 'I tutor Laura Cobb, Paul. Every Wednesday.'

The Cobbs, two teenagers and their mother, lived a block away. Marie Cobb had bipolar and didn't own a car. Laura, the younger, smarter child, probably missed many days of school caring for her mother. Hirsch looked past Clara's shoulder to the car at the kerb. Grey Fiesta. He'd seen it a few times lately, he realised. If he called Clara on it, she'd say she was in town dropping off schoolwork for Laura.

'But I can see I'm imposing on something personal and—'

'Clara, it's not personal, I'm on duty and it's a police matter.'

She tried to peer past him to the office and the connecting door. 'Always on duty, poor thing.' Pause. 'They should give you bigger premises.'

Meaning: why is that woman in your private quarters?

'Thanks for dropping in,' Hirsch said, 'I appreciate the gesture, but I'm dealing with a delicate matter involving someone's else's family and I need to get back to it.'

She turned up the light of her smile. 'I understand!' she said sunnily. 'Another time.'

'Drive carefully,' Hirsch said, hunching against the wind that whipped her skirt and pasted his trousers to his legs. 'Could be black ice on the roads.'

There was ice everywhere on Thursday morning. Hirsch tramped the streets of Tiverton in the saw-teeth of another frost. By seven-thirty he was driving through Penhale. The incident caravan was back. Four black SUVs huddled for warmth on the vacant block, one or two ninjas stamping their feet, vapour clouds puffing, dissipating, as they chatted.

Hirsch slowed the Toyota. Maybe he should tell them about the empty house he'd found with Comyn.

For what? Smug dismissal? No thanks. He made the turn and headed up Nautilus Road, passing the Ayliffe farm, engaging four-wheel drive for the steep and treacherous stretch, then on past the three occupied houses to the empty one.

Still no signs that anyone had visited the place in recent days. On the return journey, he began to feel uneasy. What if the Ayliffes had found the notes pinned to the doors of the other three houses along Nautilus Road? Three ready-made boltholes.

But Hirsch found no tracks, no broken windows or forced locks.

Twenty minutes later he was in Redruth. He sent Landy and Medlin out on house calls and a couple of thirty-minute breath-testing roadblocks and spent the day on reports and emails. Roskam was safe with his sister. Sergeant Brandl was sharp and twitchy. Graham Fuller was fine, had no intention of taking the day off, and asked if it was okay to punch TV reporters.

'Well, sure,' Hirsch said.

Whenever his phone pinged, he'd stiffen, glance at it side-on.

Late in the day, a call from Hedley Bastian. 'Constable Hirschhausen? We've never met. My daughter speaks highly of you.'

Hirsch muttered his way through the preliminaries, thinking, Christ, he'd forgotten to tell Vikki Bastian that she'd be in charge of the school for the time being. 'Is she okay?'

'Far as I know. The reason I'm calling, the festival's been cancelled, thought you should know. A weight off your shoulders, I expect. Annoying, from my point of view, but I'm trying to be philosophical about it.'

'Did Mr Quinlan inform you?'

'His secretary, forgotten her name.'

'Has everyone else been informed?'

'Everyone else?'

'The kids who bought tickets, the caterers...'

Bastian said, 'I expect so, not my concern, I just provided the venue.'

Hirsch was home by 6.00 p.m. There was a bunch of roses on his doorstep.

And a card:

I expect you're wondering if this overture means your love for Wendy is being tested. <u>*Turn that around and ask yourself how you might test her love for you.*</u> *This is how you can do that. Pretend to be an anonymous admirer and put a note in her letterbox saying how attracted you are to her and you'd like to treat her to lunch in Cousin Jack's on Monday, then watch from across the street to see if she turns up.*

Cousin Jack's was Redruth's only sit-down lunch place if you didn't want a schnitzel at one of the pubs. The least likely trysting place in the mid-north, was Hirsch's first thought.

His second was, what was he going to do about Clara Ogilvie? He had police powers of course, but that seemed a bit over the top. He felt sorry for her. Did she have family who could step in? He couldn't ask for Wendy's advice: she worked with Clara.

He was an adult with a brain. He could work it out.

Midway through Friday morning, another call from Hedley Bastian.

'I've got kids by the carload turning up. A truckload of portaloos got bogged and I had to pull it out with the tractor—and just now a semi-trailer arrives, and they want to know where to put the marquee. They all seem to think it's my responsibility. Tempers are getting a bit frayed.'

Frayed tempers was a police matter; the rest wasn't. Hirsch decided he'd leave Jean Landy in charge of the station and drive his police Toyota to the Bastian property, tailed by Tim Medlin in the Redruth patrol car.

'Two police vehicles hints at superior police numbers,' he explained.

Medlin, a soft, blurry, balding kid, said glumly, 'It seems like most of what we do is bluff.'

Hirsch clapped him on the back. 'Learning fast.'

They headed south from Redruth, then west along the Clare road for five kilometres into manicured farmland, as if into a pocket of the mid-north where the rainfall was reliable, the heat temperate, the soil and the landowners wealthy. Reaching stone gates, the words *Clonmel Run 1887* cut into a wooden beam across the top, they turned in and along an avenue of ghost gums to a broad grassy area fringed by more gums and bisected by a creek. Hirsch idly wondered if the kids would have gone skinny-dipping if the festival had gone ahead. That led him to another thought: why stage a festival in the closing stages of winter?

He parked beside a red semi-trailer, *Get Tented* in gold lettering on the driver's door. He got out, waited for Medlin to join him, and they walked downslope, passing the portaloo truck, its tyres caked in mud, and a haphazard arrangement of campervans, station wagons, panel vans and poor-student bombs. By now they could hear the shouting.

Bastian had put in a new wire fence, tight as a drum with pine posts and a massive wooden gate bearing a crest and the words *Clonmel Run Music Festival*. He stood on the far side of it, dressed in muddy workpants, an oilcloth coat and an unravelling woollen beanie. A signboard on a stake pointed to *tent city* in one direction and *overflow parking* in the other.

'I'm just as much in the dark as you are,' he said. Said it a second time, a third.

Other voices crowded him out:

'We came all the way from Port Lincoln for this?'

'Give us our money back.'

'Why weren't we told?'

'Who *can* tell us, if you can't?'

'It's your property, you're responsible.'

'I bet you're one of the organisers.'

'Piss-weak cunt.'

And so on. The voices faded as Hirsch and Medlin edged past and reached the gate. Dozens of people, ranging from a man in his fifties with *Get Tented* stitched to his top overall pocket through kids in jeans and fleece tops, to a ravaged-looking man with spaced-out eyes: Scott Clough, Redruth's sole drug dealer.

Hirsch gave him a big smile. 'Scotty, my man! With bulging pockets, too!'

Clough flushed and started to fade away.

A voice: 'You going to get us our money back?'

A sea of faces, expectant, hostile, pink-tipped in the cold air. Hirsch let his eyes roam left and right as he spoke. 'As you've no doubt gathered by now, the festival's been cancelled. It's a shame the system broke down and you weren't informed before heading out this morning. But Mr Bastian here is also a casualty. He isn't one of the organisers; he simply made this place available for the festival.'

'I bet *he's* been paid.'

Bastian was ready for a punch-up. 'That's a lie. I've spent thousands getting the space ready. I only found out yesterday.'

'Why didn't you tell us, then?'

'Refund!'

The cry was taken up. Hirsch waited tensely for it to sputter out, then said, 'At this stage, all I can do is advise you to go home, there's nothing further you can do here. Get some legal advice. Check the Ts and Cs on your tickets— or your contracts or requisition orders—and in due course seek a refund directly from the organisers or through the court system.'

One of the truck drivers yelled, 'Yeah, but *who*? It's not clear. Is the sponsor the same thing as the organiser?'

Good question, Hirsch thought, wondering if the victims would find themselves trapped in a maze of offshore shell companies. 'Please,' he said, 'go home. I'm not able to give answers to those kinds of questions. Civil litigation might be the answer. At this stage, it's not a police matter.'

'Why not? It's theft, isn't it?'

Hirsch knew he shouldn't engage, but he felt angry on their behalf. 'If theft can be shown, then it will become a police matter, I promise you. Seek legal advice, there might be a class action in it. But for now I'm urging you all to go home.'

He watched and waited as their minds shifted. Presently they drifted away, dismantled their tents, loaded up, reversed and turned on the muddy slope, creating bottle-necks on the track that led out of the property. As a last Kombi rattled away, Hirsch turned to Bastian.

'You're going to have people drifting in all day. I suggest you make a big sign and nail it to the front gate.'

'Saying what?'

What do you think? said Hirsch to himself. 'Saying the festival has been cancelled, no admission, all enquiries to the festival organisers.'

'Quinlan?'

'Quinlan,' Hirsch agreed.

He watched Bastian bump away along a gravelled track and over a small rise in the distance. A hint there of treetops and a chimney. He turned to Medlin. 'We better man the front gate until he gets back.'

His phone pinged. He ignored it but his insides went tight: a hurt-looking emoji.

An hour later, the road gate padlocked and access blocked by an old Bedford truck carrying a *Festival cancelled* sign, Hirsch and Medlin returned to the Redruth police station. A few calls had come in during their absence, but mostly what focused Hirsch's mind was Bastian's parting remark: 'Some friends and I need to talk to you later.'

What for? Tell him there was more to the story? Reveal some fresh hell?

When Bastian arrived his friends turned out to be Angela Thorburn, director of a real estate agency, Lloyd Marquand, head of Mid-North Financial Services, and Rhys Tuohy of

Redruth Glazing. Four sombre, well-heeled burghers of the district, and Hirsch at once felt a mild resentment and sense of absurdity. Patterns of influence had probably always existed in the mid-north, subtly felt, never seen. Assumptions, decisions, actions. He was a civil servant but they would expect him to be *their* servant.

He took them to the briefing room, where the smeared whiteboard, an unfinished mug of coffee and the morning's pastry crumbs underscored the divide. Thorburn and Tuohy sat on his left, Marquand on his right, Bastian at the opposite end of the table. When Hirsch placed his phone at his elbow, Bastian asked, 'Is that thing set to record?'

'No,' lied Hirsch, fishing out his notebook and a pen. 'I'm always on call.'

Bastian nodded slowly, watching Hirsch flip through to a fresh notebook page. 'It's just that we'd like this to be off the record.'

Hirsch regarded him carefully. 'I can't promise that, Mr Bastian, especially if you're reporting wrongdoing of some kind. But I will be discreet. Do you think police action is likely to flow from what you have to tell me?'

A reluctant, 'Yes.'

'Then I'll take notes.'

Bastian didn't like it. 'As you wish.'

Hirsch could see there was a good chance the four of them would pussyfoot around talking in riddles and wasting time.

Cut through all that. 'I imagine you're here because you've had dealings with Mr Quinlan, or his company, and suspect financial irregularities.'

Angela Thorburn sat lower in her chair, dry brown hair bunching around her thin shoulders, as if aware she'd been caught with her head above the parapet. Rhys Tuohy was motionless. Lloyd Marquand, straining and wheezy in a baggy grey suit, opened his mouth with a pop, thought better of it and looked to Bastian for guidance. Hirsch also looked to Bastian.

Who squared his shoulders and said, 'Okay then.' He glanced at the others and made a rolling motion with his hand. 'You all okay if I...'

'Go ahead,' Tuohy said. They all nodded.

Bastian took a breath. 'We've all known Adrian Quinlan for years. Never any trouble. Always paid in full, in a timely manner. Good stock and station agent—the best price if we were selling, the cheapest if we were buying. So when he came to us with an opportunity in Queensland, twenty-four home units on the Sunshine Coast, we went for it.' He glanced in quick embarrassment at the others. 'I put in a hundred thousand.'

'Hundred and fifty,' said Marquand.

'Same,' said Thorburn.

Tuohy shrugged and said nothing.

'And for a while it was great,' Bastian said. 'A three per cent return every month—so we invested more.'

'It didn't last,' Angela Thorburn said. 'Either the monthly return wouldn't arrive in our accounts, or it was low.'

'Or late,' Tuohy said.

'Adrian was full of excuses and promises,' Bastian said, 'but nothing changed.'

Marquand was fidgeting. 'Do you mind if I say something?' He went on, words gusting: 'When the wife and I took the kids to Noosa, the last school holidays, I asked if I could meet Adrian's representative up there, so I could eyeball the units. But could I pin the guy down? Never in the office, didn't return my calls. Eventually I learned where the units were and took a taxi there, and they were quite nice but more like twelve units than twenty-four. So I did some digging around and it turns out the units belong to a few Brisbane doctors. Far as we can tell, Quinlan never was developing home units, he just took our cash.'

'Did you challenge him?'

Bastian said helplessly, 'You need to understand, we all have to do business in this town. You can't afford to make enemies. And you do have to give people the benefit of the doubt. So, yes, the four of us went and talked to him, and he acted horrified, said he'd get right on it, but nothing's changed.'

'And he didn't really answer any of our questions,' Angela Thorburn said.

'Face it, Ange, he was shifty,' Tuohy said.

She rolled her shoulders uncomfortably. 'Well, I suppose you could say he was a bit smooth.'

They could be there forever, debating Quinlan's demeanour. Hirsch said, 'Sounds to me like a pyramid scheme. He ran out of new investors and couldn't pay you your three per cent. Then he started short-changing his regular clients.'

Like Leon Ayliffe.

'Explains the music festival,' muttered Bastian. 'He thought it'd be quick cash.'

Angela Thorburn slumped again. 'I did get a cheque from him the other day. Only for five hundred dollars. To keep me quiet, I suppose. Could it have come from ticket money?'

'Well, Angela, I think there's a very good chance of that, don't you?' said Marquand sourly.

Bastian shot them a look, then turned to Hirsch. 'What do you suggest we do?'

'First, get legal advice. Then put together a detailed account of everything, together with all the paperwork you can find.'

'What will you do?'

'Given that I can barely add two and two,' Hirsch said, 'I'll kick it upstairs.'

They didn't find him all that amusing.

19

On Saturday morning Hirsch was in the rear carpark of the Redruth police station, hosing mud away from the wheel arches of the HiLux, when John and Sylvia Fearn walked around the corner, looking for him.

'There's no one on the front desk,' John Fearn said accusingly.

Dressed up again, thought Hirsch. Morning tea, afternoon tea, going to the shops. Or the police station. Also, easily affronted by little inconveniences.

'We drove to Tiverton first,' Sylvia said, 'and found your note.' Implying that they could have saved an unnecessary trip if they'd been informed.

'Sergeant Brandl was hospitalised recently, you might have heard,' Hirsch said.

John Fearn had already stopped listening. Eyeing the hose as if Hirsch might spray him, he said, 'My wife and I need a word.'

Hirsch looped the hose around a hook on the wall,

exchanged gumboots for shoes and dried his hands. He could barely move his fingers. He tucked them into his armpits and realised he was chilled to the bone. 'Follow me.'

They declined tea or coffee. They sat in two stiff-backed chairs in Sergeant Brandl's office and told him that they feared undue influence in the affairs of their friend and neighbour, Maggie Groote.

The missing two hundred and fifty grand, thought Hirsch. 'And who is exerting this influence?'

John Fearn was disappointed in Hirsch. 'The niece, of course. Amy.'

'What kind of influence?'

'She wants enduring power of attorney, for a start,' Sylvia said, handbag in her lap, her spine upright.

'Maggie told you that?'

'She came to the house yesterday with a form Amy wants her to sign.'

'We told her not to sign it,' John Fearn said.

'If anyone should have power of attorney over Maggie's affairs,' Sylvia said, 'it's us, her oldest friends.'

'Do you think Maggie *needs* someone to have power of attorney?'

'You've talked to her. She's very vague sometimes.'

Hirsch was non-committal. 'Maybe Amy is the most appropriate choice. They're family.'

'That's a laugh,' John said. 'We've known Maggie for donkeys' years. No mention of a niece. Then suddenly we have one crawling out of the woodwork.'

'Intent,' Sylvia said, 'on taking advantage.'

'We suspect,' her husband said, 'that she's already a co-signatory to Maggie's bank account. Or accounts.'

Should be easy enough to check, thought Hirsch. His phone buzzed; he tensed and switched it off.

John Fearn watched all that as if he found it unforgivably rude. 'And there's the matter of title to Maggie's land. We have a long-standing agreement with her.'

Hirsch sharpened. 'Has Maggie signed the property over to Amy?'

Sylvia shrugged. 'As far as we know, not yet, but it could happen. Undue influence and all that.'

'What sort of agreement do you have with Maggie?'

John Fearn said, 'That we purchase the farm from her when it comes time for her to sell.'

Undervalued? wondered Hirsch. Favourable terms? 'Do you think that time has come?'

'Don't you? She's lived in the town for a year now. She's done nothing with the farm for at least five years.'

Sylvia said, 'She might as well sell and enjoy life. Travel. Things like that.'

'She's frail,' Hirsch pointed out.

'All the more reason why she should sell up. But who knows what will become of the property if the niece gets it? Hippie commune. Sold to a developer. Who knows?'

'Is there a will?' Hirsch asked, assuming they'd know.

'I expect so. Sure to be,' John Fearn said.

'Did Maggie have any children?'

'No.'

'Siblings? Other nieces and nephews?'

Sylvia Fearn said stiffly, 'I expect that's between Maggie and her lawyer.'

'Be interesting to know if her will's been altered lately,' John Fearn said, his soft, hot face sharpening.

I'll not do your dirty work for you, Hirsch thought, his own features flat.

'It's what's already happened that bothers us most,' Sylvia said. 'There was a time early in the year when Amy got it into her head to set up an online organic produce store. She asked if Maggie could lend her the money.'

'Actually suggested Maggie sign up to a reverse mortgage on the farm,' John said.

'Do you know how much she wanted?'

'Two hundred and fifty thousand.'

Hirsch had switched his phone off. Powered it on again with a kind of dread the moment the Fearns left the station—as if he might be zapped by the little slab of metal and glass.

No smiley faces. But Katie Street had sent him a text an hour earlier: *How many psychiatrists does it take to change a light bulb?*

He hadn't the heart to tell her he'd heard it. *Don't know. How many.*

She replied ten minutes later: *Only one. But the light bulb must really want to change.*

Ha ha.

Katie: *I don't really get it but Ms Ogilvie said you'd laugh. When u pick me up?*

Hirsch looked at his watch: noon. *About 1.*

Leaving Jean Landy and Tim Medlin in charge for the remainder of the weekend, Hirsch went home, changed out of his uniform, scoffed a sandwich and drove to the house on Bitter Wash Road. Wendy, distracted, studious in glasses, accepted a hit-and-miss kiss and returned to her lesson plans. 'Go off and bond,' she said, waving him away.

Hirsch only saw Katie Street on the weekends, now that she was at the high school where her mother taught, not at the primary school across from his police station. She was turning thirteen and he was taking her to Clare to buy a bigger bike.

'What colour training wheels?' he asked, as they headed across country.

'Sometimes, Aitch,' she said, 'you're just not that funny.'

She'd been calling him Aitch since the beginning of the year. Double Aitch, then plain Aitch. 'Okay,' he said, 'how many teenage girls does it take to screw in a light bulb?'

She was small, slim, dark, sometimes severe: trying to wean herself off his jokes. She shrugged offhandedly in the passenger seat of his old Nissan, but she was listening.

'Four,' Hirsch said. 'One to Instagram it, one to post it on Facebook, one to Tweet it and one to actually screw it in.'

'Ha, ha.'

'You smiled. You thought it was funny.'

'Mildly amusing.'

They rolled through farmland and up over a shallow range to richer farmland that began to merge with vine-yards. Katie, hearing his phone ping, said, 'You're getting a lot of messages, Aitch.'

'It's nothing. Ignore it.'

'Switch your phone off.'

'What if I'm needed to save the world?'

'Who's texting you? It's not Mum.'

Hirsch would enjoy being love-bombed by Wendy. 'It's just an idiot friend.'

Katie thought about it, shrugged and they were soon in the main street of Clare, looking for somewhere to park.

An hour or so later Katie was trying out her new wheels, looping around and around the hospital grounds, and Hirsch was presenting his sergeant with grapes.

'These are plastic grapes,' she said.

'Long lasting.'

'It hurts to laugh. It even hurts to roll my eyes.'

'What are you reading?'

Stroppy-looking, less pale, she shoved a Kindle off her lap as if it offended her. 'It's about a detective who sees coloured shapes come rolling out of people's mouths when they speak. He can always tell when someone's lying.'

'Useful.'

The sergeant was bored, keen to move on. 'So, what's been happening? Are you falling in a heap?'

Hirsch was economical, a few sentences each for the Ayliffes, Roskam and Quinlan. Facts—and speculations, knowing that she appreciated them. The intensity of her concentration; eyes narrowing, darting left and right as she sorted and assessed.

When he came to a stop, her face cleared. 'Excellent,

excellent. But expect some fallout from the Quinlan busi-ness, community unrest spilling over into general rioting...'

Hirsch grinned obligingly. 'There's been a bit of muttering.'

'Worrying?'

'Not so far.'

'The Irish roof scammers. Anything new?'

'No.'

'The Jarmyns?'

Hirsch realised he hadn't given the Jarmyns another thought. He was about to answer when his phone buzzed in his pocket. A text. About the eighth since he'd settled in the visitor's chair beside the sergeant's hospital bed.

'What's going on?'

'Sorry?'

'Your phone. You flinch every time it makes a sound—and that's been quite a few times already.'

With something like relief, Hirsch found himself explaining.

Brandl listened, nodding as if what he said was tedious but still to be taken seriously. 'Pity you can't tell Wendy about this woman. She always struck me as sensible.'

'They work together.'

'I know, I know. Look, there are legal steps you can take. All kinds of legislation against stalking and harassment.'

'It's just that I don't want to go in heavy-handed,' Hirsch said. 'I feel sorry for her. I'm hoping she'll get over it. Lose interest. Or if it gets bad maybe a family member can step in and get her some help.'

'You don't want it to get bad,' Brandl said, shifting on the mattress, wincing as leg muscles and tendons stretched. 'Protect yourself. Screenshot every text, keep any letters or cards she sends you, print out emails, keep a log of when you see her car, let her calls go to voicemail…Better still, block her number.'

Hirsch had done some reading. Stalkers viewed any kind of response in a positive light. If he blocked Clara Ogilvie's number, spoke to her or sent a formal warning, she was likely to see it as a link being forged, where before there'd been nothing. He'd be confirming her in her endeavours. He was damned either way.

'I will.'

Out to the carpark, where Katie was hooning across the deserted bitumen, beaming, sending light into all the dark places.

Seven o'clock, Katie's birthday dinner in the dining room of the Dugout, a newish bistro in one of the converted miners' cottages on the school side of Redruth Creek. A window table overlooking bulrushes, ducks and a grassy picnicking slope, Hirsch holding Wendy Street's hand across the table and Katie not rolling her eyes for a change, simply staring out.

A pared-down interior, just a couple of miner's picks, a sluice box, a sieve and a pan on the whitewashed stone walls. Highly polished floorboards, burly dark ceiling beams. No music, a low hum of conversation—and Cornish pasties on the menu. In Hirsch's experience, pasties were either soggy or desiccated and only edible if drowned in tomato sauce.

'That's where you'd be wrong,' Wendy said. 'They're supposed to be good here.'

Hirsch kept scanning the menu. He rejected Penzance Pie and Truro Tart, and a shadow fell over the page. Clara Ogilvie was standing hard against his shoulder, saying, 'Fancy meeting you here!'

She was vibrant in a low-cut dark dress, bristling in expectation of adventures around the next corner—but surely not with the man holding her hand? Stooped, patchy beard, tight V-necked jumper, the cuffs of baggy trousers concertinaed on blue runners with a red flash, he seemed lost, as if whisked away from a computer game.

Hirsch stood to shake hands as Clara said, 'Paul, this is Den Quigley. Den, you know Wendy of course. And that's Katie.'

Quigley's grip was firm but moist. 'Biology,' he said, and Hirsch assumed he taught it.

'Pleased to meet you.' He wiped his palm discreetly on his thigh as he sat.

After that it was a couple of minutes of step and counterstep until the newcomers were shown to a table on the other side of the room. Hirsch leaned over the table and said, 'Did you tell her we were coming here tonight?'

Alerted by his tone, Wendy regarded him expressionlessly, the planes of her face beautifully etched in the half-light of the room. 'Not in particular. I might have let it slip in the staffroom at going-home time yesterday.' Her mouth twitched. 'Why? Do you think she's stalking you?'

How did Hirsch answer that? 'Just wondering.'

'Just wondering. The big question is,' Wendy said, glancing at her daughter now, illicit humour in it, 'what's she doing with Den Quigley?'

'I know, right?' Katie was wide-eyed with delight.

Hirsch had nothing to say to that. He appreciated the pair of them. His phone pinged.

He took it out, checked the screen: *When soulmates are left to lead their lives together, it's a wonderful thing.*

He stared at Clara Ogilvie. She was leaning animatedly over the table at Quigley. Her hands were in her lap.

Hirsch switched off his phone, feeling disarranged, out of balance, as Wendy said, 'You all right?'

'His phone went off all the time on the way to Clare,' Katie said.

'Paul?'

'Just a nuisance caller.'

Wendy stared at him. Turned her head and stared across the room. Stared at Hirsch again.

Her face cleared. 'Tell me about it when you feel ready to, okay?'

Goodwill ruled the next hour, and then they paid, gave abbreviated goodbye waves to the others and went out to Wendy's Golf. Something was wrong: the kerbside rear tyre was flat.

'Shit, bugger, damn,' Wendy said.

'Way to go, Mum,' Katie said. She turned to Hirsch. 'We could do more bonding, Aitch. You could show me how to change the tyre.'

'Be careful what you wish for,' Hirsch said, opening the hatch.

Behind him Wendy said in a wondering voice: 'Hang on, there's another car with a flat tyre...Another...Another...'

20

Mother and daughter, both quick and vital in daytime, were heavy sleepers and slow to wake. Hirsch had once seen Wendy pull on a sock and then, all energy spent, collapse with a grunt on the edge of the bed and sit for a while, gloomily contemplating the impossibility of the other foot.

So on Sunday morning, when he slid from beneath her bedcovers to shower, shave, dress, make toast and coffee and listen to the news in the kitchen, not a soul noticed. Mostly his moves were automatic, but his thoughts were not. Seven cars parked outside the Dugout, seven punctured tyres, their valve stems sliced open. Box cutter? Pocket-knife? You could race from tyre to tyre and nick the rubber without leaving a trace of evidence. No point in testing for fingerprints on tyres and side panels splattered with rain, red-plains mud and road grime. Certainly not on a Saturday evening in a one-horse town.

'Kids' was the consensus of the victims, all of whom were dining at the Dugout. And maybe they were right. And maybe Clara Ogilvie had paid kids to do it. Or someone else was the target and the valve-stem slicer wanted to obfuscate or didn't know which vehicle his, or her, victim drove.

No point in overthinking it, Hirsch told himself, it'll do your head in. At least Katie now knew how to change a tyre, and Redruth Tyre Service would do a roaring trade on Monday.

Wendy staggered into the kitchen at nine, gave him a bleary, antipathetic smile, filled the kettle, stood shoulders bowed, realised she hadn't flicked the switch—that almost undid her—watched slumped as it boiled, took her tea back to bed. A considerate partner might have taken her a cup, but Hirsch had been down that road. Tea went cold on the bedside table or cups were upended in the titanic struggle of waking up.

He sat daydreaming in the weak winter sun. Made a second coffee and toast. His phone remained silent. Maybe Clara Ogilvie, too, was an inert log in the mornings.

Then Bob Muir called to say that the Tiverton CFS truck was en route to a house fire in Penhale.

'Weirdest house fire I've ever been to,' Muir said.

Hirsch's friend was burly, methodical. Never spoke without something to say. Hirsch had seen strangers under-estimate him. The locals knew how precise and shrewd he was.

'Okay,' Hirsch said.

'For a start, someone tried to put it out with that hose.'

Muir pointed. A garden hose, attached to a little Davey

pump beside a rainwater tank against the side wall of the house, ran around the corner, up over the veranda and in through the front door.

'Whoever did it probably saved the house in the sense they slowed the fire, kept it contained. The flames had just got up into the ceiling when we arrived.'

'Contained where?'

'Sitting room. Everything would have gone up quickly if someone hadn't tried to put it out.'

'You don't know who?'

'No.' He shrugged. 'Same as the person who called it in?'

'And who was that?'

'That's your job. Anonymous, that's all I know.'

'Direct to the station? Not triple zero?'

'Correct.'

A local would know the fire station number. Then again, anyone could have googled it. Hirsch and Muir stood regarding the sodden house, the hint of charring to the undersides of the tiles above the sitting room, the mess of firehoses, trampled soil, torn shrubs. The stench. The paste of water and ash. But mostly they were drawn to the body on the lawn: Maggie Groote, lying face up next to the dividing hedge, hands crossed on her chest. Beyond her was the house belonging to the neighbour who claimed to have given the Irishmen a piece of her mind.

'Smoke inhalation?'

'Could well be,' Muir said. 'Doctor Pillai should be here soon.'

She'll confirm death, Hirsch thought. Confirming means

of death would not be so easy. Only an autopsy could do that, and seeing Maggie peeled open on a slab, he swayed and he blinked.

'You okay?'

'Fine,' Hirsch said. He switched his mind's eye to Maggie's sitting room. Cramped, heavy drapes, two easily overturned electric radiators. A woman who was sometimes unsteady on her feet. Forgetful.

'The thing is,' Muir said now, pointing, 'that old lady didn't just crawl out of the house and across the lawn and lie there by the hedge and calmly wait to die.'

Hirsch had already decided that. 'She was dragged out.'

'Or carried,' Muir said. He paused. 'Check out her feet.'

Hirsch crossed to the body, drew on crime-scene gloves and crouched. Her stockings or her slippers or both had been cooked into her flesh. The rest of her looked tidy, unmarked.

Hirsch felt the loss suddenly. He breathed in and out. He didn't want to touch her. Standing, pocketing the gloves, he rejoined Muir and glanced beyond the hedge again. 'You checked with the woman next door?'

'She's out, apparently. Church every Sunday morning.'

Bob must have got his information from the straggle of townspeople standing on the other side of the road. Hirsch would talk to them later.

'Male or female caller?' Hirsch asked, wondering if the woman next door had dragged Maggie out and sprayed water all over the sitting room and then gone to church...

'Male.'

Hirsch sighed. Too much to hope for.

Muir said, 'You could check that CCTV I put in.'

Hirsch gave him a sad, crooked smile. 'The line was cut a few days ago.' He explained about the Irish roof repairers.

'Bastards.'

'Getting back to the fire,' Hirsch said. 'Did you smell an accelerant?'

Muir shook his head. 'But that doesn't mean anything. If it wasn't an accident, it would only need a small amount. I'm hoping a fire inspector can pinpoint where it started.'

Hirsch thought through some scenarios. A stroke or a heart attack or a dizzy spell. She trips over one of the heaters. A good Samaritan comes along and pulls her out and tries to extinguish the flames. Gives up. Doesn't stick around. Why not? Did this modest hero know Maggie was already dead? *Was* she already dead?

That led to another possibility—that there'd been no good Samaritan chancing upon the fire. He, or she, was already there. Something went wrong. A struggle—over money?—and one of the heaters overturned. Hirsch began to map out the questions he'd ask the niece, Amy Groote.

Eventually Dr Pillai arrived, then the fire inspector, and neither could tell him much, so Hirsch drove up into the little hill range above the town. Maggie's old farmhouse sat miserably hunched against a showery wind that came scudding up the gully from the flatlands below. He parked, got out, turned up his collar and made a clumsy run for the front door, his hands in his pockets. Pounded on it. Pounded again.

'All right, all right, hold your horses.'

Amy's voice was croaky, muffled. The door creaked open and she was saying, 'The one morning I allow myself a sleep-in.'

Already laying out her alibi? She wore a man's old-fashioned tartan dressing gown, washed-out pink pyjama legs below the hem, big bony feet in carpet slippers. Her face was creased and puffy, her hair a drooping system of knots and frizz. When she closed the dressing gown with her fist, a gust of stale bed warmth reached Hirsch.

'May I come in?'

'Is this about the Ayliffes? I haven't seen them.'

'Amy, I need to come in. It's serious.'

That frightened her. She gaped. 'Okay.'

Into the kitchen, which was arctic. 'Have a seat.'

Hirsch hovered. He said, 'Could we have some heat? A radiator? Would you like me to light the fire?'

Amy Groote was disparaging. 'I can't afford firewood. Or run a heater night and day. Please just get to the point.'

Hirsch sat, she sat opposite, and he said, 'I'm afraid it's bad news. I've just come from your aunt's house and I'm sorry, but there was a fire and she's dead.'

A long, blank moment, then a series of expressions passed across Groote's face: pain, speculation, bewilderment. Hirsch had often seen suspects do that, try for an appropriate response, but here there was no subterfuge, Amy was both surprised and unsurprised. She'd known her aunt would die sooner or later, given her age and her frailties—but hadn't thought it would be just yet.

'Was it...? Did she...?' She hugged herself. 'A fire?'

Meaning: *Was it horrible*?

'I'm afraid there are some aspects we can't yet explain, except there was a fire and it was mainly confined to her sitting room and—'

Amy uttered a moan and rocked forward and back. Hirsch said hastily, 'She wasn't badly burnt. She was found in her front yard.'

'She got out? Then had a heart attack? Stroke?' Eyes narrowing, as if she'd alighted on the only possible explanation: 'Smoke inhalation?'

'That's to be determined,' Hirsch said. 'But we think someone dragged her out of the house. Whether or not she was already dead, we can't be sure.'

Genuine wonderment. 'Who? That woman next door?'

That woman, thought Hirsch. 'She was at church. And none of the other neighbours knew anything.'

'Who, then? Why wouldn't they stick around?'

'Amy,' Hirsch said, 'I do have to ask you for your movements last night and this morning.'

She shook her head as if to say: I can't believe this. 'Last night and this morning I was in bed.'

'Alone?'

A flicker of genuine humour that anyone would think she had a love life. '*Yes*, alone. And I worked outside until it got dark all day yesterday.'

Grime under her nails. Dirt, not soot. And Hirsch saw her narrow life. Gardening, then early to bed where she could be warm. She blinked; looked about the kitchen with hunched shoulders as though the chilly walls were closing in and she'd be squeezed out. Tossed on the scrapheap again.

Hirsch was going to ask if she knew about Maggie's will when she said, 'The fire was in the sitting room?'

'Mainly. It was starting to take hold in the ceiling.'

'I told her and told her: be careful you don't trip on one of your heaters.' A pause. 'But if someone was there...'

Hirsch said, 'So, just to recap, Sunday mornings you spend in bed?'

'I'm allowed to, surely? I've always had a lie-in of a Sunday. Ever since I was little.'

As Hirsch watched from across the table, the practical woman emerged, finger-combing her hair, delicately cleaning the edge of each eye, rubbing life into her cheeks. Again, a whiff of bed staleness with the movements of her upper body, and Hirsch felt immensely sad. Can't afford firewood, he thought, can't afford to run the washing machine enough.

He gazed around the kitchen. The garlic heads and bay leaves; gardening calendar; old pale-yellow fridge; a stained tea towel hanging from the oven door. Dishes drying in a rack beside the sink: plates and bowls and a basket of cutlery and two wine glasses that could have been there for days, one used last night, the other the night before. Innocent explanation.

A few A4-size protest leaflets were stuck to both fridge doors: the Adani coalmine, windfarms, offshore drilling in the Great Australian Bight.

Hirsch was pretty sure that Amy Groote had gone to bed when she said she had, and not arisen until he'd pounded on the door just now. But did she have a protest move-ment friend? Someone who'd do what she said? Someone who thought she might inherit? He watched her. She looked lost, one thought chasing hard after the other and literally pressing her down into her chair. She gave a little shake, straightened her spine and gathered herself to face the day, just as Hirsch said, 'Amy, please quit spray- painting graffiti on the windfarm turbines.'

Gotcha, he thought. It was there in her face.

He built on it, feeling like a shit. 'Are you a signatory to any of Maggie's bank accounts?'

She blinked and the bewilderment was back. 'What?'

She didn't seem to understand the question, or its impli-cations. In some things, Hirsch thought, Amy Groote was quite unworldly.

21

Monday: Hirsch blinking awake in his own bed. Uncharacteristically reluctant to leave it. It wasn't the prospect of his bare feet on the icy floor or the dawn darkness. It was Maggie Groote inviting him to laugh with her about the mix-up at the undertakers; Clara Ogilvie; the strain of running two police stations. And the creepy sensation of the Ayliffes moving about the back country. Not in hiding, not on the run, but proactive, thirsty for revenge. Arson. Impromptu burglary. Watching and waiting from a sniper's nest.

He winced when his soles hit the lino. Dragging on socks, tracksuit, heavy fleece, beanie and gloves, he went out and prowled the town. Kitchen lights burning here and there; the grind of a distant starter motor; snatches of morning radio. A still morning, blade sharp, flaying his cheeks. But peaceful. If blood were being spilt in Tiverton, he was unaware of it.

Then Maggie Groote was in his head again, chatting fondly to a stranger's ashes as she drove around the district.

A sadness was in Hirsch. A tear froze on each cheek and he thought savagely, 'Fucking Clara,' when his phone buzzed. Another fucking emoji. The way he felt at that moment, he'd just as soon throw her arse in jail.

He walked home, jitters overlaying the sadness. Panic attack? He was in no fit state for clear thought, yet clear thought was expected of him every minute of every day.

Showered, breakfasted, uniformed, thoughts still tumultuous, Hirsch walked across the highway to the shop to collect the *Advertiser*. An ancient Land Rover towing a heaped, tarp-covered trailer was parked at the petrol bowser, a wizened bushman in a Port Adelaide beanie rattling the fuel nozzle as Hirsch approached. Happened to meet Hirsch's gaze and the eyes slid away and Hirsch made one of his snap judgments. Here was a nasty old chancer, a wheeler and dealer at the most miserable level of commerce. Love to know what's under that tarp, Hirsch thought. All he could see was a long overhang of roofing iron. Dangerous, poorly secured, but Hirsch felt just too shitty to care this morning. His phone buzzed again, and he wanted to throw it down and grind it with his heel. But in an attempt at dignity and law and order, he said to the old fuck, 'Is your load secure, sir?'

The man worked his mouth, thinking about the question. Yellow teeth and a frosting of grey and white whiskers. 'You want me to retie it?'

'That's okay, sir, just drive safely,' Hirsch said, wanting to be alone, to be left alone.

Back at the police station he sat and closed his eyes and breathed in and out, slowly, deeply, for several minutes. It helped. Maybe. Then, before he could leave for Redruth, a call came from Jean Landy.

'I've got a man on the phone I think you should talk to, boss. Paul. Your highness, whoever you are.'

It had stopped being funny. Hirsch said, 'Just patch him through.'

A crackle on the line, hesitation, a voice saying, 'Hello? Anyone there?'

Hirsch dealt with the preliminaries and asked the caller, a man named Cusack, what the problem was.

'I'm here at Belalie Waters. Know it?'

A sheep station out in uncertain country between Tiverton and Morgan, a town on the River Murray. Belonged to a Chinese agri company and operated on a shoestring, despite its size. An overseer and his wife named Waurn, and two or three jackaroos. Hirsch checked in occasionally when making one of his long-range patrols.

'I do. Is there a problem?'

'Something's not right,' Cusack said. 'There's no one here. I've poked around and it's got me a bit spooked, thought I should say something.'

'Maybe they're out mustering?' Hirsch said. Motorbikes, out in that country. 4WDs in the less treacherous parts. They contracted a spotting helicopter for the annual shearing round-up.

'Dunno.'

'Your business there, Mr Cusack? Are you a friend of the Waurns?'

'Friend? No. All I know is, Mrs Waurn was expecting

me,' Cusack said. 'We had a firm booking, this morning at nine.'

'A booking?'

'You know, airbags.'

Sometimes getting key information from people was like reading a Russian novel. You had to wade through a lot of withholding and delaying tactics. 'I don't follow,' Hirsch said.

Cusack took a breath. 'The recall, mate. Takata airbags.'

Ah. Faulty airbags. They could kill if activated in a crash, the inflators exploding with enough force to spray shrapnel over driver and passengers, but too many vehicle owners in remote areas were dragging their heels, reluctant to make a long round trip to an urban dealership to get them replaced.

'You're from Mitsubishi.' Hirsch recalled the two Triton twin-cab utes on Belalie Waters.

'That's what I said. Mrs Waurn was supposed to meet me here but there's not a soul around and only one of the utes. Plus there's a burnt-out LandCruiser—which in itself is a bit sus.'

Hirsch closed and opened his eyes. Withholding and delaying tactics. 'I'll be about an hour.'

'Yeah, well, I'm on a tight schedule,' Cusack said. 'I'll do the airbag on the ute that is here, but then I'm off to do three Pajeros in Morgan. So I may have already left.'

The Morgan road was sealed but at a lonely crossroads halfway along it, Hirsch swung left, onto a gravel surface that rattled his hind teeth. He'd taken part in endless pub debates on the subject of driving over corrugated surfaces: you avoided the worst effects if you drove flat-out, versus you avoided the worst effects if you drove slowly. Time was the deciding factor. The locals were an unhurried mob, on the lookout for a good old chinwag with the driver of an oncoming vehicle. Hirsch was often held up in the middle of nowhere by a pair of farm utes parked driver's window to driver's window in the middle of the road.

Hirsch favoured the flat-out approach on police business. The empty land unrolled on either side of him, rain-shadow country trying to be green, stunted mallee scrubland interrupted by lone cypress pine trees and tough little tussocks—saltbush, bluebush; plants he couldn't name. Spinifex? Samphire? Poverty bush? Low blue eroded hills in the distance, holding secret rock carvings; closer to, a couple of homestead ruins and dun-coloured lumps that resolved themselves as sheep.

There had been some rain, so the approaching vehicle dust was a poor cousin of the roiling clouds of summer. Hirsch slowed, pulled over. A service van loomed, slowed, drew adjacent and the driver's window rolled down.

'You the bloke I talked to?'

Hirsch nodded. 'Mr Cusack?'

Cusack neither confirmed nor denied. He was a burly fifty, in overalls, bald, a hint of ink on thick, corded fore-arms. 'Like I said, I done one of their utes, but no idea where the other one is. I need to keep going. See—'

'Mr Cusack!'

The mechanic jumped a little at the sharpness. 'What?'

'You had a look around when no one greeted you? Checked the house and sheds?'

'Yep. Knocked, called out. Not a soul.'

'Apart from the torched LandCruiser, were there any other signs something bad might have happened?'

Cusack blinked. He's a follow-the-paperwork guy, Hirsch thought. The paperwork said to be at Belalie Waters on Monday morning and that was pretty much as far as his thinking had taken him.

'Only the fire. I thought maybe an electrical fault.'

'Okay, thank you.'

'That all?'

Hirsch nodded and Cusack sped off with a spurt of gravel.

Twelve kilometres later Hirsch came to a driveway bracketed by a pair of post-and-rail fence sections painted white, a buckled iron ramp, a narrow track stretching deeper into the speckled back country. *Belalie Waters* in faded black letters along one rail. He turned in and the drive to the collection of houses and sheds that constituted the settlement took another five minutes. Overseer's house and bunkhouse and sheds of local stone and corrugated-iron. Peppertrees, sad-looking shrubs and the kind of dirt yard that ran bull ants all year round. And the burnt-out LandCruiser. The Ayliffes—Hirsch was assuming the Ayliffes—had destroyed it on a patch of soil some distance from the buildings. So that the fire wouldn't spread? But why set fire to it? Just plain nastiness? The son a budding firebug? None of that was worth pondering. All Hirsch was pretty certain of, father and son had found their way to Belalie Waters and swapped the LandCruiser for one of the property's Mitsubishis.

Did the fire indicate an escalation? Had they killed Mrs Waurn?

He parked near the LandCruiser, standing scorched and gutted on its wheel rims. A rich stench of burnt rubber, vinyl, plastics and fuel seared his sinuses and there was a hint of residual heat. Last night or early this morning.

He crossed the yard to the overseer's house and knocked on the screen door. The inner door was open. He waited, running a check on his senses. The house felt empty. He went in, searching each of the careworn, time-warp rooms he remembered from his patrol visits. A comfortable place, but marking time. You didn't plan a future here, you lived out your years one by one. Ken and Rosemary Waurn were not pampered by their employer.

The house was empty. Hirsch didn't know if the thin trace of dust on the kitchen table indicated abandonment or poor housekeeping. But the UHF equipment in the radio room had been smashed up: violence of some kind had occurred here.

He left by the back door and walked to the jackaroos' quarters, a pair of squat, back-to-back rooms. Unmade beds and dirty clothes piled on wooden chairs; in one room a guitar, in the other posters of a Tasmanian rainforest, a Formula 1 racing car and a woman in tennis whites scratching her bare bum.

The sheds: the Waurns' Falcon station wagon, a trailer, fuel drums, stacks of bald tyres, tools, ladders, ropes, axles, a blacksmith's anvil.

Hirsch stood in the yard a while, indecisive. Search a wider area? Call it in right now? The Ayliffes could be anywhere. Maybe they'd drive the Triton down into a sinkhole and the airbag would explode and slice their throats open.

Widening the circle each time, Hirsch circumnavigated the patch of buildings and stockyards. Eventually he caught, faintly but unmistakeably, a stench of death borne on the wind that gusted across the rocky ground.

22

He lifted his nose and walked into the teeth of the wind. Over stone reefs, around tussocks, trampling sheep pellets into the soil even as he searched for human footprints. He tried to work out the time lag. If the Ayliffes had arrived in recent hours and torched the LandCruiser and killed Mrs Waurn, carcass rot would not yet have set in. So, they arrived two or three days ago, killed her, then stayed on in the house? Hirsch powered along the unruly surface, seeing only the narrow scribbles left by many hooves, over many generations. Tufts of wool here and there, caught in the twigs and spurs of the region's tough little plants. Leading to water? The stench was searing now, and he played out stories in his head. Mrs Waurn is wounded, makes a run for it, succumbs to her wounds. Or she's chased down and shot in the back.

He came to a drying waterhole fringed with reeds and pockmarked dark mud, and saw, on the other bank, a pale, distended belly. He saw that because he expected to see it.

Then his brain caught up: he was looking at a dead wallaby and the stink turned him around and he retraced his steps to the house.

Then he heard a motor: acceleration. The Triton ute appeared, tearing towards the gateposts that marked the entrance to the long road out, Rosemary Waurn at the wheel. Hirsch raced to cut her off, a hop and skip kind of run across and around abrading reefs and plants that snatched at his shins and ankles. He roared; he waved his hands madly. And she saw him and put her foot down, her face pale and blindly intent.

Then it was her turn to reconfigure what her eyes were telling her: he was the policeman who called at the house sometimes. The brake lights flared. The ute stopped in the middle of the track. When Hirsch reached her, Rosemary Waurn was resting her forehead against the steering wheel. He tapped on the glass. She sat back with a jerk and switched off and he opened the door.

'Sorry, I thought those men had come back.'

'It's okay,' Hirsch said, helping her out. 'They're gone.'

'Ken and the boys left yesterday and they're not due back till tomorrow so I was alone and...'

The words tripped and tumbled like poorly laid tiles ascending and descending, but Hirsch had pretty much worked out the story anyway. The intruders had arrived early, with guns, and she'd run. Knowing the lie of the land, she'd been able to hide from them and eventually they'd given up and left. She'd stayed in hiding as long as she could, then bolted for the ute and made a break for it.

He reached into the console, grabbed a bottle of water, thrust it at her. 'Drink. Take your time.'

It worked. She gulped and the water damped down her agitation. She screwed the top back on and said, 'I think I heard another vehicle. Was it the airbag man?'

'Yes.'

She shot an uneasy glance at the house and yards. 'Oh no, is he...'

'He's fine. I met him on the road.'

'Thank God. Look, I need to tell Ken and the boys.'

'Where are they?'

She waved at a blue smudge on the horizon. 'There's an outstation hut on the other side of those hills. We've had a lot of flyblown ewes lately.'

'Do you know Leon and Josh Ayliffe?'

'From the news. It was them, yes. I'm sure of it.'

'Did they call out? Say anything?'

'Said they didn't want to hurt me, but I wasn't going to take any chances.'

'Good thinking.'

'Would they have killed me?'

Hirsch said slowly, 'I don't think so. They'd have tied you up, probably. But they're still dangerous. I wouldn't want to cross them.'

'I sneaked in the house. They've wrecked the radio.'

She grew agitated, a tired, middle-aged woman dried by the years of sun and wind. 'I really need to contact Ken.'

'We'll use my radio,' Hirsch said.

*

By mid-afternoon Rosemary Waurn had been reunited with the menfolk, STAR officers had swarmed the area—they're always going to be a few hours behind in this situation, Hirsch thought—and news programs were urging residents of the back country to be on the lookout for the Ayliffes. To lock their doors and vehicles. Report suspicious behaviour. If necessary, move away from the danger zone.

Danger zone, thought Hirsch. These guys weren't that dangerous—he didn't think.

But a kind of suppressed dread had crept in. Not surprising in country where you could drive for a couple of hours and not see a town, a house, another vehicle. Calls came in from the people on his long-range patrol routes—a woman with a schizophrenic son; an elderly man with a housebound spouse; a single mother whose car had been repossessed—all seeking reassurance.

It occurred to Hirsch as he drove back to Tiverton that he'd received no cryptic Clara Ogilvie emoji since breakfast. He hoped that was good news and expected it probably wouldn't be and, sure enough, at that moment his phone pinged. Tightening inside, he pulled over to check the screen. A text from Bob Muir: *Pop in on your way home.*

With something like relief, Hirsch rolled into town and parked outside the Muirs' neat house. Orderly garden beds, new paint, a workshop, firewood under cover and stacked in rows of such evenness you'd scarcely want to disturb it.

Muir came to the door with a small metal deedbox, buckled and blackened. 'I was with the fire inspector today. He found this.'

Hirsch took it, half-expecting it to feel hot. 'Where was it?'

'In the remains of Maggie's chair.' Muir paused. 'I had a quick look; hope you don't mind. Her will, birth certificate, insurance papers, property deeds.'

That's all Muir said. Hirsch doubted his friend had read any of the documents. He nodded his thanks, drove back to the police station and thawed out a block of bolognese sauce in the microwave as he read Maggie Groote's will. She'd left her farm to the Fearns. The house in Penhale was to be sold, the proceeds going mostly to charities except for twenty thousand dollars to Amy Groote.

First, did the Fearns or the niece know the contents of the will? Second, would the Fearns kill out of impatience, or the niece out of fury?

Hirsch checked the time: 6.00 p.m. A moment later he was speaking to Julia Galvin at Redruth Legal Services.

'I understand you're Margaret Groote's solicitor and executor?'

The voice was educated, formal, with the scratchiness of age. 'I am. And I understand that you are standing in for Sergeant Brandl? How is she?'

Hirsch didn't really know. 'Getting better.'

'How may I help you?'

'Maggie, I mean Mrs Groote, left a will and—'

'Her friends called her Maggie. You knew her?'

'Yes.'

'As did I. A dear friend.'

Stumbling, Hirsch said, 'I was wondering if you could

hold off on executing the will, or whatever the phrase is. Hold off on informing the benefactors.'

'Well.' A long silence. 'There are certain preliminary steps I'm obliged to go through, Constable Hirschhausen. Obtaining the death certificate, arranging the funeral, ascertaining what taxes and other fees and charges might be owed by the estate...obtaining probate, given that two landed properties are involved.'

She's saying yes, Hirsch realised. 'And the beneficiaries will be okay with that?'

'They'll have to be,' the solicitor said.

She paused. 'I trust you'll inform me what's going on in due course?'

'I will,' Hirsch said.

23

Soon after arriving in Redruth on Tuesday morning, Hirsch sent Jean Landy and Tim Medlin out on abbreviated versions of his Monday and Thursday patrols while he attended to paperwork, emails and walk-ins. He prowled around the town square at lunchtime: a police presence.

And made three phone calls. Sergeant Brandl was still in her hospital bed and still stroppy, but expecting to be released soon. Sophie Flynn had sent Maggie Groote's replacement bank records by Express Post the previous Friday. And the morgue, snowed under, wouldn't be performing Maggie's autopsy until later in the week.

Police life: a series of punctuation points. Mostly full-stops at the end of partial outcomes, doubtful outcomes and unfinished stories.

That's why, mid-morning, he expected it to be more of the same when Eleanor Quinlan called to say her husband was missing.

She showed him into her sitting-room. 'I didn't want to come down to the police station because, you know...'

Hirsch did know. The earlier rumours had amped up and the locals had been savaging her husband on social media and in pub, shop and dinner-table conversations.

'I can't go anywhere,' she went on. 'I've been staying at my sister's since Saturday, and now I'm starting to think I shouldn't have come back.'

'Where does she live?'

'Henley Beach.'

Hirsch nodded. An Adelaide suburb: unlikely that anyone there would know Eleanor or who her husband was. 'And you got home an hour ago?'

'Yes.'

Home was a sizeable heritage-listed stone house with deep verandas and a view over the town—over Adrian Quinlan's domain. Eleanor Quinlan had the view right now, from the other side of the sitting-room coffee table. Hirsch's view was of Eleanor and of the room itself, which to his eye proved that an expensive fit-out didn't mean a tasteful one. The main source of eyestrain was the leather—beautiful under his fingers, but that candy-colour blue seemed to have an inner glow—along with a chunky arrangement of shelves, drawers and display spaces in one corner. It housed the TV, a sound system and more photos of Quinlan with the kind-of famous...

Hirsch caught himself. Eleanor Quinlan was distressed, swiping at tears with the heel of each hand. He took a sip of scented tea and said, 'Maybe he's out viewing a property. Or he's had a puncture. Car trouble.'

She gave him a precise headshake as if to say her thinking had gone way past that. Hirsch reassessed her. Younger than her husband, without his bulk; adroit and capable, he thought; probably not recognised for it.

'It all came to a head Friday evening,' she said. 'People ringing us all day long, and I was that mad with him, our finances in ruins, money owed left, right and centre. How could he have let things get to that state and not told me? I'm sure we'd have worked something out. A management plan of some kind.'

To get her back on track, Hirsch said, 'That was Friday. You saw him Saturday?'

She nodded. 'In the morning. It was like the ice age here. He slept in the spare room. We barely spoke, I just packed up and left.'

'How did he seem?'

'Pitiful. Pathetic. Worried about his standing in the community—the good he's done, how everyone used to look up to him. I just didn't want to know.'

A landline phone rang in one of the other rooms, a hollow sound ignored by Eleanor Quinlan. 'That could be him,' Hirsch said.

'So let him leave a message.'

Hirsch heard the answering machine cut in and waited. No message.

'Any idea what he intended to do on Saturday?'

'I don't know. Round of golf? Rip off some pensioners?

Not work out how he was going to salvage our finances, I don't imagine. He seemed completely paralysed.'

'May I ask, are your own personal finances tied up in the business? Close friends and relatives?'

'What do you think? I've no idea how we'll survive. How we'll go on living in this town. How we'll go on living together, in fact.'

'Why did you come back today?'

'My sister was getting on my nerves. She's one who *didn't* invest, incidentally. The smugness was…difficult.'

Hirsch placed his cup on its saucer. Got comfortable, the leather accommodating him with a series of soft, creaky farts. Her mouth twitched. 'It does that.'

He grinned back. 'Have you called him, or he you, since Saturday?'

She nodded. 'I decided to be the bigger person. I tried his mobile and the landline. Voicemail.'

'What about the office number?'

'No one's seen him—which isn't all that unusual. He's often away, looking at stock, attending auctions, sourcing supplies. But he does call if he's going to be away.'

'I have to ask this: could he be having an affair?'

'"An affair." Sleeping around, do you mean?' She snorted. 'You've seen him.'

She said it with a kind of helpless, angry, disappointment; love still hovered at the back of it. Her husband had let her down in every way. He'd cheated, lied, been secretive and too ambitious. And he'd let himself go: florid and overweight from bad living.

'I had to ask. I realise you haven't seen him since Saturday, but do you know if anyone else has? Have you called around, staff, friends...?'

She shook her head, blinked, hooked a wing of hair behind her right ear. 'The thing is, when I got home, I found one of our suitcases gone and some of his clothes and his razor, things like that. But his heart pills are still here. His phone's on a charger we keep near the toaster. He'd never leave those behind.'

Hirsch opened his mouth to speak but she got there first. 'So I started thinking he must have taken himself off to a motel in the back of beyond to drink himself to death. Something like that.'

Or, thought Hirsch, we'll find his clothes neatly folded at a beach or a reservoir because he's stashed a couple of million somewhere, along with a spare phone and another supply of heart medication.

But he'd put out an alert for Quinlan's Range Rover, and he'd check on the whereabouts of every work vehicle registered to Quinlan Stock and Station. He left with a vague promise of prompt action floating in the air, then drove up and down the nearby streets for ten minutes or so, wondering if he'd find the Belalie Waters Mitsubishi ute parked nearby.

Passing through Penhale on his way home at the end of the day, Hirsch felt Maggie Groote's house pull at him, a black hole dragging him in. He swallowed. Gave himself a little shake, concentrated on other things.

He was north of the town when he remembered her replacement bank statements. He braked, U-turned and a minute later was checking her letterbox. Nothing but a damp flyer for the music festival.

Then it occurred to him that Penhale had no postal delivery. The nearest Australia Post outlet was a chest-high counter, a wire rack of envelopes and a wall array of private boxes in a corner of the Tiverton general store. Hirsch put his foot down. The time was 5.05 p.m. Ed Tennant's winter-closing time was 5.30.

At 5.15 Ed was saying he didn't feel comfortable letting Hirsch have Maggie's mail.

'I won't be opening it—or not at this stage,' Hirsch said. 'I'll get a warrant if that becomes necessary.'

The Tiverton shopkeeper was a precise, dour character. He'd gradually thawed towards Hirsch, but warming up would take years. Puzzled, he said, 'You just want to look at it?'

'Yes.'

'Anything in particular?'

'I'll know when I eyeball it, Ed.'

As agency manager, Ed would sort the mail from the Australia Post bag and distribute it to the relevant box in the wall behind the counter, where it could be accessed from outside, under the shelter of the shop veranda. South Australia Police rented box 19; its key was one of many on Hirsch's keychain. As Tennant ran his gaze along the rows of boxes now, Hirsch heard someone collecting mail. A key turned, paper rustled, a little flap clicked home. Curious, he moved to the main window and glanced at an angle down along the veranda. Nan Washburn stood there, sorting through half a dozen envelopes.

He returned to Ed as the shopkeeper said, 'Here we are,' and fanned supermarket leaflets and charity letters across the counter. No business letters.

'Do you know if Amy Groote ever collects Maggie's mail?'

'Is that the niece? Never met her, far as I know.'

'Do me a favour, Ed? Keep Mrs Groote's mail in a safe place until we know who her executor is? I'd like to check it every day.'

Ed Tennant stared at Hirsch, curious. His face cleared as if some kind of suspicion had been satisfied. 'Right you are.'

As Hirsch walked back to the police station, a car left the school and pulled against the kerb. Vikki Bastian wound her window down. 'Cold enough?'

Hirsch heard that every day. 'They put you in charge?'

She looked stricken. 'Until they find a replacement. Can't be quick enough, as far as I'm concerned.'

'Anyone helping you?'

'A replacement teacher.' She waved. 'Anyway, better go, I've got heaps to do. Thanks for everything.' And she was gone.

24

Wednesday. Hirsch bought Danish pastries from the deli next to the pharmacy for the morning briefing in Redruth, then walked down to the Mid-North Community Bank and asked to see the manager.

He waited—twenty minutes he'd never get back—eyed curiously by Sophie Flynn and the other teller, and apprehensively by the bank's customers. After a while, beginning to feel jumpy, he took out his phone. When would the Clara Ogilvie love-bombing start again? The screen was clear. He'd become a slave to the damn thing, taking it out, checking it, tucking it away again—almost as if daring it.

Okay, he thought, break the cycle. He took it out again and called Eleanor Quinlan. 'Heard from Adrian?'

'Not a thing,' she said. 'I was hoping you might have something.'

'His car hasn't been spotted,' Hirsch said. He lowered his voice. 'No hospital admissions, no—forgive me—suspicious deaths.'

He sensed that she swallowed. 'I understand you have to check such things.'

'I've notified missing persons.'

There was a catch in her voice, and she blurted, 'Sorry, it's just so...'

Hirsch said gently, 'I'll pop in later, if that's okay.'

'Please.'

Hirsch completed the call just as the door marked *Manager* opened and Malcolm Cater ran his gaze down the length of the narrow room as if Hirsch was concealed in a throng of customers. 'Paul Hirschhausen? Constable Hirschhausen?'

Hirsch stood up. 'Mr Cater.'

Cater blinked. 'Please, come in.'

Into a clean bland room where cash was never handled, only thought about. Cater gestured for Hirsch to sit, shut the door and settled in a swivel chair behind a plain desk. Eyed Hirsch for a moment, as if assessing his wallet potential. 'What can I do for you this morning? Do you wish to open an account with us, by any chance?'

He's already checked, Hirsch thought. Or he's the kind of man who remembers the names of every customer. 'Sorry, no.'

'Police credit union, I expect. But if you ever need more on-the-spot, hands-on, face-to-face banking, then please do consider opening an account with us.'

'I will,' promised Hirsch.

'Good to know,' Cater said. Now he directed upon Hirsch a kind of serious and paternal regard. 'Am I to take it you're here on police business, Constable Hirschhausen?'

For a bank manager, Cater would make a good undertaker, Hirsch thought. Maybe a bishop. Supreme Court judge? Reserved, calm, clean and full of ironclad convictions. Thin build, in his forties, with streaks of grey at the temples of his receding dark hair.

'One of the bank's depositors, Margaret Groote, died in a house fire on Sunday.'

Stillness, then little pouches of disapproval formed at the edges of Cater's mouth. 'Tragic, yes. It's a police matter? How is the bank involved?'

'Before she died, she was of the opinion that one of her accounts had been drained. I'm asking for your permission to view the transactions in all or any of her accounts over the past six months. It's possible a crime was committed.'

Cater took a breath and straightened his spine, faintly affronted at the impropriety. 'Not without going through the proper channels, Constable Hirschhausen. I'm sure you understand.'

'I do,' Hirsch said warmly, understandingly. 'But it would be...regrettable if an unscrupulous person withdrew Mrs Groote's savings before her estate matters were settled.'

Cater rested slender, hairless wrists on his desk blotter. With honeyed bitterness he said, 'I do not appreciate that kind of psychological manoeuvring from anyone, constable. Certainly not the police.' He sat back. 'If you'll forgive me, I have other matters to attend to. But I'll be most happy to help you in your investigation once you show me the appropriate paperwork.'

*

Life was full of gorgeous experiences. Hirsch headed for the front door and, on impulse, stopped by Sophie Flynn's window. For the benefit of the other teller he announced that he was interested in opening an account.

'I'll get you the forms,' Sophie said.

And when the other teller was occupied with a customer, Hirsch murmured, 'Sophie, do you happen to remember what address you sent Mrs Groote's replacement statements to?'

She searched her memory, looking troubled. 'Sorry, no.'

'Perhaps you could check when you have time and text it to me? No need to involve Mr Cater.'

She went very still. Her eyes shot along the room to Cater's office. 'Okay,' she whispered.

Hirsch returned to the police station and immersed himself in reports and emails. At 11.00 a.m. he drove to the house on the hill above the town and was treated to a lot of chatter and another cup of tea, this time at the table in the kitchen. It was a room that seemed to reveal the conflicting aspirations of Eleanor Quinlan and her husband. Hirsch gathered that she simply liked to potter and cook, but Adrian liked to bombard her with costly gadgets. He sat, she busied herself with the kettle. Realising he was being watched by a screen set in one of the brushed steel doors of a fridge the size of his car, he hastily changed seats. Found himself facing a block of knives, each sleek blade ready to flip out and fly at him.

A steaming mug was plonked before him with a saucer for the bag. 'It's herbal,' Eleanor said. 'Hawthorn. Gives you energy, and heaven knows I need it.'

Hirsch cringed, girded himself, sipped. Not that bad: slightly sweet, slightly sour. 'I could do with a boost, too.'

Eleanor flashed him a smile that dissolved into something more remote. A rueful memory? Of her husband; her life with him? Something in the past, anyway.

'Just a few questions, if that's all right,' Hirsch said. 'I understand your husband was developing home units in Queensland a while back. Could he have gone up there?'

Another smile, less vague: unhappy and faintly injured. 'The first I knew anything about that was last Friday, when the phone rang hot. "Where's my money?" "Give me my money back."'

The feeling intensified in Hirsch that he should notify major fraud. He said, 'Did you know any of these callers?'

'A few, yes. Bloody Adrian had me answering the phone till I got wise to that, then we just let it go through to the machine.'

'Any threats?'

'I don't know what was said to Adrian, but I got a couple of nasty comments.'

'Such as?'

'Oh, "See you in court, bitch."'

When her eyes slid away. Hirsch said, 'And?'

'One person, a man, don't know who he was, told me being a widow wasn't going to be much fun.' She looked around her. 'I shouldn't have come back. I went down the street earlier—talk about the cold shoulder.'

Hirsch visualised her, a gracious woman kept in the dark, and the rancorous undertow that followed her as she walked from newsagent to greengrocer to supermarket. 'Is there someone other than your sister you can stay with?'

Her gaze raked the room. A desperate chuckle; damp eyes: 'My daughter and her husband, I suppose...but they're on the hook financially, too. Lisa rang me yesterday—"Mum, how could you let this happen?"—all that. I didn't know what to say to her.'

Hirsch touched the back of Eleanor's hand briefly. 'I have to warn you it's possible that fraud investigators will be called in. They'll want access to your records, both here and down at the office. You might feel tempted to start shredding or throwing stuff out, but that will only make them want to dig deeper.'

He was relieved to see a tough little core of selfhood emerge in Eleanor Quinlan. 'Fine by me. Let the law take its course,' she said. Tapped her breastbone: 'I don't have any reason to be ashamed, even if I lose everything and end up living in a tent.'

Hirsch's phone vibrated. He ignored it. Eleanor Quinlan didn't. Erect, inquisitive, she said, 'It's all right, you can answer it.'

Hirsch, expecting a cryptic emoji, glumly checked the screen. Sophie Flynn had texted an address. Maggie Groote's bank statements had been going to 14 Rhynie Road, Redruth.

Over by the high school.

Had she been a canny investor, with properties all over the mid-north? But why in Rhynie Road? It was barely a hundred metres long and consisted mostly of the weedy front yards of rough-and-tumble tin or stone cottages set back far from the potholed street. Number 14 had once been a tiny corner store, boarded up now, with Bushells tea and Rosella sauce signs faintly visible on the wall; a building so faded and recessive that Hirsch almost drove past it. He parked, approached, wondering if some error had been made. Then he saw a mail slot and a new Yale lock in the high wooden side gate.

Rattling the gate experimentally, he pulled himself up, peered over the top and dropped to his feet again. The mail slot corresponded to a lidded metal box on the other side.

'There's been no one there for donkey's years,' said the next-door neighbour, sixty, with bitten-down nails; unable to meet the gaze of a policeman. 'Wouldn't have a clue who owns it,' she added.

'Have you seen who collects the mail?'

'Couldn't tell you. Mind me own business.'

A similar story around the corner in Blair Athol Street. An elderly man this time, who cracked open his door, shot a look both ways along the street and said, retreating again, 'Family named Cousins ran it back in the eighties. Went out of business when the supermarket opened.'

Exhausted, he withdrew further and made to close his door. Hirsch blocked that with his foot, feeling mean. 'Have you seen anyone collect the mail there?'

'Mail? You sure?'

So Hirsch drove back to the main street and parked behind a gracious old stone building marked District Council. His phone buzzed for a text before he could switch off. Clara

Ogilvie, breaking her silence: *Need a favour. Expect me at 4?* And a little smiley face smooching a kiss at him.

Hirsch was paralysed. He sat there thankful for a break in the clouds, the winter sun pouring down through the windscreen. He'd performed several Google searches on stalking, wanting to know what it was, why it happened, what could be done about it. Typically, he'd ended up with information that was both voluminous and unspecific. For a start, he couldn't work out what type of stalker Clara was. He could hardly call her a rejected lover, since he'd never been involved with her. Or had he been, in her eyes? Was she pursuing a relationship that she thought already existed (just because she'd made some comment on his fucking singing voice)? Seeking greater intimacy? If so, it was a strange, bipolar kind of campaign: touches of erotomania one day, notions of a higher-order love the next. And sometimes she seemed to be resentful, as if he'd failed her in some way. She did feel underacknowledged, he knew that much. And, according to Google, some stalkers were unable to recognise social cues or so narcissistic that they couldn't see they had a problem. Did that explain Clara? Narcissistic, yes. Socially incompetent? Not that Hirsch had witnessed. She seemed quite relaxed, amiable and responsive in social situations.

Predatory? That was for fucking sure.

Maybe she was a bit of every type and that made her scary. He texted back: *Sorry Clara, very busy today*.

And then winced. He shouldn't have responded at all—she'd take it as verification that a relationship existed. He shouldn't have used her name—too intimate. And he shouldn't have said he was busy: she probably loved a challenge.

She replied: *Quick favour to ask, that's all.*

Hirsch got out, locked up, went numbly in search of the district clerk.

'And how is Sergeant Brandl?'

Dean Hopper's office was tucked away in the corner of a room crammed with filing cabinets, wall charts and document tables covered in subdivision maps and planning applications under old-style desk lamps. He was alone. That morning, he told Hirsch, a fired-up property owner had come in, convinced her neighbour's new fence had shaved ten centimetres off her boundary line, but that was as exciting as the day had been so far. Or the month, for that matter.

Now a policeman, making a police inquiry. 'You've made my day.'

His stubby fingers rattled a keyboard and he eyed his monitor as he asked after Hirsch's boss. One finger would tap, he'd move the mouse minutely, scroll, tap again.

'She hopes to be back at work soon,' Hirsch said. 'But she'll need a wheelchair or crutches.'

'Good, good,' Hopper said absently. He was late sixties, a short, thin man in a collar and tie, his jacket on a hook behind his desk, a dome balding into a monk's tonsure.

'Here we are.' He swivelled the monitor for Hirsch's benefit. 'Owned by Phoenix Holdings, at that address.'

Someone trying to be funny? wondered Hirsch. A company

that had risen from the ashes of another and would rise again if closed down?

'Does it say who the directors are?'

'You'll have to ask ASIC. They keep a register of business names.'

Hirsch felt weighed down. 'How about listings of properties owned by an individual? Do you have access to that information?'

'Of course. It's a matter of public record. Who?'

'Margaret Groote.'

'Maggie? Poor woman.'

'You knew her?'

'Not well. She came in a couple of times, last year and early this year, to do with buying a house in Penhale and to check on her farm boundaries and easements and whatnot.'

'Alone?'

'Alone the first time, with her neighbours the second time.'

Hopper was busy with the keyboard as he spoke. Again he stopped, hovered, scrolled, tapped a key. 'Here we are. She owns the two properties I mentioned: the farm and the house in Penhale.'

'That's all? Nothing here in Redruth?'

Hopper looked at Hirsch, his mind working. 'Nothing here in Redruth...'

This is how small-town rumours start, Hirsch thought.

Now it was 3.30 and Hirsch considered going home. Steer clear of Clara Ogilvie every day until she gave up.

Gutless.

Besides, Google suggested she'd probably treat a delay or an evasion as a kind of foreplay. Or she'd get offended and punish him—in a loving way, for his own good.

You can't outthink a stalker, was the subtext of one article he'd found.

He stepped into the police station at 3:58 and Clara was there at 4:01. Just enough time for Hirsch to settle behind the desk in Sergeant Brandl's office, line up a pad and pen, set his mobile to record the conversation, and begin to read his emails. Then the rap on the door, and she whisked in, glowing to see him, her thin frame electric.

'Paul!'

Behind her Mr Pickett, the retiree who worked the front desk said, 'Sorry, she just—'

Clara turned to Pickett, warm and fulsome as she touched his arm. 'It's okay, Paul and I are old friends.'

Hirsch gave Pickett a reassuring nod. Clara watched him go, then gave the door a swipe to close it and settled a chair close to the side of the desk, close to Hirsch. He got up, walked behind her, reopened the door, came back around her again and sat. She was tremblingly alert to everything he did.

'Sorry, I thought, since I have something to discuss with you it would be best to—'

Hirsch gave her a huge empty smile and said, 'I understand, but I'm on duty and people need quick access to me at all times. Now, how can I help you?'

'I had a brilliant idea,' Clara said, and her eyes lit up the room.

It occurred to Hirsch that she might be nuts, but she was also artless. She was about to suggest something he couldn't possibly do, that would seem to her entirely reasonable.

He examined her more closely. Whatever game she was playing, it wasn't seduction. She was dressed plainly in pants and a jacket over a white T-shirt, and her body language in wanting to sit close to him was sexless, suggesting merely a kind of schoolyard intimacy. He thought: this woman didn't slash the valve stems of seven car tyres, or even order it done.

'What idea is that?' he said.

A broad smile. 'You come and talk to my students.'

Not too outlandish, Hirsch thought.

'Preferably once a week for the next three or four weeks. You have experience as a detective and as a uniformed policeman. Anything you can tell the kids would be invaluable, especially for our Year 12s who are contemplating a career in law enforcement. What do you think? We'll fit in with your timetable of course.'

Not too outlandish, even worthwhile, but mainly what she wanted was to reel him in. He said, 'Clara, please don't.'

She blinked. She needed a moment. Her eyelids fluttered. 'I'm sorry?'

'First, I'm afraid I'm not in a position to talk to your students. I'm rushed off my feet here, serving two police districts while Sergeant Brandl is away. I might be able to free up Tim or Jean for one school visit, but it can't be me, I'm in charge and I'm just too busy.'

She was expressionless.

'And you have to stop texting me, Clara. I have a job to do and it's distracting.'

She said flatly, 'I'm sure you get texts from people all the time. Friends, family, colleagues, your girlfriend...'

Your girlfriend...A tone in her voice. Hirsch said, 'But not every day, and not every few minutes. You sent me over twenty texts and smiley faces in the space of an hour the other day. I was in a meeting! Trying to do police work.'

'Twenty? That's absurd. I think—'

'Clara, what you're doing can be construed as stalking. There are laws against it. Severe penalties.'

She tilted her nose at him. 'I think it's quite ridiculous that a friendly text or two can be called stalking. I'm offended. And don't you think you're overreacting?'

Oh, Christ, this is going to turn into a slasher movie, thought Hirsch, seeing an ugly expression in her eyes: there and gone in a flash.

'Clara, you know I'm involved with Wendy. We love each other.' He didn't know where that came from. But there it was. He went on: 'Wendy's your friend, isn't she?'

That was a mistake; he saw it as soon as he'd said it. He'd put the crosshairs on Wendy's back.

Clara's face slackened. She spoke in a low, didactic voice: 'Did I ever, at any stage, interfere in your *relationship* or suggest going behind Wendy's back? No. What I *thought* you and I had, or might achieve, was friendship. A small thing to ask for in the scheme of things, I would have thought?'

She stood as she said this, gathering herself, gathering her things. Gathering reserves of dignity. Gave a determined, unhappy smile as she turned to go. 'You disappoint me, Paul.'

Story of my life, Hirsch thought. The ranks of those I've disappointed...

When she was gone, he stumbled through a few emails, heart pounding. And when the desk phone rang, he picked up the receiver hoping to be saved from the drifting mists and distortions of his mind.

It was the sergeant at Riverton, an hour south of Redruth. Something about a poorly secured trailer load of roofing iron and a near fatality. 'The driver said you gave him the okay. Is he trying it on, or what? We've got a kiddie in hospital, leg sliced open.'

25

The image of that trailer and the old reprobate at the bowser came back to Hirsch like a grave marker of his past. All his missteps and errors of judgment came crowding in. He was losing it. Spending too much time obsessing about Clara Ogilvie and not enough on his job. What other stuff-ups would come to light? What other fuses had he unwittingly lit?

'I advised the guy about travelling safely,' he said, feeling tentative and disadvantaged. Was that a lie? Had he said that? He couldn't remember. He didn't want to lie. He didn't want to admit culpability, either; he wasn't the one who'd been driving with an unsafe load. You weak shit, Aitch.

'Yeah, well, he didn't listen,' the sergeant was saying. 'Not that his record's covered in glory. A heap of DUI, driving while disqualified, receive stolen goods, so on and so forth.'

Then the sergeant sent a barb Hirsch's way. 'Anyway, it's irrelevant what you told him: it was his load and he was the driver. We'll throw the book at him. Thanks for your time.'

Hirsch wanted to ask about the child with the gashed leg but the guy had hung up. He thought about sweeping everything off his desk with his noble forearm and decided it was too melodramatic. Also, no one else was going to pick up his crap off the floor.

On the way home he called in at the house on Bitter Wash Road. Wendy and Katie were happy to have him there. They smiled, chatted. Looked in his eyes and touched his hands, his forearms, to make a point. And he wasn't up to it; he didn't deserve it. Opportunities to tell Wendy everything came, and he hesitated, and they went. He said goodnight and drove home with the grief and confusion still bottled up inside him.

He spent part of Thursday morning on Tiverton business then headed south and was passing through the town square in Redruth when he spotted Tilly Wanganeen tootling out of a side street on her red and white Australia Post Honda. She was swaddled in a sleeveless yellow hi-vis jacket and a white helmet, with yellow mail sacks on either side of the back wheel and her long legs, bent sharply at the knee, bracketing the little bike like quote marks.

He pulled over, tooted, got out. She braked, planting her highly polished black shoes, and flipped up her visor. 'Help you?'

'Couple of quick questions,' Hirsch said.

He knew her from the Woolpack's music afternoons. She played a ukulele in a dreamy fashion, caught up in the music—but as a deliverer of mail she was twitchy and impatient. She glanced at her watch and then up and down the street as if gauging time lost if she talked to him.

Her hand unconsciously touching the Aboriginal flag pinned to her breast, she said, 'Concerning?'

'Fourteen Rhynie Road.'

She went still, her mind sorting. Her face cleared. 'Used to be a corner shop.'

'That's it. Do you deliver much mail there?'

'Not much. Once a month, maybe?'

'Do you know who collects it?'

'No idea. I just deliver, Paul.' She paused. 'When are you going to sing for us again?'

Hirsch said, 'Genius can't be hurried. I'm working up an extensive repertoire.'

'Good, good,' Tilly said. Another one who couldn't read humour. 'Look, if that's all, I need to—'

'Last question. Can you remember who the letters are addressed to?'

A shift in Tilly's face as a thought took hold. She looked about her: no one was listening. In a soft, steady, helpless voice she said, 'I just deliver the mail. That's all I'm supposed to do.'

'I understand that,' Hirsch said, knowing there was more.

'To the *address on the envelope*. The name isn't our concern.'

A code of honour, Hirsch thought. 'I understand,' he said gently. He wasn't about to hold anything against her.

She went on in a rush, 'Four people get letters sent to that address. Mrs Groote—the lady that died in the fire—and Anne Silvester and Desmond Mannion and Freya Kroger.'

Hirsch was silent, watching her, and she couldn't bear it. 'I did wonder,' she said. 'I mean, I know where they all live and it's not Rhynie Road.'

Hirsch didn't know the names Silvester, Mannion and Kroger. 'Are they all older people, by any chance?'

Tilly's eyes went wide. 'Now you come to mention it.'

'What can you tell me about the type of mail?'

'Business envelopes.'

'All from the same business?'

That tested Tilly. She frowned, began to shake her head. 'Can't really remember.'

Hirsch went to get the morning-briefing coffee and Danishes, wondering what the mail diversion meant. Presumably the person who collected the post was the person who author-ised the diversion, and Hirsch would rather watch and wait for this person than start digging around at the bank. And what if the mail also included letters from other types of financial institutions—insurance, stockbrokers or what-ever? And what if there was a good reason for the mail drop? It was possible that a well-intentioned third party such as an accountant, a lawyer or an investment advisor—Christ, let's hope not Adrian Quinlan—was helping well-heeled elderly people to hide their assets from avaricious family members.

If bank and other statements were issued monthly, there was no point in watching 14 Rhynie every day. Hirsch was thinking of ways around this as he parked outside the

Redruth police station and walked into the briefing room. 'Morning, crimefighters. Sorry I'm late.'

He jumped when Sergeant Brandl, propped on crutches beside the whiteboard, said, 'Where's my coffee?'

She was looking spruce in a waisted jacket over a yellow T-shirt and a long woollen skirt. Thick grey tights sheathed one leg; the other was lumpen in plaster, a red ski sock over her foot.

Hirsch glanced at Landy and Medlin. 'You can have mine. The children sulk if they miss out.' Placing the coffees and pastries on the briefing table, he gave her a quick hug. 'Welcome back.'

She relaxed minutely against him. 'It's not official. Just dropping in from time to time to keep you on your toes.'

'Oh, good,' Hirsch said, sitting opposite Jean Landy.

'The children have been filling me in while you've been off gallivanting. First—'

She was interrupted by the auxiliary support officer sidling in like a shadow on a wall, his eyes to the floor. The sergeant intimidated Pickett: a woman; a woman in a position of authority; a woman with confidence and occasional prickly temper.

Yet she'd always been unfailingly kind and polite to him, and right now her smile warmed the room. 'Yes, Ron?'

Pickett cast her a troubled look, then cast his eyes down again. 'The wife,' he said.

'Is something wrong? Can we help?'

Pickett struggled. 'She's outside in the car. She's smart, she told them she was going to the bank but came straight here.'

Hirsch understood. 'Two Irish guys came to the house, offering to repair the roof?'

'Yes!' Pickett said, relieved.

Ron and Judy Pickett lived in a 1960s brick house along a sloping side street between the showgrounds and a John Deere dealership. Hirsch came in from the top end, tucking his police Toyota behind a rubbish skip. Using field glasses, he watched Jean Landy—at the wheel of the Picketts' Commodore and wearing civilian clothes—drive in from the bottom end. She said later that the men, recognising the car, gave her a smile and a thumbs-up. Even when they realised that she wasn't Mrs Pickett they were more quizzical than alarmed, and that didn't change until she'd parked nose-up to their Mercedes Sprinter van, by which time Hirsch had rolled down from the top of the street to block the rear and Tim Medlin had pulled in hard against the flank.

Beautiful police work.

The three of them got out, exhilarated, bracing for a struggle or a chase. The men were youngish, fit, tensing as they weighed the odds. One bared his teeth, ready to run or fight. The other, with a sleepy-eyed smile, said, 'Take it easy there, Fin, it's only the gardai, let's see what they want.'

The talker, Hirsch thought. Smoother, older, his words, accent and smile like honey flowing. He was about thirty, dressed in overalls and a beanie. A calm, suave, eyes-alert kind of face, unclouded by doubt.

He raised an eyebrow at Hirsch. 'Help you with something?'

Hirsch saw how it would go. This man would try to take charge. If that didn't work, he'd keep his offsider quiet while he managed the flow of information in a way that would seem polite and disarming. Separate the two men as soon as possible, thought Hirsch—psychologically as well as physically.

And one way to do that was to tune him out and rattle the younger man, who was similarly dressed but thickset and sullen. 'Your name, please, sir? ID?'

'We done nothin'.'

'Fin,' the older man said; a faint note of caution now.

'*Laurence*,' said the man named Fin, with a glance of bitter complicity. 'Time to pack up, what do you say?' he said, taking a step towards the Picketts' front gate.

Hirsch glanced at the house. A ladder against the side wall. Not that Fin would collect the ladder. He'd bolt through to the backyard and over the fence and far away. Hirsch watched him take another step. Then Jean Landy was there, her feet planted, arms folded.

'Going somewhere?'

'You serious? Let me through,' Fin said, reaching a hand to her upper arm.

She made a neat spin, ducked, tugged, and had him down on his stomach.

'Get off, bitch.'

The man named Laurence looked on. Sighed and said, 'You gibbering saint.'

He turned to Hirsch. 'I know how this plays out, constable. You have your questions; we have our answers. But I should tell you now, I am in possession of certain information and it would profit both of us to trade favour for favour.'

'Information about what?'

'That there house fire last Sunday.'

26

He said his name was Laurence Rea. Sitting in the police station interview room with a mug of black coffee at his elbow, he also said he didn't want a lawyer next to him, spoiling his flow. 'Cutting in like a woodpecker, saying you need not answer this, need not answer that.'

The accent was melodious, the man himself engaging: calm, shrewd, courteous—but with a dark artfulness to him. Hirsch wasn't about to trust him. But Rea had been cooperative during the arrest, with none of the tedious pouting of the other one, Fin.

And he claimed to have information about the death of Maggie Groote.

'If at any stage you'd like a lawyer present,' Sergeant Brandl said, 'we'll arrange that for you.'

As usual during interrogations, her manner was preoccupied but not unfriendly. When working with her, Hirsch played the emotional hand: offended, disappointed, sceptical, encouraging. The system usually worked for them.

It kept prisoners, suspects and witnesses off balance. But Hirsch didn't know how it would go with Rea. The man was a pro. In this situation he had one story to tell, and wasn't going to be drawn into anything else.

Now he inclined his head. 'Noted.'

'This so-called information,' Hirsch said. 'Will your pal back you up? Should we include him?'

'Include him out,' Rea said, twinkling at Hirsch and Brandl. 'He's an exalted piece of wreckage, you'll never get a clear fact out of him. He can turn everything around, even day and night.'

Rea turned to Tim Medlin, standing guard at the door. 'All right there, young fella?'

Tim was taken by surprise. He shifted uneasily.

Hirsch, thinking Rea was already playing a game, inflaming their curiosity with his reticence, said, 'Hey, Mr Rea, time's wasting.'

'Call me Laurie,' smiled Rea, looking from Hirsch to Brandl.

The sergeant said, 'Let's keep this formal, shall we, Mr Rea? As agreed, we won't discuss your roof repair activities. That's—'

'Alleged activities.'

'That's now a CIB matter and detectives from Port Pirie will be taking you into custody later today. Right now, as requested, we're giving you the opportunity to divulge information about the death of Margaret Groote last Sunday morning.'

'Information,' muttered Hirsch, as though the word had no meaning.

Sergeant Brandl placed a warning hand on his forearm briefly, then sat back. 'Please start, Mr Rea.'

'The boy Finbarr and I had occasion to be in that old woman's street,' Rea said, and stopped, as if expecting Hirsch and Brandl to start a series of inconvenient questions.

'Get on with it,' Hirsch said.

'And we saw a car leaving that part of the street right there. Rate of knots.'

'From outside Mrs Groote's house?' Brandl said.

'So I'm telling you.'

'What time was this?'

Rea reached for his coffee and thought better of it. 'Battery acid,' he said, with a brilliant show of teeth, giving the mug a series of fingertip nudges until it was out of reach.

Hirsch said tensely, 'What time?'

Rea gave him a sleepy look; Hirsch almost expected to be called a fine bit of pestilence.

'The time?' he persisted.

'This would be shortly after nine.'

'In the morning?' said Hirsch.

Rea looked to Sergeant Brandl for help. 'Is he always like this?'

'Please answer the question, Mr Rea.'

It was expecting a lot, but Rea said, 'Yes, nine o'clock in the morning.'

Hirsch said pleasantly, 'Can you recall what kind of car it was?'

He was rewarded by a smile. 'That silver colour they have,' Rea said. 'A fine shiny thing.'

'Sedan, station wagon, what?'

'Hold your horses. I like to canter, not gallop. It was a silver Passat sedan.'

'Thank you.'

'A new model. A fine, swooping shape to it.'

'And it drove off in a hurry?'

'It did, so.'

Here Rea grew sombre, as if the car had been easy but the next bit would be more taxing. His first genuine emotion, Hirsch thought, letting the pause do its work.

Rea looked up. 'We were passing through, you understand. Naturally our curiosity was piqued. That car streaking away. We thought: something here is not right.'

Hirsch let the bullshit go. Rea was rehearsing the story he'd give CIB. Conscious that he was adding to the bullshit, Hirsch said, 'Is it possible you smelt smoke?'

'You are correct, sir. And without further ado we parked where that car had been and went to investigate.'

'You entered the house.'

'Yes.'

'The door?' Hirsch asked, remembering that it needed a good slam.

A complicated watchfulness in Rea's handsome face. He was a man with a history of entering houses. 'The door was in a closed position but not fully shut.' With his trademark twinkle he added: 'You might say it succumbed to gentle pressure.'

Hirsch thought about the door. Maggie hadn't shut it properly the night before. Or the Passat driver hadn't shut it properly on his or her way out. 'Please continue.'

'There, in that poor woman's hall we could hear the crackle and see the flamelight dancing in her sitting room doorway. The heat on our faces and the dirty smoke swirling. I yelled to Finbarr, fetch a hose or a bucket.'

He stopped. Hirsch said, 'I saw the hose. One of you pulled Mrs Groote out onto the lawn?'

'Hold your horses, there. I touch the doorknob and it is effing hot, so I elbow it open and duck a quick look into that room and she is slumped there like this in an armchair.'

Rea flopped back, splaying head and limbs, before sitting upright again. A twist of emotion as he added, 'Her feet were burning. She had those little heaters there and they were tipped over, poor old soul.'

Tim Medlin, standing at the door, shifted his weight and somewhere outside the police station a truck downshifted for the sharp turns of the town square.

'I scooped her into my arms—sure there was no substance to her—and I ran into the hallway and collided with Fin coming in, firing water all over the place. So I put the old woman down near the front door and ran back to help him, but I was torn, help her or help Fin wet the carpet and the upholstery. I beat at the flames with a cushion, but it was all a lost cause and I grab his sleeve and we got out of that hellhole. Gathered up the old lady again and placed her on the ground and we went on our way. Called the fire station soon after.'

A bit of footwork in those final sentences, Hirsch thought. Did they know Maggie was dead—the way they'd positioned her suggested that. And they'd taken the time to search for the local fire station number rather than call triple zero. He didn't pursue it.

Sergeant Brandl, more intent now, said, 'Mr Rea, there's bound to be an inquest, and you may be asked to appear. Meanwhile, depending on what the autopsy reveals, you may find yourself talking to Homicide Squad detectives. You need to be aware of that.'

Rea stopped her with the palm of his hand. 'I did not come down in the last shower. Me and Fin did not hurt that old woman. We tried to save her. What I am doing today, talking to you, is getting out in front of all that. You have a job to do.'

'I'm not impressed,' Hirsch said. 'You could have told us this days ago.'

'I'm telling you now. You need to find a fine new silver Passat.'

'You didn't see who was driving?'

'Ach,' Rea said in disgust, 'we saw only the hind part of that car.'

One day, thought Hirsch, regional command will send us a CIB officer other than Comyn. The Port Pirie detective shouldered his way in, oversaw the prisoner transfer in his unsmiling way, then asked for an update in the briefing room. Gesturing negligently, he refused tea and coffee.

'You're saying they didn't disclose anything about their roof-repair scam.'

'Correct,' Hirsch said. 'Only their role in the fire.'

'Trying to get ahead of a murder charge?'

'Not according to them. Helping the police, in their upstanding way.'

Comyn, squat as a bear on the other side of the table, said, 'Who else can tie them to the scamming? Given that our only good witness is dead.'

Hirsch glanced at the sergeant; a look that said, can you believe this guy? She didn't meet his gaze but stared at Comyn as if at something makeshift and unsatisfactory and said, 'Three of my officers can attest to the presence of these men, their van and their equipment at an address here in town—the home of the man who works our front desk, in fact. His wife alerted us. She was told their roof needed repairs and they'd wait while she withdrew the money. Seventy-five hundred dollars.'

'Names,' Comyn said, taking out a notebook and patting his pockets for a pen.

Brandl recited the names.

'Anyone else? Other victims?'

'A job for CIB,' Sergeant Brandl said sunnily.

Comyn put a sour construction on that. 'I expect it is.'

Hirsch said, 'See if Rea will give you the other members of their crew.'

Another wearisome burden for CIB. 'Anything else?' Comyn asked, getting to his feet.

'We think Mrs Groote's death should be treated as suspicious,' Hirsch said.

Comyn replied with a kind of contained fury. 'It's suspicious that those Irish idiots were there. It's suspicious they're claiming they saw a car. It's suspicious they tried to put the fire out. Is that what you mean?'

'What if there was a car?'

'Until we have the fire inspector's report and the autopsy results, we don't have anything to go on,' Comyn said, heading for the door in his nuggety way. Creases in his jacket and the seat of his pants, Hirsch noted. A man who sat all day in a car or behind a desk.

When he was gone, Sergeant Brandl breathed out heavily. 'That man.'

She looked pinched and drawn now, as if Comyn had caused tension in her knitting bones and she was in pain again.

'Drive you home, boss?'

'Thank you. I overdid it.'

She rented a house on a leafy street behind the hospital and rode there in silence with Hirsch, a pale, diminished shape in the passenger seat. They thought their thoughts and then Hirsch's mobile rang in its dashboard cradle.

'Let me,' the sergeant offered.

Hirsch listened as she said, 'Sergeant Brandl on Constable Hirschhausen's phone...Yes...You sure? Thank you.'

The call over, she clipped the phone back in place and said, 'Preliminary autopsy findings. Broken hyoid bone.'

27

Friday. Hirsch walked the streets of Tiverton, his puny torch probing the shadows unreached by the misty streetlights, misty rain deadening all sounds and beading on his face. He curled his toes, stretched the beanie to his jawline, hunched his shoulders and wondered what kind of idiot he was to wander through such a freezing darkness.

He came down past the lucerne seed business, which maddened the Alsatian they had chained there, and turned onto the highway and was trudging past the shop, a hundred metres short of the police station, when a car came out of the heavy stillness, its headlights throwing his shadow ahead of him, and then he heard it decelerate and draw alongside him and the passenger-side window slid down and Clara Ogilvie leaned across to look up at him.

'Morning constitutional?'

She was as bright as a button. Hirsch looked around, half-fearing she'd brought reinforcements.

'What the fuck, Clara.'

It was as if he'd struck her. 'What do you mean?'

'What are you doing here?'

She stiffened, faintly affronted. 'If you must know, I'm taking a day off. My mother's not well.' She took a hand from the steering wheel and pointed to the dark reaches north of the town. 'She lives in Port Augusta.'

A longish drive. Getting an early start. But did he believe her? Challenge her? Tell her that no cop ever believed in coincidence?

'Safe trip, hope your mother's okay,' Hirsch said, straightening his spine, stepping back from the window. A negligent wave. A purposeful step towards the police station, then another. Soon he was a few metres ahead. Behind him the motor idled. Then he heard acceleration and the Fiesta pulled away, overtaking him, and he watched the red taillights all the way into invisibility. The world unpopulated again but for Hirsch entering his driveway, knuckling his old Nissan for luck.

He stripped off, danced on the icy floor until the shower ran hot, then paused. Dashed to the office and wrote it all down: date, time, place, type of encounter.

Redruth police station, mid-morning, and Comyn was not thrilled to be back again so soon. 'The Homicide Squad has tasked me with doing some digging around.'

He was with Hirsch and Brandl in the briefing room, the sergeant looking tired, rubbing where the crutches had chafed her. 'Digging around what?'

'Margaret Groote. The forensic evidence is ambiguous,

apparently, so I've been asked to see if anyone had it in for the old lady, in which case Homicide might action an investigation.'

Hirsch's capacity to think was flattened briefly. 'Ambiguous in what way?'

Comyn turned slowly to face him as if wondering who'd spoken. 'Neither one thing nor the other.'

'Don't be a dick, Detective Senior Constable Comyn,' Sergeant Brandl said.

Hirsch was relieved. He reached into the middle of the table and grabbed the last apricot Danish, knowing it would sit in his gut, a doughy lump, but he wanted something to do while he watched the main event, Sergeant Brandl and Senior Constable Comyn squaring off. She outranked the detective, but only technically. She was a small-town sergeant, he was an investigator.

'Be specific,' she said. 'Ambiguous in what way?'

Looking at her as if there was a need-to-know dimension to the case, and she didn't need to know, Comyn said, 'First, the fire inspector found no trace of accelerant. He's pretty certain an overturned radiator caused the fire. How it got overturned, he couldn't say. Not his job to say.'

'Mr Comyn, we're privy to the preliminary autopsy findings. A broken hyoid bone?'

'Not necessarily evidence of intentional violence, according to the pathologist, when he heard that Mrs Groote had been removed from the house and taken out into the front yard.' He paused. 'Bruises showed up later: neck and upper arms. Again, they could have been caused when she was moved.'

They all thought about that. Had Rea lied? He'd stran-gled Maggie and then, for reasons best known to himself, removed her body from the house? Or had he been clumsy, hasty, rougher than necessary when he removed her body? Or he'd told the truth, someone else had been there.

'Was there smoke in her lungs?'

'No. Suggesting she was already dead when the fire started.'

'Or breathing shallowly,' Brandl said. 'The fire was only just taking hold, apparently.'

Comyn shook his head. 'There was a fine layer of soot everywhere. She would have inhaled some of it, the patholo-gist reckons.'

A wind came up; the building creaked; a twiggy branch thrashed the window. Hirsch drained his coffee. 'What's likely to get the Homicide Squad more interested?'

'A big, fat motive,' Comyn said.

'Money?'

'It's a start.'

'Start with this,' Hirsch said, telling Comyn of the siphoned bank account, the missing statement and the mail diversion.

Comyn was dubious. 'Slim. We're talking an old lady, probably forgets things.'

'Or whoever was siphoning the account got worried when Mrs Groote realised the money was missing.'

'If it was ever there.'

'There's also this,' Hirsch said, removing Maggie's will

from a folder and sliding it across the table. 'And it may be connected.'

Sergeant Brandl left them to it, creaking away on her crutches, telling Comyn that Hirsch knew more about the case than she did.

Hirsch made a fresh plunger of coffee as Comyn read the will, then sat across from him as it brewed. 'What do you think?'

'Interesting. But let me play devil's advocate. Those Irish jackasses also had a motive to kill her.'

'Like what?'

'They ripped her off,' said Comyn. 'She could ID them.'

'So could plenty of others,' Hirsch said. 'I think Rea and his mate simply went back to her house to wangle more money out of her.'

Comyn shrugged. 'I got nothing out of them yesterday. They kept saying, "lawyer", like an American cop show.'

Hirsch got up, poured and delivered the coffees.

Comyn glanced at his as if he didn't want it. He slumped a little further in his chair; tapped at the will with his forefinger. 'Amy Groote was the one who tried to stab my toes with a rake?'

Hirsch grinned. 'Yes.'

'Think she'd kill if she knew she didn't inherit? Or didn't inherit enough?'

Hirsch shrugged. 'I don't know her well enough. Or her friends.'

'Sylvia and John Fearn were the people we talked to next? The old lady, Groote, was there too?'

Hirsch nodded. 'They've got motive in spades. Needed to hurry the process. Or they were worried she might change her will.'

'Aren't you the busy-minded little sleuth,' Comyn said.

Hirsch found himself borrowing from Laurence Rea's phrase-book. You glib ponce, he thought. You exalted shit.

He said, 'Amy Groote thought the Fearns were exerting undue influence.'

Comyn nodded. 'Maybe the lawyer can tell us more.'

First Hirsch took him past the empty shop in Rhynie Road. They sat in the HiLux, motor idling, Comyn gloomy and thoughtful. 'So, mail for four local people is being diverted here.'

'*Some* of their mail is,' Hirsch stressed.

'I'll take it under advisement,' Comyn said.

Smug piece of wreckage, thought Hirsch, pulling away from the kerb.

Redruth Legal Services was a one-woman outfit in Redruth North, the bay-windowed front room of a colonial-era building that had been a Masonic Lodge, a GP's surgery, a weekly newspaper office and a Bank of Adelaide branch, Julia Galvin told them.

'And now it's me,' she added, in an over-refined voice.

Aged in her seventies, Hirsch guessed, her hair combed by a gale-force wind, a snowfall of cigarette ash on her chest. Files every which way on the floor, her desk, office chairs.

A cigarette smouldered in a mountain of butts. She stabbed it out. 'Make yourselves comfortable, gentlemen.

Dump those where you will,' she said, as Hirsch and Comyn divested the chairs of their files.

They sat across the desk from her. A beautiful room otherwise, thought Hirsch, looking around at the high ceiling, window seat and pastel blue walls and white ceiling and cornices. Warm, if smoky. A storm whipped at the trees, the birds and paper scraps outside the window, but the building seemed inured to it. Galvin's office was almost silent.

'You're here about Maggie's will.'

'We are,' Comyn said. He fished in the inside pocket of his jacket and proffered the will Hirsch had given him. When the lawyer didn't take it, he let it drop. Creased, warm from its proximity to his body, it sat on the desk and Galvin eyed it with a kind of mordant attentiveness before lifting her gaze to Comyn, then Hirsch.

'I've known—correction, I *knew*—Margaret all my life. Since boarding school—country gels away from home for the first time,' she added, with an indelicate laugh.

Hirsch grinned. He liked her.

Comyn fidgeted. 'Mrs Galvin, that will was found in Mrs Groote's house after her death. I'd like to know if she talked to you at all about her reasons for making those bequests. Things that people might have said or done that influenced her.'

The lawyer picked it up, unfolded it, smoothed it and ran her gaze down the first page. 'First of all, this isn't her final will.'

'There's a new one?'

Galvin straightened. Despite her untidiness she looked

stately, reserved and patient, as if she found Comyn a bit slow. 'As I said, this is not the most recent will.'

Then, perhaps not wanting to cause offence, she gave him a transfiguring smile and got to her feet. 'Let me fetch what I believe is her final will.'

She opened the middle drawer of an old-style wooden cabinet, clacked through the files, extracted a folder and, business-like, returned to her desk. But then a twist to her features, as if a painful memory had flickered in her. 'I assume you'd like the gist of Maggie's intentions?'

'I would,' Comyn said.

We would, Hirsch thought.

'Very well. As you know, the will you found at her house bequeathed the farm to her neighbours, and the house in town was to be sold, with most of the proceeds going to charity bar twenty thousand dollars to the niece.'

'Yes,' Comyn said, a thrumming energy in him as if he could barely sit still.

Galvin wasn't to be hurried. 'My dear friend came to me Saturday morning and asked that I draw up a new will, with a major amendment.'

Comyn was terse. 'Go on.'

Galvin checked if Hirsch was similarly impatient. He smiled; gave her the minutest shrug.

She gave him the minutest smile and turned her attention to Comyn again. 'She'd had a fall in her bathroom the previous afternoon. Couldn't stand, but she was able to sit with her back against the wall and reach a landline phone she'd had installed near the sink. She called Sylvia Fearn, who promised to come, but didn't. An hour passed, poor soul. So she called Amy, who came straight away and got her to her feet and took her to see Doctor Pillai.'

Hirsch knew where this was going. 'She changed the will to favour Amy?'

'Yes and no,' Julia Galvin said. 'The Fearns get nothing. The farm is to be sold, the proceeds going to a range of charities. The house in Penhale goes to Amy.' Galvin paused. 'Maggie had old-fashioned ideas about responsibility. She wanted to award Amy, but not coddle her.'

Comyn was going to ask one of his blunt questions. Hirsch cut in. 'Forgive me, but for all Mrs Groote knew, Sylvia Fearn could have had a flat tyre, or an accident.'

Galvin seemed pleased with him. 'Indeed, but I think she'd been having doubts before this. The fact that the Fearns had paid little attention to her until the middle of last year, when Amy came to stay, for example. The way they slipped into her life and daily routines. Insinuations. Bad-mouthing Amy—who, heaven knows, was herself an absent figure in Maggie's life until last year. But, as Maggie said, what you see is what you get with Amy.'

Maybe, Hirsch thought. He would leave now with Comyn and on the drive back to the station they'd thrash through the motives. The Fearns kill Maggie to inherit the farm, unaware that the will has been changed. Or the Fearns get wind of the change and kill her out of spite. Or Amy kills her—before she changes her mind again—because a house in a country town is better than nothing.

*

But Hirsch found himself sidelined. Comyn made a series of calls on the way back to the police station, then said, 'We let Homicide deal with it. You can make yourself useful by keeping on monitoring her mail.'

And so Hirsch drove to Tiverton, one eye open for silver Passats, and, just before closing time that Friday afternoon, he was convincing Ed Tennant to let him have the contents of Maggie Groote's post office box.

Ed was dismayed. 'A suspicious death?'

'Yes.'

'She was lovely,' the shopkeeper said sadly. 'There's been some more mail for her since the other day,' he added, handing Hirsch a sheaf of envelopes, flyers and brochures.

Hirsch took them home with him. Poured himself a glass of red, sat at his miserable little table and sliced open an envelope marked Mid-North Community Bank and addressed to Maggie's post office box. An everyday savings account, balance $1,349. No major deposits or withdrawals. Meaning, he thought, that only the statements for her other account, the one that had once contained a sizeable amount, had been sidelined to the Rhynie Road address. He opened one of the charity letters. Maggie was informed that her annual donation could not be processed owing to inadequate funds, and would she care to rectify the matter?

28

On Saturday morning, conscious that he'd let too many matters slide, he made a string of phone calls.

First, the hospital, where he asked for the name of the nurse who'd bathed Lydia Jarmyn. He was put on hold and a moment later a voice said, 'Ella Voumard.' Brisk, breathless, as if rushed off her feet.

'Any relation to Rolf?' asked Hirsch, after telling her who he was.

'My dad.'

'He found a break-in at a property he keeps an eye on.'

'So he said.'

'Any further signs the Ayliffes have been there?'

'Is that what this is about?'

Note to self, thought Hirsch. Stop talking about the Ayliffes.

'No, no, I got distracted. I'm calling about Lydia Jarmyn.'

A change came over the nurse. Less brisk now, and Hirsch remembered her in the hospital bathroom that morning, her features softening to see the sores, the filth, the neglect.

'Is she all right?'

'I was hoping you might know,' he said.

'Sorry, as soon as she was fit to travel, they just whisked her away.'

'Child Protection?'

'And Della, the social worker we brought in.'

Hirsch made his second call of the day. Della Forster had little to tell him, apart from Lydia Jarmyn's location: at the Women's and Children's Hospital in Adelaide.

'She was badly malnourished. When her condition improves, she'll be placed in foster care.'

'Could I see her?'

A long pause. 'A child like that, she'll either shut down and mistrust everyone, or latch onto anyone who's kind to her. She was devastated when she had to say goodbye to Ella in Redruth, and according to Ella and Doctor Pillai, just as distressed when you had to leave. I really don't think you should see her, sorry. It might confuse her. Maybe in a few months, when she's settled.'

'But as far as you know, she's doing okay.'

'Starting to thrive, apparently.'

'And Mrs Jarmyn?'

'Wouldn't have a clue.'

'Do you know if she tried to see Lydia?'

'I've no idea. She was unfit, wasn't she?'

'She wasn't exactly mother of the year,' Hirsch said, even as he recalled that Grace Jarmyn had seemed a good enough mother—to her own child.

'It's possible she was committed after the psych eval. Don't know how you'd find out, though.'

Hirsch tried Comyn, who grudgingly supplied contact details for the social worker who'd accompanied him to the Jarmyn house. 'What are you up to?'

'Dotting *i*'s and crossing *t*'s,' Hirsch said.

The social worker was named Lisa Sandford and she was in a foul mood. 'Listen, this is a day off for me. And I can't give out that kind of information anyway.'

'Are you monitoring her?'

'Is this an ongoing police matter or an ongoing social services matter? I only ask because it's people like me who have to deal with the fallout whatever happens.'

'Lovely talking to you,' Hirsch said, thinking gloomily that society depended on different agencies like the police, the judiciary and welfare services cooperating with each other. Except their aims rarely coincided, they rarely shared information, they rarely even talked to each other. Not out of bloody-mindedness—usually—but inefficiency and failure of imagination. Even though they were all bureaucracies, their systems rarely meshed.

The floor heater scorching his trouser cuffs, Hirsch called Diana Ayliffe.

'Anything?'

'As in, am I hiding one or both of my menfolk from the police? No.'

Well done, Aitch. Ask an innocent question and get your

head bitten off. 'I saw you on TV the other day. I thought you handled it well.'

Diana Ayliffe making a public appeal, leaning into a microphone at a media conference table, senior police on either side of her. Clarity, candour, and very little overt emotion. Telling her menfolk to give themselves up before someone got hurt—but obliquely telling her son to save himself before his father got him killed.

She was partly mollified. 'They told me it might help.'

'I thought at least Josh would call you.'

Her voice caught. 'So did I. I guess it means they're really living off the land and haven't seen any TV or read any newspapers.'

Hirsch didn't know for sure, but said: 'Is it possible Josh is torn? He's found himself in a situation he can't get out of?'

Her voice grew wretched. 'I'd like to think so, but Leon's very overbearing, and as you say, Josh can't get out of it even if he wanted to.'

Depressed, Hirsch left the police station, backed the Toyota out of the driveway and headed for the Jarmyn house. Something about the place drew him. Something miasmic.

The gates were padlocked. He climbed over the fence and walked uphill, the driveway trees bending in the icy wind. He was curious to see fresh vehicle tracks where old layers of gravel had been compressed forever under the mud. Reaching the yard, he eyed the house, which crouched mute and glum as if reproaching him, as if he were coming to punish it, when consolation was needed.

No car, no chimney smoke, but the tricycle sat in the carport. Then he froze: the dog was there. It watched him from the kennel, water bowl brimming, half a dog biscuit in the dirt beneath the rim of the food bowl.

Hirsch was spooked. A neat, sad place and he'd dearly love to bring in a squad of cadaver dogs.

As he approached the front door, he noticed small patches of disturbed earth at two-metre intervals along the front of the house, a short distance out from the veranda. He made a circuit of the place: more signs of digging along the side and rear walls. Far too small for a burial. Gardening? Winter plants?

He knocked on the front door; no reply.

He checked the caravan: empty. This time he advanced more deeply into the shed, to a patch of shadowy forms against the back wall. An empty fuel drum. An old wooden wardrobe with garden stakes leaning where dresses and suits once hung; and measuring tape, hose fittings, paintbrushes and emery paper sorted neatly in a bank of drawers.

A concrete slab nearby. It looked old, dusty; oil stained. Four upright bolts cemented in one corner. Brackets for a motor? Generator? All Hirsch wanted to do was dig it up.

He walked down the track to the Toyota and drove up Hawker Road to Jonas Heneker's house. A repeat of last time: he was greeted by an apparition of whiskers, an army greatcoat, threadbare pants and an axe. But that was the only similarity: this Jonas was trembling, damp-eyed. Not the weather, Hirsch realised, but emotions. Which meant...

'Is it Ivy?'

Jonas nodded. 'She's in hospital. Pneumonia.'

'So sorry, Jonas. Let me cut some of that wood for you.'

'Could you? I've lost some of my oomph this morning.'

Hirsch chopped; Jonas stacked. 'Good quality wood.'

'I always buy redgum,' Jonas said. 'A truckload every few weeks. The stuff around here'—he gestured at hills mostly denuded of trees—'not worth burning.'

Then silence as Hirsch chopped—chopped more than was necessary. Bone weary, finally, he stopped, propped the axe against the woodshed wall, and said, 'You going to see her later?'

'I am, yes.'

'Your kids?' Two sons: one in Perth, the other in Adelaide.

Jonas shrugged. 'They know.'

Hirsch heard those words at least once a week. A friend, relative or loved one knew, but they were yet to act on the knowledge. Knew, but probably wouldn't act. Knew, but didn't care.

As Hirsch climbed behind the wheel again, he said, 'I see that Mrs Jarmyn's back.'

'Haven't seen hide or hair of her,' Jonas said, turning back to his firewood and his empty house.

Hirsch returned to town thinking that at least he had warm hours ahead, dinner and a sleepover in the little house on Bitter Wash Road.

29

At seven o'clock Hirsch was halfway through a game of snap with Katie Street when she said: 'Ms Ogilvie told me another lightbulb joke. She said you'd appreciate it.'

Hirsch was on high alert. He gave a formless smile. 'Okay, hit me.'

'How many cops does it take to screw in a light bulb?'

'Several,' Hirsch said. 'One to answer the call-out, a senior officer to kick the matter upstairs, someone at the Department of Public Prosecutions to—'

'Sometimes, Aitch, you're not that funny.'

'Okay, how many cops?'

'None. It turned itself in.' Pause. 'I've heard better ones.'

'Me, too,' Hirsch agreed.

They were on the sitting room floor with a deck of cards on the coffee table, Wendy clattering in the kitchen. Hirsch mapped her movements absently. The soft slap of table mats and the harder clunk of knife, fork, side plate. Three settings. The solid thump of a wine bottle. Water poured into tumblers.

'That dog,' Hirsch said. 'Is it new?'

A velvety tan soft toy perched on the mantelpiece behind Katie. A white patch over one eye, white paws and white tail tip. Looking over the room benignly. Hirsch quite liked it, had been eyeing it since he arrived and was only now getting around to asking about it.

'Ms Ogilvie gave it to me for my birthday. If you shake it, it says, "Walkies?"'

'Huh.'

'Do you like it? I like it,' Katie said, swivelling for a quick, confirming glance before shuffling the cards again.

'I do like it,' Hirsch said. Now Clara's worming her way into *their* lives? he thought.

Then Wendy entered in her challenging, inquisitive way. 'Right, who's for dinner?'

'Just when I was winning,' Katie said.

'A temporary glitch,' Hirsch said.

Wendy came in behind her daughter, leaned down, planted a kiss on the top of her head. 'Now you,' she said, heading for Hirsch.

He tipped up his face to receive it. His life had felt scattered until a year ago, full of small moments—many of them missteps—rather than great purpose. He puckered up. She ran her hand over his cheek. 'You shaved,' she murmured, and they both knew what that was code for.

Dinner was Irish stew and gossip and work talk, within limits.

'Heard anything more about the girl in the caravan?'

Wendy, question asked, chomped and smiled and Katie

chased a carrot dice with her fork. Hirsch tasted his wine, a Clare Valley shiraz. 'Far as I know,' he said, 'she's still in hospital. Psychologists, nutritionists, I suppose. But I think Mrs Jarmyn's home.'

'Poor thing,' Wendy said, and Hirsch didn't know which of the Jarmyns she meant.

'And the husband?'

'Haven't been able to track him down,' Hirsch said.

A car passed on Bitter Wash Road, slowing as if to evaluate a light burning in the darkness of a quiet back road, and Wendy saw the tension in Hirsch, his bottom jaw pausing, head tilted. Then the car accelerated and presently he returned to the food on his plate and she saw that, too.

'Everything all right?'

'Sure.'

She said, 'Aitch,' with the flattest of looks.

Mother as well as daughter called him 'Aitch' these days. In fondness, but also when they wanted him to pay attention. Hirsch looked at Wendy across the table, her face set as she waited for him to respond.

'Yeah?'

But then she seemed to have second thoughts. The opacity deepened and she speared a cube of lamb and said, 'Nothing.'

They ate and the silence deepened, until Katie said, 'I saw Mrs Ayliffe on TV.'

Relief all round. 'I saw it, too,' Hirsch said.

'She was kinda, I don't know, kinda saying Josh should think about what he's doing,' Katie said.

'You're not dumb.'

'No, she isn't,' Wendy said, snaking her hand between water jug and salt and pepper pots to Hirsch's. 'And neither am I.'

She wasn't talking about any media conference analysis. They resumed eating and the kitchen bench cordless phone rang. Katie jumped to her feet. 'I'll get it!'

Hirsch thought nothing of that until he saw how still Wendy was. Listening.

Katie returned to the table. 'Another hang-up.'

'You've been getting hang-ups?'

Wendy said, some acid in it, 'We have, Paul. One a night since last weekend.'

She was saying: *There's something you're not telling us.*

Deep in the night, Hirsch confessed.

Wendy listened, lying on her back, concentrating as if she had her arms folded. When he was finished, she was clear and adamant. 'For a start,' she said, 'you need to take out an intervention order.'

The darkness enfolded them in the bed and the wind rattled the window and Hirsch snuggled close to her, seeking comfort. 'She'd feel humiliated,' he said.

'Fuck that, Aitch,' Wendy said, and her bones were unyielding. 'You're being too nice. Forget her hurt feelings.'

This was a strict and maternal kind of love and Hirsch couldn't bear it. He wanted to forget Clara Ogilvie for a few hours. Women are better at making hard judgments, he thought; hard decisions. They know when to save and salvage, and they know when to cut their losses and move on. 'What if she goes completely off the rails?'

A faint yielding in Wendy's body, as if she regretted her harshness. Relieved, he ran a palm over one of her breasts; felt the nipple rise into his hand.

But she wasn't ready for anything weak or soft to fall into line. She grabbed his wrist very firmly and gave him back his hand. 'Why did you take so long to tell me what was happening? Are we in a relationship or not?'

He struggled to answer adequately. He told the truth. 'I thought I could handle it. I thought it was just a phase, just her having a bit of a crush on me. I thought it was harmless.'

Wendy accepted that. He could tell from the responsiveness of her body beside him. It was as if her flesh could love, ignore or rebuke as effectively as her eyes, her voice.

'And I thought it would upset things at work for you,' he went on. 'You have to see her every day. And I hated the thought of her having to leave her job or move away or go to court or jail or anything like that.'

Wendy turned onto her hip to face him and she was warm, she soaked him up. 'The thing is, it's having an effect on you. You're tense. Forgetful. And that business with the old man and his trailer: what if you mess up again?'

'I know.'

'I can tell you've become hyper-vigilant—I have, myself, just from a few hang-up phone-calls. You seem heaps more obsessive and withdrawn. What if it leads to depression? Do you feel depressed?'

That shocked him. 'Umm, bit panicky,' he admitted. 'I've had one or two panic attacks.'

He wanted to touch her, but she went on in her practical way. 'Awareness is an important first step. When Glen died, I was a mess for quite a while. It wasn't good for Katie. I started seeing a really good therapist and she said I don't have to stop thinking about him, just start asking myself, does it improve my life to dwell on him so much, what can I be doing instead, what's most important, where do my responsibilities lie.'

Hirsch knew full well how lovely Wendy Street was—in all respects. Sentimental, unsentimental, wise. And he was just another man, floundering. He hugged her tight and presently they made love and it salved him, to a degree; brought him back. Then she fell asleep and in the deepening hours he asked himself what mattered most. The answer included being a good copper and recognising that he was loved, and ranged all the way down to being able to do something as small and pleasurable as giving Wendy's kid a bike for her birthday.

Then a random thought, a strange tension growing, and it wasn't panic. The talking dog on the mantelpiece. At the very darkest hour of that night he made his way to the sitting room and took down the dog and squeezed it and it said, 'Walkies?' And he was squeezing the abdomen, feeling for the voicebox, and he was examining the bead eyes by the spill-over light from the hallway, and suddenly Wendy was there, shivering, saying, 'What on earth are you doing?'

He waggled the dog in the space between them. And her mind was quick. A speculative look hardened her bleary face. 'Spy camera?' she said.

30

Sunday morning was storm-tossed. Bark scraps, leaves and petals riding the wind, Hirsch daydreamed in the sunroom while the others slept. A grey day until sunlight broke through and banded the earth—and he barely registered it before clouds closed over again. He saw, without seeing it, a willie wagtail ride the slender branch of a little silver princess gum. He was incurious about a stubby red drum-shaped object caught against the side fence. A floppy-eared soft toy was what he saw. And a Hollywood psycho blonde snarling out of the darkness, light glinting on the blade in her hand.

Then the little red drum was picked up and bowled along by a wind shift and it was only the plastic bucket from the back veranda. That woke him up. Hirsch fixed another coffee, fetched the toy dog from the mantelpiece, returned to the sunroom. The house creaked around him. The dog squeaked, 'Walkies!' as he kneaded the abdomen, his fingers tracing a well-padded rectangular shape. Most spy cameras transmit to a nearby receiver. Wondering where it was, he pulled on his jacket and prowled around the house, peering up at the eaves, under the veranda, inside the garden shed.

Nothing. Freezing now, he went back inside. Wherever the receiver was, had it been Clara's intention to retrieve it in the dead of night, when mother and daughter were asleep? Or during the day when no one was at home? And what kind of footage did she hope to find? Wendy beating her daughter? Wendy and Hirsch pashing on the sofa? Katie watching TV or doing her homework? She couldn't have been sure that Katie wouldn't toss the toy into her wardrobe.

Now Hirsch examined the stitched seams of the dog. Picked at them experimentally. One proved to be a Velcroed flap, and there in a pocket of foam was a small black box with a tiny lid over a battery compartment. The hoodwinked owner would simply believe it was the voicebox. No need to remove it. Maybe lift the lid to replace the battery once or twice a year, that was about it.

Hirsch tugged; it came free; he turned it over. There was an SD slot on the hidden side. So there was no remote receiver, storage was on the SD card. You'd slot it into your computer and play back the recorded footage. How on earth did Clara expect to gain regular access to the dog? Find an excuse to visit the Streets every day?

He couldn't work it out; he returned to his formless daydreaming. But thoughts of Wendy intruded. Her anger last night, raw and vengeful, as she took in the enormity of a spy camera in her house.

'That fucking bitch.' Wendy rarely swore. 'What does she think she's playing at?'

Hirsch gave her his opinion: there was an emptiness in Clara Ogilvie's life. Or realising she couldn't have him, or wasn't having any luck getting him, she wanted to know more about the opposition.

Wendy had clicked on that. 'Opposition. As in, feed her hate. Learn where Katie and I are vulnerable.'

Hirsch had conceded it.

'Arrest her, Paul. Chuck her in jail. Throw the book at her.'

'She needs help.'

'Yes, she needs help, but who's going to convince her of that?'

She saw the look on his face and added: 'She needs to be shaken out of her delusions. Arrest her, charge her. This'— Wendy pointed at the toy dog—'is serious.'

They'd taken the argument back to bed with them.

Wendy emerged at 10.00 a.m., came in silently and kissed the top of his head. He stood, they embraced, they found the ways to say they were sorry.

'I need coffee.'

'I'll make it,' Hirsch said.

She was there in the kitchen wherever he turned, getting in his way, trying to explain herself. 'I've been thinking about what you said. She does need help.'

'Yes,' he said.

'Otherwise she could lose her job. Big media splash.'

'Yes.' Hirsch told her about the inadequacies of the spy camera. 'I have no idea what she hoped to record or how she hoped to access it—let alone what she'd do with it.'

'Is she, whatever the term is, unstable?'

'Who knows? It's not rational behaviour, that's for sure—but perhaps rational to her.'

'Would a reality check work?'

Hirsch ducked around Wendy for the milk in the fridge door. 'What kind of reality check?'

'Realising that you're unattainable. Absolutely unattainable.'

That stopped Hirsch. 'You'd think she'd have twigged by now.'

Wendy was in a silk dressing gown of many colours. It vitalised her. Now she took her left hand from a deep pocket and displayed her fingers.

Hirsch took a moment. He said, 'I don't recall proposing marriage in the middle of the night...'

'It's mine. I stopped wearing it a couple of years ago.'

They were silent and they thought, in their separate ways, about the man now dead who'd given her the engagement ring.

'Don't worry, it's just a stupid thought I had, middle-of-the-night brainwave.'

'My life is full of those,' Hirsch said. 'You were thinking you'd let Clara see you wearing the ring at work?'

'Actually go around to her house and wave it in her face,' Wendy said. 'Insist she stop what she's doing. And look—you and I are engaged.'

She paused. 'Luckily, I came to my senses.' She laughed, an unhappy bark. 'Here we are, wanting to change her behaviour, and the opposite's happening, she's changing *our* behaviour, we're buying into her madness.'

Hirsch wrapped her tight.

'We should still go and talk to Clara,' Wendy said, her mouth against his chest. 'Today.'

'I think she's at her mother's,' Hirsch said, going on the explain.

Wendy went rigid. 'Her mother died last year. She told me about it at the time. She had to take a few days off.'

They dropped Katie at a friend's house near the Redruth mine museum and drove the short distance to Hayle, one of the original settlements among the little hills that ringed the town. They were in Wendy's Golf, not his Nissan.

She wasn't speaking, and that unnerved Hirsch a little. He said conversationally, 'You've been to her place before?'

Wendy gave a little shake, as if emerging from sleep. Slowing for a man on a mobility scooter, she said, 'It's a granny flat behind someone's house.' Pause. 'A bit depressing.'

Hirsch realised that with the abatement of her anger, Wendy had begun to see the paltry dimensions of Clara Ogilvie's life: a lonely woman, a little unhinged, looking for love but going about it the wrong way. And living in two or three rooms originally tacked onto the back of a house for an elderly relative, now dead.

Clara was home; Wendy had called to check. Maybe she's usually home, Hirsch thought, as the car took them uphill into a network of little streets. He pictured her seated in a corner, her face flickering in his imagination: gleeful, hurt, wily, open, pensive.

And right now she was forewarned, she'd been told they were coming.

'Aitch, it's only fair,' Wendy had said.

Hirsch was more for the police approach—a surprise raid—but hadn't quibbled.

The house was on a street lined with huge silvery gum trees that seemed too grand for the modest Californian bungalows behind them. Wendy parked and Hirsch followed her down a driveway and around a carport to a sodden, weedy back lawn. Here the ground sloped away steeply, so that Clara's flat stuck out from the rear of the house above an open brick storage bay: lawnmower, rubbish and compost bins, garden tools. Concrete steps and a rickety black wrought-iron handrail led to a water-damaged plywood door. Hirsch guessed at the view from the rooms up there: damp backyards, tree canopies and rooftops.

Carrying the spy-camera toy dog, he followed Wendy up the algae-slick steps. Wendy knocked. Clara appeared, hectic and warm. 'Come in out of the cold!'

She speaks in exclamation marks, Hirsch thought, following both women into a small living room. Clara gestured. 'Sit, sit.'

She'd effaced herself. Baggy jeans and woollen jumper; Ugg boots; no makeup; hair pulled back so tightly it stretched her face. 'Tea? Coffee?'

'We're fine.'

Hirsch looked around at Ikea-style bookshelves, a small TV, a laptop on a card table in the corner and three old club chairs.

Clara saw him examining a Turkish rug that took up most of the floorspace. 'Like it?'

'It's lovely.'

'It's about the only rug my husband—*ex*-husband—didn't pull out from under me.' It was obviously a well-rehearsed quip. Steadfastly not looking at the dog in Hirsch's hands, she added, 'Sit, for heaven's sake.'

He sat in one of the chairs, thinking about the ex-husband. A gambler, or so Wendy had heard.

Wendy, taking one of the other chairs, said, 'Clara, there's something we need to talk to you about.'

Now Ogilvie eyed the floppy-eared dog, all her bounciness gone. 'What?'

'Please sit.'

'I'll stand, thanks.'

So Hirsch and Wendy got to their feet again and they found themselves at three remote points of the room, or so it seemed.

'I think you know why we're here, Clara,' Hirsch said. 'Things like this toy dog'—he set it down on the coffee table, a slab of cold, clean glass—'and the texts, the phone calls, the running into each other all the time. It has to stop.'

Feeling behind her carefully for a chair, Clara sat. One after the other, they followed suit.

Her expression wasn't insensate, exactly—there was a touch of dignity in it, if anything. It was as if she feared she'd provoke further accusations if she showed her emotions. They waited.

'You think it was inappropriate of me to give Katie a birth-day present?'

'With a spy camera in it? Come on, Clara,' Wendy said.

'I beg your pardon?'

'What did you think you were going to see?'

'I don't know what you're talking about.'

Hirsch found himself nodding. How often did the police hear that? Only every day of their working lives.

Wendy went on: 'It has to stop, Clara. It's bad for you, it's bad for us. It's wrong. It's also illegal. What on earth is the point of it?'

Clara Ogilvie said, 'This posturing is unattractive in you, Wendy. I'm disappointed, frankly. And I'd like you both to leave now.'

A tormented rip as Hirsch undid the Velcro flap. He removed the little box and pulled out the SD card. 'We haven't watched what's recorded on this, not that it would be of any interest to anyone. What the fuck, Clara? Did you think it through? How were you going to get hold of the recording, for a start?'

She was still channelling the victim of a cruel injustice. 'I have no idea what you're talking about, cards and recordings and whatnot. I bought a talking dog for a child I'm fond of. So what?' Something slipped in behind her guileless eyes. 'A child whose wellbeing I have sometimes wondered about.'

The universe tilted and Wendy said, 'Oh, you bitch.'

Hirsch, looking around the room again, saw dogs. A little pastel drawing on one wall, glass and china dogs, even two velour basset hounds asleep in a toy basket in the corner.

Barking mad, he thought.

'Clara,' Wendy said, 'you do know Paul would be within his rights to charge you for this? Stalking him? Installing a spy camera in my place? The courts take things like that seriously. And think of the public humiliation. Your name in the paper. You could easily lose your job. It has to stop.'

Hirsch, looking at Ogilvie, saw a glitter of spite and decided to cut in. Offer her a good-choice, bad-choice scenario, he thought; see what happens. 'This isn't really about you stalking us and breaking the law, though, Clara. It's about your needs as a person, right? Everybody needs love... and, er, appreciation.'

Wendy wanted to glare, he could tell, but thought better of it. They both watched Ogilvie.

She rubbed her face with both hands. 'You don't know what it's like,' she said eventually, a whine of entreaty in her voice. 'I'm so lonely! I can't meet anyone. Just these idiot hayseeds and drones like Den Quigley. Don't you think I'd like a normal life? A child? Someone I can love? Someone to love me?'

She was rocking in her chair, a huge overstuffed old thing that diminished her. 'That damn dog!' She dropped her hands from her face and pointed at the toy. 'I just went on eBay and bought it and realised I had no idea how I was even going to use it.'

She flopped back, depleted.

'I'm sorry. I'll stop, I promise. I'll move away. Find another school. Please don't take this any further.'

There was nothing they could say to that. Wendy and Hirsch stood to leave, and for a brief moment it seemed that the two women would embrace. Hirsch slipped on the steps going down, clutched the loose handrail for dear life and almost kicked Wendy in the back as Clara's voice drifted from above: 'Paul, I do hope you keep singing. Wendy, I didn't mean it, you're a wonderful person, a wonderful mother.'

They both kept their backs to her, negotiating the treachery underfoot: they couldn't read her face at all.

In the car, Wendy said, 'What were we thinking?'

31

Hirsch returned to Tiverton late afternoon, knowing he'd need an early start on Monday. He'd just rolled into town, through the long shadows cast by the silos and past the Sunday-quiet, tucked-away houses, when he spotted Ed Tennant standing with his assistant, Gemma Pitcher, and a couple of others outside the police station. Swivelling their gaze from the building itself to his police Toyota, which he'd left at the kerb. Then, as he slowed and turned in off the highway, they were staring at him in his clapped-out Nissan.

As soon as he'd parked, he saw what they'd been looking at: blood-red slogans dripping on the front wall and on the inside flank of the Toyota. He switched off, got out and checked the building first:

A hard and impenitent heart, a worshiper of the beast.

Shouldn't that be a double *p*? Hirsch turned to the Toyota. *Imperfect man depart from me.*

Gladly, thought Hirsch. One thing was clear: Clara Ogilvie

hadn't been here with a spray can—unless she was subcontracting her loony obsession. He gave the little throng a sunny smile and said, 'Caught you all red-handed.'

Waited a beat. Nope, this mob didn't appreciate his jokes either. Maybe Gemma did: he saw a shift in her eyes from awe and bemusement to a kind of appreciation.

She said, 'You been upsetting the Callithumpians?'

She thought there was a religious-nutter element to this? Could be right. 'Been upsetting someone,' he said.

None of the Toyota's tyres was flat, but he knelt anyway. The valve stems were unmarked. Then he creaked to his feet again, spat on a corner of his handkerchief and rubbed at the capital *I*. Water-based paint, thank God.

'I'll help,' Gemma said, then his other neighbours went to fetch rags and buckets of warm, soapy water and helped him clean off the graffiti, before saying their goodbyes as the shadows lengthened and the light slid away, leaving Hirsch alone in the pokey rooms that were his home.

A call from Sergeant Brandl before he left for Redruth, Monday morning. The doctor said she'd overdone it and had to take a couple of days off.

'Help the Homicide Squad set up in the briefing room,' she said. 'And keep the world safe.'

'No pressure, then,' Hirsch said.

A team from the Homicide Squad reached Redruth from Adelaide at 10.00 a.m. Six officers in two cars: a senior sergeant named Stolte, a collator, and four senior constables, all about Hirsch's age. He set them up in the briefing room—phones, their own laptops, two whiteboards—and received no thanks for it, only a grilling that lasted until late morning. They wanted facts, they were even open to speculations, but their expressions were flat, eyes grey as river stones. As if they neither believed nor disbelieved, trusted nor distrusted. They asked all the right questions, though.

After that, he was released to run the police station. 'Don't get in our way and we'll get along fine,' said Stolte, a paunchy, harried-looking man.

So Hirsch got out of the way. As far as he could tell, Stolte and the collator would run the investigation and file the results, while one pair of detectives questioned suspects and witnesses within the station and the other pair pursued a roving brief outside the station—meaning the bank, he assumed, the Rhynie Road corner shop, the lawyer's office, and perhaps the homes of Maggie Groote, Amy Groote, and John and Sylvia Fearn.

He received one text, just before lunch. Wendy, saying that Clara Ogilvie had quit. *Came in, collected her things, left. End of.* Hirsch was certain that those things had happened. He was less certain that was the end of it.

Amy Groote was interviewed first. She gave Hirsch a look of peevish befuddlement as she strode into the police station. She'd dressed up—a long dress and a tailored jacket—but looked ungainly, smudged. As if heart, body and soul were still in her side yard, digging out weeds. She didn't speak to him as she was ushered through to the rear of the police station; merely asked a detective if she needed a lawyer before she was sealed behind the interview-room door.

They released her at 12.30 and she hissed at Hirsch on her way out, 'A waste of time. A complete abrogation of my rights.'

He didn't reply. She hadn't expected a reply.

He was chatting to Ron Pickett at the front counter when John and Sylvia Fearn arrived. Typically neat as two pins, they were bereft of their poise now. Tidy still, but formless, as if clean hands, combed hair, good clobber were their only resources.

The interviewers took Sylvia in first. Hirsch, seeing John standing irresolute, said, 'Come and sit here, Mr Fearn.'

The waiting area was opposite the reception desk: two stackable plastic chairs, one with a widening split in the seat, under a rack of brochures and community notices. Fearn gazed at it. 'I'll stand, thanks.'

Hirsch shrugged. He'd come in for a file related to the probable theft of a stud ram worth $72,500. Sold by a breeder in Hallett to a breeder near Farrell Flat in a deal brokered by Adrian Quinlan. He closed the filing cabinet, turned to open the door leading to the main part of the station, and caught an expression on Fearn's face. Vulnerable? Haunted? It was there and gone again.

Using his brisk official voice, Hirsch said, 'Tea, Mr Fearn? Coffee?'

Fearn blinked. 'Coffee would be good.'

'I'll take you through to the tearoom,' Hirsch said.

Maybe he'd break the case. Maybe he wouldn't. Maybe all

he'd do was rattle the man and add another layer of grime to his soul with his devious cop games.

The tearoom was barely larger than an ensuite bathroom: sink, bench, cupboards, a scarred laminate table and three chairs. An empty kitty jar. Sticky tape on the walls where Christmas tinsel had hung until at least April. A sign curling in the steam above the urn: 'Treat this room as you would your own kitchen.' Well, they'd done that. Crumbs; turdy little dried-out teabags on saucers; unwashed cups and mugs.

'Must get the cleaners in,' Hirsch said brightly, but before he could start opening and closing cupboard doors and tossing Fearn the kinds of questions that might get him talking, his phone rang: Amy Groote.

'I need to take this, Mr Fearn.'

'John.' He paused. 'Why don't I make the coffee?'

'White, strong,' Hirsch said.

He walked through to the back door of the police station, a region of cheerless scuffed walls and chilly air. 'Ms Groote?'

'Did you put them up to it?'

Background noise, a low rumble. She's driving, he thought. 'Amy, it's out of my hands. Your aunt's death is being treated as suspicious, and that means questioning everyone close to her. You, Mr and Mrs Fearn, her lawyer, people at the bank...'

'I was in bed when the fire happened. You saw me.'

'Not quite accurate,' Hirsch said. 'I saw you afterwards.'

'Splitting hairs,' Amy Groote said. 'I don't tell lies, constable.'

He shrugged inwardly. It was possible that Amy Groote

didn't, in fact, ever lie; but she could be evasive. The way her eyes slid away when he'd mentioned the slogans painted on the windfarm turbines.

'Is it true about the will?' she said.

Hirsch hesitated. What will had the Homicide Squad detectives referred to when they questioned her? The earlier one, in their bland, devious way? To gauge her reaction?

'I can't comment on that, Amy.'

'Why not?' Sudden anguished sobs halted her voice. 'Oh, suit yourself. Everyone does.'

'Where are you?'

'What do you care?'

Hirsch realised he knew very little about her. Her life before she'd moved north; where she'd lived, who she'd been married to, her job...

'Is there someone you can call when you get home? Maybe—'

'They asked me what I did with the money. *What money?* Was someone ripping Aunt Maggie off?'

'I really can't comment, Amy.'

'Useless.' Hirsch heard a downshift of gears, acceleration, and then Groote went on: 'I'll have you know I don't believe in internet banking. Too risky. The internet's almost non-existent at the cottage anyway and Aunt Maggie could barely do anything beyond email on her computer. What I'm saying is, I had no online access to her accounts and I doubt she did either. Those neighbours of hers, though, that's a different kettle of fish. Probably offered to handle all that kind of thing for her. I mean, have you even checked?'

'I'm sure everything's being looked into.'

'I don't mean those police there today—they clearly didn't believe me—I mean *you*.'

'Amy, you've mentioned undue influence several times. Do you have hard evidence of that? Or is it gut feeling?'

A pause that told Hirsch she had suspicions, not proof. 'You don't believe me either.'

The icy morning air was seeping into Hirsch the longer he stood beside the back door. 'Look, if it's just a feeling you had, it must've come from somewhere?'

'Auntie Maggie said Sylvia would write things down for her so she wouldn't get muddled. And Sylvia told her to cancel some of the charities she gave to, said there were people better off than her to support things like the lost dogs' home, et cetera, et cetera. And then she told me she didn't feel pressured by the Fearns when I hadn't even asked, she just volunteered it, and I wondered if that meant in the back of her mind she did feel pressured. Another time she said, "I want my money to go to people I know"—and that was out of nowhere too. As if she was arguing with herself.'

That was Amy Groote's way of saying goodbye. Hirsch made a mental note to call in on her later and returned to the tearoom, where John Fearn was seated at the little table, blowing across the surface of his coffee and jiggling his leg.

'Didn't know how much milk to put in.'

Too much, by the look of it. 'That's fine,' Hirsch said, sitting opposite.

'Did we really have to come in? Couldn't they have talked to us at the house?'

Hirsch sipped his coffee—weak, lukewarm—and set the mug down. 'There's nothing to be worried about, Mr Fearn. They need to speak to everyone concerned. Standard procedure.'

'You didn't answer my question.'

'Manpower limitations, that's all,' Hirsch said.

He wanted to get Fearn talking but would need to be very careful. He couldn't second-guess or circumvent the Homicide Squad: he'd risk alerting Fearn and be hauled over the coals himself. Even innocuous questions could be construed as relating to the Fearns' relationship with Maggie Groote.

Keep it circumspect. 'I didn't know Mrs Groote all that well, but she struck me as a nice woman.'

Fearn laughed sourly. 'She could be an old witch.'

Hirsch sipped his disgusting coffee. 'Like I said, I only knew her in passing. I expect you've known her for years.'

'*Neighbours* for years. Not the same thing.'

Hirsch said, 'True.'

'Right now my wife is telling your colleagues just exactly what kind of woman she really was.'

Hirsch stroked his jaw. 'I see.'

'I know what you're thinking, what a stupid thing to be telling them—motive, right? But we talked it over.'

Hirsch saw a flicker of doubt. Maybe the wife had talked it over, but he didn't think the husband had. Trouble in paradise, obviously—but which paradise? Their marriage? Their relationship with Maggie Groote?

Hirsch said nothing and eventually John Fearn filled the silence, his voice low, almost inaudible: 'Wouldn't have killed Sylvia to go and help her.'

Say nothing, Hirsch warned himself. He raised a questioning eyebrow.

'Maggie called us the other day. She'd fallen over in the bathroom. Sylvia said, "Let's just see what happens." Quote, unquote.'

John Fearn. A round, soft, man. An overgrown schoolboy with a lifelong habit of throwing his pals under the bus to deflect blame.

How to tell Stolte's crew? Hirsch wondered.

Speak of the devil. Voices in the corridor, a shape looming, cutting half the light. 'There you are,' Stolte said, arms propped on either side of the door. 'We've got a missing bank teller.'

32

Still hooked to the door frame, he realised Hirsch wasn't alone. 'Sir, may I ask who you are?'

'John Fearn.'

There was something shadowy and unreadable in the look that Stolte shot Hirsch. He said to Fearn, 'Then I must ask you to wait at the front desk until we call you.'

Fearn left the table and, drawing in his shoulders, sidled past the senior sergeant, who stepped back into the hallway to watch his progress through the police station. 'Keep going, sir, through that door. Yep, that's the one.'

Then Stolte was standing over Hirsch, taking up all the air. 'You were questioning him?'

'I offered him a coffee, senior sergeant, that's all. We barely spoke.'

Stolte wasn't mollified. 'Why would you bring a civilian back here? Who, by the way, is awaiting questioning as an interested party to a suspicious death?'

Fuck it. Hirsch stood, and now they were eye to eye. 'I

was careful not to mention any of that, senior sergeant.'

Stolte looked as if he hadn't finished, but he changed tack. 'This teller: she didn't return from lunch. My people are there interviewing the manager, but they'd wanted to interview her first.'

'Sophie Flynn?'

'Yes.'

Hirsch rinsed both coffee mugs, dried his hands on a rank tea towel. 'Did she know you wanted to talk to her?'

'We confirmed it with both of them late morning. I'm stretched. I need you to track her down,' Stolte said.

Hirsch called Sophie's mobile: voicemail.

Then he called the bank. The older teller answered and gave her name as Tina Russo. Sophie almost always ate a cut lunch in the tearoom, she said. 'She's saving up for an overseas holiday.'

'And the times she doesn't eat there?'

'She and I go out sometimes, usually on a Friday.'

'The deli?'

'Usually.'

'Anywhere else?'

'Pub lunch once or twice. Her birthday. Mine.'

'Do you know where she lives?'

An address in Kooringa, thirteen kilometres south of Redruth.

'She lives with a partner? Friends?'

Tina laughed. 'She still lives with her parents. She's just a kid.'

'Do you have a number?'

'I've already rung it. No answer, so I doubt Sophie's there. Both her parents work in Clare and I don't have their numbers.'

But Hirsch would need to check. Leaving Tim Medlin temporarily in charge of the police station, he and Jean Landy took the Redruth patrol car to Kooringa, Landy driving, Hirsch checking the on-board computer terminal. Sophie Flynn owned a blue 2009 Jetta: a VW, but not a late-model silver Passat by any stretch.

On an impulse, he checked the manager, Cater: a black 2016 Volvo SUV.

He pushed the terminal back against the dash. Sat and thought as Jean took them through flat, sodden farmland. He barely registered the damp highway rushing at him, the wintry greenness slipping past. He didn't stir until clumps of trees appeared above the ribbon of bitumen, then rooftops clarified, hedges, low-slung garden walls. *Kooringa. Population 19.*

Jean Landy seemed to rouse too. 'What's the thinking?'

'I don't want to think Sophie had any part in Mrs Groote's death,' Hirsch said. 'That's my thinking.'

'Looks suspicious, though. Told to make herself available for interview by the Homicide Squad, she does a runner.'

'In my role as mentor to young and/or inexperienced constables,' Hirsch said, 'I would like to suggest that there is such a thing as being too suspicious.'

'You?' She knew his bullshit by now. 'You're suspicious of everything.'

What Hirsch suspected right now wasn't Sophie Flynn's guilt but something more unpleasant.

The house was anomalous: about twenty years old, sprawling, possibly constructed of mudbrick or rammed earth, with a line of north-facing clerestory windows along the shallow roofline. A couple of older gum trees at the rear. In the front, newer, smaller gums of the weeping variety, along with native shrubs, grasses and ground creepers in garden beds bracketed by redgum sleepers. A short driveway led to a closed garage at the side of the house.

They parked in the street, Jean saying, 'Doesn't look like anyone's home.'

'But we check,' Hirsch said, getting out of the car.

Landy followed him along a path of small flagstones and collided with him when he halted abruptly, one hand up. 'Hear that?'

A motor running, muffled. Coming from inside the garage? Hirsch veered off the path and pulled on the door handle. Locked.

There would be side-door access from inside the house, he thought. From the kitchen? He eyed the shed again. Maybe there was a window on the hidden side, or the rear.

By now Jean Landy was pounding on the front door. She tried the knob, knocked again, and a dog flung itself against the door, a frenzy of barking.

'Shit.' She recoiled in alarm.

'We'll try the back,' Hirsch said.

'You go in first. Dogs don't like me.'

'So much to learn about police work,' chided Hirsch. Not so much of the light touch this time.

He wondered later if the dog was smart. It fell silent, as if tracking their progress down along the side of the house and up onto a set of concrete steps leading to the back door. It remained silent when Hirsch knocked, waited, and finally opened the door.

Opened it wider. No scrabbling claws or bared teeth or barrelling body. He stepped over the threshold, into a dim kitchen. He registered these things: a door to the garage; chairs at skewed angles to a table and one on the floor; a blood smear on a floor tile and the tap lever; the sound of the motor clearer now.

He took another step, Jean hard on his heels. Now the dog charged, a lump of short-haired black muscle rocketing across the room at them from a passageway in the inner wall. Landy yelped, flung herself out onto the back steps and slammed the door. Then, looking mortified, she reopened the door a notch, her head in the gap, the tip of her pistol probing the room as Hirsch fended off the dog with a chair.

He spotted her. Backing towards the garage door he shouted, 'No shooting—ricochets! See if you can distract it.'

She didn't reholster her pistol but stepped into the kitchen and whistled, the fingers of her free hand to her lips. Hirsch took a moment to appreciate the sound: a lovely, piercing rip in the air. He'd never been able to whistle like that. As the dog swung around on her, a quivering vision of teeth and drool, Hirsch took the opportunity to retreat and open the door to the garage. The last thing he saw was

Jean giving him a thumbs-up as she slipped outside, the dog slamming after her.

Hirsch didn't know how much time he had. The air was thick; he was cooking in the poisonous exhaust of Sophie Flynn's blue Jetta. Taking a breath, holding it, he jerked open the driver's door and switched the engine off. Then he raced to the garage door, pressed a wall switch, and as it rose and sweet air poured in, he returned to the car.

Sophie was slumped at the wheel, her seatbelt fastened.

Seatbelt?

Three of the car's side windows were fully closed. The fourth showed a small gap stuffed with rags and one end of a hose, the other end attached to the exhaust. Hirsch had studied suicides at the police academy. Not many women chose this method. He touched Sophie's neck, her wrists. He was certain she was dead. She'd probably died within minutes, but could have been here for up to an hour.

On the seat next to her, a couple of bank statements. Hirsch didn't touch them, just leaned across Sophie's body for a closer look. Saw the name Margaret Groote, the Rhynie Road address. A balance of $260,500 in March; $100,000 withdrawn in May and again in July; $50,000 withdrawn at the beginning of August. Then $7,500 for the conmen.

Hirsch, trying to breathe shallowly, felt sleepy. He wanted to drag Sophie out onto the grass but knew he should leave her intact, and then the decision was removed from him as the dog came skidding into the shed. He barely had time to clamber onto the workbench before it lunged at his thigh. It tried to scrabble onto the bench. He grabbed a hammer from a peg on the wall, feeling the impulse to bash its brains in, but there was a little window, just below the roofline, and he smashed out the glass and drank sweet air again. He was sleepy; been inhaling carbon monoxide. He might just succumb and fall to the ground and become tucker for that damn dog.

He fumbled out his phone, called Landy and said dazedly, 'Where are you?'

'Back in the house. I was behind the door and when the dog shot right past me, down the steps, I went back inside and shut the door on it. Look out for it, Paul.'

'Yeah, well, it's found me,' Hirsch said.

'You okay?'

'I'm standing on a bench in the garage. Sophie Flynn's here, dead in her car, carbon monoxide poisoning. We need to call a few people.'

It was decided that she would call an ambulance, Dr Pillai and a vet. He would call Stolte and the bank.

Stolte first.

'You're sure she's dead?'

'Yes.'

'Absolutely sure? Check again.'

Hirsch explained about the dog. 'If the vet can tranquilise the dog, then yes, I'll check for a pulse. But I think she's been in the car for a very long time.'

'Shoot the dog.'

'I am not shooting the dog,' Hirsch said. 'There are houses nearby. And it's only doing what dogs do. Plus I think we'll find forensic traces on it. Blood and fibres.'

'Your thinking is...?'

'She was murdered. Made to look like a suicide. The dog attacked whoever killed her.'

Hirsch cut the call before Stolte could run a string of objections past him. He called the bank.

'Mr Cater was here,' Tina Russo said, 'but he went out again after his police interview.'

'Did he say where?'

'No.'

'Are the detectives still there?'

'No. They said something about going to see a lawyer.' Tina paused. 'Did you find Sophie?'

Hirsch said, 'What were your impressions of Mr Cater today?'

'Mr Cater? What do you mean?'

'How did he seem? What was he wearing?'

'Now you've got me worried. He changed his suit, I know that much. He said he slipped in the mud when he went home for lunch.'

'What about his mood?'

'I'm not sure that I should be—'

Hirsch said gently, 'This is very important.'

'He seemed a bit tense about being interviewed. Who wouldn't be?'

'He changed his clothes between late morning and being interviewed?'

'That's what I said. He'd fallen over. He was limping and had bandaids on his hands.'

33

Bitten by the dog, Hirsch thought.

It was pacing below him now. Stopped, gave a queer, human-like cough, resumed pacing. Snarled if it caught Hirsch's eye. And it had the sense to keep mostly near the open door, where it took an occasional gulp of fresh air.

It seemed to know something was wrong, though. Hirsch watched it stalk down the side of the car a couple of times, in its hunch-shouldered way, stand on its hind legs and scrabble at Sophie Flynn's window glass, before sloping back to the front of the shed. And it would always return to Hirsch, stand below him and remind him he was a carcass in waiting.

Hirsch called Stolte again.

Stolte sounded like a man with too many plates in the air. 'Yes, Constable Hirschhausen?'

'The Cater interview: did your people say anything about his appearance?'

'It's one of the things we look for, you know that. Body language. Why do you ask?'

'According to the other teller, he returned from lunch limping. Bandaged hands. Wearing a different suit.'

Stolte was silent. He's absorbing it, Hirsch thought. A vehicle pulled up outside, the forest-green Nissan twin-cab that belonged to Redruth Veterinary Services. Two women got out: Cathy Duigan and a colleague. He waved but they didn't spot him there on a workbench in the dim reaches of the shed.

Stolte said, 'You think he was attacked by the dog that's got you bailed up?'

Faintly mocking. Hirsch said, 'Sophie Flynn was no embezzler. She was the one who discovered money missing from Mrs Groote's account. If Cater was behind it, maybe he felt he had to silence both Mrs Groote and Sophie—framing Sophie at the same time.'

'Can't spare anyone just this moment, we're still interviewing Sylvia Fearn,' Stolte said, as if thinking aloud, sorting through his priorities. 'Strange, not very nice woman. And my other team's up in Penhale.'

Talking to Maggie Groote's neighbours, Hirsch guessed. 'The vet's just arrived. As soon as the dog's secured, I'll go and look for Cater.'

'And?'

'Arrest him.'

'On what charge? What evidence? He could claim he slipped over in the wet.'

'At least talk to him, senior sergeant,' protested Hirsch. 'And with the greatest respect, may I suggest we get Crime Scene to look at Sophie Flynn, her car, her house—particularly the kitchen—and the dog?'

'The dog,' said Stolte flatly.

'For traces of human blood,' Hirsch said, as patiently as he could manage. 'Fibres. And maybe Cater's mobile phone will tell us if he was in Kooringa at lunchtime today.'

'Let's not get ahead of ourselves. Find Mr Cater and see what he has to say for himself. You have to admit, the dead girl does give us a plausible alternative story. She commits suicide and leaves the bank statements next to her as a kind of apology and explanation. It's not unusual for people not to leave suicide notes, as it happens.'

'I understand, but if—'

'Just go easy, okay? I'll free up some of my team when I can. I suggest you locate Mr Cater, but don't approach him. Leave that to us.'

'Senior sergeant,' Hirsch said.

Next, he called Tim Medlin; told him to go to the bank. 'See if the teller can close up. But you stay there, and don't let Cater in. Don't let anyone start shredding documents.'

'I don't know if anyone would listen to me if—'

'Tim,' Hirsch said, with some grit in it.

By now the vets had something planned. They were at the garage entrance—Cathy Duigan waving nonchalantly at Hirsch—placing a wire cage, open at one end, on the ground. The dog crouched, hackles up, as Cathy feinted with a blanket like a matador with a bull. The dog sprang—and jerked back, choking, as the other vet came in from behind with a catchpole and snared it around the neck. Now Cathy rushed in, blinded it with the blanket, and they bundled it into the cage. Inflamed, thwarted, it howled and snarled.

Hirsch climbed down, called Jean to say it was safe to come outside, and left the shed.

'Saw you perched up there,' Duigan said.

'A career highlight,' Hirsch said. 'Look, it's complicated, but there could be crucial evidence on the dog, like blood and fibres.'

She regarded him solemnly. She knew what he was asking. 'I don't like to sedate unless it's absolutely necessary.' She gestured at the cage. 'He can't harm anyone now.'

Hirsch gestured at the garage. 'Sophie Flynn's in there. She's dead. I think it was a staged suicide. I think the man who killed her was attacked by the dog.'

After a long moment, Duigan said, 'Okay. How's Hilary?'

Duigan and the sergeant often jogged together. 'She came in to work a couple of times. Still recuperating.'

'Tell her I'll visit soon,' Duigan said, preparing a syringe.

As she sedated the dog, Hirsch collected evidence bags from the police car. Then, with Hirsch, the other vet and Landy as chain of evidence witnesses, she took swabs from the dog's mouth, teeth, ruff and collar. The collar was removed, placed in a separate bag. Signed and dated.

Just then, Jean Landy leaned in. 'Look there.'

A tuft of fabric was caught on the buckle. 'Cater's suit?'

'Find the suit,' Hirsch said. 'Find the man. Not necessarily in that order.'

He called Tim Medlin. 'Anything?'

'Quiet as a mouse.'

'Is the bank open or closed?'

'Still open.'

'Put Tina Russo on,' Hirsch said.

Russo gave him Cater's address. He left Jean in charge and drove to a house on a sloping side street near four attached cottages named Tiver Row. Cater's home was built of local stone: broad and roomy, with a deep veranda and topped by a faded red roof. No Volvo in the driveway or the carport or on the street.

Hirsch got out, stood a while, surveying the house, his hands on his hips, and a voice said, 'Thinking of making an offer?'

Hirsch peered; it took a moment. Deep in the shadowy regions of an identical house next door was an elderly man in a bulky, high-backed wooden chair, a rug over his knees. He wore an overcoat and scarf, mittens on his hands and a cap with sheepskin earflaps. An outdoor gas radiator, familiar to Hirsch from sidewalk cafes in the city, hissed next to him.

'Couldn't afford it on my salary,' Hirsch said, walking the short distance along the footpath and in the old man's front gate.

'The bank owns it anyway,' the man said, viewing him wryly. He had papery thin skin, watery eyes, a faint hand tremor visible despite the mittens. 'All the managers live there.'

'Nice part of town,' Hirsch said.

The old man ignored that. 'So you're here to arrest Mal for embezzlement?'

Hirsch froze. Saw that the old geezer was joking and almost said aloud: *Among other things, sir.*

What he did say was, 'Have you seen Mr Cater today? His wife? Kids?'

'Bachelor,' the old man said. 'But I did see him an hour ago. Maybe two hours. He burned some rubbish.'

Hirsch registered it then, an acrid tinge in the air. He looked across at Cater's house.

'Not there. Here, in my backyard,' the old man said.

Seeing Hirsch's confusion, he added, 'Incinerator. An old forty-four-gallon drum. Had it forever.'

Cater incinerated the suit, thought Hirsch. 'Would you mind if I had a look?'

The man stood, twinkled at him, removed a mitten and offered a crooked hand. 'You can have a look once you're no longer a stranger. Des Mannion.'

Embarrassed, Hirsch shook and gave his name, even as a bell rang. Mail for a Desmond Mannion had been going to Rhynie Road. 'Do you bank at Mid-North, Mr Mannion?'

Mannion grabbed a walking stick. 'Not as spry as I was. Yes, I do. Malcolm persuaded me. There's a reason you're asking...?'

As Mannion turned and led the way to the front door, Hirsch said, 'We've had reports of bank statements going to the wrong address. Privacy concerns. Have you experienced missing statements, by any chance?'

'I'd better check, hadn't I?' Mannion said. 'You've got my mind working.'

He shuffled along a dark passageway, Hirsch following. The floor creaked. It was a house of heavy dark furniture and shadows. The only modern touch was the heating: hydronic panels. The air was stifling. Down a step into a kitchen, across a worn lino floor and out to the backyard. It was like any yard. Lawn, garden beds, dank little shed, rotary clothesline; a wheelbarrow propped against the back fence. An incinerator in the form of a rusty fuel drum, a curl of smoke rising.

And a car shed, oddly situated, facing the opposite side fence, not the driveway. Parked in it was a black Volvo. 'Your car, Mr Mannion?'

'Malcolm's. He's had a problem with dirty diesel, so he's borrowed my car.' Shrug. 'No difference to me. I bought a new car last year, and since then I've had both hips replaced, so it's not as if I'm going to be driving up the Birdsville Track and back.'

'Shame. What kind of car?'

'Passat. Lovely thing. An indulgence.'

'Passat,' Hirsch said. 'Silver? I'm sure I've seen it around town.'

Mannion was sharp. 'Not that often, I shouldn't think. Except a handful of times when Malcolm borrowed it.'

'Like today?'

'This morning.'

'He has a key?'

'Saves him having to knock on my door all the time. What's this about?'

'I won't lie to you, Mr Mannion. We do need to speak to Mr Cater about certain matters. I'd consider it a favour if you could call me if he shows up again, either to burn rubbish or return your car.'

They'd reached the drum. Hirsch peered in. Ash, mostly:

black, oily, lumpy. You could sift through it and find molten buttons, he supposed. A fly zip. All the dog and human evidence burnt away.

He glanced again at Cater's Volvo. 'Is there a reason why Mr Cater parks his car in your shed?'

'To keep it out of the weather. He hasn't got a shed.'

'So, it's driveable?'

'He said something about dirty fuel. It goes, but he doesn't want to rely on it. If he has to go down to Adelaide, for example.'

'He wouldn't have given you a key for it, by any chance? In case you needed to move it?'

Mannion stared at Hirsch, a line of calculation in his eyes. He said, 'Wait there,' and returned to the house. He was back a moment later. 'Help yourself,' he said, thrusting a key at Hirsch.

Hirsch thanked him, unlocked the Volvo, lifted the bonnet, disconnected a few cables and hoped for the best. The engine didn't start when he tried it, so he must have done something right.

They returned to the house. 'On second thoughts,' Hirsch said, 'perhaps there's someone you can stay with for a few hours, Mr Mannion?'

The old man said promptly, 'My daughter, at the hospital.'

The hospital's business manager, as it turned out. Hirsch drove, parked, and they went looking for the daughter. She was in her office, peering short-sightedly at a PC, and raced to the door when she saw her father there with Hirsch. Grinned and asked, 'What's he done now?'

'Robbed the bank,' Mannion said.

'Caught him after a particularly dangerous car chase,' Hirsch said.

'You wish, Dad,' the daughter said.

'This youngster wants me to lie low for a few hours.'

The woman listened attentively as Hirsch explained, and said, 'I'll dump him in with all the other old geezers here.'

'That'll be dull,' Mannion said. 'They're all senile.'

'See it as an opportunity to brag and fib and get away with it,' his daughter said.

Hirsch shook hands and returned to the HiLux to fire up the on-board terminal and issue an alert for Mannion's Passat. He'd barely entered the information when his mobile rang.

Eleanor Quinlan's voice. Sounding tense. 'Adrian?'

'Er, actually you've—'

She overrode him. 'Ade, sweetheart, I need you to come home right away, okay? Soon as you can.'

34

Hirsch opened and closed his mouth. The scope of what was happening took shape, but before he could tell Eleanor Quinlan he understood, she went on: 'Malcolm Cater's here. Ade, sweetheart, he'd like a word with you. It sounds important...Uh-huh I'll tell him. Your office at two o'clock...'

Smart woman. But Cater must have snatched the phone from her. 'Fuck that, Adrian. We meet right here, understood? Your place. I'm not budging till you get here. Fucked if I'm taking the fall for this.'

Hirsch grunted, hoping he sounded like Quinlan, and cut the connection.

The situation went downhill after that. He called Stolte's mobile: out of range or switched off. He called the station landline; according to Ron Pickett, Stolte and his detectives had just left.

'Did they say where they were going?'

'No.'

Pickett was a civilian. Hirsch couldn't leave the police station in his hands for long. Move Tim Medlin from the bank, or bring Jean Landy back from Kooringa? 'You okay holding the fort, Ron? I'll get someone there as soon as I can. You've got my number.'

Hirsch regretted not taking two vehicles to Sophie Flynn's house. Maybe Jean could hitch a ride back with the vet—if Cathy and her offsider were still there. But even if Jean left now, it could take her up to twenty minutes to reach the Quinlan house.

Tim Medlin was closer. Hirsch called, gave him the Quinlan address. 'I'll meet you there.'

Finally called Jean to tell her what he was planning, only for her to say, 'You'll never guess who showed up.'

Hirsch knew. 'Stolte and his crew.'

They must have been in a signal blackspot when he called. 'I don't have time to talk to them. Tell them I'm heading straight to Adrian Quinlan's house. His wife just called me, pretending she was calling her husband. She's under duress. Malcolm Cater is there, sounds like he's coming apart.'

'Wait for us, Paul,' Jean said, a thread of anxiety in her voice.

'I can't, no time. We know he's a killer.'

'Be careful,' she said, and Hirsch visualised the intensity in her pale features.

Drawing bleak sustenance from it, he raced down the hill, left onto the highway, left again after the town square and up to the big house on the hill.

A silver Passat parked in the street. And Tim Medlin had beaten him there.

As Hirsch reconstructed it later, Malcolm Cater had come steaming out of the house and down the driveway when Tim pulled up. And, before good sense could kick in, Tim, baby-faced, incurably polite and trusting, had got out with a warm smile of community relations, only to be spun around, slammed against his police SUV and relieved of his service pistol and handcuffs.

All Hirsch saw when he arrived was the SUV, driver's door open. A wind moaned up the hill and tossed the trees, some in new leaf. A windchill-factor day. Pallid light. He sneezed: pollen on the wind.

Then he saw that the main door to the house was also open. He went in cautiously and was almost to the end of the hallway, kitchen lights blazing ahead, the edge of the island bench visible, a pair of legs visible—a woman's, outstretched—when Cater tucked the tip of a pistol behind his ear and said, 'Remove your gun very slowly and drop it on the floor.'

He must have been behind one of the hallway doors. Hirsch sensed Cater stepping back a couple of metres, out of range of any sudden move, so he complied. The pistol landed with a soft thump on the carpet.

'Kick it away.'

Hirsch kicked it away.

'Move,' Cater said, prodding him again.

Into the kitchen. Tim lay on the floor, trussed in gaffer

tape: arms behind his back, his legs wrapped from knee to ankle. He looked up at Hirsch, red with misery and humiliation.

Cater would have forced Eleanor to bind him at gunpoint, Hirsch thought, and then to manacle herself to the oven door handle with Tim's handcuffs. A nasty gash on her forehead.

'Okay, Tim?'

'So sorry, boss. Paul.'

'*Shut up*,' Cater shouted, slamming the pistol against the back of Hirsch's head, a burst of blinding pain. 'See that sly bitch? Go and sit with her. Cuff yourself to the oven like she is.'

'Take it easy.'

Another slam; Hirsch felt his face go white. 'Do it.'

He levered himself onto the floor, one eyelid fluttering uncontrollably, Eleanor Quinlan watching in concern. He tried a smile, cuffed himself to the oven door. Then, a little recovered, he looked up at the banker.

'Everything's falling apart for you, Malcolm. The others know I'm here.'

Cater tensed; advanced across the kitchen floor and kicked Hirsch's ankle. Winced, hobbled back a couple of steps. Blood seeped where the leg of his trousers was bulked up—by a bandage, Hirsch supposed.

'Get bitten by a dog, Mal?'

'Shut up. I have to think.'

They were drowning in electric light: a row of halogens on the ceiling, a spotlight above the sink, another above the island bench. A stark, unforgiving environment for an unravelling man. Cater paced, limping, not trying to hide it, stress furrows carved into his face, his clothing. His tie hung loosely below his agitated throat. He was sweating; rank with it.

Hirsch turned to Eleanor. 'He hit you?'

She nodded as Cater screamed at them to shut up. Ignoring him, she said, 'After I called you, he checked my phone and—'

Cater was in her face, spittle flying. 'Shut up. Please shut up. I can't think.'

'Okay, okay.'

'I just need to think.'

Cater paced again, sometimes jabbing the pistol at his prisoners, at the air. Warning off phantoms, Hirsch thought. A man like that might simply start shooting. He caught a glimpse of his pistol in the corridor. He'd need to be six metres long to hook it with his shoe. So he amused himself by choreographing another ridiculous move: angle his hip towards Eleanor so she might fish around in his pocket for the handcuff key.

Eventually Cater ran out of steam. He pulled a chair away from the table and sat down with Tim Medlin's pistol awkwardly in his lap. Probably never held a gun before, Hirsch thought. If he did decide to start shooting, he'd waste time looking for the safety catch.

'Malcolm, police are going to be—'

'Shut up. I'm talking to Eleanor. You really don't know where Adrian is?'

'I really don't. He just left without telling me where he was going. That was a few days ago.'

'Ran off like the dog he is.'

'Ran off with a lot of the bank's money, hey Malcolm?' said Hirsch. Anything to get Cater talking. 'With Sophie Flynn's help?'

Cater's eyes grew half-lidded as he considered that. Hirsch saw him seize on it. 'I did notice certain irregularities.'

Then he looked down at his leg; shook it.

'You should get that seen to, Malcolm. Germs. Rabies. Sophie's dog's a filthy-looking thing.'

Cater's eyes slid away. 'Don't know what you're talking about.'

Then he stood, trembling, stabbing the gun towards the huge refrigerator. 'Just look at that thing. Would've cost a load of someone else's money, right, Eleanor?'

'Fiftieth birthday present.'

'Oh, is that right? Old Adrian turned human for a few minutes, did he? Humankind needs to watch its back when that happens.'

Full of disgust, Cater sat again.

They were all seated, and for some time nothing was said or done. The harsh light aged them. It encouraged Hirsch's other senses: the dryness in his throat, the stink of the man with the gun, Eleanor Quinlan's body warmth, the soft click of car doors closing.

He was running out of time. He had witnesses to Cater's answers. 'Why did you go to see Maggie Groote, Malcolm?'

Cater looked away again. 'What?'

'I've spoken to your neighbour, Mr Mannion. You borrow his car sometimes.'

Cater looked as if he hadn't seen that coming. 'He's an old man.'

'His car was seen at Mrs Groote's house around the time she died.'

Cater hunted around for an answer. 'So? Two old people. Friends? I don't know.'

'Easily checked. We think the fire was an accident, by the way. She kicked over a radiator.'

'There you go.'

'Why she kicked it over is the key question. Was it when you started choking her?'

Cater waved the pistol at Hirsch. 'No you don't. No, no you don't.'

'Don't what?'

'Put that on me.'

'What?' Eleanor Quinlan said. 'You only killed her a little bit?'

Hirsch was careful not to smirk, but it set Cater off again anyway. 'Keep out of it, you bitch.'

Hirsch cut in. 'I'm sure you had a valid reason for visiting Mrs Groote, Malcolm.'

Cater didn't trust the kindness, the mildness of Hirsch's tone. But the urge to justify himself was overwhelming. 'I'll only say there were certain account irregularities that I was hoping to help her reconcile in due course.'

It was a bummer, Hirsch thought, as Cathy Duigan slipped in behind Cater with the catchpole, Jean Landy covering her with her firearm, both of them alight with calculation and glee, that Cater still hadn't admitted, in front of witnesses, to being at Maggie Groote's house.

35

Hirsch had to endure a lot of childish shit in the corridors of the police station afterwards, everyone smirking, clamping their wrists together if they encountered him. 'I *allowed* myself to be captured,' he'd say. 'As part of a complex and delicate psychological manoeuvre.'

Or, 'I came *this close* to dying.'

And they'd laugh and walk by, waving their imaginary handcuffs above their heads.

'No one's finest hour, really,' Stolte said, beginning Hirsch's debrief in the mid-afternoon.

Hirsch wanted to say, *But if it hadn't been for me*...He knew better than to protest, though. Instead, he sat at one end of the briefing room table, Stolte at the other, with the collator on one side, taking notes, facing two of the homicide detectives. The others were escorting Malcolm Cater to police HQ in Adelaide.

Stolte began: 'We have a preliminary result on the samples taken from the dog's neck and muzzle. Positive for human blood.'

'Cater's,' Hirsch said.

'That remains to be seen.'

'You saw his leg.'

'You saw his leg, *senior sergeant*,' Stolte said. 'And yes, I did see his leg. And let's hope he left other evidence behind—like in the car or on the body of the girl.'

'And on Mrs Groote's body.'

'We know what to look for, Constable Hirschhausen. What I want to know is, how you put it together, whatever it is you *did* put together.'

Meaning you weren't listening to me earlier, Hirsch thought. I told you what I thought. Comyn would have told you what we both thought. Explaining about Adrian Quinlan's debts, he said, 'How these tie to Cater or the bank, I don't yet know, but Cater went to Quinlan's house for a reason, and I clearly heard him say, "I'm not taking the fall for this."'

'What do you think he meant by that?'

'I think Cater was stealing from the bank. To benefit himself, or Quinlan, or for their mutual benefit, I don't know.'

'What do you mean, "from the bank"?'

'From a few elderly clients, like Mrs Groote, who had large sums of money in accounts they wouldn't monitor regularly. Term deposits, for example.'

'Intending to pay it back?'

'Presumably. Meanwhile he altered the records so that the statements went to the wrong address.'

'Rhynie Road.'

'Yes. Mrs Groote and the others continued to receive statements for their everyday accounts and were probably reassured by that.'

A chipped jug of water sat at the centre of the table. Hirsch poured a glass, watched in fascination by the others. 'Enter a pair of Irish conmen,' he said. 'Mrs Groote went to the bank to withdraw cash and because she'd already withdrawn a few thousand a week earlier, and because Cater had swiped the rest, she suddenly didn't have enough money in the account, and was sharp enough to realise that. And Sophie, the teller, also had her suspicions.'

'So he killed them both,' Stolte said.

'Yes, although I don't think the first murder was intentional. Sophie's was. He staged it as a suicide. We were supposed to believe she felt guilty for ripping off the bank's clients—maybe even felt guilty for killing Mrs Groote. He hoped that's how we'd read it when we saw the bank statements lying there on the passenger seat.'

'And Mrs Groote wasn't intentional?'

Hirsch paused. 'There's something too...messy, spontaneous about it. I think he went there to reassure her or something and lost his temper and shook her or found himself strangling her and she kicked over the heater, starting the fire.'

'What proof do we have that he was there?'

'A bit thin,' Hirsch admitted. 'A newish silver Passat was seen leaving her house at the time of the fire. Cater's neighbour owns one and Cater's been borrowing it from time to time. There might be forensic traces—ash if his clothing got a bit burnt, for example. There's probably a lot more evidence tying him to Sophie Flynn's murder, though. Blood and saliva from the dog transferred to the car seat...'

'What makes me uneasy,' Stolte said, 'is that your witness to the Passat is a conman. As for Flynn, Cater could argue he went around to check on her welfare and found her dead and got attacked by the dog.'

'But he borrowed the Passat both times.'

'Because his own car was playing up. I think we need to find this Quinlan character. He might be able to fill us in.'

'I've no idea where he is,' Hirsch said. He felt faint. Nothing to eat since second breakfast.

'You believe the wife when she says she doesn't know either?'

'Yes.'

'She's not in on it?'

'Doubtful.'

And Stolte was doubtful about that. He said, 'If you're right about all this, it clears Mrs Groote's neighbours and it clears the niece.'

'Yes.'

'Not nice people.' He shook his head. 'The neighbours. The niece is just an idiot.' He stood, a signal for the others to stand. 'Thanks for your time, constable. We all need to hit the road. If you could monitor the Rhynie Road mail over the next few days and weeks, I'd be very grateful. We need to know who else was ripped off. Forensic accountants will go through the bank's records, of course, but it'll help to have separate confirmation.'

He gave Hirsch a nod as he left the briefing room. No calculation or derision in it. A simple goodbye and thank you. Maybe even a skerrick of respect.

Sergeant Brandl called Hirsch on Monday evening. 'I'll be back on deck tomorrow, so there's no need for you to grace us with your presence. I presume you've left the place in a shambles?'

'Au contraire,' Hirsch said. 'I've arranged all your files according to location rather than surname or topic, switched your operating system to Linux and replied *yes* to all your emails.'

'That's the spirit. You going to catch up on your back-country patrols?'

'Out west tomorrow, out east on Thursday.'

'Keep your eyes open for the Ayliffes.'

Tuesday dawned with a squall straight from the South Pole and Hirsch prowled the town half-blinded by his pulled-down beanie and jacket hood, rain beading on his eyelashes. A chill rose from the ground, another came lancing in on the wind, and he was trudging past the shop, head down, when a vehicle decelerated behind him.

Please God, not Clara Ogilvie.

But in the next instant, even though deafened by his hood and the wet, driving wind, he knew it was larger than a car. He stopped, blinked, as a van marked *Mid-North Removals* drew alongside. The passenger window slid down and Darvesh from the servo stuck his head out. 'Fancy meeting you here.'

'You'll get your turban wet.'

The grin was too irrepressible for the hour, the weather. He jerked his head, indicating the driver. 'Helping my cousin. We were hoping you'd point us in the general direction of the primary school.'

'You're nearly there,' Hirsch said. 'Go on past the school oval, then turn left. You're moving stuff out of the teacher's house?'

'Yep.'

'It's behind a hedge at the back of the school,' Hirsch said.

The truck moved on; Hirsch followed it and found it parked behind a station wagon, doors open. Darvesh was bumping a trolley down a set of metal ramps, the cousin unfolding old blankets. 'If you're after the people that live here, they're out the back,' Darvesh said.

Hirsch nodded his thanks and entered the icy dankness of the little house. Along a passageway—packed cartons and plastic tubs in some of the rooms—to the dismal kitchen, where Julian Roskam was emptying the fridge and his sister was wrapping crockery in newspaper. Avril gave Hirsch a 'what now?' look and went back to her wrapping but Roskam almost wept to see him there. He clenched his fists, shifted into high hysteria and stamped a foot. 'Leave me alone. You've done enough.'

'Julian,' Avril said.

'I am not going to talk to him. He can't make me,' Roskam said, stalking out.

Avril called after him: 'Do the bathroom cabinet.'

She turned to Hirsch, wrung out, looking as if she'd been

dragged through a hedge by the ankles, her eyes heavy behind smudged and crooked glasses. 'Can you believe we actually spent the night here?'

Busy sounds came from the other rooms: bumps, scrapes, the soft screech of a wonky trolley wheel. 'How's it going?' Hirsch said, feeling inadequate.

'How do you think?'

There was no answering that question. 'What will Julian do now?'

'Well, he's resigned from the Education Department. Only a matter of time before they found out. He's got a court appearance in a few weeks.'

'I wouldn't worry,' Hirsch said. 'He won't get jail time. Probably a fine and community service.'

She gave him a stare. 'Please.'

Hirsch looked away. She probably knew all her brother's secrets, and, once again, she was getting him out of a bind. Had CIB investigated Roskam's earlier department postings? Tied historical snowdropping reports, even sexual assaults, to them? Hirsch knew he couldn't ask Avril Roskam.

There was a crash, breaking glass, from one of the other rooms. Julian Roskam the head teacher might have shouted, 'Careful!' Julian Roskam the snowdropper didn't utter a whimper, not that Hirsch could hear. He glanced at Avril. She glared as if he, not her brother, was responsible for everything.

After breakfast, Hirsch headed north, then west into the Tiverton Hills, up Hawker Road to the windfarm depot.

There had been a frost: the roadside grasses glittered; his tyres cracked across ice puddles; spiderwebs trembled, intricate filigrees that spanned one fence wire to another.

He pulled over to let a mini convoy of service vehicles leave the compound, then drove in, parked, pulled on his cap. Stamped his feet uselessly as he crossed the yard to the main shed.

Graham Fuller was there, rummaging in a tray of greasy bolts and washers and his hand flew out, sending a spanner flying, when he heard Hirsch's boots and felt Hirsch there behind him, blocking the weak, wintry daylight.

He whirled around. 'Jesus, Paul.'

'Sorry.'

Fuller was one of those quiet, solid, competent men. He'd lost a little of that solidity when the Ayliffes tied him up at gunpoint. 'Sorry,' Hirsch said again.

Fuller breathed in; smiled; gestured casually. 'Oh, it'll pass. What can I do for you?'

'Just checking in. Back to my regular patrols.'

'Is it true? About Malcolm Cater? You can be sure I checked my bank balance last night.'

'You won't be the only one,' Hirsch said. 'I'm assuming you didn't have a couple of hundred thousand in term deposit?'

Fuller grinned. 'Who knows what I've got stashed away.'

'Meanwhile,' Hirsch said, 'anything out of the ordinary here? Missing fuel? Missing vehicles, for that matter?'

'Christ, you don't think they'd hit a second time, do you?'

Hirsch thought exactly that. The Ayliffes were nearby, he

was sure of it. They might have gone on the run after shooting Andrew Eyre but they weren't behaving like fugitives; probably didn't see themselves as fugitives.

He stayed for a coffee—instant, the granules shovelled into a mug of questionable cleanliness from a Maxwell House tin the size of a fuel drum—and headed downhill to Jonas Heneker's house. This time there was no old man and no rusty Valiant. He headed down to the highway and sped north, then west, beginning a long loop around through the back country. He stopped at shacks and farmhouses and the gas pipeline camp, giving consolation where he could, giving advice, issuing a mild warning here and there. He didn't enforce the law because no one was flouting it. The day was too cold, too dispiriting, too lacking in scope and opportunity.

Mid-afternoon he was in a region of sticky backroads when a call came in from Sergeant Brandl. Katie Street was missing.

36

Hirsch and Katie shared a taste for disaster films. Headlong rescue missions across landscapes arid, ablaze or icebound and populated by the outcast, the cut-adrift. One-step-forward-and-two-steps-back stories. Don't stop for that forlorn hitchhiker. Don't enter that town, that room. Don't trust the fuel gauge. Don't drink the water. And always a time imperative to ramp up the tension.

He was reminded of that as his own mad dash went wrong. Reminded because Katie filled his head every step of the journey out of the dips and rises of that country, trying to reach the highway. Her wisecracks and her side-eyes. Her expectations of him. What she meant to him. How she was an indivisible part of his life with Wendy.

But he wasn't in a disaster film. He was in a perverse comedy. Five minutes after receiving the call he came around a bend and found the road ahead seething with sheep in full fleece. He slammed on his brakes, the Toyota twitching, losing traction as two teenage kids on mustering duty wobbled to safety on their little Hondas and gaped at him, kelpies at their heels.

Heart hammering, Hirsch wound down his window. 'Is it okay if I drive through?'

They glanced uneasily at each other, their long, booted legs propping up their bikes, little breath clouds showing their agitation. The question overwhelmed them.

Hirsch breathed deeply in and out, close to panic. Tried conversation. 'Pretty big mob. How many head?'

'Two thousand.'

He didn't know what that represented. All he knew was, broad brown rumps filled the world for as far as he could see and he was late, far from home.

'Shearing?'

One boy nodded.

'Is it far to the shed?'

The second boy said, 'Up the road a bit,' as if confirming that the world was indeed round. Hirsch knew these back roads but for him, a country copper, knowing a back road meant knowing who along it had light fingers, a mass of unpaid fines or a sick husband, not where the shearing sheds were located, or how far 'up the road a bit' was.

He drummed his fingers on the steering wheel. 'Is it okay if I drive through slowly? They won't stampede?'

The boys looked at each other, a silent demarcation of authority. Eventually the first boy gestured towards the outer reaches of his world. 'Dad's up ahead.'

Waiting on the other side of an open farm gate, thought Hirsch. One of those slow-talking men, sitting quietly in his ute in the middle of the road, listening to the ABC news, a third kelpie curled on the passenger seat. Eventually this kelpie would prick up his ears and the farmer would turn down the radio and they would wait for the vanguard to materialise. Man and dog would uncoil from the ute and— barely moving, barely uttering a sound—turn the head of the lead sheep. Where it went, the others would follow. Two thousand sheep. It would take as long as it took. It would take a long time.

Hirsch could feel his heart fluttering. 'What do you reckon? If I take it slowly?'

They shrugged. This wasn't epic cinema. No life in peril. No deadline. Just a cop in a cop vehicle and you didn't say no.

'Go for it,' the second boy said, not confident, just help-less. 'The other police car did.'

Other police car...

It took twelve minutes for Hirsch to get clear of the mob. He accelerated along a road that mostly ran high and dry but sometimes dipped to cross creek beds and patches of sodden, low-lying ground. Here he'd crawl across in four-wheel drive, his tyres churning already-churned mud so sticky and deep it would snag you, glue you in, if you were careless.

Or ignorant.

He came around another bend and had time to brake gently and roll to a halt behind the STAR Group SUV that he recognised as Inspector Merlino's. Bogged to the axles.

No way around it. Hadn't they put the vehicle in four-wheel drive? Hadn't they seen the rutted treachery of the road? Then Hirsch thought: easy for me to say. Eighteen months ago he'd have tried to sail through. Not now. An old hand now.

He switched off, stepped out and, jittery again, approached the SUV at an angle. Merlino was in the rear, working his phone or tablet. Didn't acknowledge Hirsch. Another shape in the passenger seat. The driver was Beulah; he opened his door but didn't get out. Mud from shoes to kneecaps. He'd tried pushing the SUV or maybe just been walking around it hopelessly.

'Here to pull us out?'

Hirsch shook his head. 'Don't have a cable. And there's no point going back the way we came; we'd have to wade through those sheep again.'

'That's just lovely.'

'What are you doing out here?'

'What are *we* doing out here?' said Beulah, with an insinuating singsong in his voice. A man who'd never had a sense of his own incapacity. 'Just doing our job. Some idiot thought he saw the Ayliffes back there. Remember them, the Ayliffes? The ones you let go?'

Jesus Christ, Hirsch thought. He looked at his watch: 5.00 p.m. on a trembling wrist. 'I need to get past,' he said, and immediately wished he hadn't.

Beulah looked lazily down at the mud. 'Is that a fact.'

'Have you called anyone?'

'Like who?'

'RAA, Redruth Motors...someone from your freakin *team*?'

'Now listen—'

They heard it then: someone had fired up a tractor. 'Help comes to those who only stand and wait,' Hirsch said.

'Fuckwit,' Beulah said, but he was turning his head in the direction of the sound, a farm driveway beyond the bogged SUV.

A tractor appeared over a slight rise, the tops of trees behind it suggesting a house and sheds. It spluttered closer, a little grey Massey-Ferguson, a woman at the wheel. She wore an army greatcoat, rubber boots and a beanie, hair corkscrewing around cheeks flushed with cold. Came bouncing out onto the road, then U-turned and reversed, aiming the towbar at the radiator of the SUV. Hirsch waited, watching. Beulah got out and waded across the mud to greet her. She barely acknowledged him. Ran a steel cable from the tractor to the SUV and got down into the mud to fasten it.

Hirsch realised how tightly wound he was. He tried to slow his mind, his body. Slow his breathing. He guessed he'd have a five-minute wait. Checked his phone for something to do and, wonder of wonders, had two signal bars.

Climbing back into the Toyota, he ran the engine and the heater and called Wendy.

'Where are you?' She sounded ragged, and he knew her well enough to hear the suppressed dread.

'I'm about half an hour away. Stuck behind a bogged car but the farmer's here with a tractor.'

She had no time or use for that news. 'Please hurry.'

'Tell me what happened?'

'It's sport this afternoon. She went off to netball; didn't come back to school.'

Every Tuesday the high school kids would troop down to the town's sportsground after lunch. A football oval, tennis and netball courts, swimming pool and a skateboard ramp. Then troop back at 3.30.

'You talked to the other kids?'

'No, of course not...*Jesus*, Paul, what do you think? No one saw anything. Nor did their parents. Nor did any of the coaches. Still got a couple of calls to make.' She paused. 'Sorry.'

'That's okay, you're entitled.'

He saw the tractor belch smoke; imagined the cable tightening. 'One thing: tell Sergeant Brandl or one of the others to check Clara Ogilvie.'

'I know, I know, first thing I thought of, in fact,' Wendy said. She was close to tears.

'And?'

'Hilary and I both went to her place. She's not home. Or her car's not there but there's music playing but no one answers the door.'

Hirsch was at a loss now. 'Did you check the netball changeroom?'

'Katie's not there, Paul.'

'Is her bag there?'

A long pause. 'Oh. I'll go back and check.'

'Take someone with you. I'll be there as soon as I can.'

'Please hurry. I'm losing my mind. I've almost run out of people to call.'

'Are you still at the school?'

'I'm in my car, driving around and around.'

'I'll soon be there. We'll find her.'

He saw the SUV jerk and begin to climb out of the mud, the farmer half-turned in her seat as she watched and steered.

A quick call to Sergeant Brandl.

'Paul, where the hell are you?'

Hirsch told her.

'If it doesn't rain, it pours,' she said. 'Okay, update. We've asked for reinforcements and brought in volunteers and started a sweep out from the sportsground and near the school, looking in empty houses, garden sheds, that kind of thing. Calling kids, other parents, the teachers.'

'Wendy told you about Clara Ogilvie?'

'She did. The stalking got worse? Why didn't you tell me?'

Hirsch cut her off. 'There's music playing in her flat, but no car?'

'Correct. And no answer when we knocked.'

'We need to check inside.'

'But her car's not there.'

'Put out an alert, boss. Meanwhile: we need to go in.'

Brandl was exasperated. 'I haven't been able to track down the O'Mearas.'

'Who?'

'Her landlords.'

Hirsch felt defeated. He knew Brandl would need a compelling reason before she broke down someone's door. She'd want to use a key. She'd want the landlord to be there. 'Don't know what else to suggest.'

'If we assume Katie's not just skiving off, meeting friends, this could be payback for something you've been working on, you know. The Ayliffes, for a start.'

Hirsch went cold. 'Oh, God. But they wouldn't have it in for me, would they?'

'Are we talking clear thinkers, Paul?'

He couldn't answer.

Brandl went on: 'Who apart from Ogilvie have you upset lately?'

'Quinlan, but I don't think he's around anywhere. Cater's locked up. The Irish guys are locked up in Port Pirie.'

'John Fearn and his wife. Amy Groote.'

'Can't see it.'

'CIB gave them a hard time, remember.'

'Can we just look inside Clara's flat before we do anything else?'

A pause. 'I'll see what I can do. How long will you be?'

'Half an hour.'

'Okay, meet you at Ogilvie's flat,' the sergeant said. Another pause and she said, 'How about Julian Roskam?'

Hirsch could see it, the man's sullen misery. 'I'll try his sister,' he said, cutting the call, searching for her number.

'He's not here,' Avril said.

Hirsch stiffened. 'Where is he?'

'Hospital, thanks to you.'

Not thanks to me at all, thought Hirsch. He let silence work for him.

And she added: 'Sleeping pills.' Then her voice altered. 'Actually, I don't blame you at all. Sorry. I'm just sick of it, frankly.'

'When did it happen?'

'After lunch. I thought he was having a nap.'

The SUV was free and Hirsch got off the phone. Beulah remained behind the wheel while the farmer unhitched the cable, then, with a flick of the wheel, he accelerated past the tractor and disappeared.

Hirsch drove to the edge of the mud and got out. 'Afternoon.'

The farmer was seamed and weathered, an old face, but she moved like a young woman. Straightened her back and said, 'I suppose you want a tow, too?'

'I'd be grateful, thanks.'

She came across the mud with the cable. 'At least you said thanks. More than I got from that prick,' she said, gesturing in the direction of the departing SUV.

'Cop royalty,' Hirsch said. 'I'm more your peasant class.'

She gave him a look and sank to her knees and fed the cable hook under the front bumper. 'You're the Tiverton policeman.'

'Paul Hirschhausen. I'd have got around to calling in on you one of these days.'

She whipped her head around. 'Why?'

Hirsch filed that away. Hiding something? Didn't matter right now. 'I hope to call in on everyone out here eventually. Part of my patrol duties.'

She grunted and slid under the Toyota again. A clank and a thunk, giving Hirsch time to gaze across at the entry gateposts. A CCTV camera: that's how she'd known Beulah was bogged.

'Hop in, go with the flow, don't use your brakes,' she said now, getting to her feet.

Then Hirsch was jerking, rolling, following the little tractor across the mud and onto terra firma.

37

Hirsch was rolling over elongated shadows by the time he reached Redruth: blockish buildings, spindly power poles and the amorphous clumps of tree canopies. Here and there a last flare on west-facing windows before the sun winked out.

Through the town and up the side street to Clara Ogilvie's flat. Sergeant Brandl wasn't there. Wendy was.

'Oh, God,' she said, and threw herself against him. She was warm, tight and trembling with emotions she couldn't control. Hirsch was little help, but he was all she had.

Eventually he tilted away, arms still around her. 'Where's the boss?'

'She tracked down the O'Mearas. She should be here any minute.'

'Do you know them?'

'No.'

'Where were they?'

'Getting the church hall ready for a wedding on Saturday.'

A small town ticking over, thought Hirsch. 'Did you find Katie's backpack?'

'It wasn't there.'

Hirsch didn't know what that meant. 'Let's check out the flat.'

'We already have. Like I said, music on but no answer.'

Hirsch looked both ways along the street, hoping to see the grey Fiesta. Wendy realised what he was doing, and her voice expressed an overflowing pool of helplessness. 'Clara could be anywhere. She could be halfway to Adelaide by now.'

Her eyes were wet, her thin face sharper than Hirsch had ever seen it and close to despair. She had deep, instinctive reserves of wisdom and practicality but they were useless here. He wrapped her in another hug, briskly. A way of saying don't give up.

'Let's check again,' he said. It was something to do. It was better than waiting.

They walked down the side of the house to the backyard. A motion-activated light came on, struggling against the gathering darkness. Looking up at the flat, Hirsch saw that curtains had been drawn but light leaked out—the rooms were not in darkness. He could hear music, very faint. 'Adieu False Heart': track one on the album of the same name. Maybe someone had just inserted a CD? Maybe it was a playlist.

He thought of Clara Ogilvie in there, a woman who'd waited so long for her life to start, and just seen it stop. He thought of Katie Street in there, lying drugged on the floor.

He couldn't think beyond *drugged*.

He wanted to look in the main window, but the litt
balcony only extended a metre past the door. Ladde
He crossed to the storage bays under the flat. Stepla
der, mower, fuel cans, rakes, spades. No proper ladder. H
found himself staring steadily, helplessly, at the stepladd
knowing it wasn't tall enough.

'I know what you're thinking,' Sergeant Brandl called.

Hirsch turned. She came creaking in on her crutche
trailed by a couple in their sixties: grey-haired, plump, ner
ously smiling.

Making the introductions, she said, 'If you could do tl
honours, Mr O'Meara.'

And looking at Wendy with infinite tenderness, she sai
'It might be best if Paul checks first.'

A tightening of Wendy's face and body. She opened h
mouth to protest. Then, just as quickly, recovered ar
nodded.

Hirsch had never felt such a visceral sense
someone's fear. He followed O'Meara up the greasy ste]
and waited for him to unlock the door. 'Best stay outsid
Mr O'Meara.'

But before he could go in, Brandl called up to him: 'Ti
sent a text. He's found her car.'

He looked down; she waved her phone at him, her fa
ghostly in the glow of the screen. That dash of technology
the dank darkness felt anachronistic to Hirsch. It frighten
him.

He found his voice. 'Where?'

'Parked behind the Woolpack.'

'Tell him to see if she's in the bar. Or if she's rented a room.'

'Will do.'

Now Hirsch entered the flat. The air was stuffy, over-warm. Lived-in smells, not death smells. He hurried through to the sitting room. Empty. The source of the music was an iPhone docked with a speaker. Too loud: he turned it off, couldn't think. Three empty wine bottles, an almost-empty Smirnoff vodka bottle; a lonely drained wineglass, a centi-metre of vodka in a tumbler.

He found Clara on her bed. Didn't need to touch her neck but did so anyway: warm and pulsing. The snoring was enough to announce life. A harsh sound, like a cotton sheet being ripped into a hundred pieces.

He checked the bathroom and kitchen. Inside cupboards. Under the bed. Behind the sofa. A home so small it offered few hiding places.

Returning to the balcony he leaned over the railing and said, 'Clara's here. She's been on a bender, must've walked home from the pub or taken the taxi.'

Hurrying down the steps, he said, 'No sign of Katie.'

Before he could reach her, Wendy sank to the damp grass. It was relief. It was also fear prolonged.

Brandl took Hirsch aside. Her face was pinched with pain and fatigue in the half-light. 'We can both see what this is doing to Wendy.'

'Yes,' said Hirsch cautiously.

'She feels useless. Dead-end phone calls, driving up and down streets...'

'What do you suggest?'

'I'm going back to the station; the crutches are killing me. I'll coordinate. Tim and Jean can run the search in town. You take Wendy with you.'

Hirsch opened his mouth to reply but she raised her hand. 'I'll handle any fallout. You go and talk to Amy Groote and the Fearns.'

Hirsch gazed across at Wendy, who stood with the O'Mearas, all three watching anxiously from the cone of weak yellow light cast by the bulb above their heads. 'Okay.'

'News on Roskam?'

'Hospital.'

'Off you go, you know what to do.'

'Thanks,' Hirsch said, crossing the yard. He held Wendy close against him and said, 'You're coming with me.'

They raced north along the Barrier Highway, into greater darkness, the air icily still, signalling a frost in the morning. Wendy was calmer now. Thinking. 'Amy Groote's a long shot, surely?'

Hirsch dimmed the lights for an oncoming car. 'Yeah, but she really gave me the evil eye yesterday when CIB were done with her.'

'How would she even know about your involvement with me? With Katie?'

In Hirsch's experience, there were few secrets left in the mid-north. Admittedly, though, Amy Groote seemed too self-involved, too garden-involved, too uninterested in others, to know what was going on in Hirsch's life.

'We rule her out and move on,' he said.

Penhale was no more than a faint smear of light in the distance, with shapes resolving as they slowed for the outer limits: houses hunched against the cold; a couple of icy streetlights too stunned to move. Hirsch turned right, taking Hubert Wilkins Road into the foothills above the town.

Amy Groote wasn't home. No lights, no car.

'Next on the list, the Fearns,' Hirsch said, getting behind the wheel again.

'Can you put out an alert on her car?'

'Too soon,' Hirsch said. Too curtly?

Wendy's voice was small, defeated: 'Okay.'

He rested his hand on her thigh and steered back onto the road, turning left towards the driveway for the house on the hilltop, which was lit up like a cruise liner. John Fearn stepped out onto the veranda as Hirsch parked. He was neat as ever in trousers, slippers, a business shirt and a V-neck pullover.

He hugged himself for warmth as Hirsch and Wendy got out. 'I thought we were finished with you lot.'

Unsmiling. Peevish. Not anxious or diminished this time. Sylvia's listening in, Hirsch thought. Or he's had time to let his grievances marinate.

Wendy stepped closer. Said warmly, 'Mr Fearn? I'm Wendy Street.'

Fearn's good manners took over. Courteous and seemly, he almost gave a little bow as he said, 'How do you do, Mrs Street. You teach at the high school.'

'Yes. You might be able to help us. My daughter's missing and...Look, I won't lie to you, we're desperate and we're contacting everyone Paul's had dealings with lately.'

A nice bit of defusing, Hirsch thought, but Sylvia Fearn shouldered her husband aside, her voice harsh and shrill. 'We don't deserve this. We've done nothing wrong. Clear out. Go on, get lost the pair of you.'

'Standard procedure, Mrs Fearn,' Hirsch said.

'You think we'd kidnap a child to get back at you? Who do you think we are? Who the hell do you think *you* are?'

'Sylvie,' her husband said, letting his fingertips touch her upper arm.

She shook him off violently. 'Don't you Sylvie me.'

And, just as quickly, she was weeping. Hiccupping and heaving with it, as if she'd reached the far edge of the slights and pain she'd been traversing over the past few days.

John Fearn embraced his wife and stared at Hirsch over her shoulder. There was hostility in it, jaundiced and irrevocable. A complex marriage here, Hirsch thought. The meshing of different types of strength.

'Thank you both for your time,' Wendy said, taking Hirsch's hand and leading him back to the Toyota.

They drove away shakily. 'Scratch them off the list?'

Hirsch nodded. 'Scratch them off the list.'

Down the road to Penhale. Hirsch was about to turn back to Redruth when Wendy said, 'How about Maggie's house?'

'Good thinking.'

And Amy Groote was there, huddled inside a coat, scarf and beanie, standing on the veranda as if she'd been there for days. She came down the steps when Hirsch pulled in at the kerb. Walked up to his door and made a wind-down-your-window motion with her hand.

'Amy,' he said, looking up at her. She was shivering.

'I just want to apologise for yesterday. I was out of sorts.'

'Understandable,' Hirsch said.

Then she stuck her head part-way in and said, 'Are you Mrs Street? I'm so, so sorry.'

Wendy's hand went to her chest. 'You know already?'

Hirsch shot her a look, then gently opened his door, further, further, so that Groote had to step back to let him out.

'Amy, you know about Wendy's daughter?'

'It's on the news. I heard it on my way here.'

Hirsch looked past her at the house and its still intact, lockable rooms. 'What are you doing?'

Groote said helplessly, 'I'm in two minds what to do with the place. Sell? Fix it up first? Fix it up and live in it? That'll take money I don't have.'

'May I ask where you were this afternoon?'

'In Adelaide. There's a nursery I go to in Norwood for rootstock, then I worked on a mail-out for the Wilderness people...' Her voice trailed away. 'You can't t̶ ̶k I'd do a thing like take someone's child from̶ ̶ulder. 'We have

Hirsch didn't think it. He patted h̶ to check.'   she stopped him from

He got behind the wheel a̶ ̶said, 'I hope there's good closing his door. Lookin̶ news soon.'

327

'Thank you,' Wendy said, her smile bleak.

Hirsch U-turned and headed back onto the highway and was five kilometres down the road when his phone rang. 'You take it.'

He heard Wendy say, 'Hilary, it's me...Okay...'

She completed the call. Looked at Hirsch strangely and said, 'A man tried to snatch Lydia Jarmyn from hospital this afternoon.'

38

'Has to be the husband,' Hirsch said, finishing a U-turn, accelerating. 'I thought he was dead.'

'They don't know who it was,' Wendy said. 'According to Hilary, he ran off when security appeared.'

She leaned forward as if to spur the Toyota through the night. Both hands on the dash, then back to her lap, then on the dash again. She wanted Hirsch to put his foot to the boards, and she wanted him to keep them safe, and she could not reconcile the two.

Hirsch checked his speed: 130 k's per hour. Farm fences and seedling crops flashed by on either side, painted briefly by the headlights. There was evening dew, tiny diamonds winking as they sped north. A rabbit froze in the headlights, dashed halfway across the road, then back to the verge, and at the last moment in under the wheels. A couple of slaps as the loosely wrapped bones knocked the underside of the Toyota and Hirsch eased off the accelerator, shrinking a little inside. Bad omen.

Wendy touched his thigh fleetingly. 'Assuming it was the father, he drove up here and took Katie because he failed to grab his own daughter? But why her? To get back at you somehow?'

Hirsch could see it, a screwy mind growing hard, deliberate. Increasing his speed again, he said, 'Maybe he's been around this whole time. His wife was hiding him.'

'Why, though?'

He shrugged. 'Mental illness?'

Wendy brooded. 'Religious?' She patted the Toyota's dashboard. 'Maybe he was the one who painted that Biblical graffiti?'

Hirsch felt a slow creep of dread. 'Could be.'

'And let down everyone's tyres outside the Dugout? Was he *watching* us?'

When Hirsch didn't reply, she folded in on herself. 'Will he hurt her?'

Hirsch wished he knew. A man maddened by God and isolation. 'Not if we can help it.'

He reached the Hawker Road turnoff and threw the Toyota off the sealed surface and onto the mix of greasy mud and gravel. Halfway up, the driveway loomed, and he threw the vehicle into another turn, straight through, the front of the Toyota smacking both gates aside.

Reaching the yard, he braked and slid, narrowly missing a pale blue van. Stopped with the bull bar nudging the rear of the station wagon. All of the outside lights were burning: veranda, yard, sheds.

They got out. The wind had picked up, a glum lowing in

the pine trees, but not enough to drown voices, one shrieking, the other lower and pleading. Not in the house. Around the back. Hirsch made to run, and Wendy shrieked, 'Wait for me.'

He was metres ahead. Hurried back and gathered her to him. 'Sorry.'

'Please don't do anything stupid. Don't get him agitated.'

They ran together down the side of the house, passing the precise line of freshly disturbed soil that Hirsch had noticed on his earlier visit. And now he had a strange intimation. He stopped before they reached the corner. Knelt, dug with his fingers.

Ten centimetres below the surface was a magnet as large as his hand. New, horseshoe shaped, red tipped. He tossed it aside, climbed to his feet, and now the voices at the rear of the house were more agitated.

'What on earth?' Wendy said, staring down at the magnet.

Hirsch clamped his arm around her; steered her to the end of the wall and around to the backyard.

Grace Jarmyn was there, digging up magnets in a fury, tossing them onto a heap beside the veranda steps. '*You bring her here? You bring her here?*'

The man partly concealed behind the back door, as if fearful of the night, said agitatedly, 'Grace, please. You're letting in the forces.'

Half-expecting some kind of wild-eyed Rasputin, Hirsch saw a small, neat figure dressed in tracksuit pants, Ugg boots and a fleece. Clean shaven. The madness was in a finger-painted blob of yellow paint in the centre of his forehead and an eruption of hives over his entire face. Red, swollen, about to burst.

He saw Hirsch and shrank back. Screamed at his wife: 'Now look what you've done, let the outside in! Don't dig any more of those up, put them back. Put them back!'

'You mean these?' his wife said, tossing another magnet onto the heap.

She turned to Hirsch. 'He thinks we need a magnetic field to protect us. Windfarm rays, electrical fields, cops, social workers...'

'Grace, please. Put them back. I can feel a weakening, a breaching of the portal.'

'To hell with the portal,' his wife said. 'To hell with the Controller and to hell with the cycle.'

A sad, fucked-up story, thought Hirsch. Sad, fucked-up people. To cut through the insanity he stepped out front and centre and shouted: 'Mr Jarmyn!'

Jarmyn jumped in fright. Hid until only one eye was visible behind the door. 'You don't speak any truth I recognise.'

'Mr Jarmyn, this is Mrs Street. We've come to collect her daughter. Her name is Katie.'

'*You took my daughter,*' Jarmyn howled.

Wendy was trembling. 'Is Katie all right? Have you hurt her?'

'*Hurt* her? You were the one hurting her. With the end of the cycle, she can be saved.'

That got to his wife. She bent over as if in pain and screamed up at him, 'You had to bring her here? Expected me to look after another one?'

Wendy said, 'I've had enough of this.' She took a step towards the house. 'Katie!'

Jarmyn reacted as if she'd punched him: reeled and clapped his hands over his ears, eyes squeezed shut. '*Stop it. It hurts.*'

Hirsch shouted. 'Katie! You in there?'

Alex Jarmyn staggered and moaned but remained behind the lintel, still in fear of the corrupted environment outside the doorway. He'd be hard to take down. A millisecond too late and he'd dart back inside and barricade himself. We can't let him regain any composure, Hirsch thought, just keep bombarding him.

He leaned close to Wendy and murmured, 'Continue shouting, loud as you can. We want him off balance.'

She walked up to the steps and screamed her head off. With Jarmyn doubled over in apparent agony, Hirsch leapt lightly onto the end of the veranda and sidled along the wall. Reached the door. Checked with Wendy. She nodded okay, so he surged into the gap, grabbed a sleeve and whirled Jarmyn off the veranda. Followed him down onto the grass. Pinned him there, cuffing his hands behind his back while Jarmyn clenched himself into a ball and wailed.

Hirsch darted back onto the veranda and in through the door, shouting, 'Katie? It's me, Paul. You're safe now.'

A small, clear, distant voice: 'In here.'

He found her in a child's room among soft toys and pink bedding. She was huddled on the floor, her arms wrapped around a small child. Naomi Jarmyn: she wouldn't look at him.

'She's frightened.'

'I know,' Hirsch said. He felt like crying. 'You okay for a moment? Your mum's here.'

39

Hirsch made a series of calls: an ambulance for Alex Jarmyn, who was catatonic, Port Pirie CIB and Sergeant Brandl, and the Muirs, asking them to collect Katie and her mother and drive them home.

'All sorted,' Hirsch said, pocketing his phone.

They were at the Jarmyns' kitchen table, Katie on Wendy's lap. An ordinary house, predictable: a table where a table should be, beds where they wouldn't crowd bedroom space, a sitting room set up for TV watching. But a strangeness had lodged here, a bad feeling creeping into the corners. Hirsch would bulldoze the place if he could.

The others felt it, too. Grace Jarmyn was sitting in an armchair, nursing her daughter, both staring at Alex, who lay unmoving on the sofa, his back turned. Still. Silent. Cold.

Hirsch shivered and returned his attention to Katie. 'There'll be more questions tomorrow, official questions. But till Bob and Yvonne get here, are you up to talking more about what happened?'

Katie lifted her head from beneath Wendy's chin. 'Ask away,' she said; a low, quiet voice that seemed older.

'You say he didn't hurt you?'

'He said he wouldn't, and he didn't. Except when he pushed me in the van. I banged my shins.'

'And you'd seen him waiting around after school recently?'

She'd seen Jarmyn several times and assumed he was a parent, waiting to collect his kid. She usually mucked around in the playground after school, waiting for Wendy to finish up, and she'd found herself chatting with Jarmyn once or twice, no big deal, he hadn't come across as creepy.

'Except those sores on his face. Kind of like mosquito bites.'

Wendy had been silent. She gave a little cough in the cheerless room. 'Hives.'

'Hives. Anyway, I hardly spoke to him.'

'And today he was waiting near the netball court?'

Katie tucked her head under Wendy's chin again. Hirsch waited.

'Yeah.' She added slowly: 'I should've realised that wasn't right. He said his son was playing football, but the oval's on the other side of the swimming pool. Anyway, Naomi was with him and he said she wasn't very well, and would I please take her to the van and put her in her car seat while he waited for football to finish.'

She'd taken Naomi by the hand and was just reaching for the van's passenger door when she realised that Jarmyn had followed them. Before she could react, he'd opened the sliding door and bundled them both into the back.

'He climbed in after us and shut the door again. It was so quick.'

'You didn't scream?'

'No.' She dug deeper against her mother. 'It was too quick.'

'No one's blaming you, sweetheart,' Wendy said. 'It was a shock. And you didn't want to upset him.'

Katie started nodding. 'Plus Naomi was crying. She was scared.'

'You put her first,' Hirsch said, feeling a sting of pride. 'Good for you.'

Katie gave him a complicated look, as if relieved, grateful—but recasting the experience in her mind, looking for her missteps.

'No one saw it happen?'

A quick little shrug. 'Don't know. There were people around. But he'd parked under the trees with the sliding door facing the other way.'

Hirsch visualised it. Even if there were witnesses, their imaginations had probably configured it as some kind of odd family thing. Nothing violent or criminal.

'Did he say anything, then or later?'

'I was cuddling Naomi in the back and we were both trying not to slide around all over the floor, but he did say something about the end of a cycle and a gateway.'

Headlights swept the windows, a knock on the door. Hirsch opened it to the Muirs, who bundled Wendy and Katie into their car and drove off into the cold night. Then Hirsch spent another few minutes out in the icy air when the ambulance arrived to collect Alex Jarmyn.

Now the wait for CIB. He sat a while in the dreary sitting room, one ear on Grace Jarmyn putting her daughter to bed: murmurs, tears, more murmurs. He realised that the window had been covered in aluminium foil.

Finally Grace came in, winding her hands around each other. 'I think she's asleep. We'll need to be quiet. Tea? Something to eat?'

Hirsch realised he was starving. 'Yes, please.'

Five minutes later, nursing cups of tea, nibbling oat cakes, Grace Jarmyn said, 'Do I have to go through the same thing again?'

'I don't know,' Hirsch said. 'But a crime's been committed.'

'Nothing to do with me,' she said, putting down her cup, hugging herself. 'I hate that detective. Comyn. And that social worker.'

'I don't know who they'll send,' Hirsch said. 'For the moment, you're not under arrest. But that might change. In the meantime, can I ask you a few questions?'

'If you like.'

He'd have to tread delicately. 'You received some counselling?'

'If you can call it that,' she said.

'Are the police going to...?'

She looked away; shrugged.

Had a court date been set? 'They said it was okay for you to come home?'

She was offended. 'Of course.'

'With Naomi?'

'Yes, with Naomi.'

The system working at its finest, thought Hirsch. 'Tonight it looked like you were trying to...' He paused. 'Trying to stop your husband from what he was doing.'

'I had to. This is where I live! Plus—he brings another kid for me to look after?'

'I understand,' Hirsch said. 'Where's he been all this time?'

'A retreat with the Controller. Outside Sydney somewhere. I honestly thought I'd seen the last of him.'

Hirsch suspected that was a lie. 'When did he come back?'

'He was already here when I got home on Friday. He knew about Lydia and he was blaming me for it. Said I lost her to the other side.'

'He tried to take her from the hospital.'

A shrug. 'Nothing to do with me.'

Hirsch wondered about Grace Jarmyn. Her strange mix of naivety, outrage and self-absorption. Had that primed her for manipulation by Jarmyn? Or had life with Jarmyn made her that way?

'How long have you known him?'

'Five years. An anti-vaxxer rally. He was different then. He wasn't as strange as he is now and, you know, reasonably good looking. But after Naomi was born, he started to talk about how he could communicate with other worlds. He said it was how his spirituality manifested itself. It was hardwired in him.'

'This retreat: he's been away for a year?'

Her gaze slid away. 'Yes.'

'What about you? Did you ever go on these retreats? Visit him there?'

'No.'

'Who is the Controller?'

Another shrug. 'Don't know. Alex was always on the computer with those people. Chat rooms and that. Research. Every night, sometimes all night long. Had no time for me. Probably why he got sacked from the mine.'

'He said something about a cycle...'

'It's a higher consciousness that's going to sweep the world as soon as the current cycle ends,' she said, her face solemn, as if she'd spoken a deep truth. 'Seventy-thousand-year cycle.'

'Affecting everyone?'

'A select few.'

'Fascinating. You know quite a lot about it. Alex kept you up to date while he was away?'

She shook her head—too vigorously. She was lying. 'I've had years of it and it's too much. I come home and there he is, burying magnets all around the house. You saw his face? He breaks out in hives when he gets stressed. He said it was the windfarm turbines and the electricity poles.'

She glanced at the covered window.

'About Katie, the girl he brought here this afternoon...'

'He said the balance got upset when Lydia got taken away. How it was my fault.'

'And Katie was meant to restore the balance?'

'Yes. But he used Naomi to lure her and I couldn't have that.'

Hirsch wrapped his hands around his mug of tea. The comfort was scant. The coldness of the house and the woman had reached right through to his spine. 'We don't think Katie was a random choice.'

Grace Jarmyn rolled her neck as if to ease some stiffness. 'It's possible Alex was watching me for a while.'

Her eyes slid away again. Hirsch remembered her calmness, her tendency to answer obliquely, as if she were hearing questions other than those put to her. 'Who knows what that man was doing?' she said.

You, thought Hirsch.

He heard vehicles pull up in the yard, a welcome end to his day.

40

It was past midnight before Hirsch reached the house on Bitter Wash Road. Finding mother and daughter asleep together, he crawled into the spare room bed and lay for a while, mind racing, heart still.

He woke at six. Showered and breakfasted, he stood for a moment in Wendy's doorway.

'I'm awake,' she croaked.

He crossed the room, stooped, planted a kiss. 'How did she sleep?'

Wendy turned to look at her daughter, whose limbs took up two-thirds of the bed. 'Restless.'

'You going to work today?'

She shook her head.

Another kiss and he stood to go. 'Reports to write, crime to fight.'

'Stay with us tonight?'

'Definitely.'

Not something he could always promise.

'And you'll see if Clara's okay?'

'On my list,' he said. 'I'll call you during the day.'

'If I know you,' Wendy said, 'you'll call every hour.'

'I'm no stalker,' Hirsch said, and immediately regretted it. 'Sorry.'

'One or two calls would be nice,' Wendy said, before burrowing deeper into her bed.

Sergeant Brandl had left a message: 2.00 p.m. briefing in Redruth.

So Hirsch spent Wednesday morning in the Tiverton police station, catching up on paperwork. He welcomed it, after all the madness. Work had been piling up.

At 8.15 he walked across to the primary school and Glenys the admin assistant took him through to the office that until recently had been Julian Roskam's. She knocked and poked her head in. 'Someone to see you, Vikki.'

She said it without grace, as if she disapproved of a youngster being in charge of a school, even temporarily. Vikki Bastian, who'd had been on her knees flicking through bottom-drawer files, stood awkwardly, red-faced, brushing at her skirt. She came forward as if to shake hands. Had second thoughts and stood there paralysed.

'I'll leave you to it,' Glenys said with an air of satisfaction.

Bastian watched her go, then turned to Hirsch and this time completed the handshake. 'I live for the day I'm just a nobody again, back teaching the bubs.' She gestured at the filing cabinet. 'I didn't know there was so much involved.'

343

'Same here,' Hirsch said, telling her about his stint over-seeing the Redruth and Tiverton police districts.

'At least you've got a few years under your belt. I've only been teaching for five minutes.'

'Any idea when the new principal arrives?'

'No.'

'Mr Roskam had the removalists in early yesterday morning.'

'No one tells me anything.' Bastian's young face was baffled, as if the world piled mystery on top of mystery. 'Is it true, he stole, you know, women's underwear?'

Hirsch nodded; he couldn't see any point in denying it. 'How's your dad?'

'Oh, you know, muddling along. He still can't believe about Mr Quinlan.'

'Has Quinlan been in touch with him?'

Her eyes narrowed. 'Is that what this is about?'

Hirsch reassessed her: she could be sharp when she needed to be. He held up a placating hand. 'No. no, just checking in. We'd like to know where he is. Even little bits of incidental information can paint a picture.'

Wondering quite why he'd gone to the school, he returned to the police station. Mid-morning he received a landline call from Andrew Eyre, the environment protection officer, who said without preamble: 'I've been speaking to a lawyer. He says if the police had accompanied me to the house, I wouldn't have got shot.'

Or we both would have, Hirsch thought. But his mouth went dry. He could see himself tied up in court for a few years. No help from police command. No help from the union...

'Conferring with a lawyer is your prerogative, Mr Eyre. Are you back at work?'

'He said a million dollars, as a baseline figure.'

'I see.'

'But you know what I told him? I went charging up to the house without waiting. My fault.'

Hirsch didn't respond immediately. He thought: you're a bit of a prick really, aren't you? You want thanks? You wanted to watch me squirm?

He gave a little cough and said, 'How's the shoulder?'

'I won't be swinging a tennis racquet anytime soon, if that's what you're asking,' Eyre said, and hung up.

Then a call from Adelaide: an *Advertiser* reporter named Bec Dewhurst asking for his comment on a link between Adrian Quinlan, the Ayliffe manhunt and goings on at the Mid-North Community Bank.

'I can't comment on that.'

'I can think of one possible link,' Dewhurst said. 'And that's you.'

'I can't comment on that.'

A smirk in her voice. 'Really? Leon Ayliffe says you're the man to talk to.'

Hirsch waited a beat. 'He called you.'

'He did.'

'Any information as to his whereabouts, Ms Dewhurst? You may be aware that he's currently wanted in connection with a shooting incident...'

But she would say only that Ayliffe had seen a couple of her articles and phoned her that morning, full of insinuations. Hirsch, knowing he'd get nothing more from her, no-commented until she went away. Then he ate an early lunch and drove down the Barrier Highway to Redruth.

He'd long believed that an occupied dwelling emits a minute atmospheric charge. He didn't feel that when he knocked on Clara Ogilvie's door.

He made his way down the steps and around to the O'Meara's front door and was told, 'She packed up and left. There was a removal van here first thing this morning.'

So he climbed behind the wheel again, ran the heater for warmth, checked in with Wendy for the fourth or fifth time and drove across town towards the police station.

He was driving slowly around the square when he saw Brian Cottrell leaving the antique shop carrying a small hallway table. Did the sergeant know her ex was in town? Cottrell stowed the table in a classic old Rover and didn't look in Hirsch's direction.

Nice car, thought Hirsch, turning into the police station side street. Pity it belongs to that shithead. The time was 2.05: he was late.

Nodding to the civilian clerk, he walked through the connecting door and along the corridor to the briefing room. Jean Landy and Tim Medlin were already seated, attending to Sergeant Brandl, who sat at the front of the room, a laptop in front of her, a whiteboard and a wall-mounted flat-screen monitor behind her. A quick warning look from

Jean as he settled into a chair at the end.

'Good of you to make it.' Brandl's gaze raked him.

'Sorry, sarge, checking on Clara Ogilvie.'

'And?'

'Packed up and left this morning.'

The sergeant wasn't interested. 'I had Fraud Squad officers here just before lunch. They finished interviewing Malcolm Cater yesterday and spent the morning at the bank. If I could get this damn technology to work, I could show you a diagram of the mess they've uncovered.'

She tapped a laptop key, craned her head around, saw only a calming blue field on the screen. Tried again. 'Damn. I had it going before.'

'Let me, sergeant?' Medlin said, bracing to rise from his chair.

She shut him down with a slashing gesture of her hand. She was in a mood: Hirsch thought he knew why. Her lean face looked more tired than it had last night, if that was possible. Hollowed by strain.

He glanced at Jean. Slight, dark, serious, she'd already started taking notes. Tim, still embarrassed, was gazing across the table at her notepad, a worried crease in his shiny face. He picked up his pen, put it down again. Hirsch began to draw a series of interlocking box shapes. He usually enjoyed the Redruth briefings, but the atmosphere today felt weird. Urgent but rudderless. He eyed Sergeant Brandl again, reading distraction in her, as if she found her own thoughts unwelcome.

She gave a little shake, saw that the wall monitor was still blank, and said, 'Oh, bugger it. I'll précis, all right?'

'Sarge,' they chorused.

'This is what I was told. Adrian Quinlan's a long-standing client of the bank. Business loans from time to time, all legitimate, nothing risky, always repaid before they were due. Eventually he and Cater became friends. Business partners. They got greedy and started investing in risky ventures like Sunshine Coast real estate. When the economy tanked, Cater began arranging loans to shell companies he created, just so he and Quinlan could keep paying their investors their monthly three per cent. Eventually there was no more money coming in. Quinlan was facing bankruptcy. Meanwhile Cater looked like being audited by his own people, so he started siphoning money from some of the bank's clients. Elderly, well-off.' She looked at Hirsch. 'Like Mrs Groote.'

He nodded.

'An act of desperation, really. He used the money to pay the interest on some of the loans—five thousand here, ten there—but the rest probably went into his pocket, and Quinlan's. And Quinlan was doing the same thing, just managing to keep afloat, paying staff wages, electricity bills, a night out with the wife, that kind of thing, and slipping his wealthier creditors a few thousand now and then to keep them quiet.'

'Eleanor Quinlan was quite revealing,' Hirsch said. 'She often heard him on the phone: "Oh, the cheque's in the mail." Or, "There was an error at the bank," "There was an accounting software glitch." He said to one of them, "Eleanor usually does the books, but she has the flu."'

'Grade-A douchebag,' the sergeant said. 'The thing is, look what it's led to. Cater's not admitting anything but it's pretty clear he committed two murders to cover his tracks. And because Quinlan couldn't be bothered looking after his small creditors, we have Leon Ayliffe on a rampage.'

She looked desolate, as if still assessing the fallout. They waited.

Then she surprised them. Lifted her face from her laptop, treated them to a beautiful, broken smile, and said, 'Dismissed. Thanks for all your hard work, sorry I'm such a grump.'

She was blinking as they packed up and filed out. Hirsch, the last one to leave, heard her murmur, 'Paul? Got a minute?'

He took Landy's chair. 'Sarge?'

'Brian came to see me. We had lunch down at Cousin Jack's.'

Hirsch guessed she'd walked out on him. He put up both hands, as if to say he understood. 'It's okay, boss, no need to explain.'

She gave him a look. 'You're my friend, you idiot.'

That made him blink. A flicker of warmth in some corner of him. 'What did he want?'

'A talk. Return my *Mamma Mia* DVD.' She shook her head.

Hirsch grinned, and she grinned back, exasperated. 'Anyway, he said he felt bad about the way we'd left it.' Pause. 'What he meant was, he couldn't bear to think there was anyone, anywhere in the world, thinking badly of him.'

'All about him,' Hirsch said.

She nodded. 'Seems he met so-and-so three years ago but she was married then. When she finally separated...' She gave a strangled laugh. 'I was a stopgap.'

'Didn't exactly act honourably, boss.'

'You got that right.' She gathered her laptop and note-books and made for the door. Over her shoulder she said, 'You're a tonic.'

Which reminded Hirsch to call Wendy. Who said, 'We're fine. For the hundredth time.'

41

Thursday, early, Hirsch walked across the road for a copy of the *Advertiser*. A van dumped bundled copies outside the shop at six every morning and they sat there until Ed opened at eight. Hirsch needed to hit the road, so he went over with a kitchen knife, sliced through the poly strapping and carried a copy of the newspaper back to the police station to read during breakfast.

He hadn't given Bec Dewhurst anything and was relieved that although she named him as a local policeman, she hadn't placed him front and centre. Instead, she opened with a question: 'Is there a rottenness at the core in the sleepy wheat and wool town of Redruth, in the state's mid-north?' She went on to answer: 'Yes, according to local farmer—and wanted gunman—Leon Ayliffe.'

Hirsch scanned the rest of the article. Ayliffe and his son, currently on the run from police after a shooting incident in which a local council inspector was wounded, didn't shy away from his own actions, but, in a long and sometimes rambling call to Dewhurst, claimed that two murders in the Redruth area were tied to financial irregularities at the town's branch of the Mid-North Community Bank and the 'shoddy' business practices of 'prominent local business-man, Adrian Quinlan'. Quinlan, she could now reveal, had disappeared owing hundreds of thousands of dollars.

No hard facts, noted Hirsch, just a tidy line of specula-tion and innuendo, but the story did knit together many of the matters confirmed and explored in yesterday's police briefing.

He wondered when his phone would start ringing off the hook...

Stolte was first. 'Seen the paper?'

'Yes, senior sergeant.'

'She's getting a lot of this from you, right? You thought you'd stir the pot? Grandstand?'

'I declined to answer her questions, senior sergeant.'

'Where's she getting it then?'

'Ayliffe. He rang her.'

'So she says. Where's *he* getting it? For example, how does he know Quinlan's missing?'

That's what Hirsch wanted to know. He placated Stolte, drained his coffee and called Eleanor Quinlan.

She sounded croaky. He'd woken her. 'I haven't read the paper yet. But a reporter kept ringing me yesterday. I didn't say anything.'

'I suggest you don't. But she knows Adrian's gone walkabout.'

'Plenty of people know that.'

'But she says Leon Ayliffe told her. He hasn't called you, has he?'

'No.' She sounded offended. 'I'd never tell him anything even if he did.'

Then calls from Merlino, Comyn and Sergeant Brandl. Deny, deny, deny.

And, finally, Dewhurst herself. 'Did you see my story?'

'A bit light on, I thought.'

'That's because you wouldn't tell me anything. Have you had an opportunity to reconsider your position?'

'Plenty of opportunity; no inclination.'

'Come on, we can help each other. You can tell me things I can't otherwise uncover, and I can do likewise for you.'

'Sorry, I'm late, I need to go.'

'If you don't want to say what *you* think, what's the general police position?'

'I suggest you call the media office.'

'Do you think the Ayliffes are unhinged?'

'Well, they shot someone and went on the run,' Hirsch said. 'How did Leon sound to you? Voice of reason?'

A long pause. 'Obsessed, more than anything.'

'So, try digging around in what he's obsessed about.'

'I intend to. But what do *you* think—off the record?'

'Sorry, try the media office.'

'Lies, damn lies and bullshit,' Dewhurst said, not without justice.

Almost eight o'clock by the time Hirsch could set out on his long Thursday patrol. Paul Kelly on the CD that Katie had burnt for him: 'Roll on Summer'—and Hirsch thought it seemed apposite on this icy clear morning.

The first leg took him north to Terowie, then east into marginal country, where stone reef eruptions bisected the back roads and he crawled in low gear down switchback roads and across creek beds, some in flood for the first time in years. Down a rutted driveway to a farmhouse and a cup of tea and an Anzac biscuit, then, if he was lucky, a blessed few kilometres of sealed roads and graded gravel roads, before another side track to another isolated station property, another cup of tea and a chat about sheep missing, believed stolen, or mysterious headlights in the night, or a grown son not taking his meds. He helped a widow start her ute with the police Toyota's jumper leads, held a ladder so a man could fish his grandson's cricket ball out of a gutter, helped an elderly woman change a tap washer.

The long loop east and south took him to Belalie Waters, the northern approach this time, crossing the low hill range where Rosemary Waurn's husband Ken and his jackaroos had been tending to fly-blown sheep a few days earlier.

He rolled into the yard and it was empty of farm vehicles. He looked towards the house with a feeling of unease. Bathed in wintry light, no moaning wind. But some kind of disturbance had occurred, he thought. He turned on the dashcam.

He was both relieved and alarmed when Rosemary came running from the car shed, darting her head left and right. He got out and she skidded into him as he opened his arms instinctively. She flung herself against him, briefly tense as a board, until there was a great unlocking and she relaxed. She sighed, relieved, and stepped away.

'They came back!'

I knew it, thought Hirsch. 'The Ayliffes? When?'

'No more than ten minutes ago.'

'Where are Ken and the boys?'

'They went off in the truck to buy hay. Won't be back till tonight. Ken didn't want to leave me, but we couldn't all fit, and I told him lightning doesn't strike in the same place twice. Ha!'

Hirsch looked around. The only vehicle in sight was the family station wagon. 'So now the Ayliffes have both your utes?'

'The other ute's in Clare having the airbag done; Ken's picking it up on the way back this afternoon. No, they were in a Range Rover. They must've dumped the first ute somewhere.'

Hirsch tingled. 'Black Range Rover?'

'Yes, one of those posh ones.'

'Was anyone with them?'

'Adrian Quinlan. I recognised him from the ram sales.'

'Did he look all right?'

'No. He had a black eye and he looked frightened.'

She added, in a helpless, uncomprehending voice, 'It was strange. Leon said they gave up on the first ute because it had a slipping clutch, like it was my fault. But he said the Range Rover wasn't right, either, not for where he wanted to go—rough country, I assume. It was like we were chatting about the weather.' Pause. 'He'd been drinking.'

*

Hirsch called Inspector Merlino and was given the go-ahead to track the Range Rover but not to engage.

'If you find it, I'll need you to coordinate ground vehicles and a chopper—if we can get one.'

'Will do, sir.'

'I mean it when I say don't engage,' Merlino said, with the unpleasant grittiness of every muscling-in cop Hirsch had ever encountered.

'Understood, sir,' he said, but Merlino had already cut him off.

Hirsch turned to Rosemary Waurn, and pointed along the driveway. 'You're sure they went out that way?'

'Positive.'

He tried to step into their shoes. Would they go as far as the Redruth–Morgan road? Turn left and make for the river? Turn right and head for Redruth? Or lose themselves out bush again? That seemed their most likely decision, given they were after a better off-road vehicle.

Waurn was watching him with a troubled, concentrated expression. 'I don't really want to stay here.'

'Don't blame you,' Hirsch said. 'I suggest you take the car and leave the back way. Go as far as you can, maybe all the way around to Tiverton and stay in the shop.'

'I need to tell Ken.'

'Did you get the radio fixed?'

'We splashed out on a couple of sat-phones.'

'Call him and tell him and the boys to stay away for a few hours. We'll get word to you.'

Rosemary Waurn's whole life was waiting for a word from

someone, Hirsch thought, watching her return to the house. He waited, and presently she came out with a small overnight bag, tossed it on the back seat of her car and headed out. Watching until she was a speck receding to the line of low hills behind the property, he swung the HiLux around. Headed it across the yard and down the long driveway to the gravel road where he'd encountered the airbag mechanic.

It was a stop-start hunt. He'd speed over the corrugations then brake to a crawl to check a farm gate or a side road, trying to read the soil for fresh tyre impressions. The hunt sharpened his senses. It didn't matter that it was touch-and-go country; it was a living landscape. He'd been formed by a city, its exact delineations of asphalt streets and bricks in orderly rows, but out here the angles were unpredictable. Roads shot off in unlikely directions, buildings decayed at a lean and the endless flatland was neither endless nor flat, throwing up stone reef patches or plunging into gullies. And it was a landscape charged with unheard testimony: an ochre hand stencil in a cave; a stick figure carved into a rockface; a grinding tool laid bare after a flash flood.

Not empty, not even sparse. But still, there were long stretches between the side roads, farm gates and driveways. He stopped twice to examine tyre tracks. The first had been left by a truck, he decided: too broad, too knobbly, too deep. The second confused him: the width suggested a car the size of a Range Rover but there were two sets. Two vehicles? Or one that had gone in and come out again?

He investigated. Half a kilometre along a farm track he came to a fold in the earth, a little rift, the track bisected by a creek in flood. If the Ayliffes had come this way, they'd evidently decided not to risk a crossing. The driver had made a meal out of turning around in the narrow space: a series of short, full-steering-lock manoeuvres; spinning tyres and mud sprays; deep ruts in the spongy verge.

Hirsch made his own dog's breakfast of turning around and raced back to the road and along it for another few kilometres until he came to fresh tyre marks on either side of a stock ramp that marked the entrance to a station property: *Willalo Downs 13 km* painted on a weathered board nailed beneath a milk-churn letterbox.

No tyre marks leaving the place.

He called it in and headed down the track, pitching about like a little boat in choppy waters, sometimes bottoming out on the high crown. Five minutes, ten, twelve...

His radio crackled: Merlino, telling him that Willalo Downs was abandoned.

So maybe the Ayliffes intended to camp there. Or—discovering it was abandoned—would come back this way?

Hirsch felt indecisive, suddenly. Keep going; see who'd left the tyre marks? Assume it was the Ayliffes and wait? Wait where he was, or go back and block the main gate?

He travelled a few hundred metres thinking these things, then came to a natural hollow in this land of stones and struggling grass. Nestled down there was someone's mouldering empire of dirt: a sad old house with sightless windows and a rusted roof; falling-down sheds; pine trees and a garden gone wild. A movement caught his eye a hundred metres away and to the left of the house. There was only a wintry sun to light the day, but it was strong enough to seek out and arc off reflective surfaces. Off the windscreen of a black Range Rover, bogged in treacherous grass. Off the eye of a rifle scope. And then the world seemed to fall in on Hirsch.

42

The Toyota shook with it; the noise was stupefying. Hirsch blinked awake and looked up for the boulder that had dropped on him.

No, his mind caught up: it was a shot. It must have scored the roof—had probably torn off the antenna array.

The second shot took out the rear passenger-side tyre, but by then he'd switched on the dashcam and tumbled out, seeking the cover of the engine block and driver's-side wheel. Poor cover if Ayliffe started placing shots between the chassis and the ground, but Hirsch had nowhere else to go, only rocky outcrops downhill from where he was crouched, shaking in his boots. He could retreat along the track but would be visible for a crucial few seconds. And he wanted to know more.

Ayliffe started that ball rolling. 'Paul! Constable Hirschhausen!'

Hirsch darted a look. 'What?'

'First things first: I don't want to hurt anybody.'

'Funny way of showing it,' Hirsch said. He felt suddenly acutely annoyed.

'If I'd wanted to hit you, you'd be dead,' Ayliffe said.

Dickhead. Hirsch stuck his head out and shouted, 'What do you want? You're bogged, right? And you go and shoot out one of my tyres?'

'This is what's going to happen. I come up there and watch you put the spare tyre on, then you drive down here and pull us out.'

Leon had thought it through, Hirsch realised. Temporary disablement, giving him time to control the situation. 'I don't know what condition my spare tyre's in.'

'You're wasting time. Start now or I'm gonna hurt Quinlan.'

Merlino and his crew know where I am, thought Hirsch. More or less. But how far away were they? Play for time. Play dumb. Negotiate.

He darted another look. All he could see of Ayliffe was a small, hunched shape. He was on the far side of the Range Rover, using his elbows on the bonnet to prop and sight the rifle. Hirsch could feel the eye of the scope; feel it trained right on his nose. Range, one hundred metres. Years of hunting experience.

Meanwhile, at the rear of the Range Rover, Josh Ayliffe stood with a sawn-off shotgun in the small of Adrian Quinlan's back.

'Not sure if I have a jack or a wheel brace,' Hirsch yelled. 'Can I come down and fetch yours?'

Ayliffe put a bullet through the prisoner transport

compartment above the back wheels and the Toyota rocked and again Hirsch was stunned by the raw violence of it. He had no agency here. Everything had been irretrievable long before he arrived. His service pistol was puny against a rifle and a shotgun; against a confused kid and a man who'd surrendered himself to his grudges.

He called, 'Is Mr Quinlan all right?'

'He's fine. Now shut your mouth and change that fucking tyre.'

Hirsch, crouched in the shelter of the front wheel, took deep and deepening breaths and unfolded his limbs. He was visible now, from the chest up. 'Coming out.'

'Slowly.'

When Hirsch was standing in the open, Ayliffe moved away from the Range Rover. Still training his rifle on Hirsch, he shouted, 'Take out your gun—*slower*, slower. Now throw it away. That's it.'

Hirsch waited, disarmed now, hands held away from his sides.

'I'm coming up to you,' Ayliffe said. 'If you run, I'll shoot you and then I'll shoot Quinlan, got it?'

'Loud and clear.'

As Hirsch watched, Ayliffe began the climb, stopping twenty metres short of him. 'Okay, now get out the jack.'

Delay, delay. 'I think we should talk about this, Leon. My colleagues know where I am. I left Mrs Waurn not that long ago and called it in. There's a team of police on the way as we speak. Helicopters. You can't get out. Why not give up while you can—before anyone gets hurt.'

Ayliffe's answer was a shot fired above Hirsch's head and the quick flick of the bolt ejecting the spent shell and loading another.

'I see,' Hirsch said.

A part of him was frightened to the bone, the other part was still sour. He made to move but his attention was caught. Something was happening in the hollow. His glance downhill was brief, he swung his eyes back a millisecond later, but that was enough.

Leon Ayliffe the hunter read it in him, turned and saw what Hirsch had seen, his son urging Adrian Quinlan to run.

'*Hey*. Josh! What the fuck're you doing?'

Josh sent his father a frightened look, prodded Quinlan's bulky spine. Made shooing motions. Quinlan, slow to realise he was being given a way out, that he wasn't prey in some sick game, ran stumblingly towards the house, where a track at the rear led up and out of the hollow. He lurched clumsily, shaky with panic. Fell, rested on his hands and knees, stood, stumbled off again.

'You little shit,' Leon screamed. He began to charge downhill, driven by fury, hopping and skipping over the stone reefs.

Josh stepped away from the Range Rover, hands up placatingly. 'Dad, don't.'

For a moment, Hirsch was a metronome, his body ticking one way, towards his service pistol in the grass, then the other, towards the three men in the hollow. Finally he moved: scooped up his pistol and made his own hectic run over grass tussocks and quartz outcrops, slipping, twisting his ankle, barking the palms of his hands on a hidden spine of stone. His pistol flew into the grass. He scouted around for it, found it, lost valuable time.

And he was seconds late. Years late.

Leon barely paused before he smacked the butt of his rifle into his son's face. The boy's body went slack. He simply dropped.

Leon, nestling the rifle into his shoulder, snapped a shot at Quinlan. Quinlan made a stumble-run of two or three steps. Fell to the ground.

Hirsch drew closer, a limping, half-crouched, nervy potential target. Tried to train his pistol on Ayliffe, who was closing in on Quinlan. Quinlan, facedown, was trying to lift his heavy torso. Blood: he'd been shot in the upper right leg.

Hirsch screamed: '*Leon.*'

It seemed to work. Ayliffe halted. A great shudder ripped through him. His shoulders slumped. His arms flopped, loosening his grasp on the rifle until the barrel tip trailed in the grass. When he turned around, he didn't see Hirsch, only his son. He hurried to the boy, rested the rifle on the ground—careful, like a craftsman with a valued tool—and knelt.

'Josh. *Joshy,*' he said.

Hirsch, scarcely breathing, darted in, grabbed the rifle and backed away. He ejected the spent shell, removed the clip and stood ready for what came next.

He didn't know what that would be. They were alone, not even a moaning wind in the pine trees for company. Quinlan had flopped again, and Josh Ayliffe was a heap of bones splayed on the ground, Leon keening over him, continually reaching out his hand to the distorted skull and jerking it back again.

The shotgun. Hirsch took a step.

It was as if Ayliffe read that in him, too. With a wail that curdled Hirsch's soul, he scuttled around to the other side of his son's body, grabbed the shotgun and tucked the shortened barrel under his chin, and all Hirsch could do was flinch. Snatch a look afterwards and listen to the echo repeat, repeat, and fade to nothing.

After a while Quinlan spoke, a waver in his voice. 'Hello? I need help.'

As if blind or lost in a desert. 'Keep still, Mr Quinlan.'

Quinlan was still facing away from Hirsch, out across the unprepossessing hollow. He attempted to roll onto his left hip and prop himself on one elbow. Groaned as things moved in his damaged leg. Flopped again, face down, head on one side. 'Is someone there? It hurts.'

When Hirsch moved into view, he blinked, reassessed, began to comprehend. 'Oh, Constable Hirschhausen, yes, of course...'

Hirsch knelt beside him, said, 'Just lie still,' and peered at the sodden trouser leg.

Ayliffe had snapped, barely aiming, and the bullet had gone through the flesh below Quinlan's right buttock. A hunting round, though; plenty of tearing force in it. Had it missed the bone? If it had hit the bone, wouldn't there be more trauma? Wouldn't Quinlan have gone into shock?

Hirsch stood. 'Remain still, Mr Quinlan. I'll call an ambulance.'

No, he wouldn't. His phone had no signal and the radio was kaput. Change the tyre and drive Quinlan to Redruth? Wait for Merlino?

He fetched the first-aid kit from the police Toyota. Knelt beside Quinlan again, rolled him onto his back. Scissored off the trouser leg, washed the blood away and splashed antiseptic over the entry and exit points. Stuck on a couple of bandages, wrapped the upper leg in a metre of crepe dressing, and tucked a space blanket around the stock agent's big form.

Some time later Quinlan said, 'Am I going to die?'

He looked as if he'd woken from a dream and found himself in a nightmare. Hirsch said, 'Can you curl your toes?'

He waited. Quinlan's shoes, just visible beyond the hem of the space blanket, moved a little.

'Yes.'

'It's a flesh wound. Nasty one, but you'll be okay.'

'Hurts like buggery,' Quinlan said, his large round face bruised, greasy and pale with pain.

'Help will be here soon.'

Ten minutes? Fifteen? Someone on Merlino's team could take Quinlan to hospital, possibly meet the ambulance halfway. Giving me ten or fifteen minutes in which to tease out a story, maybe even the truth, Hirsch thought.

'Quite an adventure you've had.'

A long silence before Quinlan said, 'They just came barging in and grabbed me.'

366

'Did they say why?'

Quinlan looked away, a touch of the backslapper appearing in his eyes. 'Leon said I owed him three thousand dollars. If he'd only been a bit patient, he'd have got his money, and all this could have been avoided.'

'Patient.'

Quinlan shook his head. 'The market. Cashflow. The state of the economy.'

'People have died, Mr Quinlan,' Hirsch said.

Quinlan looked over his shoulder. Saw the bodies; winced and recoiled. 'You can't think I had anything to do with that?'

'Margaret Groote,' Hirsch said. 'Sophie Flynn.'

Quinlan's face went blank. He closed his eyes. 'I don't feel all that well, to be honest. When's the ambulance getting here?'

The wind seemed to answer him. It had risen in the past few minutes, lonely in the pine trees around the deserted farmhouse.

Time passed. Quinlan decided he wanted absolution. 'I've let everyone down,' he said, his voice low and hoarse.

Hirsch could hear vehicles now. Soon they would appear on the rim of the hollow. He squeezed Quinlan's shoulder, surprised at its solidity under the space blanket. 'When the time comes, just tell the truth.'

The words gave Quinlan strength. 'If Malcolm hadn't been so impatient...I was actually getting through to Mrs Groote, she was listening to me.'

Hirsch stood where the consoling air flowed. Up there

on the ridgeline a black SUV was nosing past his shot-up Toyota.

'I can get past this,' Quinlan said in his salesman's voice, a man lying on his belly in the dirt, his pants stiff with blood.

Yeah, well, Hirsch thought. Good luck with that.

Acknowledgments

Deep and abiding thanks to Michael Heyward, Mandy Brett, Chong, Kate Lloyd, Jane Watkins, Stefanie Italia, Shalini Kunahlan and all at Text Publishing, who have nurtured my career for many years now, steadily finding me new readers and helping me to push at my creative boundaries with every book.

About the Author

Garry Disher has published fifty titles across multiple genres, and is best known as Australia's King of Crime. He has won the Deutsche Krimi Preis three times, the Ned Kelly Award twice, and his novel *The Sunken Road* was nominated for the Booker Prize. In 2018 he received the Ned Kelly Lifetime Achievement Award.

garrydisher.com